Acclaim for Rosemary and Juliet

"An outstanding first novel. . . . A work of intelligence and passion. . . . Offers some new insights into the human mind and heart."

—Arthur J. Blaustein
Author, *Make a Difference* and *The American Promise*

"Beautifully written. Judy MacLean's graceful prose and storytelling power make this book a page-turner."

—April Sinclair
Author, *Coffee Will Make You Black*

"This wonderful coming-of-age novel has everything—memorable characters, a great plot, suspense, drama, and humor. *Rosemary and Juliet* is lyrical, political, and sexy."

—Margaret Cruikshank
Adjunct Professor of Women's Studies,
University of Maine and University of Southern Maine

"Finally, a Romeo and Juliet story updated for today's young lesbian—and a great read for family and friends of all ages. This beautifully written book is lyrical and exciting, funny and fierce, with lots of drama and adventure. It's fresh and inventive.

The core of this book is the blooming of mind and heart, and the coming together of two different, appealing, smart, and vibrant young women. This is a book that could save lives and prevent heartache, with its moral and social vision of tolerance, but most of all it is a compelling, endearing, sweet, and exciting love story that rings so very true. I guarantee you, too, will fall in love with Romey and Julie—and with their love for each other—and beg Judy MacLean for a sequel."

—Torie Osborn
Author, *Coming Home to America*;
Former Executive Director, National Gay and Lesbian Task Force
and the Los Angeles Gay and Lesbian Center

Rosemary and Juliet

HARRINGTON PARK PRESS
Alice Street Editions
Judith P. Stelboum
Editor in Chief

Rosemary and Juliet

Judy MacLean

Alice Street Editions
Harrington Park Press®
An Imprint of The Haworth Press, Inc.
New York • London • Oxford

Published by

Alice Street Editions, Harrington Park Press®, an imprint of The Haworth Press, Inc., 10 Alice Street, Binghamton, NY 13904-1580.

This is a work of fiction. The town of Divido is fictional. Its residents, geography, plants, animals, and economy are based on a composite of several towns in northern California.

Cover design by Jennifer M. Gaska.

Library of Congress Cataloging-in-Publication Data

MacLean, Judy, 1946-
    Rosemary and Juliet / Judy MacLean.
        p. cm.
    ISBN 1-56023-483-0 (soft : alk. paper)
1. Teenage girls—Fiction. 2. Lesbian teenagers—Fiction. I. Title.
    PS613.A2737R67 2003
    813'.6—dc21
                                                                        2003012309

For Kathy

Editor's Foreword

Alice Street Editions provides a voice for established as well as up-and-coming lesbian writers, reflecting the diversity of lesbian interests, ethnicities, ages, and class. This cutting-edge series of novels, memoirs, and nonfiction writing welcomes the opportunity to present controversial views, explore multicultural ideas, encourage debate, and inspire creativity from a variety of lesbian perspectives. Through enlightening, illuminating, and provocative writing, Alice Street Editions can make a significant contribution to the visibility and accessibility of lesbian writing and bring lesbian-focused writing to a wider audience. Recognizing our own desires and ideas in print is life sustaining, acknowledging the reality of who we are, as well as our place in the world, individually and collectively.

Judith P. Stelboum
Editor in Chief
Alice Street Editions

Acknowledgments

For reading part or all of the book and giving me helpful feedback, thanks to Arthur Blaustein, Debra DeBondt, Pam Drake, Peg Hites, Sherrie Holmes, Lois MacLean, Joan Mandell, Carolyn Matthews, Jan Richman, Martha Shelley, Peggy Shinner, and April Sinclair.

For research assistance, thank you to the San Francisco Public Library Interlibrary Loan service and Peg Hites. For helpful advice about getting published, thank you to Suzanne Corwin of Boadecia's Books, Peg Cruikshank, and Anne Farrar. For math inspiration, thank you to *From Zero to Infinity* by Constance Reid, *Fractals: The Patterns of Chaos* by John Briggs, and *More Joy of Mathematics* by Theoni Pappas. For excellent copyediting, thank you to Julie Ehlers and Peg Marr, and thank you also to everyone at Alice Street Editions/The Haworth Press who worked to turn my manuscript into this book.

For love and support, for encouraging feedback at every stage of writing, and for insightfully reading every draft all the way through, thanks to my life partner, Kathy Hess.

Chapter 1

No one, she told herself, ever died from speaking in front of a crowd.

Romey dug her long fingers into her palms and wrapped her ankles around the legs of her chair until the cool metal bit into her shins. Her lungs felt like they were being mashed in a garbage compactor. She had to keep from getting tongue-tied, or squeaky-voiced, or forgetting part of her testimony, or starting to cry, or getting rattled by a heckler so she said the wrong thing, or blurting out something stupid—*stop it,* she ordered herself. *Just stop it.*

All over the high school cafeteria, little groups of people talked with worried frowns. A loud, unamused laugh erupted above the voices, echoing off the concrete walls, along with the wail of a pitch pipe. The high overhead lights glared down on small children running up the aisle, shrieking.

At least 150 people were at the school board meeting already, and more were still arriving. Volunteers banged extra metal chairs into rows and shoved more tables against the back wall, the legs screeching against the scuffed linoleum floor.

The side door opened, letting in a puff of cold, rain-scented air. Romey turned around, but when she saw it was just a group of parents, neither Elliot nor Amina among them, her shoulders sank.

Outside, a chilly wind whipped gray eucalyptus leaves and grit around the parking lot. Although the sky was clear, it felt as if rain clouds were massing over the Pacific, boiling up just on the other side of the California Coast Range, ready to call an end to the calm, hot days of early fall and hit Divido with the season's first storm.

Inside, the cafeteria was warm; the big ceiling heater fan kept up a low background hum. The air smelled of deodorant, bodies, makeup, spilled baby formula, take-out french fries, and the little sour candies one dad was handing out. Above the hum and clatter, the authoritative and tired voice of Iris Bernstein, the school board president, rang out through the sound system. "Take your seats, please. We'll be starting in five minutes. If you wish to speak, please put your name in the fishbowl up here now."

Romey tore a sheet of yellow lined paper into four pieces and wrote her name on one. On the others she wrote her mother's name, then Elliot's and Amina's. She had a desperate urge to pee, but she'd been to the girls' rest room twice in the past ten minutes, and nothing had come out. She stood up and walked toward the fishbowl, holding her back straight and setting her jaw with what she hoped was a look of determination. She expected stares because of her hair, red-brown, cut close to her head, short as a boy's, shorter than plenty of boys', cut in a way that felt good and looked right to Romey. Now, at the sight of her, she was sure people were nudging each other, whispering, "That must be her; that's the one."

The cafeteria seemed bigger to her than during the day, cavernous. She failed to notice that no one was paying her much attention and that, in any case, her athlete's stride concealed her jangly queasiness. Romey was a junior at the high school, a member of the girls' track team, and she imagined herself on the track now, how safe it would feel to be running through quiet air, one foot after the other hitting the predictable flat dirt.

When she got up to the front table, she crossed out "Romey" on her piece of yellow paper and wrote her full given name, "Rosemary," instead. It would sound more adult. Then she dropped all four pieces into the fishbowl.

School board meetings in Divido were normally sleepy and short, with an audience of less than ten. That had all changed since June, when the Divido Bible Church members had banded together to elect Louise Stubbs to a seat. Mrs. Stubbs immediately put forth a resolution to change the science curriculum for all grade levels, so the Book of Genesis creation story would get the same instruction time as evolution. The two theories would be presented as equally valid, neither able to be scientifically proven. The proposal kicked off two meetings of outraged debate, which had climaxed the previous month with its being voted down. Undeterred, Mrs. Stubbs immediately introduced a second measure to ban gay teachers. The board was hearing testimony on it tonight.

Romey walked back to the seats her mother was saving in the third row. They had come a half hour early, planning to save four seats in the very front row, but others had come even earlier. Her heart knocked around her ribs.

Janis, Romey's mother, was feeling pumped up and ready. She looked forward to speaking in front of a group—something she did regularly on her job—and had several pointed barbs ready for hecklers. She knew her arguments were solid, sure to sway the undecided. But now she noticed the group of people clustered on the far right side of the room, and remembered the Santa Rosa police department's recent advice, which she hadn't followed, that on the job she should be wearing a bulletproof vest.

She'd seen several of those people from the local fundamentalist church before, picketing in front of the clinic where she worked, thrusting their pictures of mangled fetuses in the faces of women arriving to have abortions. One of them could well be the reason for the police warning.

But no one could be idiotic enough to shoot a gun in front of all these witnesses, Janis decided. She watched her daughter walk back and fold herself into her chair with that tentativeness people have when their arms and legs have only recently grown long. The back of Romey's bare young neck, and that short hair the color of new redwood—it emphasized the shape of Romey's head and made it look somehow vulnerable—gave Janis a quick flashback to a bygone apartment, to holding the sleepy toddler Romey, wisps of damp hair stuck to the baby forehead, the fresh-bread smell of very young sweat.

Janis had felt like a mama bear then, ready to claw and lunge at any threat. She seldom let things stand in her way; she was used to barging in, to bluffing through when necessary. But now her abdomen was cold with dread. She fought an urge to grab Romey and take her back home. It was one thing to bluff her way through while people jeered at her, but she hadn't faced until now the possibility that she might have to watch Romey, her tender sapling, be hit by a withering blast of humiliation. She reminded herself that it might not happen.

Still, a noose of anxiety tightened around her throat. And what if this were one of those times she was always seeing on the news, when some man, or even a boy, burst into some unlikely, crowded place, shooting an automatic rifle? The old mama bear's body wouldn't completely shield her daughter anymore. Romey was a head taller.

Janis shook her head. *Where* were these thoughts coming from? She didn't usually imagine disaster. The taste of the salad dressing from dinner rose sour in her throat.

She looked down and saw her daughter's long fingers methodically tearing up the top margins of three pieces of lined paper in her lap, notes for the testimony Romey planned to deliver tonight. The girl's black jeans were covered in yellow confetti. Janis brushed the paper scraps to the floor.

After many years at various barricades, Janis had honed her techniques for getting through experiences like the one that was coming. The best thing she could do now was to pass those strategies along to her daughter. She decided Romey needed to hear again all the things Janis had told her the night before, when they'd gone over their testimony together. "Remember," Janis put her hand on Romey's shoulder, felt the tension in the firm young muscles, "speak about three inches from the mike. Go slow. Say the important words louder. If you get nervous, take a deep breath and remember you have every right to be here. If you get heckled, repeat what you have just said. Repeat it again until you make yourself heard. Don't let them drown you out. Meet the eyes of a couple of people in the audience, and keep looking back at them."

Romey stopped tearing at her notes. Overhead, big cracks loomed in the ceiling. At the back of the room, a child fell down with a wail. Romey's hands shook. "Mom, I think it'll help if we don't talk about being nervous, okay?"

Romey heard a banging on her left. She looked over and saw her friend Elliot clumsily pushing his way down the row of chairs, past extended legs and knees, panting from exertion, finally knocking down the empty chair next to her. He smiled at Romey and Janis and swung his head in an exaggerated arc toward the same knot of people Janis had noticed earlier. "We're throwing ourselves to the lions tonight," he said, "but in this case, the lions happen to be the Christians."

He picked up the chair he'd knocked over, held it knee high. "I don't want to talk like those people are prejudiced against us or anything, but when two men sit down next to each other in that church, it trips off the automatic ejection seat." He hoisted the chair up above his head.

Elliot was a year older than Romey, a senior at the high school. He had plans for a future career as a gay studies college professor. He'd found a niche for himself in the school drama club, where he was cast in character parts, grumpy fathers or villains or comic bumblers. He was tall and broad; tonight, as always, his clothes were rumpled. Even just after a haircut, his hair somehow looked shaggy around his open, square face.

He set the chair back on the floor. His stainless steel eyebrow ring glinted in the fluorescent light. "But fear not, by the time the two of *us* finish, all bigots present will fall on their knees, calling, 'I repent! I repent!'"

Elliot dropped to the floor on his knees and held his big square hands in a pose of prayer. "Your testimony, Ms. Romey, has opened our rusted minds. Your oratory has moved our stunted hearts. We will discriminate no more. Forgive us. Before this night, we knew not what we did."

From the row just in front, two men who had driven over from Guerneville twisted around to watch. They wore pink triangle lapel pins on their suit jackets and big grins on their faces.

Elliot nodded in quick acknowledgment at the one he thought cutest, who had an eyebrow ring.

"In fact," Elliot went on, playing to his larger audience, "the local press will report Romey's words. Her electrifying performance will be front-page news in San Francisco. Gay activists will make pilgrimages up to Divido to learn how to give a speech from a pro. The TV networks will jump on the story. There will be a media feeding frenzy here in Divido, with Romey booked solid for interviews eighteen hours a day.

"As Romey's words ring out on the six o'clock news," Elliot stood up and threw out his arm, narrowly missing the head of one of the men with the pink triangle pins, "gay bashers will run sobbing into the streets, throw themselves onto the pavement, and beg forgiveness. Counseling centers will open round the clock to help people deal with a newly identified constellation of psychological symptoms, Post-Homophobic Instant Guilt Syndrome, or PIGS."

He clicked his heels together and gave a military salute. "The U.S. Army will hold grand parades honoring all gay members, past and present, of the armed forces. Two members of the Joint Chiefs of Staff will announce they are longtime companions. The Marines will parade in high heels, evening gowns, and feather boas. It will give a whole new meaning to the term *dress uniform*."

Elliot relaxed into an "at ease" stance. "Mother's Day will be changed to 'Coming Out to Your Mother Day.' Satellite TV will beam your message around the globe. It will be translated into forty-four languages. Europe will declare a continent-wide Gay and Lesbian Appreciation Day. In China, open homosexuals will be appointed to high government posts. People will embrace their gay neighbors and urge them to come out of their closets and onto the streets of Moscow, Sydney, Rio, Addis Ababa, Manila, Tehran, Bombay . . ."

The men from Guerneville exchanged a smile with Janis.

Romey stretched out her legs and leaned back. "Don't worry, Elliot," she said, "I'll still be your friend when I'm famous. But now, better sit down."

Iris Bernstein was banging her gavel and calling the meeting to order.

Elliot leaned over and whispered loudly and confidentially behind his hand, "I didn't even get to what will happen on other planets."

The racket of voices died down. Mothers and fathers pulled children in mid-run from the aisle and scooped them onto their laps. Throats cleared. Chairs scraped.

Iris sat behind a microphone at a long table on the small raised stage. The four other school board members sat beside her. Another mike was perched on a pole at one side, next to the American and California flags. A quiet punctuated by coughing settled over the audience. Iris welcomed everyone, the board secretary read out the minutes of the previous meeting, and Iris introduced the first order of business, a motion from Louise Stubbs. Mrs. Stubbs rose from her chair. She wore the weight of her considerable responsibilities and a suit the color of pigeon feathers. She settled her half-glasses over her nose and read firmly: "Resolved, that no homosexuals shall be hired or retained as teachers, counselors, principals, or in any other capacity by the Divido California Unified School District."

Hissing and booing rang out from some parts of the room, cheers from others.

Iris slammed her gavel onto the table so hard her clipboard jumped. "If you applaud every speaker, we'll be here all night. I would hope booing would be beneath the dignity of this meeting. This is your last chance to put your name in this fishbowl. Please remember, the time limit is strictly three minutes. First up—"

Iris reached into the fishbowl and pulled out a piece of lined paper torn from a yellow legal pad, the same kind Romey had put in earlier. Romey dug her fingernails into the fleshy pads of her hands and willed herself to ignore her stomach's weird flopping.

"Janis Arden," Iris called.

At the far side of the room, Connie Wright turned to her husband, the Reverend Jim Ed Wright, pastor of Divido Bible Church. The corners of her mouth were tight with annoyance. "Oh, great. This is all we need," she whispered.

"The first shall come last," he whispered back to her. Then he repeated it a little louder, to buoy up the nearby members of the congregation.

Janis, wearing jeans and a multicolored Guatemalan embroidered vest, walked forward briskly. Her big feet slapped the three steps as she climbed up to the stage. She felt better to be doing something at last, instead of just waiting. Her old confident buzz was coming back, her readiness for a fight. Tonight held a deep resonance. Memories speeded her blood, memories of a hundred marches, vigils, public hearings, lobby days, mailing parties, guerilla theater stunts, of knocking on doors, collecting petitions, winning sometimes, losing a lot. Now she was here with her daughter, activists together for the first time, if you didn't count Janis pushing Romey in a stroller years before, carrying a sign that read "U.S. Out of El Salvador" or "Take Back the Night," and Janis didn't count those times, because Romey hadn't chosen to go. Tonight was Romey's choice; in fact, it was Romey's idea, and damned if Janis was going to let anyone spoil her passing to her daughter the torch of rebellion and activism.

Of course, she wasn't really passing the torch. Janis wasn't ready to retire yet. They were just going to run for a few laps, side by side, holding the torch together. And now she was getting to speak first, icing on the cake.

Janis still wore her hair late 1960s style, parted in the middle and hanging straight halfway to her waist. It was about equally gray and brown. She impatiently pushed it over her shoulders, raised the microphone a few inches, placed her hands on her hips, and thrust out her chin.

Romey's stomach felt like an elevator plunging ten floors. Everything her mom planned to say had sounded okay last night at the kitchen table, but there were so many people here.

"I live here in Divido. My daughter is a student at Divido High." Janis's loud, gravelly voice brought the whole crowd to silent attention. She liked to say her voice had come from yelling herself hoarse at the barricades, but in fact it had been gravelly even when she was a child. "I am also director of A Woman's Decision clinic in Santa Rosa."

"Baby killer!" someone called from the back.

Romey clenched her fists and dug them into her stomach.

Iris pounded her gavel. "We are not here tonight to discuss Ms. Arden's work, but to address school board business. If you can't be quiet, you'll have to leave. Go on, Janis."

"Thank you, Iris." Janis's long hair swung around as she turned to face Iris, then the audience.

Among the cluster at the far right of the room, Janis spotted Connie Wright, the preacher's wife, the most dogged of the clinic picketers, the most determined to talk women out of getting abortions, Connie with her helmet of dark hair in regimented waves, dressed in what the clinic staff called the Standard Issue Pest Uniform — a navy blue skirt, white blouse, and a red bow. Connie showed up in sun or rain for a four-hour shift every Thursday afternoon and walked beside every woman who arrived, especially the young girls, clutching her Bible and her crisis pregnancy leaflets, intoning, "God does not want you to kill your baby!"

Now, Janis calmly met Connie's eyes.

"I'm here tonight to speak against the measure proposed by Louise Stubbs. I'd like everyone here who is over twenty years of age to just think back a minute to when you were eleven, or twelve, or thirteen, or whenever you first hit that rocky stage of life known as puberty. Remember what it was like? All those hormones bouncing around your system for the first time, your body changing, it seemed, every day?"

In the harsh fluorescent light, Romey saw how wrinkled her mother looked, with circles under her eyes. Romey clutched the metal seat on either side of her thighs and leaned forward.

"Now, imagine for a minute, adding to all the puberty confusion, that you also feel attracted to your own sex. It would be pretty tough, wouldn't it?

"Kids going through this need to be able to talk to gay teachers because their parents . . ." here, Janis shot a look toward the part of the crowd that had booed her, the group from Divido Bible Church, and then bored her eyes into Connie Wright's, ". . . their parents may or may not be available to give their children support and understanding."

"How about being available to punish them when they need it," Reverend Wright called out. A couple of men nearby clapped him heartily on the back.

Iris glared at him and banged her gavel. "Reverend Wright, you hold a position of authority in this community. Please set an example by showing respect for this board and do not interrupt. Your turn to speak will come. Go ahead, Janis."

Janis looked steadily out at the audience. "Children who are brave enough to admit their gay feelings don't have an easy time."

Romey put a hand on each knee and squeezed the bones hard. Mom was talking about her, now. Romey looked cautiously around, but no-

body was staring at her. Last year, her sophomore year at Divido
High, Romey had decided that no one had the right to make her hide
who she was. She would become the school's first and only open lesbian. She'd face the consequences, whatever they were.

Romey didn't recognize most of the people here tonight. There
were hardly any kids, and she knew few parents. Maybe no one here
knew about her. When she stood up and told them, they would probably be shocked.

Janis's voice grew oratorical. "Gay teenagers are more likely than
straight ones to attempt suicide. And what message does it give a
young gay boy or lesbian girl if people like them are not allowed to
teach at the school where they spend all their days?"

Romey let out a loosening sigh. She could feel the audience and it
wasn't all hostile.

She looked to her side and saw Amina, threading her way between
the chairs. Elliot moved over to the seat they'd been holding vacant,
and let Amina sit down between him and Romey.

"Your mom's on a roll," Amina whispered. Just as it did during the
day at school, her cocoa-brown face stood out in this crowd with
beige-pink skin, and the few golden faces of the Mexican-American
parents. Amina's mother was white and her father black, but since she
was the only person of African descent in the high school, most kids
referred to her as "the black girl." This annoyed Amina; she felt part
of her was never seen.

Romey hugged Amina. "I'm so glad you finally got here."

"It was Lyle. He was late. I couldn't leave the kids." Amina, her
mother, and her stepfather had a tight schedule that revolved around
taking care of her twin toddler brothers.

"I put your name in the bowl. To speak."

"Gulp."

Up at the microphone, Janis swiveled toward Reverend Wright
and his followers. "I would like to point out that many of the young
people here tonight in support of this resolution do not attend Divido
public schools. They're being taught at home and at church. The sexual orientation of public school teachers is not their business, and none
of their parents' business."

From the back, one of the church teens yelled, "Pervert!"

Elliot stood up, pushed his way out of the row of chairs, and stomped over to the boy who'd yelled. Romey watched Elliot's face twist with sarcasm. The other boy balled his fists and moved closer. Elliot was taller and heavier, but his body seemed soft next to the Christian boy, who had a military haircut and all those coiled muscles, reminding Romey of a bulging metal can, marked "Contents Under Pressure," left out too long in the sun.

Romey looked at Amina and could tell Amina was thinking something similar.

Without a word, Romey and Amina rose up and pushed their way between the chairs to the back, took Elliot from each side by his arm, pulled him away, and dragged him to their seats.

"Nicholas Daggett," Iris called.

The boy who had just argued with Elliot gave two other church boys the high five. His black T-shirt was decorated with a white cross and the motto, "This generation marked for the living God—Ephesians 1:13-14."

Nick walked up to the stage like a cowboy on the way to a shoot-out.

"If homosexuality isn't a sin," he spit into the microphone, "then how come God said it was a sin in the Bible?"

The two men from Guerneville stood up and turned their backs to Nick at the mike. They stared off over the heads of the rows of people behind them. "Cool way to show he's an asshole without getting ruled out of order," one of them whispered to Elliot. "We saw it at a hearing in San Francisco."

Nick clenched his hands and raised his fists chest high. "K-k-k-k-k . . ." Nick's face reddened with the effort he was making to get the sound out of his throat. His breath sounded through the microphone. He drew his eyebrows together and his face held desperate concentration, as if he were trying to remember the word his mouth struggled to form. The pause lengthened and the audience shifted uncomfortably.

"K-k-ids!" the word exploded from Nick's mouth, "are just learning what's right and wrong. So if you put s-s-s-s . . ."

Romey felt the audience tense when Nick's hiss died into silence, but this time, the pause lasted only a second.

"S-sinners in charge of little kids, how are they going to learn what's right?"

Nick's face swung toward the reverend, who threw him back a thumbs-up sign and a big, calm, encouraging smile.

"If you don't teach kids what's right and wrong, there's gonna be more kids who commit crimes." Nick's arms dropped to his sides. "So I say to h-h-homosexuals, you shouldn't be allowed to be teachers." He glanced back at the reverend. "I . . . I guess that's all."

Elliot popped up and turned his back to the mike just as Nick finished.

Romey steeled herself, in case her name was called, but next up was a local Episcopal minister. "The Bible says homosexuality is a sin. But on a nearby page, it says receiving interest on your savings account is a sin, that those who commit adultery must be stoned to death, and that slavery and harems are perfectly okay. I want to talk about the danger of taking the Bible literally," he began.

After he finished his turn at the mike, two members of the Divido Bible Church were called in a row. Elliot and the pink triangle men from Guerneville stood, stone-faced, their backs to the speakers. Here and there around the room, a few others joined them and stood silently the same way.

Outside, the wind lashed the trees. A big eucalyptus branch screeched against the cafeteria's wire mesh-reinforced window.

A shaky high school senior from Petaluma spoke next. She told the story of her biology teacher, who took them on field trips and "made us all see how cool the natural world is. Mr. Petronelli had us all doing independent science research, and his students won thirteen statewide science fair prizes over the years. He helped us figure out what college to go to, and he volunteered his own time on weekends so we could have wilderness field trips. He let us use his sea kayak."

The girl breathed noisily into the mike, her words tumbling out fast. I have to remember, Romey thought, to talk slower when it's my turn.

The girl went on, describing this past semester, when her teacher had grown gaunt. He'd explained that he was gay, he had AIDS, and that the miraculous treatments which were keeping other people alive were failing for him, "and we learned more that day than in a whole month in some classes." Tears glittered in her eyes. "Mr. Petronelli died three weeks ago, but for a lot of us, he was the most important teacher we'll ever have."

Romey, Amina, and Elliot all clapped and were admonished by Iris.

The big heating fan hummed on. Papers rustled and people shifted in their seats as the next speaker, another member of the Divido Bible Church, walked up the three steps to the stage.

Elliot stood and turned his back.

"With all due respect to the grief of the young lady from Petaluma," the man began, "does anyone here seriously want to argue that we should hire homosexual teachers so our kids can watch them die of AIDS? I guess I'm just old-fashioned. It seems to me that's the best reason *not* to have homosexuals teaching our kids."

Then Iris called Amina.

Amina had a cloud of springy brown hair, a couple of shades lighter than her skin, with loose bits that poked from the edges like question marks. She whipped an elasticized velvet band out of her pocket, rapidly pulled her hair into a tight bun at the back of her head, popped up and walked toward the stage. Her head was pushed so far down that her neck seemed to disappear into her shoulders. She hated to speak even when called on in class, but she was here out of loyalty to Romey.

Tickly sweat ran down Romey's ribs as she watched her friend. Amina stared into the microphone as if it had her speech printed on it in tiny letters. Her mouth moved, but no sound came out.

"Amina, speak a little closer to the mike." Iris smiled encouragingly.

Amina laughed with embarrassment and moved forward. She still didn't take her eyes off the microphone. "My name is Amina Porter and I am a junior at Divido High." She looked quickly out at the crowd and then back to the mike. "Some people testifying here are, you know, like, 'You're gonna get cooties if you're around gay people.' That's how we used to talk about some kids in first grade. Like there was something you could, you know, catch if you hung out with them."

Some of the audience chuckled appreciatively. Romey looked around with a grateful smile.

"That's okay for first graders, but grown-ups should know better," Amina continued. "It's all, you know, just different kinds of love. Why should people be scared of love?"

The crowd coughed, scraped chairs. Amina walked back and sank down between Romey and Elliot, who both hugged her. Janis reached around Romey, touched Amina's shoulder, and said, "You did great."

Last year, Romey had told just enough kids she was gay to get the news around the school. She prepared herself for all kinds of reactions. If she got expelled, her mom was ready to fight for her, even to call in the ACLU. If Romey got insults hurled at her in the hallways, she was going to resolutely ignore them. If kids tried to beat her up, she'd go to the principal. If parents yanked their kids out of school, well, that would be their problem. If the TV news covered it, Janis rehearsed Romey until they were both sure Romey was ready with something to say. Still, Romey had no plan for what actually happened.

Some kids at the high school, when they first heard the news, thought they were being nice to her by not believing the gossip. One girl from the track team even came to Romey to tell her what people were saying and to give Romey a chance to clear what the girl saw as Romey's good name, and the team's good name. Later, Romey thought of a million ways she could have handled it, but at the time, she stammered and talked around the whole subject until, when she finally said yes, she *was* gay, it sounded stupid, like she was ashamed or something, when the whole idea behind coming out was to show the school she wasn't ashamed at all.

Then, gradually, things settled in to everyone just quietly avoiding Romey. In the hallways, she became invisible. At track practice, the other girls were careful to run far behind her, or far ahead. In the locker room, especially in the shower, there was a four-foot forbidden zone around Romey. No girl would enter it. When Romey sat down before a class began, the students around her looked away, or were busy with their homework, or absorbed in conversation with someone else. It was the same when class was over.

Her friend Amina stuck with her. But Amina had second lunch hour while Romey had first, and day after day no one would sit with Romey. Romey sat alone at a big square table for eight, refusing to eat more slowly and slink away, insisting by her posture that she had a right to be there. Kids would come up, smile, and ask if it was okay to drag the metal chairs away, the same chairs now arranged in rows for this meeting. Then they would crowd ten or eleven chairs around other tables, not looking at her the whole time. Gradually, all the chairs but Romey's would disappear from her table.

It made her mouth dry. She couldn't chew something like potato chips, so she brought wet things, carrot sticks and tuna fish sandwiches soggy with mayonnaise, yogurt in little plastic cups. After about a month, Elliot, a year ahead of her, the school's only other gay person—or, at least, the only other one who'd admit it—discovered her and started eating lunch at her table. This year, things were better. Amina, Elliot, and Romey all had the same lunch hour. Three chairs at a table and it almost looked occupied.

The next two speakers opposed the proposal to ban gay teachers. One harked back to the integration of public swimming pools in the 1960s; the other defended tolerance in general. Both of them mentioned Amina's point about "cooties" approvingly; one said it hit the nail on the head. Each time Amina was quoted, Romey elbowed her friend in silent congratulations. Elliot, from the other side, raised his big square hand with pantomimed emphasis and clapped Amina on her back.

A woman held a little girl up to the microphone. "My name is Ashley and I'm six," she said. "Please don't stop gay teachers."

Meredith should be here, Romey thought. The class president should come to something like this. Getting ready for the meeting, Romey had dreamed of her speech stirring people, and of Meredith watching, eyes full of new respect and admiration. She'd also clutched in fear of stumbling, of Meredith seeing that, too.

Romey had assumed that announcing she was gay at school would free her to express who she was. It hadn't turned out that way. When the track team girls giggled conspiratorially about how cute various boys were, Romey didn't have the nerve to say Meredith was cute, too. She still had to watch herself around everyone except Amina and Elliot. But tonight was a chance to express herself—not to say Meredith was cute, of course, but to say something serious and responsible, to have an effect in the wider world of adults and at the school too, to move the audience and make the school board decide in favor of gay teachers. That's why she had to do it, no matter how much her hands shook. Romey slid her hands between her jeans and her chair, sat on them to stop the shakes.

Reverend Wright was called next. Dressed in a blue suit, white shirt, and red tie, he moved toward the mike with the confidence of a TV talk show host.

"Ooooh, I'll bet a lot of those folks in his congregation just loo-ove to look into those blue, blue eyes on Sundays," Elliot leaned over to whisper to Romey. "And not all of them are ladies, either."

Reverend Wright swept those eyes, fortified under the sharp ledges that defined his brows, across the crowd. He snapped the mike expertly off the stand and moved to the edge of the stage, toward his audience.

"For those of us who believe in God, the cornerstone of American freedom is the freedom to raise our own children as moral people. *Moral* people. Now I have a daughter. Her name is Julie. Julie will be fifteen next month. She's the light of my life. I love her with all the love a father can feel."

He whipped the microphone cord and paced across the stage.

"Julie isn't here tonight. Can I tell you why? Because I didn't want to expose her to the filth we've heard here in this room. I didn't want to have to explain to her why some people want her to be taught by sodomites with AIDS." He paused and stared at the two pink triangle men and Elliot, who were standing, their backs to him. "In fact, we at Divido Bible Church brought only our young people eighteen years and older here tonight."

"Now, Mzzzzz. . ." he drew the word out until it was repulsive, snakelike, "Mzzzzz. Arden suggests that we of the Divido Bible

Church have no standing to speak here, because many of our children do not attend the public schools.

"Well, I'd dearly love to send Julie to public high school. My wife, Mrs. Wright," he intoned the "Mrs." reverentially, a proper and holy sound, "bless her heart, Mrs. Wright has set up a wonderful home school. Julie is getting a first-class education. Julie is a whole year ahead in math, for example. But my wife should not have to work so hard, on top of all the duties that fall to the wife of a clergyman. I'd like for my daughter to receive an education funded by the taxes I pay—"

"Church property is tax-exempt," someone called from the crowd.

Iris banged her gavel.

The reverend boomed, "I said, I'd like for my daughter to be educated here at Divido High, but I keep her home because of the immorality rampant here. Did you know our children are being taught how to use condoms? Condoms!"

Elliot, standing with his back to the speaker beside Amina, clutched his head in mock horror. Then he pantomimed unrolling a condom with much difficulty over his up-thrust fist. Romey and Amina stifled their giggles.

The reverend halted his pacing and stood still. His blue eyes locked on one audience member after another. "When children still want to ride Big Wheels and play with dolls, teachers are showing them how to have sex. Now, we all know that homosexuals cannot reproduce. They have to recruit new homosexuals. What we are proposing here is a modest and moderate reform."

Romey saw how most people, unless they faced the back wall in protest, were turning their shoulders, following the reverend as he paced across the stage. He wasn't even as tall as Romey was, but his motions and voice compelled attention. She wondered if she could pull it off when her turn came, if she could pace with the mike and stop to hammer home her strong points, instead of standing still, reading. Or would that look like imitating the enemy? Would she stumble over the cord? Probably safer not to try.

"We are saying to homosexuals," the reverend intoned, "you may not use our schools to recruit our children. The measure proposed by

Mrs. Stubbs is a simple way to stop it. I've been scratching my head all day trying to figure out why some parents—*parents*—in our community want their kids to learn how to be perverts."

The reverend walked down the three steps, still holding the mike, and moved a few feet into the right side aisle, toward where his church members were clustered. "In fact, I've been scratching so hard, I noticed this in the mirror as I was getting ready to come on over here tonight." He pointed toward his bald spot.

The flock laughed.

"Why would anyone oppose Mrs. Stubbs's sensible measure, unless they want homosexuals to teach acts of perversion in our classrooms? Openly in our county—"

Iris gave her gavel a crisp tap. "Time's up, Reverend."

"Well, now, just to wind up—"

Iris banged again. "Sorry, we strictly enforce a three-minute limit."

With an exaggerated air of obedience, the reverend crossed the stage and set the microphone back on its stand, producing a loud thump that reverberated with a three-second feedback screech.

Iris called Virginia Waldrip next. Virginia, the Divido Bible Church choir leader, walked slowly up from the back of the room. She was close to sixty, with quivering, round cheeks and glasses that magnified her sensitive eyes with their perpetually red rims. In a calm voice, she spoke into the mike. "I yield my three minutes to Reverend Wright."

The audience buzzed and stirred. Reverend Wright strode upon the stage once more.

"I thank you, Virginia," he said. "Now, as I was saying, homosexuals want to come right in here to Divido High and teach our children how to become perverts." He had a look that came over him during his Sunday sermons, when he fixed sin in his blue eyes and made it squirm like terrified prey. "You may not stand in front of our students and explain to boys who are still Cub Scouts how to perform sex acts that are unspeakable, ugly—"

One of the pink triangle men burst into loud giggles.

"—too disgusting to be mentioned here with all the children present. I know of no homosexuals teaching right now in the Divido schools. This measure merely puts into law the situation we now enjoy."

With a loud sigh of frustration, Janis stood up and turned her back. But Romey's eyes were locked on the row in front of her, where Nick Daggett was standing beside the two pink triangle men. "You laugh again, fag, you'll be real s-s-s-s-sorry," Nick snarled. A little spray of spit came out when he stuttered, "Sh-sh-sh-show some respect."

The man looked right at him. Unsmiling, he said, "Ha. Ha. Ha. Ha."

The reverend's voice rang out. "Now Mzzzzz. Arden, a mother who doesn't think a daddy is necessary to a family, who makes her living killing babies—"

"Stick to the point!" Iris shouted. Her gavel banged.

Nick grabbed the pink triangle man by the shoulders and tried to turn him around and force him to sit. The man's leg knocked against his empty metal chair. Romey caught it before it fell over.

"Mzzzz. Arden says our kids have no right to be here because they don't go to Divido High. Well, the little girl from Petaluma who told us about her biology teacher with AIDS doesn't go to Divido High, and I didn't hear Mzzzz. Arden objecting. And those two men . . ." the reverend swung his body around to point his arm at the two men with pink triangle lapel pins, "Nicky, go on back to the other side of the room. Those two men—go on, Nicholas . . ."

Nick took his hands off the man's shoulders and moved a few feet back.

Sneering, the reverend pointed his arm again. "*Those* two men over there came *all the way here from Guerneville.* Why is it okay for homosexuals to come here from Guerneville to testify about our community's schools, but not okay for Christian kids who live right here?"

With a crash, the wind broke off a big eucalyptus branch and hurled it against the west window.

The reverend turned and paused for a few seconds, looking at the window with respect. "Even the tree seems to have some doubts about the wisdom of letting pervert outside agitators testify here tonight. If we listen carefully, we can hear when the Lord is trying to tell us something."

The group from Divido Bible Church chuckled.

Janis leaned over and whispered to Romey, "The message, dear preacher, is that the trees need trimming. The school board can't get to its regular business because every meeting they have to hassle with fundamentalists."

"Bigot! Shame!" One of the pink triangle men yelled.

Iris banged for order.

"Big-got! Shame! Big-got! Shame!" The two men from Guerneville chanted. "Big *Gut.*" With his arms, one of them pantomimed a stomach extending out twice as far as the reverend's.

Nick Daggett grabbed him by his jacket and swung him into the aisle, sending a chair clattering to the floor.

"Bigot! Shame!" Romey, Amina, and Elliot joined the chant.

Virginia Waldrip raised her arm and blew a long blast on her pitch pipe.

"Order! Order! Stop that chanting." Iris's gavel rat-tat-tatted above the din.

The contingent from the Divido Bible choir started up in unison: *"What a friend we have in Jeeee-sus, all our sins and grief to bear—"*

Nick punched wildly at the pink triangle man, who kept chanting "Bigot!" and ducked.

"Shame!"

"What a privilege to carry everything to God in prayer!" sang the choir.

"Quiet! Stop this singing!" Iris's voice was hoarse. Bang, BANG, went her gavel. "Stop that chanting!"

"Big-*got!*"

"O what peace we often forfeit, O what needless pain we bear, all because we do not carry everything to God in prayer." Virginia beat vigorous time with her arm.

"Shame! Bigot! Shame!"

Iris was almost shouting now. "This is no way to conduct business. I'm sorry, but I have to declare this meeting officially adjourned."

"Have we trials and temptations? Is there trouble anywhere? We should never be discouraged; take it to the Lord in prayer."

"All those who didn't get a chance to speak will be called first during next month's meeting." Iris slammed down her gavel and turned off all the mikes.

The choir finished the verse and sang another chorus. Others gathered in angry clumps. Small children were released to run around.

For a few moments, Romey looked up toward the stage, not understanding.

So it was over. She wasn't going to be called to speak. Relief surged through her, then disappointment, then a slow, small dread. She had a whole month to be nervous, then she'd have to go through this whole thing again. She was suddenly sleepy. She slumped down in her chair and yawned.

Janis collared the two men from Guerneville. "Listen, you guys," she said sternly, "you've got a lot to learn. Never, never disrupt a meeting when the majority is with you. That's bad tactics. Bad strategy." Her face brightened. "It *was* kind of fun, though, wasn't it? Well, see you next month, same place, same time, I hope."

She walked around the room, giving the same message to others who'd yelled, "Bigot!"

A few people left, then a few more, then buzzing groups drifted out to the parking lot.

Reverend Wright stood amid his followers by the red-white-and-blue Divido Bible Church van. "We have not yet begun to fight. Tonight, we saved our measure from defeat. I'm proud of all of you who spoke up. We'll be back next month, stronger than ever. I want to report that two ladies and one gentleman asked me for the address of our church and the time of our services."

The group applauded.

"And did you hear that three-part harmony, even with many of our choir members not present? That Virginia is something else.

"Nicky," the reverend pulled his nephew to his side and held the boy's neck in a playful hammerlock, "we appreciate your fighting spirit for Christ, but you know we don't use our fists. Hear?"

Reverend Wright released the grinning Nick and patted him on the back. "Now, Nicholas, I want you to follow me home. The way you've been driving lately, I can't trust you not to speed 'cause you're wishing you could whip those sissies from Guerneville." He ran his hand over Nick's crew cut.

The wind was dying. Intimations of frost sharpened the autumn night air. The long, curved, pointed leaves of the eucalyptus trees hung down, barely stirring. Ignitions started. Cars pulled out, engines droned, and tires crunched dry, fallen eucalyptus berries, leaving a medicinal scent. An almost-full silver moon lounged over the eastern treetops.

At the other end of the parking lot, Janis hugged Romey. "I'm so disappointed you didn't get called. If I'd known the meeting was going to break up so soon, I'd have yielded my time to you."

Janis and the two girls got into the car, slamming doors.

"It was hard to get up there and speak. I was scared at first," Janis said.

Romey turned to her. "I sure couldn't tell."

"Me, neither," Amina said from the backseat.

"You can't let 'em see you're scared. Just have to talk louder. Amina, you did great. You were both brave tonight. You know, I was just your age when I went to my first anti-Vietnam War march." The gravel voice took on a softer edge. "But what you did tonight was braver, because it's so personal. I thought I was brave, but all I did was get arrested with about three hundred other people. They crammed us into cells so there was no room to sit down—"

Romey twisted around and rested her chin on the seat back, facing Amina, grinning, and finished her mother's sentence, "—for ten hours. And they got only half a baloney sandwich. And each person had only thirty seconds to pee."

Janis started the car. "Okay, okay, so you've heard that story about ten times before."

"Mom," Romey patted Janis's arm, "*Amina's* heard it ten times. For me, it's more like a hundred."

Janis pulled the car into a line of departing vehicles. "Amina, want me to drop you at your house or you want to come over?"

"Come over."

"Okay, but call your mom when we get home and tell her where you are."

"My mom's at work."

"Then call your dad."

"Stepdad. Like he's pacing the floor wondering about me."

"Call him anyway, okay?"

"All they care about is if I'm there when I'm supposed to baby-sit."

"Just call."

"Yeah, okay."

Janis stopped the car next to Elliot, who was on the sidewalk, talking with the men from Guerneville. She rolled down her window. "In the future, Elliot, no breaking up a meeting when you're ahead. Got that?"

"Got it, Janis."

"And don't hang around this parking lot too long. You don't want to meet up on a dark road with that kid from that church."

Elliot leaned his head in the window, toward Amina. "All these people are asking for my autograph because I sat with the orator of the 'cooties' speech, the fabulous Ms. Amina."

"See you tomorrow, Elliot," she answered.

"Yeah. Well, good night, sweet ladies."

A long line of golden headlights and red taillights glided along the county road, curving with the riverbed. The wind was gone, leaving the night crisp and starry. Iris Bernstein locked up the cafeteria door and commented to her husband, as they walked toward the lone car left in the parking lot, that it looked as though the first storm of the season had blown on by.

The moon held so much fiery brightness, it looked like it might burst. While the reverend addressed the school board meeting, his only child, Julie, six weeks shy of fifteen, lay on her white eyelet bedspread in her pink nightgown (both homemade by her mother) and let the moonshine wash in the window and along her body. She felt that liquid sensation, new to her these past months, blushing over her again. She had a private name for it: Yearning.

She savored this rush of sweet longing for something unknown. An invisible cord of feeling connected the center of her body to the moon; moonlight set the cord to humming, vibrating. She couldn't make

Yearning come when she wanted to, though she'd tried; she had to wait patiently for it. Now, it rose within her in great, lush swells.

Her window was open. Outside, the wind tossed the lemon tree around and blew into the bedroom a powerful fragrance of lemon blossoms. Julie stood up beside the bed, facing the window. She opened her arms wide to the wind and the moon. When Yearning came over her like this, it felt good to sigh deeply, out loud, letting the sigh linger tenderly in her throat and merge with the voice of the wind. Then she fell diagonally backward onto the moonlit bed. She knew this feeling was a force larger than herself, something elemental. The almost-full moon's face seemed to tilt and lean closer. She buried her fingers in the silky softness of her black hair. It gave her a shivery thrill to wander around the edges of Yearning, to taste, to probe.

Until now, only two other experiences had been this strong. The first had happened to her when she was nine. Daddy and Mom and Virginia had been telling her for years what it would be like for Jesus to come into her heart. She'd waited and prayed for it. That Sunday, she'd been sinful because she'd said something mean to her mother just before the service, and when the altar call came, she walked up the blue carpet on the aisle, faces from the pews a blur at her side, the stained glass shimmering above her, feeling as though she wasn't the one moving her own legs. Instead, she was being pulled up to the front of the church by an inescapable force. There she was at the altar, as she'd seen so many others before her, sobbing with remorse and relief, accepting Jesus as her personal savior. His light streamed into her, mixed up with the sun coming through the big red and blue stained-glass window. The whole congregation embraced her with a song of welcome. She felt as if she were coming home to a place she'd never known she'd left, and that Jesus would be in her heart forever.

Since that day, Julie had accepted Jesus into her heart again and again. She knew she could count on Him. All she had to do was pray to feel His presence.

Yearning was different. Yearning swelled up inside her at unexpected moments and she could never tell when it would vanish. But when Yearning arrived, and for as long as it lasted, it felt as right as her love for Jesus, something like her conscience, a conscience of another kind, a strong feeling from deep within, guiding her toward goodness.

Julie stretched her hand out toward the moon and turned it slowly, watching silvery light and shadow glide along the curve of her forearm. Gusts of wind made the white curtain surge in toward her, and then out into the night. She rubbed the back of her leg against a ruffle on the bedspread and wrapped her fingers in the satin ribbon at her nightgown's throat.

The other feeling as strong as Yearning came certain Sundays (but not all of them), when Julie sang in the choir, and the harmony throbbed through the whole congregation. Every heart pumped to the same rhythm, and the stream of voices rose together toward the sunny stained glass, up and up for that moment when Julie hit the highest note, her velvet voice soaring above it all, big and true.

She understood what happened then in the choir. It was the Holy Spirit coming into her soul, and out of her through her voice. The sense of soaring came because she practiced her singing, developed the gift of the voice God had given her, and followed Virginia's direction. But nothing she did could make Yearning come. It arrived in thrilling waves for no reason at all.

She sat up and reached for a glass of water from the nightstand. She sipped the moonlight shining gold on the water's surface. Below the moonlit glass, her new breasts swelled under thin pink cotton. She liked having breasts, their rosiness in the shower, the sight of them under her clothes, solid, all the time. Julie put back the glass, lay down, moved her hand until her fingers lay softly curled on her nightgown, in the warm space between her breasts. The moon glazed both hand and breasts with pale light.

She'd asked her mother about Yearning, stumbling over her words, trying to describe the excitement and longing, embarrassed.

Her mother, who was sewing a button back on one of the reverend's shirts, jabbed the needle hard through the blue cloth. The two lines that led downward from the corners of her mouth got deeper. "It probably means you're going to be interested in boys soon," she said. "But you're still too young for all that. You know what your dad and I have told you. No dating until you're sixteen."

After that, in church, Julie tried fixing her eyes for an entire service on a boy—a dark-eyed, shy tenor from the choir, who was on the short side, like her—to see if Yearning would arrive. At youth group, she sat attentively next to one boy one week, another boy the next, waiting hard for Yearning to break over her. But, nothing.

She asked Virginia, the leader of the choir. "Yes, I've had that feeling," Virginia answered. Her red-rimmed eyes focused on some distant point far behind Julie. "You pull that feeling right into your singing and you'll sound like an angel from heaven."

But Julie knew there was more to it. Yearning was beautiful, just like the choir-singing feeling, but also more fierce and complicated. She turned on her side, smoothed the pink nightgown over her hip. When she lay this way, her breasts touched each other. Moonlight was almost a feeling tonight. The cool wind, with its breath of lemon blossom mixed with faraway rain, blew over her hot skin.

She hadn't asked her dad about Yearning, and she wasn't sure why not. But last Sunday, she'd been excited to hear him make a comment in his sermon that she knew applied to Yearning. "If we accept Jesus as our Savior, if we truly allow Him to enter our hearts, we will surely receive blessings, but *we cannot choose what blessings we receive.* Jesus does that part for us," Reverend Wright said.

Lately, Julie had begun to see depth in her father's sermons, to understand how they told each person something different, always just what each one needed to hear. To her mother, last Sunday's sermon said not to question God because there had been no more babies after Julie. To Virginia, it said to be thankful that she had a gift for bringing out the best in her singers, and that the choir won prizes, and not to feel bad about never getting married. And now, Julie was old enough to understand what her dad's sermons had to say about her own life. To Julie, the sermon said that this new Yearning was her own special blessing, chosen for her by Jesus. Its mystery would be revealed in time, or not. Either way, she should thank Jesus for the inner joy bestowed upon her, welcome Yearning, and protect it.

But now, Yearning was flying off into the night. That was the sad part. Yearning came and went on its own inner time. She couldn't make it stay, even though she took a deep breath full of moon and lemon blossom.

Julie stood and closed the window. The room went still. She got down on her knees, clasped her hands against a white eyelet ruffle, thanked Jesus for Yearning, and asked Him to send it back again. Soon.

Back on her bed, staring at the wall where the lemon tree branches danced in a moon shadow, Julie was left with only the pallid memory of Yearning, a ghostly longing for longing itself.

Chapter 2

Twenty-five years earlier, Janis had been part of a lively women's consciousness-raising group, which still met twice a month. One of the members, Pam, owned a cabin, all glass and redwood, high on a ridge outside Divido, accessible only by a half-mile walk on a bumpy dirt road. Every summer the group held a retreat there during the weeks Romey was away at her father's in Oregon. The group had dwindled, after all the years, down to three, affectionately known as the Remnant.

Janis had urged the Remnant to come to the school board meeting, but Pam had to see her therapy clients and Peg had to meet with the board of the small organization she ran. As soon as Janis arrived home with the girls, she got on the phone, first with Peg, then with Pam, to describe how disgustingly the fundamentalists had behaved and to indulge in a little ranting about the gay rights supporters' strategic errors.

Romey and Amina headed for Romey's bedroom. Seated cross-legged on the floor, Romey glared at a stack of books, her poster of women runners, her poster of Gay Freedom Day in San Francisco, an old gash at the bottom of the door, her limp running clothes hanging from a hook, the brown comforter on the bed, compact discs piled up in front of the boom box, the same stuff that had been there forever and would be there forever.

"Elliot'll probably go home with that blond guy from Santa Rosa tonight, the cute one," Romey said. "Welcome to the least interesting life on the planet, the life of a teenage lesbian."

Amina shook her head, and her cloud of hair, which she'd let loose again, stirred, stray bits rising up and settling back down. "You don't really want to go home with some girl you just met."

"Just watch me if I ever get the chance. It would be better than nothing." Romey sighed. "No, not really, I guess I don't. It's just— I don't get to try out anything."

She stood up and walked to her dresser, struck a match, lit a candle. It glowed in a lavender glass bowl. Behind it was a picture, cut out from last year's high-school yearbook, of Meredith at a podium, giving her serious class-president election speech. Beside the photo, three stems of honeysuckle curved up from a little vase. Romey pinched off a wilted flower and tossed it in the wastebasket. "Maybe Meredith will show up at the school board next month."

"You stay so in love with her when she'll hardly even speak to you. Plus, she's totally into Brian."

Romey touched the gold picture frame lightly. "Ameens, I figured out something. You know what going on dates is all about? It's so kids can get practice at love."

"I think it's mostly about having fun."

"But during the fun, the main thing is to practice *love*. And people like that reverend tonight, who try to keep us gay kids from getting any practice, they're trying to make us into lonely grown-ups who won't know how to love." Lately, Romey had worried that the lack of practice could harm her the whole rest of her life.

"Not all straight kids get practice. I'm not getting any."

Romey rearranged the honeysuckle and, not looking at Amina, said quietly, "Getting your heart broken is still some kind of practice."

"Oh, give me a break. No way what happened to me was a broken heart. It wasn't that real. Not even close. You make it, like, better than it was. What I got practice at was being stupid."

"At least you won't still be a virgin when you graduate from high school."

"Well, give me a gold star."

"Easy for you to say. I'm gonna be a virgin. And the only other virgins in the whole school will be church kids. That preacher would be shocked to find out how much I have in common with his youth group."

Romey felt excluded from the whole cycle of flirting, dating, or even collecting sympathy during a break-up. It filled her with sick envy to see some girl walking down the hall at school, reveling in the drama of losing her boyfriend, surrounded by a knot of other girls delivering condolences. It was a higher order of pain than Romey's. Far better than being locked completely out of love's candy store.

Romey flopped down on her bed. "There may not be another lesbian in the whole school, but no one can stop me from loving Meredith." She glared at the ceiling. "They say it's better to have loved and lost than not to have loved at all. Well, I say, better to love and get nothing back than not to love at all. What harm does it do? It doesn't hurt Meredith. It doesn't change her sterling heterosexual record. And at least I love somebody."

"Your friends love you. I do. Elliot does. Your mom."

"That's different and you know it."

Amina picked at the brown bedspread. She looked cautiously at Romey. "Sometimes I think when you find a girlfriend, you won't be friends with me anymore."

Romey jerked her head up stared at Amina. "How can you say that? We're best buds. If I didn't have you for a friend, I'd be one of those gay kids who kill themselves, like my mom was talking about. You're not gonna stop being friends with me when you get a boyfriend."

"Like it's gonna happen next week."

"Well, you're not, are you?"

"No, but it's different for you, because she'd be a girlfriend. There are things you can't tell a boyfriend, but you could tell your girlfriend all the same stuff you tell me."

"If another girl who's got a white mom and a black dad moves to Divido and you guys get to be friends, will you stop being my friend?"

"The chances of *that* are about one in infinity."

"Still, what if? Would you drop me for her?"

"No way."

"So I'm not going to stop being your friend, either. You stood by me when I came out. You just went to that meeting and spoke up 'cause of me, and you hate talking in class. Plus," Romey reached over and tickled Amina's arm, "you're over here spending the night with me when most girls would be afraid they'd get *cooties*."

Romey lay on her back, propped one leg on the other knee and pointed it in the air. "If we ever stop being friends, it won't be because I wanted to."

"Well, I won't want to, either."

"Then I guess you're stuck with me for life, Amina-beena."

Their sophomore year, Amina, who had never been to a movie or a dance with a boy, got invited to a basketball game by a tall, white senior football player. He started coming to her house and taking her out to Burger King.

Amina went over to his house on a Saturday night to watch videos. His parents weren't home. They drank a little beer, the boy told Amina he loved her, and quick as punching "fast forward" on a remote, they were having sex on the scratchy tweed couch.

She wasn't even used to having a boyfriend when another football player taped a yellow rose and a note to her locker. He showed up frequently to walk her from class to class. Soon she was at his house, and again there was beer, and again, sex.

"I don't know how I'm going to juggle my two boyfriends," she told Romey, giddy, cheeks aglow. "They're both going to want a lot of time. And I better get to your mom's clinic for some of those pills."

Then both the football players vanished. Amina went over to the first boy's house one night, needing to talk to him, sure that if he would only tell her what was wrong, they could work it out. She sat on the edge of the ottoman in the TV room, trying to say the magic words that would rekindle the looks he'd given her before, those looks like a character on a TV drama who was tormented with love, and bring back his tender flirting. But he looked away from her, made it sound like she was a kid who didn't understand sex, broke off the conversation to answer a phone call from another girl, and then just didn't come back into the TV room.

Amina sat frozen on the ottoman until the boy's mother came in and said, "Oh, are you still here?"

How pale the woman's skin looked to Amina then, compared to her own cocoa color. The difference felt glaring in a way it never did with the kids and teachers at school.

That "Oh, are you still here?" somehow echoed loudest in Amina's memory, digging into her more than the recollection of rushed sex on the couch. Whenever the tone of that voice came back, she cringed and flushed.

Yet another football player started to ask Amina out. Before their first date, Amina heard via the school rumor mill that five boys had a bet they could all "get the black girl to fuck us before spring break."

She'd had no dates since. Boys didn't ask her often, but when they did, Amina wasn't about to be the fool again. She turned them down.

Now, lying across Romey's bed, Amina could feel this bright room around her, like strong arms, secure amid the dark night. Amina looked up at Meredith's picture. "Except for the fact that she's straight, Meredith would be perfect for you."

Romey grinned. "Wouldn't we look good together? I'm an inch and three quarters taller."

"You're as smart as Meredith, too. She got early admission to UC Berkeley and so will you."

"'Cept I might not go there. Mom found out about a bunch of colleges in this town in Massachusetts, Northampton? There's supposed to be a ton of lesbians at all the colleges. I might go to one of those."

"Wherever you go, there'll be lots of girls like Meredith."

"There aren't lots of girls like Meredith."

Romey was quiet for a minute, looking out the window into the darkness. She was being selfish, going on about UC Berkeley versus some expensive private schools in the east, because Amina's mother and stepfather had told her she couldn't count on any help with college. And Amina's grades were as good as Romey's. Amina's SATs were even a little higher. It wasn't fair.

Amina was not only the only brown-skinned girl at school, but also the only one in her family. Her father, his skin the color of walnut wood finish, was just a memory. Her mother had one of those pale English complexions that show a blush easily. At home, Amina felt like a relic of something past and tried not to bother her harried mother, who was preoccupied with the family's tight finances, rotating shift work, Amina's blond stepfather, and the towheaded twins who had been born two years before.

"Maybe your parents will change their minds," Romey said.

"I doubt it. Want to hear what Lyle said yesterday? If I want to stay home and go to college, I have to get a job and pay them *rent*. He said he joined the Army to get an education and I can, too. He says that's how it was in his family, and that's how you learn responsibility."

"But does Lyle have a degree?"

"Does a worm have a computer?"

"What does your mom say?"

"Oh, she pretty much goes along with Lyle."

Hard knocking sounded on the bedroom door. Janis stuck her head in. "Amina, if you need a place to live when you graduate, you just move in here for free. Don't let yourself get cheated out of college. I won't charge you rent. You can ride into Santa Rosa with me and go to classes at the junior college. It might go four-year soon. I'll be rattling around in my empty nest with Romey gone. I'd love to have you."

"Oh, Janis, that's won—"

"*Mom!* That's great, but we're having a *private conversation* here, okay? How many times have you yelled at me for listening in on you and the Remnant?"

"Stop exaggerating. I hardly ever yell. And I wasn't listening in. I was just coming back from the bathroom and overheard one little bit. It's a standing offer, Amina. Now, I know the meeting got all of us hyped up, but tomorrow's a school day. Settle down in there and go to sleep."

"Right, Mom. We need our rest to lead our fascinating social lives."

"Just remember, all interesting people had a bad time in high school. If you were enjoying high school, you wouldn't want to be the kind of people you'd turn into when you grew up. Now, good night." Janis closed the door with a thump.

Romey threw Amina a smile that meant "Mom can't help it" and tossed Amina an extra-large T-shirt.

After they lay down, Romey wondered, not for the first time, why she never felt attracted to her friend. A fear lurked on the edge of her thoughts that deep down, she might be, well . . . racist.

But then, she didn't think Amina would want Romey to be attracted to her. Amina liked boys. If Romey were attracted to her, it would probably make Amina uncomfortable.

Still, Romey wondered, wasn't it kind of insulting to Amina that she didn't feel attracted? Maybe Amina wanted Romey to be attracted, just so Amina would know she was attractive, even though she wouldn't really want Romey to do anything? Maybe it hurt Amina's feelings, but she was just keeping quiet about it, because she was embarrassed. Except that would be selfish for Amina to want Romey to be attracted to her and yet not want to respond at all. It couldn't be. Amina was too nice.

Romey turned over on the bed, trying not to disturb Amina. The strange part was that when Amina moved to Divido all those years ago, when they were still kids, Romey had been fascinated by the way the airy brown of Amina's hair was a lighter color than her cocoa skin. Partly, Romey had been drawn to Amina's looks.

Yet when Romey got older, she felt an arc of excitement in her body when she saw blonde Meredith, and a milder version, sometimes, for other girls. Not for Amina.

Romey didn't want to be racist. If someone said or did something that seemed racist to her, she always asked Amina if it really was. But in this case, she couldn't ask. It sounded insulting: Am I being racist because I'm not attracted to you (even though you don't want me to be)?

Maybe she knew Amina too well? There was no mystery there? Love—not the sisterly love she felt for Amina, but grand love—was supposed to need mystery.

Maybe something inside Romey tuned in to the part of Amina that liked boys, and prevented Romey from being attracted to Amina?

But that couldn't be right. Meredith was straight, too. And the feeling of attraction to Meredith was as uncomplicated as knowing when you were thirsty.

Of course, that could be because maybe Meredith wasn't really straight. Meredith could be gay, deep inside, and only Romey could detect it. Now, here was an appealing theory . . .

Romey flopped over, shoved more pillow under her face.

As a friend, she really loved Amina. Loved Amina a whole lot more than her stepsisters up in Oregon. Without Amina, at school, she'd feel like a speck of floating junk, constantly in danger of being swamped.

True, Romey had Elliot. But as Amina had just said, there were some things you just couldn't talk about with a boy. Especially one a year older.

Maybe it was kind of like an incest taboo. Even though she desperately wanted a lover, maybe she needed a best friend more, and that need stopped her from ever feeling attracted to Amina.

Or did all this wondering why she wasn't attracted to Amina mean that deep down she really was, but she couldn't admit it, because Amina's rejection would devastate her? Was she in denial?

But if that was so, why was it so easy to tell she was attracted to Meredith? Meredith wasn't exactly calling up and asking Romey to the prom.

She rolled over again and untwisted the sheets with a loud sigh. Love, caged inside her, clicked its little clawed rodent feet in her brain, relentlessly spinning its plastic wheel.

Romey wondered if Amina ever had the mirror image of these thoughts. There was no way she could find out. But clearly, Amina wasn't lying awake about it now. Amina's head was already still and heavy on the pillow, her breathing even, her mouth a little open, her eyes moving under her lids in that way that signals a dream.

Closing her eyes, Romey started a trick for inducing drowsiness, powers of two. Two times two is four, times two is eight, times two is sixteen . . . thirty-two . . . sixty-four . . . 128. At some point after two to the twentieth power, 1,048,576, the numbers dissolved into meaninglessness and floated off. Romey slid into a pool of sleep.

The following Sunday, at the eleven o'clock service at Divido Bible Church, the choir was singing the final hymn. As love for Jesus poured through Julie in song, she always picked out someone in the congregation and sent them extra blessings through her eyes. Today, it was an old man in the third row who'd been out of work ever since the sawmill downsized, and next to him, his trembly wife.

When Julie smiled, her cheeks rose and her eyes appeared, paradoxically, slightly sunken and sad. The bigger her smile, the sadder her eyes. Those sad eyes set in a joyful face made her look wiser than a fourteen-year-old can be expected to be, gave the impression that she understood life's sorrows in a deeper way than she actually did. The old couple took the succor she offered, sighed, and sat back more comfortably in their pew.

After the service, Connie walked her sister Patty and the boys up the aisle. Wayne, Patty's husband, wasn't with them.

Connie noticed how Nick, Patty's oldest son, was looking like a real man these days. She smiled at him. "You did a real good job at the school board meeting."

Nick looked at his shoes. "Th-thanks."

She turned to Patty. "What a pretty dress," she said. It was green and silky, a good color for Patty. "Is it new?"

Patty smiled, and twirled so the skirt flared out a little. "Brand new."

"And I got a new shirt!" Teddy, the youngest in the family, tugged on Connie's hand. "We all got new shirts."

Patty held him to her hip. "We sure do, don't we?"

Teddy wriggled and ducked, trying to get out of his mother's grasp, then broke free and lunged toward a tall side window, bumping into parishioners' legs. He climbed up onto the broad windowsill, grinned with satisfaction at being momentarily taller than anyone else, and flexed his legs to jump.

With a couple of deft steps, Nick was in front of Teddy. "Whoa there, Tiger. Let's walk outside as quiet as we can, and then I'll swing you like an airplane." He lifted the boy and carried him away.

Patty smiled apologetically at Connie. "Ted got thrown out of kindergarten for kicking the teacher last week. He's a real handful. And the only one who can do a thing with him is Nicky." Patty and her middle boy turned to go, leaving Connie to wonder where Patty was getting all this money for clothes. Wayne had been out of work for more than three months now.

The reverend stood at the sanctuary door, talking to one of the Wrights' closest family friends, Bob Gahl. High time Bob showed up here, Connie thought. In her opinion, Bob was getting carried away drilling with the volunteer militia he'd organized, parading in the woods weekend after weekend, neglecting his ranch and missing church more Sundays than not.

The congregation mingled in the lobby. A group of people clustered around the reverend, another around Connie, and the largest of all around Julie. After a while, Connie's group dispersed and she stood alone, watching people talk to her husband and daughter.

Julie was standing near the coffee urn, wearing a blue dress Connie had made to match Julie's eyes. In the muted sunlight from the stained-glass cross overhead, Julie's black hair gleamed. She had her choir robe draped over her arm. A steady stream of people trooped by to tell her how beautifully she sang. The praise polished Julie to a rosy radiance. The parishioners were tired for the most part, weighed down by diabetes, money worries, heart trouble, cars that needed new engines; they were angry about the cutbacks at the lumber mill, bewildered by the way the old town was changing, by the new people moving in with master's degrees, with their jobs in Santa Rosa or even San Francisco (to which they "telecommuted"), those arrogant newcomers with their high gloss of assurance about their good taste. Julie's sparkle, tinged with sadness, connected the parishioners to a time when they themselves were younger, and everything seemed, looking back, less complicated. Sunnier.

But to Connie, there was something disturbing and unhealthy about Julie's beauty, about that smile that promised an understanding Julie couldn't possibly have yet at this young age, that trick of Julie's cheekbones. Connie could see plainly that people were projecting onto Julie something that wasn't there. It worried Connie. She walked back into the sanctuary, gathered up programs, and returned hymnals to the backs of the pews.

Connie remembered her own teenage years, the attention and praise she'd received for her organ playing. She knew all about being the young star of a congregation. But those ladies at the church had to explain only once about beauty being God's gift, meant to be used as a balm for others, and about how important it was to be modest. Connie hadn't needed to be told over and over.

It was grating on her, the way Julie was carrying on today. "Lord, I'm proud of her, but don't let her head get turned with all this fuss," she said softly, looking up at the red and blue stained glass.

Connie walked up the aisle and stood in the archway to the lobby. "Juliet Christine," she called sharply. "Come on over here and help me straighten up."

In Reverend Jim Ed Wright's twice-yearly weekend workshops on Creating Zest in Your Christian Marriage, and when he counseled couples about to marry, he advised making a place in this busy world, where often both husband and wife must hold jobs, for "special sex time." Monday night—with the words of his sermon from the previous day still ringing, the busy Sunday over, and the reverend relaxed from his only day off—was a traditional special sex time for the Wrights. The adulation the reverend had received on Sunday lent an extra gusto to the marriage sacrament.

He felt especially buoyant tonight. He'd received in the mail the official Call from a Christian congregation in Lubbock, Texas. The congregation was almost twice the size of his present one, he would have an assistant pastor, and, while the compensation package was smaller, Lubbock had a lower cost of living. The reverend wasn't going to accept the Call, for several reasons. First, his daughter had been born here in Divido; he and Connie had sunk roots. Second, his wife had family here, troubled family who required the reverend's spiritual guidance. Third, this was a Godless part of the country. He was needed.

But it made a man feel good to be sought out by a faraway church, spiced up his evening.

As he shaved, he transferred his weight jauntily from foot to foot and hummed to himself with the cheer of a man who knows without doubt that sexual enjoyment is imminent. Shaving was one of those little ways to create zest. His face didn't scratch Connie when he rubbed it freely over whatever part of her body he chose, and he'd learned a shaven face heightened his own sensations, too, particularly if he was careful not to cut himself. Above all, a fresh shave made Connie feel cherished.

When he stepped from the bathroom into the bedroom, Connie was standing by the bed. The three-way lamp was set at dim. Its soft glow revealed, beneath her filmy nightgown, the shape of her breasts, the curve of her waist, the fullness of her hips.

"You're still as beautiful as the first day I saw you," he said, and it was true, except maybe for the two deep furrows that ran from the corners of her mouth down to her chin. Connie's intensity, nervousness, and heavy schedule just burned the calories off her, so that now she was only slightly plumper, and to the reverend, becomingly so. Her hair, though shorter, was still as black and still undulated in the same firm waves as the day when he, a shy seminary student, finally wangled an introduction to the vivacious girl from the Bible college across Seminary Road. Back then, she already played a ravishing church organ. One of the many pleasures of his family life was watching his daughter's features transform themselves, day by day, from a child's to a copy of Connie's lovely face as it looked in their courtship days, except that in place of Connie's dark eyes, Julie had his own blue ones. "You sure had the boys buzzing around you then," he reminded Connie now. And she'd chosen him out of them all.

Connie smiled at his familiar praise. "You're still just as gallant as you were back then, too."

A pastor's wife is always sharing her husband with someone who needs his comfort and guidance. Tonight, he was hers. The door to the bedroom was locked. Julie wasn't likely to interrupt them, but, as the reverend counseled in his workshops, a lock protects a couple from inhibitions.

He walked toward her, caught her in his arms, and held her for a minute, inhaling her perfume. He lifted the filmy nightgown up over her head. She untied his bathrobe belt and pushed the robe down his shoulders. They embraced and sank onto the bed, the reverend carefully avoiding any move that might irritate his back.

Sex, the reverend taught the couples who came to his workshops, is too beautiful and good to be an accidental by-product of the cold, impersonal force of evolution. Something as sublime as the sex act, something so powerful and yet so delicate, must have been lovingly and intentionally created by God.

And to fully enjoy what God has bestowed, the reverend advised, couples should begin with plenty of tender foreplay. He ran his hand slowly along his wife's thigh and nibbled her neck.

Connie was very organized. She had to be. She had so many responsibilities to the church, to her home school for her daughter, to the Right to Life group, and to her husband. Sometimes, when they began making love, her mind would frantically run over the agenda for a church committee meeting, or the lessons she needed to give Julie the following day. Tonight, she was replaying an encounter from last Thursday in front of the abortion clinic, thinking of something different she might have said to that one woman who looked hesitant, but who had gone inside anyway. Connie didn't want these thoughts to intrude now, while Jim Ed was stroking her body. She pushed them away and concentrated on kissing him.

Some couples who arrived at the reverend's weekends in search of zest had armed themselves too strongly against the temptation of sex before marriage. Once married, once sex was blessed and encouraged, they had trouble achieving sexual pleasure. The reverend helped them claim the healthy, exhilarating sex life that was their privilege and right through Christian marriage. For instance, he taught that modesty is good in many places, but not in the marriage bed. And that the heavenly Father placed the clitoris upon woman's body for her enjoyment, provided that enjoyment takes place between sanctified marital sheets.

Paying attention to his wife's enjoyment, he always said, a husband reaps a rich harvest of pleasure himself. After some minutes, their whole-body loving condensed around their most sensitive places, heightened, and built steadily to that moment just before climax becomes unstoppable, with both of them panting and Connie crying out, "Jim Ed, *Jim Ed.*" Then, as the reverend phrased it in his workshops, the two became again one flesh in a release that reflects, on this earthly plane, the Christian soul, on the spiritual plane, bonded to Jesus in rapture.

But even the most devoted Christian couple rarely achieves rapture at exactly the same moment. This is when, the reverend pointed out to the husbands who came for the marriage weekends, the hand comes in handy. The reverend was tender and knowing with his. Soon Connie quivered, moaned his name, became still, and clung to him, suffused with soothing afterglow. She pressed her cheek against his chest.

"Connie Belle, Connie Belle," he said, stroking her hair, "you sure are something, after all these years."

If you can just remember one thing, he told husbands-to-be, don't roll over and go to sleep afterward. Your wife needs sweet talk and cuddling.

Over the bed hung a framed sampler, embroidered in blue and gold by Connie's sister Patty. Their wedding date was picked out in French knots; below it Patty had cross-stitched: "On this day Jim Ed and Connie Wright put their marriage in Jesus' hands."

Connie fingered a tuft of her husband's wiry chest hair. "It breaks my heart to see those young girls at the abortion mill, to know they're ruining their chances for this kind of lovemaking. They think they've made love, but they haven't, really. They've just had sex. Empty sex."

"Not to mention dangerous sex." He patted her rump.

"Those diseases," Connie agreed, thinking with a shudder of running sores and wasted bodies. She pulled up the clean sheet and snuggled closer.

"And even if they don't get sick," the reverend pointed out, "they don't realize that the guilt they are bound to feel will corrupt their married pleasure later. If they do get married."

The reverend liked to quote a survey at his workshops showing that born-again Christian couples made love more times per week than the average secular couple. He was sure that those who stuck to God's plan of marriage as the holy channel for the tumultuous force of sexuality had better sex, too. He believed abstaining before marriage heightened the pleasure of sex even further after the wedding bells. But since quality of pleasure was hard to measure in a survey, he had no data. This part had to be taken on faith.

Going farther, it could be speculated that a man who had dedicated his whole life to the church and his loving wife might enjoy the topmost order of sexual pleasure, but the reverend didn't let his thoughts wander in that direction. Pride, after all, is a sin.

Connie lifted her head and planted a kiss on his bald spot. "I have a hunch some of those girls at the abortion mill didn't even enjoy the sex that landed them pregnant at fourteen or fifteen. I can see it in their eyes."

"And then to throw away the most delightful result of married love. The gift of parental love." He stared at the opposite wall, where Jesus looked out, eyes full of compassion, at a point just above their bed.

Tears trickled from Connie's eyes at the thought of the four miscarriages that had followed Julie. "I wish I could make those girls understand. If they really knew how good married love *feels,* they'd realize what a poor substitute they've gotten stuck with."

His arms encircled her more tightly. "Shall we pray, Connie Belle?"

She blew her nose. They put on their bathrobes and knelt beside the bed.

"Father, we thank you for the beautiful sexual expression of our marriage and the abundant love You have blessed us with," the reverend began. "We give thanks to You for our lovely daughter, Juliet. And, if it is Your will, we humbly ask You to bless our union with another baby."

Connie's tears gushed out. It touched her for him to ask for the pregnancy she had always included in their prayers. Lately, she'd stopped. It just plain hurt too much. The word "miscarriage" was so impersonal. It didn't describe what had happened at all. Each one was a child, a child she planned and hoped for. She thought about those four babies every day, always knew how old each one would be. Tonight, they would be nine, eight and a half, six, and three. The eight-and-a-half-year-old had been a boy, would have been Julie's little brother. The others, she didn't even know if they were boys or girls. She'd lost them when they were that young.

The reverend continued, "Thank You, Lord, for giving us a good daughter and guiding us to teach her right from wrong."

Connie drew a ragged breath. "And we thank You, Father, that she's not boy-crazy, the way even some of these girls who've been saved are."

"We thank you for her singing voice, and her beauty."

Connie lifted her head. Her voice grew stronger. "Help us understand, Lord, the times when she needs a firmer hand." Silently, she asked Jesus to guide Jim Ed away from the temptation to spoil his only daughter. And to help Julie not to get her head turned by being so pretty.

They asked God's blessing for their relatives, near and far.

"Help Wayne to find work, help him be a good father to his sons, and help Patty not spend money on foolishness," Connie asked.

The reverend added, "Lord, guide their boy Nicholas now. He's a good boy. Nicky wandered away from righteousness and got into trouble these past two years, but now he has come back to the church. The boy was brave at the school board, spoke up for Your Word even though he's got that stutter. Help him. Keep him away from drink and the bad boys he was running with."

Next, they prayed for members of the congregation, then for the whole denomination, then for those who ministered in the missions abroad. After their "amens," they took off their robes and cuddled up again to fall asleep in the nude.

A misty thought drifted through Connie's mind, that waiting to fall asleep was a little like waiting for your husband to give you an orgasm. In both cases, you could do plenty to make it more probable, but the timing of the final event was in someone else's hands. With orgasm, Jim Ed's. With sleep, God's. She relaxed her arm, let it slide down Jim Ed's side into a little trough formed by their two bodies, and waited to be carried off in God's firm hands.

The streets had no sidewalks here. Romey churned up dust as she ran along the shoulder, doing her regular three-mile route at twilight, when the air had cooled down. Starting the uphill part, she breathed harder. The high point of the run, both in altitude and interest, was the street with Meredith's sprawling old ranch-style house. Often Romey had passed the first corner window and seen Meredith there, in what must have been her bedroom. As Romey rounded the bend, the first glimpse of that window felt like a giant hand, lifting her up the hill, quickening her pace. Tonight, the window was dark, the shade down.

Her breath evened out and the burn in her shins receded as she passed Meredith's house. At the opposite end from the room she thought must be Meredith's, a big picture window was lit up. In the purplish dusk, the dining room inside glowed, a bright gold box. Meredith and six other kids jostled around a table, elbowed each other, and pulled away slices of pizza, trailing long, gooey strings of cheese. Meredith wore a tight-fitting tank top. It showed off her graceful shoulders, her breasts. She laughed at something Brian said. Rock music thumped and moaned.

Romey missed a breath. Her stride got ragged. There were sweat circles under the arms of her old yellowed T-shirt. Her legs were streaked with dirt. She turned the corner and ran toward her own empty house. Her mom was at the health club, Amina was baby-sitting the twins, and Elliot was on his way to his support group in Santa Rosa.

She'd seen plenty of stories on the TV news about kids having sex too young, the damage that caused. But what about having to wait until you were too old—eighteen or nineteen or even in your twenties—until you felt a hug that wasn't parental or friendly, until someone touched you in a sensual way? Wasn't that a social problem, too? Didn't it shrink the soul?

Her arms felt gangly. Romey pumped her legs harder and headed back down the hill toward her empty house, a thin sweaty figure disappearing into the darkening night. No cars passed, and no one was out in any of the front yards. Her running shoes hit the gray asphalt and kept a steady, lonesome rhythm under the bruise-colored sky.

Chapter 3

Heat waves shimmered off the dry grass in the open meadows at Divido County Park, but the County Fair food booths stayed cool all afternoon under a dark green canopy of live oaks. Whole turkey legs and sausages sizzled on an open grill as big as a king-sized bed. At nearby booths, teenagers in white aprons heaped mounds of curly fries on paper plates or piled alfalfa sprouts onto tofu burgers. People from age five to age ninety crisscrossed from booths to tables carrying corn dogs, pesto pasta salad, vegetable burritos, ice cream cones, locally brewed beer.

Business was brisk at the Divido Bible Church's apple pie stand, set up as a fund-raiser. Julie and Connie had just finished their shift, and now Julie carried half a pie to one end of a long table covered with red-checked oilcloth. The bench beside it, made of hay bales topped with a long 2 × 12 board, scratched the back of her legs as she sat down. Her attention got snagged by a young mother, two tables over, who jerked her toddler by his arm and shrieked, "Zachary, I told you to stay here," with a series of hard slaps on his rear. Zachary burst into tears.

Connie walked up next to Julie, balancing a Diet Coke and two paper boats containing baked potatoes smothered in cheese, sour cream, salsa and black olives. Her daughter appeared to be staring into space. "Julie, what are you doing?"

"Saying a blessing for that little boy and his mother over there. They look like they need it."

Connie turned. The little red-faced boy screamed, then whimpered. Connie slid the paper boats onto the table and bent to hug her daughter. "Good girl. Let's say a blessing together."

The reverend and Virginia arrived from other booths and spread out more food. Connie smiled at Julie. "Now, how about a blessing for our family?" Noisy groups of people eddied around their table. The four bowed their heads as Julie spoke a quick, quiet prayer.

The reverend picked up a barbecued turkey leg. He bit into the crisp, caramel-colored skin. "Don't we have a fine daughter, Virginia?"

"Sure do, praise the Lord."

"A year ahead of herself in math, and that truly must come from Jesus, because I'm no good at numbers and neither is Connie."

Virginia tunneled her fork through the sour cream to scoop up some baked potato. Julie smiled.

"And so grown-up," the reverend went on, "her best friend is twenty-five years her senior."

He meant Virginia. She squinted over the top of her glasses. "Only twenty-five? Careful about shaving your figures around our math whiz here, Rev."

The reverend smiled at his daughter's glossy dark head, watched her lift her eyes from her pizza. He always enjoyed the surprising lightness of those blue eyes, surrounded by the darkness of her hair. He wiped barbecue sauce from his cheek. "And she's a beauty to boot."

Connie swallowed fast. "It's her character that Jesus cares about."

"Yes." The reverend nodded, face serious. "I was just getting to that. The Lord is forming a character of beauty within her."

"Oh, thank you, Daddy."

Connie looked pointedly at Julie. "Still, it wouldn't hurt you to have more friends your age. You don't want to be stuck-up."

Julie looked down. Her dark hair fell forward on either side of her face, shielding her like a curtain. Little beads of grease were congealing on her pizza slice. She did try to hang out with the girls her age in youth group. They talked about makeup: how the ones who weren't allowed to wear it got around their parents' restrictions, where they hid it, what brands were best; they talked about boys: which ones were cute, who said what to one of the girls, which girls had kissed one; and they talked about what had happened on the few TV programs they were all allowed to watch. Julie would get bored, lose the thread, start daydreaming.

The youth group girls thought Julie was an overzealously virtuous preacher's daughter and didn't appreciate the way most of the adults in the congregation showered Julie with attention as if she were a movie star. With Virginia, Julie never got bored. They had grown-up conversations about choir music and life.

The rest of the Wright party chewed their food until Virginia broke the little silence. "I'll never forget the first time she got the Holy Spirit."

She turned to Julie. "You were just a little thing, about nine, and you sang your first big notes in choir practice, like you do all the time now. Your voice surprised everybody, even you. I could tell you felt something was different."

Virginia waved her plastic fork at Julie and swallowed a bite of potato. "I heard the Holy Spirit coming out of you, and I told you that's what it was. Then, in the break, I found you in the girls' bathroom with your blouse off, by the mirror. I asked what you were doing and you said, 'Looking at my back to see the hole where the Holy Spirit came in.'" Virginia guffawed.

"Well, I thought if it came out of me, it had to come in somewhere," Julie said.

Virginia laughed more and shook her head. "Looking for the hole where the Holy Spirit came in."

Julie smiled across the table at her father. "Remember you said I could go on the rides?"

"Angel, you know I never go back on my word. I'll be ready to take you in a minute. I just need to let my food settle some."

"You don't need to take me."

"Well, I don't know about that. I don't feel right with you running around on your own. There are all kinds of people here. I'll come with you in just a minute."

"But the rides make your back act up."

"Angel, I didn't say I'd ride. I'll walk along with you and watch you."

"Daddy, I'm almost fifteen."

"If we run into Nicky, I'll let him take you."

"Nick'll want to be with his friends, not me. There's so many church people here, I'll bet there's some in every ride line. Please let me go. I'll be fine."

"All right, angel." He reached into his pocket, pulled out his wallet, and handed her a ten-dollar bill.

"That's okay, Daddy. I've got some money from baby-sitting."

"Let her use her own money, Jim Ed," Connie said.

"Hey, you take this and have a good time, but stay in the ride area, hear? And come over to the rodeo by seven. I don't want you running around by yourself with all these people after dark."

"All winners in all prize animal divisions come to the rodeo arena, please. In fifteen minutes, we begin the Parade of Champions." The announcer's voice boomed over the sound system.

Nick Daggett closed the gate on Bullet's stall. He walked out of the cool, damp darkness of the fairgrounds barn, away from the sour stink of urine and manure, into the grassy light. The sun's heat hit his shoulders. Bullet—the bull he'd raised, or mostly raised, at Uncle Bob's ranch just a couple of miles outside Divido (Uncle Bob was not really his uncle, but a close family friend he'd always called "Uncle," a man who tried to be there as another father figure because, Nick could tell, everyone thought Nick's own dad needed improvement in the fatherhood area), the brown and white bull Nick had raised up to its present size, the massive equivalent of a teenage bull, not quite full grown yet, with little triangle stub horns, the bull he'd been given by Uncle Bob as a newborn calf last spring, with Uncle Bob's gruff, "Here's a little project to keep you off the streets," Bullet, the bull Nick had just shown, had come in, out of five animals in his division, last.

The other four bulls had been shown by girls he was sure must be as young as his cousin Julie, or even younger, all dressed in white 4-H pants, white shirts, and those dorky green 4-H neckerchiefs.

Nick was glad he hadn't brought Teddy along. The kid would be all torn up, probably crying. But Nick himself could deal with it. Bullet's losing was no biggie. At nineteen, he was kind of old for that stuff. The kids leading their sheep, goats, and cattle now to the Parade of Champions (Nick could tell they thought it was soo-oo-oo cool) were early high school age, even middle school. That boy clutching the glossy white champion rabbit, stroking its black ears, looked about eleven. It would have been embarrassing to parade Bullet the bull by the grandstand along with all these kids. Like being held back a grade in school. Nick didn't need a bunch of applause from 4-H kids' parents. He knew who he was.

He adjusted his baseball cap with the logo, "Team Jesus." He accidentally brushed the back of his neck, irritating a pimple that felt an inch wide, an "undergrounder," not visible yet, but throbbing beneath his skin, ready to erupt. He could use a cigarette. He wished he hadn't given them up for Jesus.

Another reason Nick felt okay was that as soon as Bullet was sold, Nick was going to get a twenty percent cut. As his dad told him, this was not bad, considering Uncle Bob supplied barn, pasture, feed, water, inoculations, supplements, Bullet himself, everything, even the leather harness Nick had just used to yank Bullet around the corral to display the animal's fine qualities to the judge.

And the main reason Nick was feeling okay was that in just three days, he'd be off probation. A free man. Raising Bullet hadn't exactly been a condition, but when Uncle Bob proposed the plan in court, it had been part of why Nick hadn't gotten a jail sentence. Nick had held up his part of the bargain, showing up every day at Uncle Bob's. He'd gone out to the woods one weekend in the pickup with Uncle Bob, listened to Uncle Bob's jackhammer voice the whole way—a long speech about the value of discipline—then marched and drilled with Uncle Bob's volunteer militia. He'd even shown up today at the fair. Not going to jail was a heck of a lot bigger prize than a cheap blue ribbon, which was, Nick could clearly see now, just another one of those things adults dreamed up to "build self-esteem." Let the kids who needed a shiny ribbon to feel good about themselves have one. Or several, which some of the kids passing seemed to have collected. It didn't matter, Nick told himself. He felt just great.

Romey and Elliot stood and gave an exaggerated, clapping-hands-over-heads ovation to the last chorus of "You Don't Have to Call Me Darlin', Darlin'." The bluegrass band took a bow from the meadow stage, Elliot's mom stepping out from behind her washtub bass, Elliot's dad holding aloft a guitar.

The two friends then headed over to the midway, on a mission from Romey's mother. Janis's friend Peg (one-third of the Remnant), ran a small nonprofit organization. It tried to alleviate the economic distress caused by the layoffs at the downsized Divido lumber mill by helping Dividans start small businesses. A feasibility study had shown that a promising area for business development was food processing. Peg had a stand this year where her fledgling business owners were handing out free samples of their artichoke pasta sauce, fat-free chocolate topping, chutneys, relishes, jams, and honeys.

"Peg is having nightmares about no one coming to her stand. Go there and hang out, look enthusiastic about the food, make it look busy," Janis had instructed Romey at breakfast, four or five times, and then, when Elliot arrived to pick Romey up, Janis had told him, too.

Romey and Elliot wandered in and out of sunlight and shade, past the prize 250-pound pumpkins, so heavy they had spread out and finished their growth lying on their sides, past the patchwork quilt raffle, the tie-dyed clothing tent, the sculpture of a liberty bell made from animal feed, dried beans, alfalfa pellets, pumpkin seeds, and prunes. They stopped where the path to the rodeo arena crossed the booth area, to let pass boys and girls who carried champion chickens and lambs, led prize horses, and tugged the harnesses of winning goats and calves. The procession churned up fine dust. A few halfhearted bleats and moos sounded in protest.

"Watch where you step," Elliot said as he and Romey pushed through a break in the kids and animals, "there's champion goat shit down there."

Just past the fire prevention display, Romey spotted Peg, red-faced and sweating in a tan business suit, standing behind a table covered with jars. Peg had asked all the new businesswomen to dress professionally, even if it was the fair and most people wore T-shirts and shorts. Peg rushed around the table to hug Romey and Elliot. "It's fantastic. People are *ordering case lots.* A distributor from *San Francisco* is even interested." Peg loaded up two paper plates with samples of everything and turned breathlessly to a woman who wanted to pay for two carafes of herbed olive oil.

Romey and Elliot stepped back and stood out of the stream of foot traffic. Lifting a crispy wafer spread with apricot-flavored honey, Romey said, "Meredith's hair is this exact color, isn't it?" She had studied Meredith's hair in the hallways between classes, watched it pour, liquid butterscotch, from shoulder to shoulder as Meredith walked. She'd spent hours two seats behind Meredith in French, noting how the girl's hair was really warm brown underneath, with an overlay of light gold. Romey bit the cracker. "I bet Brian doesn't really appreciate her. Do you think he does?"

"No, I'm sure all he notices are Meredith's tits."

"Elliot!"

"Like you don't notice them."

"Don't talk about her like that. Meredith's going to be famous someday. She could be the first woman president of the United States. She's good-looking enough. She's articulate enough. And she's already great at politics."

"Ay-yi-yi!" Elliot's plate, balanced on his big square palm, wobbled, and half the food slid to the ground. "That one's really hot." He pointed to a dollop of Spicy Sun-Dried Tomato Salsa, now lying in the dirt. "I wonder which will come first, a woman president or a gay man president?"

"I bet a woman."

"If we had a gay man president, wouldn't I make a great," he made his voice deep and smooth, "First Gentleman?"

"I wonder when we'll see Meredith."

"Can't you just see me presiding over those White House dinners? With lavender china, of course."

"She's got to come by nighttime."

"Or rainbow china. White with tasteful rainbow rims."

"I'm surprised we haven't seen her already."

"I can hardly wait. Watching you torture yourself following Meredith and Brian, now that's my idea of how to enjoy the fair."

"I'm not going to *follow* her. It would just be nice to see her. Say hello."

"I know what. When we meet them, we'll ask them to have a Coke with us. Then, I'll do a subtle switcheroo and give Brian a beer. Then another beer. We'll ply him with beer after beer after beer until he has one and only one thought left in his head. Peeing. He'll be so desperate, he'll leave Meredith with us and we'll quickly maneuver you two onto a scary ride. As the whirling car speeds around the starry sky, Meredith will be thrown into your strong and welcoming arms. Then, you make your move."

"Oh, we both know I can't 'make a move' with Meredith."

"Why not?"

"Look, I love her, okay? Love means treating someone with respect. I'd have to . . . get a sense from her that she wanted me before I could—"

Elliot hit his forehead theatrically with the back of his hand. "Alas, my plan is just another tale told by an Elliot, signifying nothing."

Romey punched his arm lightly.

He put the arm around her. "But how's Meredith ever going to find out if she likes it if you don't give her the chance to try it?"

Romey shrugged. "I don't know. I know I'm going to like it and I've never tried it. You knew you wanted to be with another boy before you ever tried it."

"But not everyone's that way. Some people don't know what they want until just the right person kisses them. You should come with me to the support group. Find out all the different ways people can come out. Get some perspective."

Romey gave him a skeptical look. "Perspective? You go to the support group for perspective? *That's* why you go home with those guys afterward? For perspective? I'll bet they give you lots."

"I only went home with one of them. Tim lives with his parents. It was in his car."

"Perspective," Romey muttered. She popped an olive stuffed with an almond into her mouth.

"This is why I like to talk to you about the support group, Romes. Because anyone else would think, here's this guy who's been going for a whole year and only got lucky twice. But you make it sound like a

Romey looked back at the girl, who cast her eyes down toward the ground, cheeks blazing. Romey imagined herself lying beneath her, Romey having just fallen from piloting a stunt plane, those concerned eyes making sure Romey wasn't hurt, that small hand reaching down for hers.

"Howdy." A man with extremely neat and puffy hair stood in front of her, shook her hand, tried to give her a card, told her his name, and asked for her vote in the county supervisor race.

"I'm not old enough," Romey said, trying to see around his wide shoulders.

"You will be in a few years. Have a card anyway. Pass it on to your mom and dad."

Now a large family group walked past, all clumped together. When Romey could see clearly again, the dark-haired girl was gone.

Julie sat on a bench under a redwood tree, the crowd flowing around her. Specks of dust swirled dizzily in a sunbeam. So this was it. At last, she'd felt what they were all talking about, the feeling you were supposed to feel about boys. She just hadn't seen the right one until now, that was all.

She replayed how he'd looked at her, all shy and deep, yet seeming to see clear to her soul, brushing his hand across his hair. Her blood was dancing. The feeling was almost unbearably intense, but she wanted it to keep coming. Big, happy waves gathered and broke inside her. It made her feel like lolling forever on this bench, lost in silky sensations, and at the same time, she could barely sit still. Oh, it was fun to be growing up!

Romey walked down the line of booths, searching the other side, but she couldn't see her. At the far end, carnival rides flashed neon lights. Romey drifted in their direction. The sun was moving closer to the western hills. Shadows grew longer. In the spaces between the trees, sunlight gilded the tops of people's heads.

The rides were circled in a meadow. A carousel set with white lights rotated slowly to music. There was a miniature dragon-shaped roller coaster for toddlers, and high school boys smelling of aftershave were lined up to ride the Tilt-A-Whirl. Colored lights blinked from the House of Horrors, the Whirling Dervish, the bumper cars. At one booth, kids Romey recognized from Divido High threw balls, hoping to win a stuffed dog. Inside the booth, a horn ooglahed. By far the tallest ride, with a star of lights radiating from the center in rainbow colors, the majestic Ferris wheel turned gracefully in the deepening blue sky.

From the Ferris wheel, it might be possible to see the dark-haired girl again. Romey bought some tickets at the booth in the center of the meadow and got in line.

Julie stood up and wandered dreamily toward the rides. "A woman now, a woman now." The words were the rhythm of her step.

There he was, the last person in line for the Ferris wheel.

She studied the line of his hair against his T-shirt collar. The rainbow lights of the Ferris wheel blinked and twirled. It was like the first time she felt the force pulling her to the altar. Her feet took her on their own, and in just a minute, she was close enough to feel the warmth radiating from the T-shirt across his back. She might burst soon.

Julie drew in the kind of breath she needed to reach the high notes on Sundays. "Beautiful day," she said.

He was turning around. Julie looked down, feeling a blush again. His look wrapped itself around her, and she had a tingly awareness that he liked what he saw. Slowly, she raised her eyes up to his.

Romey turned, and there was the dark-haired beauty, looking down at the ground again. She smelled like soap and flowers. Life wasn't going to be a long, dull slog to college after all, it was going to have beautiful girls in it who smiled at you and then turned up in line behind you and even said something. White lights whirled on the carousel, growing more luminous as dusk spread. Romey could see the curl of each dark eyelash, curved into the tender hollows beneath the girl's eyes. Like a velvet curtain in an ornate theater on opening night, the girl's lashes slowly rose.

"Oh! You're a girl," Julie blurted out.

Now would be a good time for an earthquake to open up a fault big enough to swallow her, she thought. If only she could undo the last two minutes and live them over. She wished you *could* die of embarrassment, that would be better than standing here, feeling stupid. The girl was thin and tall and probably athletic, she had broad shoulders, but she also had breasts, and her hips definitely flared out from her waist. It wasn't a boy's haircut, just a short one. Even from the back, Julie should have seen she was a girl. And to go and say, "Oh, you're a girl." If she'd just kept quiet, the girl wouldn't even have known.

"Yeah, did you think I was a boy?" She was smiling at Julie now, like she didn't completely mind.

"No, not really, um, cool Ferris wheel, huh?"

"Step on up, girls," the man at the controls called.

Romey climbed up the three steps into the red vinyl seat, handing him her ticket.

"Oh, I forgot about buying a ticket," Julie said. She was messing up every which way. She turned to go.

"That's okay, I've got another one," Romey said, handing it over.

"Here, I can pay you."

"Settle that later, girls. Get in," said the man.

Julie sat down beside Romey, between two poles glowing with turquoise neon. The man banged down the heavy safety bar in front of them, and the chair swung free.

"It's okay. You don't have to pay me," Romey said.

The seat creaked.

"My name's Romey."

The chair rose up into the air. "Mine's Julie."

Having tickets for both of them gave Romey a pleasant, worldly, in-charge feeling. She squared her shoulders. A thrill rose in her pelvis as the Ferris wheel mounted the sky. She imagined guiding beautiful Julie on some adventure, a safari to save the rain forest, Julie looking up at her with trust as Romey parted the jungle foliage.

The fine-grained, cream-and-rose texture of Julie's cheek was just inches from Romey's eyes. How long, Romey wondered, were you allowed to look before it was staring? This girl was like candlelight made into human flesh.

The Ferris wheel jerked and turned slowly. The sun was already behind the forested hill, but as they glided up, it rose again and warmed their faces. Turquoise neon poles passed behind them and down until their chair seemed suspended on pure air.

Below, booths were lighting up orange lanterns. A high-stepping palomino horse pranced around barrels in the middle of the rodeo arena. The grassy hills to the northwest, tinted blond in the last of the sunlight, swelled like the muscled haunches of a mountain lioness.

Romey and Julie's shoulders were touching.

Even though Julie was sitting next to a girl and not a boy, here came that liquid excitement, that familiar inner thrum—an unmistakable surge of Yearning. She drew a big breath. Her mother said Julie was still too young for boys, and she decided it must be true. Yearning was here to lead her to something else, to a special kind of friendship she was now old enough to have, a friendship with thrilling depth.

A space filled with soft evening air, no wider than a finger, separated their blue-jean-clad thighs. Romey gazed down at Julie's creamy arm, the roundness just below the elbow. Romey was exactly the right height to slip her own arm over Julie's shoulder. If she had the nerve. Which she didn't.

Their seat floated downward. A breeze ruffled Julie's hair. Romey gazed sideways at the shorter, delicate swirls of hair that caressed Julie's temples, then forced herself to look at the sky.

Just above the dark silhouette of the redwoods, the first star gleamed on the pale lavender horizon.

"Look," Romey stretched her hand toward it, making the chair sway gently. "Sometimes when I look at that, I get this feeling—"

"Oh, I know." Julie turned to stare at Romey, wondering if she'd found someone else who knew about Yearning. This girl could be the friend she would tell the feelings she'd never dared to voice, the friend who would have amazing, deep thoughts of her own to share.

Down on the ground, Elliot and Sean were at the far end of the booths, by the Native Plants display, doing a replay, with gestures, of the high points of the school board meeting.

Nick ambled by, fresh from trying to get served at the wine-tasting booth and being turned away for lack of I.D.

"Neanderthal alert!" Elliot said to Sean.

"Fags," Nick muttered. More loudly, he asked, "What'd you say?"

Sean turned, squinting with disdain. "To you? Nothing."

Nick took a step closer. "Th-they were asking for you g-g-guys over at the archery demonstration."

"Huh?" Elliot and Sean both spoke at once.

Nick's face reddened. "Yeah. They're sh-sh-sh-short on targets."

Elliot waved him away. "What is your problem? Go find some first-graders. Your jokes are about at their level."

"T-t-t-t-t . . ." The sound exploded from Nick's mouth. His face got even redder and he balled his fists. The muscles along his arms sprang into definition.

"Oh, give it a rest." Sean took Elliot's elbow and the pair walked away.

Nick lunged after them and threw a punch, but they evaded it by taking a slightly larger step.

"Nicky!" Reverend Wright's voice boomed out. "Get on over here and walk with us over to the rodeo. And I don't want to see you making any trouble."

Nick shot the boys a sneer, wheeled, and walked away.

When Nick was clearly out of earshot, Elliot sighed. "Okay, there are guys that talk like him. I faced it a long time ago. I'm so over it. But I ask you, Sean, how can you keep up faith that there's any justice in the world when he's that cute?"

Romey and Julie whirled through the air among bars of neon light, rose almost to the dark tops of the redwoods, then plunged down near the bright carousel, where music drifted out, "Love Me Tender."

A jet headed into the sunset, leaving a peachy gold trail across the sky. Cotton-candy clouds glowed in the west. The forested ridge was almost black, but the gently mounded meadow hills were still the color of champagne.

The wheel halted abruptly and reversed direction. Julie and Romey's seat, at the very top, swung up, creaked, and clanked back down, hard.

Julie grabbed Romey's hand.

The swaying stopped. Julie didn't let go.

Stars blinked on. The littleness and softness of Julie's hand intoxicated Romey. Someone had let a helium balloon escape, and it rose high in the sky, one side sunlit like a half-moon. The Ferris wheel plunged down for the last time, and their seat stopped at the bottom. The operator clanged open the safety bar.

Julie let go of Romey's hand and they walked down the three metal steps, legs unsteady.

"Makes you kind of dizzy," Romey said, knowing it wasn't the Ferris wheel.

Julie's body pulsed. She felt as if they were walking in a bubble made of colored lights and sunsets, nothing but goodness possible inside it. Always before, Yearning had left on its own schedule, but now Julie understood with a rush of new power that if she could keep Romey with her, she could keep Yearning with her. She prayed silently, *Please, Jesus, just let us be together a little longer.*

Romey walked, newly tall and capable, someone who'd had the foresight to buy a bunch of ride tickets and had been able to gallantly offer Julie a ride, someone who didn't have to settle for just waiting and waiting, because she could make things happen. And now, she was going to make things keep happening. She saw the caramel apple stand just ahead, glowing with orange lanterns, and said, "Do you like caramel apples?" at exactly the same moment Julie pointed to a bench in a little redwood grove and said, "Want to sit down over there?"

They stopped walking, turned to face each other, laughed awkwardly, looked at the ground, looked back up, and Romey said, "Sitting there is fine" just as Julie said, "I love caramel apples."

They laughed again and caught each other's eyes. Romey moved toward the bench.

"An apple's okay," Julie said.

"No, let's just sit."

Carousel music throbbed, and the blinking jewels and mirrors on the carousel tipped the ends of the redwood branches with silver. They talked, but more important than any words was the force of being near. The new night air had a breath of dew and enchantment.

After just a couple of minutes, Julie looked up at the now-black sky. "I have to go. I'm singing with my choir on the main stage tomorrow at two," she said shyly. "Not the meadow stage or the arena, the main one."

"I'll be there."

When she got to the rodeo arena, Julie walked up and down the wooden bleachers searching for her parents. Finally she found them, and sat down between her dad and her cousin Nick.

Her mother leaned over her dad and hissed, "You're late."

The reverend sighed with relief and leaned back, elbows braced on the empty bench behind him. He'd hardly been able to pay attention to the calf roping, wondering where Julie was. And what a fascinating stage she was in now, this beginning of adolescence. One minute, a grown-up young lady; the next, a little kid. Even in the dusty, dull light from the rodeo ground, he could see she was exhilarated from riding a few simple amusement park rides. Her eyes glowed, her cheeks were rosy; even the motion of her body as she sat down beside him was a simple dance of happiness. It all made her exceptionally beautiful. Incandescent. He sat up and put his arm around her, thinking how she was still, in many ways, just a child.

Chapter 4

Back home in her bedroom, Julie knelt by her bookshelf until she found a picture she'd recently downloaded from the Internet. It was a graph of a complex mathematical formula for a fractal, a colorful swirl of paisley in emerald, tangerine, and violet, edges bursting with tiny gold fireworks, a mathematical portrait of the unpredictable. At the bottom of the sheet its intriguing name was printed in black type: Strange Attractor.

She ran her eyes along the graceful curves of the Strange Attractor for several minutes, then dropped the paper to the floor. She opened the curtains wide. The wind sang a soft chorus through the trees. She took off her nightgown and let silver moonlight pour over her body. Now she understood what Jesus meant when He said, The Kingdom of Heaven is within you.

Then doubt stabbed her chest. What if it was a mistake to ask Romey to come to the choir? All she'd thought about was Romey seeing her do what she did best. But kids from the high school probably thought choir singing was for dweebs. Why did she always have to blurt things out? She put her nightgown back on and pulled the covers over her head.

On the front porch, Romey watched a wisp of a cloud caress the wise silver face of the full moon. She felt too jumpy to sleep, or even to sit any longer.

She went into her bedroom, put on her running clothes and shoes, and stretched her legs. As she was walking out, she turned back. She took the picture of Meredith off her dresser and tossed it on the floor of her closet. She threw out the flowers, put away the candle and the vase, got rid of everything.

Romey ran into the soft night. With every stride, she sensed the moment when both of her feet were off the ground, that moment she was airborne. It was a way to trick relentless old gravity, which, unlike a parent, never lets its attention wander for even half a second, but obsessively keeps you pinned down. Without engine or wings, for moment after moment, perhaps a fifth of every stride, a minute out of every five, twelve whole minutes out of every running hour, she was flying. Gliding on air.

She ran three miles. Above her, light flung itself across the wide black sky, lost in starry exaltation.

At the fair the next afternoon, Julie filed onto the outdoor stage with the choir. People were sitting on blankets spread out amid the flattened, dry, brown grass. The sun was in her eyes as she searched the audience, saw people not as tall as Romey, or bulkier, or with hair the wrong color, or holding a baby; an exasperating number of not-Romeys. But maybe it was better if Romey didn't come; then she wouldn't think the choir was stupid. Still, Julie kept looking.

Virginia blew her pitch pipe and raised her hand to begin the first hymn.

Julie followed Virginia for a few bars, then her restless eyes moved back to the audience. There was Romey, right in front, sitting on some newspapers, hugging her knees and grinning.

"Hallelujah, hallelujah," sang the choir. Then Virginia nodded toward Julie for her solo.

Romey hadn't slept all night. Jangly energy danced through her body. She was also worried that the people surrounding her might be some of the same ones who'd disrupted the school board meeting. While she'd been waiting in the bright sun, what had happened under last night's carnival lights had begun to seem dreamlike. She worried she'd read too much into the look in Julie's eyes, into Julie's words, that it had all been induced by loneliness, just Romey's own desperate fantasy.

Now Romey heard Julie's rich, velvety voice, surprisingly strong amid the rest of the chorus, and Romey was pretty sure she could understand what made people think up the idea of heaven. It must have been a voice just like this one. Julie's lips sent each rounded note to Romey, Julie's eyes singing a more playful melody than the hymn, each phrase carrying a second meaning, just two words, *"You're here. You're here. You're here."*

Romey's heart picked up speed. She'd heard few hymns in her life. She hadn't been to church often, just for some weddings and for a few months in the sixth grade, when she'd briefly wanted to find out about religion and Janis had patiently driven her to the Unitarian Church every Sunday. This hymn had been embellished with a harmony invented by Virginia Waldrip. To Romey, the tune sounded like something she'd maybe heard over the radio at someone's house long ago. It held the memory of something distant, hazy, yet familiar. The harmony made it intriguing. Just when Romey thought she knew where the tune was going next, a surprise note met her ear.

Julie's powerful soprano soared above all the others. The mellow word "love" flowed directly from Julie's throat to Romey's ear, streamed down on her like melting honey butter.

Listening to those words, all about love for God, Romey made a discovery she thought was entirely original (she couldn't wait to tell Amina about it). It took just the slightest shift in thinking to hear in the lyrics not praise for holy love, but rapturous celebrations of a love much more earthly.

Julie's eyes held hers. The sadness at the corners of those blue eyes seemed to tell Romey that Julie understood, with words not even necessary, exactly how it felt to be the only lesbian at the high school, understood, in fact, everything about Romey. The sun hugged Romey's shoulders. Promise zipped through the air from Romey to Julie and back again, along the arc of their eyes.

When the performance was over, Julie hurried down the steps at the side of the stage and headed straight toward Romey, her blue choir robe billowing behind her. She took Romey's hand, panting.

"I have to go talk to some people. Can you meet me in the field behind the stage in ten minutes?"

Flushed cheeks and happy-sad blue eyes. As if Romey wasn't already willing to walk to Santa Rosa—to San Francisco, even, if necessary—to have a few minutes together. "Sure."

Julie squeezed Romey's hand and flew back toward the stage. Romey stood still in the sun, watching Julie's animated answers to congratulations on her singing. Overhead, green and purple swallows made thrilling dives and winged back up, on their hunt for something invisible in the air.

Romey walked behind the stage scaffolding and across a little road to the broad trunk of a live oak tree. She felt around the ground for stickers and, finding it clear, stood on her hands, feet against the trunk. She bounced back down, stepped to the side, and rotated into an exultant cartwheel.

She brushed off her hands on the side of her shorts and leaned against the tree. In the heat, the cracked dry earth, the bleached-out grass, the tree's crisp leaves all seemed to beg the sky for the coming rains. A red ladybug crawled on Romey's finger. Looking around, she saw that the foot-high gold grass was covered with ladybugs. A river of orange and red ladybugs was flying through a gap in the trees and settling in the meadow. Now Julie walked quickly toward Romey, dressed in jeans and a T-shirt with wildflowers painted on it, and with each step, Julie stirred up little puffs of ladybugs.

"Hi," Julie said, breathless.

"Hi. You have a beautiful voice."

"Was it too much like church for you?"

"No, no. I liked it. I mean, I don't *go* to church—"

"That's okay," Julie said, at the same time Romey said, "But I liked the way you sing."

They stood together under the silent sun, looking at each other, then down at the ladybugs in the gold grass. Now that Julie was near again, Romey seemed to have exhausted her stock of things to say. Fool, she told herself, you should have thought of something while you waited. Romey's arms just hung there on each side of her. Finally she said, "Have you ever seen so many ladybugs in one place?"

"No," Julie said eagerly. "Isn't it amazing?"

Romey looked down again. The grass was flattened where she'd just been standing. Silence lengthened like an afternoon shadow.

"What's your favorite subject in school?" Julie looked up at her, blue eyes pleading.

"Trig, well, math."

"Math's mine, too. I'm a year ahead," Julie said, and then they were off, talking about math, Julie telling Romey about her advanced placement Internet class.

They sat on the lowest part of a thick live oak branch that curved down almost to the ground, then back up into the sky. It rocked gently with their weight. In that perfect fall afternoon, with the sun tender, the air sweet and herb-scented, their talk flowed on without effort. It meandered to the fair, to Julie asking Romey what high school was like, telling Romey she'd never been to school at all, but always studied at home, "and I think high school would be intimidating. Do you ever feel intimidated or are you so used to it you don't notice?"

"Sometimes it can be hard if you don't have someone to eat lunch with," Romey said, prickling with guilt because she didn't say why only two people in school would share her lunch table.

The last of the season's pink and gold asters were blooming near their feet. A ladybug got caught in the swirl of hair at Julie's temple and Romey reached up and held her finger there, waiting for the ladybug to crawl on. Romey's own hair was sturdy, textured, every strand individual. She'd never felt hair this satiny, like thistledown. She met Julie's blue eyes and wished she could look into them and not talk for about three days, but she nervously turned to let the ladybug leave her finger for the tree trunk.

"I have to go," Julie sighed.

Romey stood up. Her hands brushed something sticky on the back of her jeans. "Oh, no, sap's leaked out of this tree. Did it get you?" She turned Julie around, looked for sap along the curve of Julie's jeans, found a small sticky spot, touched it feather-light. "You've got some, too."

Julie felt around behind her. "Darn." She lifted her fingers to her nose. "Well, it smells good, anyway."

Romey smelled the sweet sap on her own fingers.

They walked back toward the stage. "Look." Julie halted, pointing. At the edge of the trees, two half-grown fawns browsed among the ferns. They sensed the girls watching, looked up, and one lifted its slender leg and took a tentative step toward the other. It nuzzled its twin's delicate, pale neck. Julie and Romey, silent, also moved closer together.

The fawns' eyes were so liquid and soft, it made Romey want to quit school and spend all her time keeping them safe.

"Your hair is the same color as the fawns' spots," Julie whispered. "My mom doesn't like deer because they eat her flowers. But I like them. It makes me feel like wild things still have a chance, if deer can walk right up to our house."

A doe emerged from the shadows, and the three deer leaped into the trees.

Julie looked at the dusty ground. "I've only known you one day, but you're already my best friend." She raised her head, almost jumped, and her lips quickly brushed Romey's cheek.

Then Julie turned, all pink-faced, and walked across the golden meadow toward the back of the stage. Romey followed in a force field of kiss vibrations. Ladybugs rose up around them like clouds of orange confetti. Julie spun around and looked up at Romey, radiant. "My family's over at the tables near the food booths," she said. "Come and meet them."

Romey walked beside Julie past the stage, past the audience now gathered to watch some young gymnasts, and onto a path of wonder between the booths. She liked the way her tall body felt next to delicate Julie, liked the shape of the space between them. Their steps kept time like a dance.

Julie and Romey threaded their way under the spreading live oak trees, among the long tables covered in red-checked oilcloth and hay-bale benches. "Daddy, I'd like you to meet my new friend, Romey," Julie said.

"Pleased to meet you, young lady." Connected to the hand shaking Romey's was the face of the preacher from the school board meeting.

Something was happening at the sides of Romey's vision, a dark wavering. She grabbed the sticky oilcloth at the corner of the table for support. Julie was introducing Romey to her mother and the choir leader, Virginia. Somehow, Romey's mouth was smiling and saying hello.

"Well, sit down, have a curly fry," the reverend said, pushing a paper plate Romey's way.

"Oh, I . . . No, thanks. I . . . I have to go meet my family. Bye, Julie."

Romey kept her steps slow, didn't run like she wanted. As soon as she passed the bushes that separated the food area from the walkway, she speeded up and zigzagged through the roiling, heaving crowd. Somehow she had to get rid of this feeling that a hammer had been shoved into her stomach. A stroller with a little boy in it bumped into her shin. His face had been painted at the face-painting booth, splotched with greasy purple and green flowers. Romey looked up in panic at the woman behind the stroller, veered away and lunged for a bench, sat, put her head between her legs, and breathed hard.

"Rides got you dizzy?"

She raised her eyes. "Elliot!" His familiar voice and his solid, rumpled, everyday presence were like waking up in her own bedroom from a scary dream. "Listen, if you thought Meredith was bad, wait till you hear who I'm in love with now."

"My ears are the radar in every airport in the world, beaming in on your signal. My mind is every e-mail server in the USA, waiting for your message. Tell me quick, or I'll pee in my pants from suspense."

"I met her last night. Her name's Julie." It was the first time she'd spoken the name "Julie" out loud. Even knowing what she knew now, Romey savored the taste of the name, the way her tongue touched her palate on the first syllable and her lips almost formed a kiss. "I swear, Elliot, love at first sight isn't just a myth. It's real. Julie's beautiful, and it feels right to be with her, and her favorite subject is math, too, and she *kissed* me. On the cheek, though."

"Sounds great. *But,* I can hear there's a but."

"Yeah. A hella but. Remember that preacher on a crusade against us gay sinners at the school board meeting?"

"That blot on humanity? That scummy growth on the evolutionary tree? That reptile two steps above plankton?"

"Well, he's her dad."

"*Reverend Wright's* daughter kissed you?"

"On the cheek."

He fell backward across the bench. "Excuse me while I swoon; the news is giving me the vapors."

Romey tried to smile.

"Well, you can't hold who her dad is against her," Elliot said, sitting up. "He didn't kiss you; she did."

"Yuck, don't even bring up the concept of him kissing anybody. I'm not holding anything against *her*. But to think that getting to see the person I love depends on that, that . . ."

"I believe the term you are seeking is self-righteous hatemonger."

"If it could only be anyone else."

Smirking, Nick walked over to the table where the Wrights sat. "You know who that girl was? Her mom runs that baby slaughterhouse in Santa Rosa."

Julie stared at him. Could that be her heart moving into her throat, that sudden icy lump? But she felt her voice coming out hot. "So what? You can't judge her by her mother! What if she wanted to come to church? Would you keep her out because of what her mother does?" She was surprised at her own arguments. Love must be good for her, she decided; it helped her think fast.

"You say Janis Arden's daughter wants to come to our church?" Julie's mother put down her hot dog and bored her stare into Julie.

"I just meant, what if? You should wait and see what Romey's like herself, and not judge her by her mother."

A blue jay hopped onto the table and tried to peck at a pizza crust. Virginia shooed it away. "Apples don't fall far from the tree," she said. "But what a victory for Jesus if that girl came to Divido Bible Church."

"Julie, if she wants to come to church, of course she's welcome. But we can't have you running around with someone like that." The reverend put his Coke down on the table, hard.

"This is way better than Meredith," Amina said thoughtfully at lunch the next day.

"Oh, yeah." Romey sighed. "Meredith seems like puppy love now."

"I mean, this girl likes you back."

"Yeah, and a lot, I think."

Julie had said, "You're already my best friend," and Romey felt an uneasy wiggle of guilt in her abdomen, not repeating this part to Amina now. It was exactly what Amina had been afraid of the other night after the school board. Well, I didn't tell Julie she was *my* best friend, Romey thought now, in her own defense. But she also hadn't told Julie she already had a best friend. The guilty feeling spread out and squatted in Romey's stomach, like too much food.

"Okay if I sit here?"

Romey, Amina, and Elliot all looked up at once. It was the first time someone else had wanted to sit with them all semester.

"Sure," Elliot and Romey said.

"Hi, Matt." Amina motioned for him to sit next to her. "This is Elliot, and this is Romey. Matt Rodriguez. He's in biology with me."

Matt was dressed in a crisp blue shirt, the kind men wear under business suits, and neatly ironed tan slacks. The other three all wore T-shirts and jeans. Romey thought with sympathy that he must have dressed up to sit with them the first time. Or she guessed it could be that he dressed like that because hardly any of the Mexican-American kids were in the college-bound classes. He probably felt like he had to try harder.

Matt's eyelashes were so long, his smile so shy, his manner so deferential, and his movements so gentle that Romey and Elliot exchanged a long, knowing look.

It was Thursday. Connie was at her regular picket duty in Santa Rosa, dressed in her blue suit with the white blouse and red bow, striding in front of the clinic where Romey's mother sat inside, hunched over backed-up paperwork. Connie wouldn't be home until after six. Julie always made dinner Thursdays, and it was done, a pan of meat sauce cooked, taco shells laid out, tomatoes chopped, cheese grated, salad in a bowl, frozen potato balls ready for the microwave. Julie pedaled her bike two miles, up a big hill, then down to the high school, a long exhilarating glide.

Inside Building A, Mr. Goldfarb, the chemistry teacher, gave his class the last fifteen minutes to start on their homework. Romey drew the formula for sulfuric acid, then paused, pencil in midair. Her eyes drifted toward the window. A breeze stirred a long, dangling branch of eucalyptus. The pointed leaves, pale with sunlight, darkened with shadow, then turned light again, with a gentle, hypnotic rhythm.

Another flood strikes Divido. Julie and Romey row a boat to a family stranded on the roof of their garage. Churning water has almost swamped the roof. The littlest child hugs the chimney. Romey and Julie get the family into the boat, and while Romey's strong arms row them to shore, Julie wraps the children in warm blankets. Afterward, in front of the fire crackling in the fireplace (where? oh, headquarters for rescue volunteers) their kisses . . .

Julie is dying of an incurable disease, and her parents agree she shouldn't die without knowing the most important human experience of all: sex. So Romey is brought to the hospital. They make love on the white sheets of the hospital bed, surrounded by banks of flowers. Romey kisses Julie everywhere. Their passion ignites Julie's immune system. Julie has a complete recovery. And her dad, the reverend, comes and thanks Romey. But then Romey catches the disease, and wastes away with Julie tenderly nursing her. . . . No, with Julie's love, Romey recovers, too, and they go to college together.

A famous minister, the world's foremost authority on love, comes to Divido to deliver a public lecture. He talks to Romey and Julie and tells them he has never, in all his experience, met two people who are more in love. He can tell just by being in the room with them. It's that strong. The famous minister speaks with Julie's parents about how an exception must be made for them because their love is so pure, so obvious, so true. It shatters all human records for love. And Julie and Romey are allowed to spend every other night in each other's houses after that. The first night, in Julie's room, they take off their clothes and Romey kisses Julie everywhere . . .

The bell rang. Books were slammed closed and gathered up, kids shuffled out of the room, talking. Romey found Elliot in the hall and they walked around Building A together.

Elliot pointed toward the doorway of Building B. "Look, it's Good Cop and Bad Cop, together again." Ms. Chakirian, the school counselor, and Mr. Grant, the assistant principal, stood talking in the wide doorway. "When Good Cop isn't busy trying to get the depressed kids to express themselves, and Bad Cop isn't busy trying to *keep* the disruptive kids *from* expressing themselves, they have a steamy romance going."

"Oh, Elliot."

"They've been seen. She has a couch in her office. They lock the door."

"She does not have a couch."

Julie hadn't realized the school was so big and sprawling. There were five low buildings made of glass and brown-painted wood, with big eucalyptus trees between them, blocking some of her view. She'd pictured everyone coming through a front door and down some steps, but kids were walking out of the different buildings and taking off in all directions. Romey could be anywhere. So many kids, laughing, talking, knocking books to the ground, calling across the walkways, bumping each other. Belonging.

The sun shone on the dusty air, turning the atmosphere into a golden haze. Julie felt small, clutching her handlebars by a tree, a river of kids tumbling around her. She was embarrassed to be alone, afraid that when Romey saw her, she'd seem insignificant, not worth knowing. She tried to look inconspicuous so no one would pity her in her isolation. Her T-shirt and jeans must be okay. Lots of other girls wore something just like them, although many girls also wore miniskirts. But Julie's hair. It felt plain, cut the wrong way.

She caught sight of some girls from the Divido Bible youth group. No miniskirts in this bunch. Julie didn't want to explain what she was doing there, or have Romey find her talking to these girls. She turned away, pretended she didn't see them. They walked off. Maybe they hadn't noticed her.

Waiting for Romey was like being a child on Christmas morning, forced to wait for her parents to get up before she could touch the presents under the tree.

Romey and Elliot turned onto the sun-dappled walkway. Something drew Romey's eyes to the tree in front of the school. Small fireworks detonated in the vicinity of her heart.

Intent on the crowd in front of her, Julie didn't see Romey and Elliot hurrying from the side.

Romey got close enough to notice little drops of sweat on Julie's velvet upper lip. "Looking for someone?"

Julie turned with gratitude and relief. "Hi."

"Julie, this is my friend Elliot."

Elliot threw out his arms, miming surprise, letting his book fall to the ground. "So this is the fair Julie Romey's been talking about. Romey told me you were more dazzling than the lights of New York City, that compared to you, Cleopatra, Helen of Troy, and Marilyn Monroe were dowdy—although they might have had better press agents—and that your beauty surpasses a thousand models. But I see she was lying. You're much better looking than that."

Julie smiled up into his big square face, color flaring in her cheeks. "Thank you." She felt an extra surge of excitement when she noticed his pierced eyebrow. It was the first time she'd ever talked to someone who had one.

"You two look good together, you know that? You go together like a vase and a rose, like Superman and Lois, like a hubcap and a tire, like a TV and a remote, like a mouse and a computer, like a mouse and a cheese, like —"

Julie turned to Romey with a laugh. "Does he ever stop?"

"— like a lawyer and a lawsuit, like a lawyer and a three-piece designer suit, like California and —"

"Actually," Romey reached toward Elliot's ear, "there's a switch right here. Boink." She twisted her hand.

"— earthquakes." Elliot froze.

Jittery happiness was causing a sweet pressure to build up in Romey's chest. Julie's presence made it hard to stand still.

"I was afraid I wouldn't find you," Julie said, eyes wide, upturned. "Do you have to go somewhere?"

Everything around Romey got blurry. "No. We were going to do chemistry homework, but we'll do it later. Come on over to my house with us. We can stop at the creek on the way."

Elliot shifted his weight and intoned in a machinelike voice, his lips barely moving, "Permission to speak requested, Captains."

Romey and Julie turned to him and said, together, "Speak."

Elliot gave them a courtly bow. "Fair ladies, I wouldn't think of intruding into the beautiful picture you paint just by being together. Besides, I've got to get that chem done so I can get to a hot meeting in Santa Rosa tonight. Talk to you later, Romes."

A few blocks from the school, Romey and Julie walked down the creek path in redwood shade, balancing Julie's bicycle between them. Their shoes crunched fallen leaves that released a sweet, mild fragrance. On either side, tall green bushes were studded with late huckleberries. Romey picked a few. "Ever had these?" she asked, emptying the tiny purple fruits into Julie's palm.

Julie tasted. A sweet explosion in her mouth. "Like blueberries. More intense."

They laid the bike on the ground, picked huckleberries, and ate them until their lips were stained purple.

Then they bumped the bicycle down the trail to the creek. From the edge of the shady banks, bright yellow-green plants leaned out over the water into a narrow strip of sunlight.

Romey set the bike against a madrone tree. Bark had peeled off the lower trunk, exposing wine-colored underbark. "I love to touch these," Romey said.

Julie ran her hand along the tree. "Smooth." The surface swelled out and indented gently under her hand.

Romey's hand rested on the tree beside Julie's. "Tree muscles," Romey murmured.

They sat down side by side on a rock, took off their shoes, and slid their feet into the stream, shallow and lazy-flowing in this late season. A gusty breeze sent a shower of dry leaves onto the creek. The leaves floated downstream, twirling in the soft current.

Julie wiggled her toes. "I went down to a creek once when I was little, but my parents got mad and wouldn't let me go again. They said I might fall, or a skunk might spray me. Or a snake might bite me. Or a tick might bite me and I'd get Lyme disease. Or a squirrel might give me rabies. Or bubonic plague." Julie gestured with her hands at the trees, the water. "This is nice."

"I come here a lot. I saw a snake once, but it wasn't the kind that bites."

"Do you know the difference for sure?"

"Oh, yeah. Most of them don't bite. You can stay away from skunks and squirrels. And you just have to look all over your body and make sure you don't have a tick." Romey looked across the creek, her face suddenly hot with embarrassment. She stuck a leaf into a bigger leaf, making a little boat with a sail. She set it on the creek and they watched it bob around the bend amid flashes of silver light. Cool water eddied around their ankles.

Something about the fresh line of Romey's shoulders, the planes of Romey's face, and her serious, cinnamon-colored eyes reassured Julie. "Dear Jesus," Julie prayed silently, "please let me come with her. On all her walks by creeks. And everywhere." Romey seemed strong, with those long legs stretched out, toes lightly teasing ripples in the creek. Yet that shyness in Romey's eyes made Julie want to smile her Sunday smile, the one she gave to downhearted members of the congregation. Was that, Julie wondered, what made Romey so fascinating? Some combination of muscles and softness? Romey had so much vitality, she was so . . . physical—yes, that was it. Romey was somehow more deeply physical than ordinary people.

Julie turned her smile on Romey's toes. "You're more physical than me."

Romey looked at her. "How do you mean?"

"Well . . ." Now that Romey asked, Julie couldn't figure out how to explain. All she could manage was the lame and obvious, "like, you're on the track team."

They both stared at a rock in the creek, Julie telling herself to figure out what she meant before she said things.

Romey tossed a pebble at the rock. "Is it bad or good to be more physical?"

"Oh! Good, good." Julie looked at Romey's profile, shocked that Romey might have thought she was getting criticized. "It's really, really good. Oh, I almost forgot. I brought you a present." Julie pulled a piece of paper out of her pocket, unfolded it, handed it to Romey.

Romey smiled down at the bright colors. "A fractal. Cool."

"I thought you'd know what it was."

"It's beautiful. Thanks. It's a great present."

They both gazed at the multicolored swirls.

Julie leaned back on her elbows. "Is it hard, having your parents be divorced?"

"Well, they got divorced when I was two, so I don't really remember when they were together. I'm used to it, I guess."

"Do you ever get to see your dad?"

"We talk on the phone. And I go up and stay about a month where he lives, in Eugene, every summer."

Romey tried to think how to explain all the ways it had been, the summers she was small when her dad swung her on the swings and took her to McDonald's for almost every meal, the bad year when he had the mean girlfriend, Karen, and later, when he moved in with Lois and told Romey she had two new sisters.

"Do you miss your mom when you're at your dad's?"

"When I was little I used to. I'd cry the first few nights at Dad's."

Julie put her hand on Romey's arm, triggering a happy flutter inside Romey's chest.

Romey leaned toward her. "My dad has a new wife now, and she has two beast children, who are sort of my stepsisters."

"Do you hate them?"

"Actually, not anymore. They're okay now. But the first summer, it was awful. I was used to it being just me and my dad. He had to get some writing done for his job and was at his office all day, and he just expected me to be happy staying home with these three strangers. I guess I was kind of bratty about it. I mean, I was nine years old."

Julie rested her hand on Romey's shoulder, eyes full of sympathy. For a second, the thrill caught Romey's breath.

"Are your sisters older or younger?"

"Younger. They kind of look up to me now. And my dad and I go jogging together, just us. And this summer, we all went to this cabin at Glacier National Park for two weeks, and . . ." Romey's voice trailed off. She was about to say her dad was proud of her for deciding to be openly gay in high school.

A silence descended. From the corner of her eye, Romey could see the delicate hairs at Julie's temple.

Sunlight flickered over the water. On the far bank, a soft gray rabbit, smaller than a cat, stepped timidly from the underbrush, noticed the girls, and went still as a statue.

Julie touched Romey's arm softly and turned her eyes to the rabbit. "It thinks if it doesn't move, we can't see it," she whispered. Romey felt Julie's breath brush her ear.

"I think if we don't move, it can't see us."

All three stayed still. Then the rabbit turned and disappeared with two gentle, low hops.

The silence thickened and got sticky in the way silence does when something needs to be said. Romey fumbled inside, trying for the courage and the best words to start talking about what she knew she had to tell Julie. She stared at the spot where the rabbit had been.

"I want to always be honest with you," Julie said.

Romey's stomach lurched. Had Julie read her mind?

"I'll be honest with you, too," Romey managed to say. Except about one thing, she thought, the thing I had the courage to tell the whole school, but not you.

Julie looked down, breathed in. "I'm in love with you," she whispered. "I don't think I could even love a boy any more than this."

Romey stared at the top of Julie's head.

"I mean, you have something," Julie continued, eyes on the flowing creek, "whatever it is that makes girls love boys. Only you have a lot more of it."

Julie raised her eyes to Romey's. "Don't worry. It's not like I'm gay or something." A dry, embarrassed laugh. "I'm just in love. Is that okay?"

"Oh. Yes. Yes! I'm in love with you, too."

Now was not the time, Romey felt certain, to announce she *was* "gay or something." Yet how could she not tell the girl who was in love with her? *In love with her.*

Julie moved her face closer and put her lips, still slightly colored with the huckleberry juice, on Romey's.

Romey stiffened, pulled back. It was automatic. She didn't know how much to kiss back without betraying her desire to go on kissing, her desire to slip her fingers under the back of Julie's hair and stroke Julie's soft neck. She couldn't let her kiss scare Julie, couldn't allow her lips' eagerness to expose her dream of kissing Julie all over. Or maybe she was just scared herself; she couldn't tell. Something had turned her to wood.

Julie looked down at the brown water.

Romey instantly wanted to turn Julie's chin back toward her and move their lips together again. Or would that be bad? Romey's hand stayed paralyzed in her lap. Was the kiss a spontaneous thing that couldn't be made to come back? She'd probably waited too long to do anything now. Better be ready the next time. If there was one. What bothered her most, the stupidest part, was that Romey had been thinking so hard about what to do, she hadn't even felt the kiss.

Finally she moved, touched Julie's hand. "I really love you, Julie."

Julie smiled like dawn in paradise.

They stayed a little longer by the creek. Then they walked through golden sunlight to Romey's house, where Romey's stomach churned with fear that Julie would ask to see her room, with its poster of San Francisco Gay Freedom Day up on the wall. But Julie didn't ask. And so they sat on the sun-warmed wood of the front deck, drinking sparkling berry juice, copying down each other's e-mail addresses, looking at old baby pictures Romey brought out, and telling each other lots of things that happened when they were little.

Chapter 5

Here was a delectable conundrum for Romey: had it been her First Kiss? Even though Romey drew back in fear? Julie did, after all, tell Romey she was in love and put her lips on Romey's.

She sat on the floor in her bedroom, under the women runners, their muscles exuberantly propelling them along the track. Beside them, the brightly colored picture of the fractal was tacked to the wall. She'd consulted Amina and Elliot. Amina had said, "It was your first kiss if you think it was." Elliot had said, "People like us have to take our first kiss anywhere we can find it."

But here was the stumbling point: Could it be Romey's First Kiss and, at the same time, not Julie's First Kiss?

To Julie, Romey was pretty sure, the kiss had been a token of deep friendship. Nothing more. And how could it be your First Kiss if you couldn't talk about "our first kiss" with the one who kissed you?

Romey considered the possibility that the kiss might have approached the limit of being the First Kiss, without actually getting there. Sort of like when you add: $1/2 + 1/4 + 1/8 + 1/16 + 1/32 \ldots$ And then you keep doubling the bottom number of the fraction, adding them up, but after adding an infinite number of fractions, you've gotten closer and closer, but you never quite arrive at one, the first number. Some distance always remains, even though it is infinitesimally small.

But then, Romey had another kind of evidence. Even though she had been unable to feel it at the time, every time Romey replayed that kiss, the memory spiraled down into her core, set it tingling, and produced new, amazing, beautiful sensations throughout her body.

Julie walked the two blocks to Virginia's house in the hot, hazy fall afternoon. Dry leaves spun around her ankles. The wind held a taste of rain soon to come.

She crossed the neatly mowed front lawn, ducked under the limbs of an acacia tree, and arrived at the small one-story house with its white siding and brown shutters.

"Hey, Virginia," Julie called through the screen door.

"Come on in, Jule."

Virginia's drapes were drawn. Stepping inside from the glaring sun, Julie could barely see the small, dim living room. Virginia gave a hard tug on the lever that heaved her worn recliner chair up into the sitting position. She planted her hands on the chair arms, let out a small grunt, and raised herself to her feet. "These bones sure don't move as fast as they used to. Want some lemonade? I just made a fresh can."

"Sure," Julie said, her eyes adjusting.

On the wall was a framed photo of a deer in thigh-high grass on the edge of a dark wood. Burned into the clear sky were the words, "As the deer pants for the water brooks, so my soul longs for Thee, O God.—Psalms 42:1"

Julie sank into the squishy faded plaid sofa. An upright piano loomed against one wall. Stacks of sheet music, records, tapes, and CDs closed in around her. Virginia's calico cat, Leviticus, picked at a strip of silver duct tape Virginia had used to mend the arm of the recliner chair; the other cat, the gray one, wandered in and leaped up on Julie's lap.

"Hi, Revelation," Julie whispered. She stroked the comforting fur. Being a cat seemed secure and easy.

"Here you go, sweetheart." Virginia bustled back into the room with the lemonade. "What's up? You want some extra coaching?"

Lately, Virginia and Julie had been working together once a week to create a smoother blend between Julie's head voice and chest voice.

Julie took a gulp. "I have something I want to talk to you about."

"Well, bless your heart."

"Will you keep it a secret?"

"Sure, if you want."

"Even from Daddy and Mom. I'm going to talk to them about this soon, but I have to be the one who tells them. Will you promise not to?"

"Promise."

"Sure?"

"I promise, honey. On the Bible. Now, what's on your mind?"

Julie's eyes held Virginia's in a beam of dreamy excitement. "I'm in love."

"Well, it was just a matter of time, you so pretty and all. Who's your boyfriend? Is he saved?"

"It's not a boy. I'm in love with my new friend, Romey."

"The Arden girl?" Virginia made a noise that was a combination of a laugh and a snort. "For sure, she's not saved."

"But she's really a good person. You'll like her when you get to know her. It's not like I'm gay or anything. I just love Romey, kind of like a sister, if I had a sister, except it's so strong, I have to call it being in love."

Virginia's red-rimmed eyes wandered distractedly to the wall opposite the recliner.

"I know this is love, Virginia. I want to be with her all the time. Just thinking about her, I feel like, like—"

"Like you have a Fourth of July sparkler inside you?"

"Yes, that's it! And Virginia, this is good for me. I have so much energy, I get all my school stuff done in about an hour. I can hardly sleep at night. I just keep remembering things she said. She's so pretty, too. Pretty in a strong way." Julie stroked Revelation vigorously.

Virginia smiled.

"I've prayed and prayed about this," Julie continued. "I believe this love is a blessing from Jesus. But I'm afraid other people might not understand. And, I don't know, I thought you would?"

"She love you, too?"

"Yes. She told me so. We've told each other. But somebody else might think it's wrong. Do *you* think it's wrong?"

"Well, let me see. Now, Julie, would you ever . . ." Virginia paused.

"What?"

"Do anything . . . *homosexual* with her?"

"Oh, no! No!" Revelation meowed sharply, protesting Julie's clutch.

Virginia looked thoughtfully at the wall. "Well, then, loving her is not wrong. It is not a sin."

Julie sighed and sat back on the sofa.

"So when you gonna bring her to services? Can she sing? Ask her to a practice. Maybe she'll want to join the choir."

"Well . . ." Julie's voice broke off. Her stomach flopped like a just-caught trout on a boat deck. She'd thought about inviting Romey to church. Thought about it lots. Knew it was the right thing to do. But if Romey didn't want to come, Julie couldn't take the rejection. It would be like Romey was rejecting Julie herself.

"Come on," Virginia said. "Where's your Christian spirit? Your relationship with Jesus is the most important one in your life. Of course you want to share it with the person you love."

"I . . . I'm just waiting until we know each other better."

"Well, don't wait too long. Growing up in a household like that, the girl is probably thirsting for Jesus like a man in a desert at high noon thirsts for water. You'd be doing her a big favor. In this life, and the next."

"I know, it's just . . ." Even if Julie could face the prospect of Romey rejecting her, Julie knew that wouldn't be the end of it. She would be duty-bound to either keep trying to convince Romey, and risk driving her away, or stop being in love. It was too cruel to have to choose between Romey and Jesus. Like a choice between breathing and eating.

"Sometimes a lot of us are shy about gathering new souls for Jesus when we're young. But as you get older, you understand that the people you bring into the church are grateful to you. Romey will be grateful, too, if you just get up your nerve."

"You're probably right."

"Of course I'm right. You're offering her the gift of an eternity of heaven. There's no gift greater."

Julie took a big drink of lemonade and ice cube. She crunched her teeth on the ice. Revelation jumped down and walked lightly out of the room.

Virginia took off her glasses, slowly polished them with a tissue, and put them back on. "Jule, I want to tell you something now."

"Okay."

"But this time, *you* have to swear never to tell anyone."

"I swear."

"You have to absolutely promise on the Bible."

"I promise. Virginia! I'm just like Daddy. I always, always keep my word."

"It's kind of like with what you told me. Other people might mis-understand."

"Well, nobody's gonna find out from me. I wouldn't tell if they tried to torture it out of me."

Virginia chuckled. "Well, I guess that's not too likely. This is real important to me. I don't want just any old person talking about this and thinking about this. Lots of people have sacred places in their lives. The only ones you can share them with are friends who show proper respect."

"I will. I *promise*. Tell me."

"All right, then." Virginia pushed herself up out of the recliner and crossed to the far wall. She took down a faded photo in a heavy brass frame. It showed a young woman, her hair cut in a style that had been popular in the 1970s, short on top, sides and back in varied lengths, carrying a hint of rebellion, shaggy. The young woman sat at the Divido Bible Church's big organ, wearing a shiny purple shirt, a grin on her face and her head cocked to one side, raising her hand as if to signal a rowdy crowd to sing along.

"That's Sandy Galloway," Virginia said. "You wouldn't remember her. She played the organ for the church a long time ago, before you were born. Before your daddy was even our minister." Virginia's hand rose to her head and she gently smoothed back her gray hair.

"She looks lively. Like she'd be fun."

"Oh, she was. We had a wild time in the choir then, I tell you. We could get those folks to sing! The choir sounded just as good as now, and we didn't even have anyone with a voice like yours. It was all holy spirit and Sandy's and my love pouring through those people. Their voices just shined."

Virginia drank the rest of her lemonade. "I loved Sandy Galloway, just the way you're talking about loving Romey. Not like homosexu-als. Just pure, true love." She smiled down on Sandy's picture. "I feel blessed to have loved her so, even the way things turned out. It's not the kind of love most people feel, but I believe it is one of the most beautiful and holy things on this earth. I never had a husband and children, but if I had, I cannot imagine loving them more."

"What happened?"

"Sandy and I had four years of love together. Four years, five months, and thirteen days. That was when the choir won prizes for the first time. We were so good for each other and so good for this church. The congregation grew in those years. I learned how to make that choir stop being a bunch of people and turn into a single musical instrument, and I learned that because of Sandy's love. And her organ playing—oh, my."

Virginia rubbed her knees. "We had picnics. We rode a canoe down the Divido River one time."

"You? In a canoe?"

"Well, Sandy was the expert in that department. We'd play piano at night and sing, just the two of us. Then we made hot chocolate and cinnamon toast. Our favorite song was 'On the Wings of a Dove.' Our love was like that song says about Jesus' love. Pure, sweet. And it came down from heaven."

"Did she die?"

"No. Sometimes I think it would've been better if she did, I don't know. Sandy loved me, but after a while, she decided she loved me in a different way." Virginia looked down at her lap. "Like . . . like homosexuals do."

Through her eyes, Julie beamed silent sympathy across the coffee table to Virginia's bowed head, where pink skin showed through the thin hair on top.

"We had always kissed and hugged. Like best friends do. Like sisters who were closer than sisters."

"I kissed Romey like that, too," Julie said dreamily.

"Did she try to make it a homosexual kiss?"

"Oh, no. In fact, she kind of got all stiff. I think she was scared."

"Well, that is certainly a good sign. With Sandy, after a while, she'd try to kiss me just like she was a Hollywood leading man."

"What did you do?"

"Prayed. I prayed a lot. I told her, in my eyes, kissing that way was a sin. She would stop. But as time went on, she wanted to do . . . other homosexual things, things best not to mention, you being only four-teen and all."

"Oh, Virginia! That must have been hard for you."

"Our love was strong, though. I was sure we'd survive her being tempted like that. I just kept doing all the things with her we both loved, the music, the choir, the picnics. We'd sit on the sofa where you are now and watch *The Waltons* on TV. And we talked. Lord, how we talked." Virginia's voice caught.

Julie stood and walked around the coffee table to the recliner. She perched on the armrest. Her small arm reached only partway around Virginia's shoulder. They both looked at Sandy, smiling up young from Virginia's lap, in her purple shirt, surrounded by gleaming brass.

"After a while, Sandy was saying all the time she was a homosexual. She tried to get me to say I was one, too. I always told her it was not true. I was just in love with her. Only her."

Virginia jerked off her glasses and dabbed her eyes. Julie leaned over, tugged two more tissues out of the box, and handed them to her. She put her arm back on Virginia's shoulder. Crying turned the rims of Virginia's eyes, which were usually red, an even harsher shade. They were the color of a stop sign.

"Then Sandy decided she wanted us to leave Divido. She wanted to go someplace like San Francisco or even New York, where there would be more homosexuals. She even found some dance once for girl homo-sexuals. Over in Santa Rosa, I think. Tried to get me to go."

"But you didn't?"

"I refused. So anyway, she asked me to go away and try it for a year, living in a city with homosexuals around us. See, she thought if I saw lots of homosexuals, I'd want to be one with her. But it wouldn't have mattered to me if I saw a million homosexuals. Sin is sin."

Virginia set her glasses back on. Julie patted her shoulder.

"Sandy said she wanted to find a lesbian community. I told her, 'Our community is the Divido Bible Church. We grew up here. We belong here. We don't need to go off and find a community of sinners. We got a saved community right here.'"

Virginia blew her nose. "Finally, she told me she was going to San Francisco, and she wanted me to come with her, but she was going whether I came or not. She went down there, found a place big enough for both of us in case I decided to come later. I helped her pack all her stuff into a U-Haul truck. And Jule, both of our tears were on every box in that truck. We slept that last night in my bed in there." She waved her hand toward the bedroom.

"You used to spend the night together?"

"Oh, all the time. Like girlfriends. A slumber party."

"Weren't you afraid she might do homosexual things while you were asleep?"

"Jule, Sandy loved me. She kept pestering me to do sinful things, but she would never have gone ahead and done them without me saying yes. She was a lady."

"So it's okay, if you love another girl, to spend the night?"

"Oh, absolutely. It's okay to sleep with your arms around each other. But if two girls ever do homosexual things, well, that's crossing the line to sin. Jesus will know. Anyway, that last night, I didn't sleep at all. I watched her breath come and go. Every one of the happy days and nights we had been blessed with passed before me. I knew all I had to do to keep her by my side was wake her up and kiss her like they do in the movies. I looked at her lips a long, long time. Or I could touch her . . . well, never mind. The point is, Jule, I knew the only way to keep her was to cross over that line into sin. And that I would not do."

Virginia set the photo on the coffee table as gently as if it were a new baby or an antique crystal glass. "The next morning, I made us cinnamon toast and hot chocolate for the last time. I had a picnic lunch ready for her to take on the drive. Her favorite things, deviled eggs and homemade apple turnovers and all. She drove away in that U-Haul."

The choir leader cried quietly. Julie felt like she shouldn't be there, but it didn't feel right to leave. She pretended not to see. This was embarrassing and an honor at the same time. No one had ever trusted her with such a grown-up story before.

"Sandy called me almost every night at first. Tried to get me to come there. And those were the days when people didn't call long distance much at all. I was lost in the wilderness, Jule. I could only just barely choke down my food. Couldn't sleep, but then I couldn't hardly get out of bed in the morning, either. I felt like my heart was nailed to a cross right alongside Jesus' hands. And the spirit went out of the choir. I lost my touch. Plus, we didn't have anyone who could play organ worth beans. Praise the Lord, we got your mom, now."

"So is Sandy still in San Francisco?"

"Yep. She calls me every year, without fail, on my birthday. One year we were over to Sacramento for that choir tournament on my birthday? She called the next day when I got back. In all these years she's been calling, she's had four different homosexual girlfriends, one after the other. That's one of the things wrong with that life, Jule."

Virginia punched the recliner's arm with the side of her fist. A puff of lint shot out from a tear in the vinyl upholstery. "Those sinners do not understand commitment. The last three years, Sandy told me she got with a girl named Paquita. Paquita's parents are Mexican, but Paquita's an American. A teacher. That Paquita has two little kids, and Sandy lives with them. Like some sad imitation of a family. I don't believe in it." Virginia rubbed her eyebrow, then closed her thumbnail and fingernail around an eyebrow hair and yanked it out.

"And you know why I don't? Because every year, on my birthday, when Sandy calls, she's been drinking liquor. Now she never drank here in Divido. Never drank with me. There, she drinks. Sandy puts that phone near her piano and plays 'On the Wings of a Dove.' Then, through all these years, and four different girlfriends, even this one she claims she's being a mother to her kids—Sandy tells me she's still in love with me."

"Oh, that's sad."

"Yep, she's a sad one."

"What do you say when she says that?"

"I tell her the truth in my heart. I tell her what Jesus wants for her is a life without all this sin. I tell her I do what my church teaches. I hate the sin. And I will hate the sin forever. But, Julie, love like I feel for Sandy does not just get up and go away. As long as I live, with all my heart and soul, I will love that sinner. I'll always, always be in love with Sandy."

Julie had been sitting with her legs dangling from the arm of the recliner for so long her thighs had gone numb. She dropped her feet to the floor, walked back to the sofa, and sank down. They were both quiet. Julie sipped her lemonade and looked down at the photo of Sandy's face, full of vitality, her hand waving from long ago.

Finally, Virginia sighed and pushed herself up from the recliner. "Let's work on a few voice exercises, sugar."

They both moved to the upright piano. Its dark wood had become almost black through the years. Virginia pulled open the cover above the keys. The places her fingers grasped were worn to a leathery light brown, with a pattern of tiny cracks, like crazed china.

Julie started with a scale, the grown-up seriousness of all Virginia had told her reverberating inside her. Later, she'd remember this afternoon and wonder why it hadn't seemed important that Virginia and Sandy hadn't had a happy ending. But now, as the exercise took her voice through the transition from chest to head, rising higher each time, the notes seemed to ride effortlessly on the thrill of what she'd found out today: It's not a sin to spend the night. It's all right to kiss. All right to love.

It was Connie's day to visit members of the congregation who needed a little extra support. She slammed the door of her car and hurried up the front walk to the Kulp's house. She noticed how scraggly the lawn looked, since Henry was down with a stroke, and decided to see if one of the Youth Group boys could come over and mow it. Helen Kulp opened the door before Connie knocked. "Lordy, you're taller every time you come over here," Helen said. "Either that, or I'm shrinking."

Helen did seem tinier to Connie, just frail bones and papery skin. Although Connie was often the shortest person in a group, next to Helen she felt tall and bulky. But she answered, "Oh, it's probably just these new shoes."

Helen asked if Connie wanted anything from the Safeway.

"No, you just go along and shop and don't wor—"

From the bedroom came a large, mushy thump.

Connie and Helen rushed in. Henry lay on the floor beside the bed, pushing his good arm on the floor in a useless effort to lift his massive chest, one side of his face like a scared child's, the slack side looking hopelessly puzzled.

"Let's see if we can get you back up, Henry." Connie kept her voice loud and cheerful. She wasn't too sure how much Henry understood anymore. She wriggled into the space between Henry and the bed, motioning Helen to the other side.

Helen looked doubtful, but she sat down beside Henry.

"Now Henry, when I count three, you help us out with your good leg, okay?" Connie slid her hand under Henry's bad arm and motioned Helen to do the same under the good one.

Henry grunted something. Helen said, "I don't know about this."

"Come on, give it a try. One . . . two . . . three."

Everyone let out a breath. Henry's shoulders rose a few inches, but when Connie tried to slide him into a sitting position, he wouldn't move further.

"Oh, fudge," Helen said, and let go of her husband's shoulder.

Now that they were down on the dusty wooden floor, Connie realized how impossible it was to move this inert heap of Henry's body. It was as if two chipmunks decided to move a fallen bear, and she couldn't help it, there was something funny about it. She clamped her mouth around a laugh, but it came out of her nose in a snort, filling her with shame that Henry might think she was laughing at him. She peeked at Helen's face, only to find that Helen was pursing her lips around her own giggles. Helen's stomach was shaking.

Another helpless snort escaped from Connie's nose. Then she realized that the deep, panting, unmistakable chuckle in the room could only be coming from Henry. She stole a look down at his face. The slack side still looked helpless and puzzled, but the other side was laughing as hard as half a face could laugh. He pointed his good arm at Helen's face.

The sight of Henry's drooping, lopsided laugh was like being tickled. Connie gave in and let giggles just take her over. She rocked back on her heels, and the three stayed on the floor, shaking and choking on laughter.

"Oh my," Helen said finally, handing Connie a tissue and dabbing her own eyes. She looked around the room with a distracted air. "There's a nurse coming at six," she said tentatively.

"Henry can't stay here for four more hours." Connie's voice was brisk. "I'm calling the fire department."

"Oh, I hate to bother them."

"Don't be silly. That's one reason we pay all these sky-high taxes."

Four burly firefighters in dark rubberized jackets answered the call, lifted Henry into bed, and told Helen to call any old time. Helen left for the supermarket, leaving Connie sitting in a chair by Henry's bedside, reading to him from Psalms. She continued reading for ten minutes even after he'd shut his eyes. Then she got up quietly and went to the kitchen. She ran a sink full of hot water, added a good squirt of detergent, and washed a pile of dirty dishes. She emptied the garbage, swept the floor. Helen arrived home and they put away the groceries together, then sat talking over a cup of coffee.

By the time Connie left for her final visit of the day, she was late. It was the one that always left her feeling so upbeat, too, a family who'd adopted three little disabled kids, two in miniature wheelchairs and one who scooted around the house in a helmet, using a padded walker on wheels. She'd just made the turn off South Divido Boulevard when the car phone rang.

"C-c-connie?"

The reception on the car phone wasn't the clearest in the world, but she could hear a ragged edge of tears around her sister's voice.

"Hey, Patty. Are you okay?"

"I think so, it's just—I did something really silly." A nervous laugh. "I'm afraid maybe my arm's broken."

"Oh, Patty."

"And I need you to give me a ride to the emergency room? Wayne," Connie could hear Patty stop and take a deep breath, "Wayne went out with the car, and well, he was kind of pissed off when he left and, and I'm not sure when he'll be back."

Connie made a quick turn. "I'll be right over. How'd it happen?"

"I'm sorry, Connie. I know I'm bothering you. I'd get Nick to take me, but he's off somewhere."

"It's okay. I want to help." Connie thought it was a good thing she was available. Nick was still just a kid, really; it would probably scare him to take his mother to the hospital, though Lord knows, he wouldn't admit it. "Tell me what happened."

"Oh, it was just so stupid. I fell on the kitchen floor. I turned around too fast and there was this wet spot."

Connie noticed how streaky her windshield looked with the hazy sun at this angle. "I'm on my way, honey."

"Oh, thanks, Conn."

"What's Wayne upset about?"

"He got the MasterCard bill today." A dry, joyless giggle.

Connie thought about all the new clothes Patty and the kids seemed to have lately, all store-bought. Especially Patty's new dresses. "Well, Patty, you know you *do* need to be a little careful with money, now, with Wayne not working—"

"Just cool it, Connie. You don't know the first thing about it. When money's tight, that's when you need nice new things the most. It keeps you from feeling like garbage."

"Still—"

"I get everything at the outlet mall. It's cheaper than sewing clothes yourself. And it's just a credit card. It'll get paid off. I don't need a lecture right now."

"Okay, Patty, okay. You just lie down and keep your arm rested till I get there."

"Fat chance. Lie down, with these two little boys running around here? And I've got to do another load of laundry or nobody'll have anything to wear tomorrow."

"Tell you what. I'm just going to stop by the house first. Won't take even five minutes. I'll get Julie and she can stay with the boys."

As she turned around, Connie remembered being maybe ten years old, with her mother passed out on the sofa, a sour, vomit-wine smell lifting off her. It was breakfast time, and Connie's dad was gone, as he often was for weeks. Connie got out the cereal and milk, but the milk was sour, so she and Patty just ate their cereal plain. Connie told Patty to change her shirt, it didn't go with those pants with the pandas on them (Connie was proud then that she'd recently mastered the concept of "go with" when it came to clothes), told Patty she couldn't wear that combination to first grade—it must have been then—or maybe even kindergarten. Patty hugged the shirt to her stomach and said, "You're not the boss of me." Then Connie tried to brush Patty's hair and Patty cried because it hurt, and Connie cried because she couldn't get the tangles out, and then her mother made a little snoring sound from the sofa. Connie went over and shook her mother's shoulder. Her mother's quivery chin was wet with drool. "Mommy?" Her mother's eyes opened and she grunted, raised a limp hand, and waved Connie away. Connie wished then for someone to watch over her and Patty, especially Patty.

Not too many months after, Connie found the local Bible church. At home, everything was messy and she never knew what was coming next. At church, there were rules, order. And there were ladies, ladies who taught her to sew her own clothes and Patty's clothes, ladies who noticed her talent for music and made sure she had lessons on the church organ. There was Sunday school, youth group, choir, a community of people who opened their arms, who knew right from wrong, who stuck with Connie all through her teenage years and helped her win a scholarship to Bible college.

And then at college, with the seminary nearby, Connie understood she could marry a future reverend, and she could live her life in the church community, amid the body of God here on earth, surrounded by—and even helping to create—the comfort of order and rules.

It had all come true, her dream marriage. Here she was, today on her visiting day, bringing comfort to families from the congregation. But when it came to Patty, she still felt as if she were trying to get out those tangles with stubby child's fingers. Patty had never been any good with money. In Connie's opinion, Wayne should have put his foot down about it years ago. But not like this. Connie thought Wayne probably had something to do with Patty's arm. She couldn't poke her nose into Patty's business if Patty didn't want to tell her, especially not with Patty so touchy, but Connie didn't see how it could have been some accident.

"Dear Jesus," she prayed aloud, "please help Patty and Wayne."

When Connie arrived at the redwood-shingled parsonage, Julie wasn't in the study, or her bedroom, or the backyard. Connie walked across the parking lot to check the church, but the reverend was out, the church locked up.

She crossed back over to the house and looked in every room and every closet, calling Julie's name. The table was set for dinner, bread rolls already in the basket. Kidnapping popped into Connie's mind, but nothing seemed to be out of place. "Julie!" she yelled in frustration. She could picture someone somehow luring Julie away, maybe by posing as a member of the church in another town, someone who'd watched the house for weeks, a drifter, who saw when Connie left and waited, biding his time, then just walked brazenly up and rang the bell and enticed Julie away, a big man with dirty hands and a greasy mustache, but dressed in a suit, maybe—Connie almost felt it all again, the pain in her insides that had come after every miscarriage, and that other harsh, terrible pain, in her soul. She whirled around the kitchen, called out the back door another time. Not Julie, too. She couldn't lose Julie.

A scrap of paper was taped to the refrigerator. Relief collided with anger as Connie read that Julie was over at Virginia's.

Driving the short blocks, Connie realized this was part of a whole pattern. The congregation's praise was making Julie full of herself, and Jim Ed treated the girl like a princess. Now Julie thought she could just ignore the house rules. It was going to lead to something bad, Connie just knew it.

The ladies at church had only had to have one conversation with Connie, back when Connie was Julie's age, for Connie to understand that her organ playing was a gift from God, given for the purpose of service to God. It wasn't hers to take pride in. Connie had understood immediately that she must be modest, always. Not that it had been easy. She loved all that attention, she drank it in so thirstily. But the ladies saw what was happening. Praise had made Connie start feeling she was better than the other girls in the congregation, secretly maybe even better than almost everybody. And so Connie prayed to Jesus to take her conceit away. And after a lot of prayer, He did.

Conceit wasn't only a sin, it was darned unattractive to boot. But Connie had told Julie at least twenty times about modesty, and it had never sunk in. Julie positively wallowed in praise, she preened.

In front of Virginia's house, she cut the ignition with a jolt. From clear out on the sidewalk, Connie could hear Julie's luxuriant soprano reaching high on some singing exercise, not even a hymn, just notes for music's sake, each note thickly coated with vanity. She rushed to the open door and rapped her knuckles on it at the same time as she walked in.

At the sight of Connie's purple face, Virginia's piano and Julie's voice stopped in mid-note.

"Young lady, when you're told not to leave the house, it's for a good reason. Your Aunt Patty's got a broken arm, I've got to drive her to emergency in Santa Rosa, and I need you to watch the boys."

Julie looked at the floor. "I'm sorry, Mom."

"Your aunt's been sitting home in pain while I'm chasing around looking for you."

"I got though with my work early and I thought I'd be home before five, and that's when you were supposed to come home."

"Don't tell me what I'm supposed to do. Come on, let's go."

Virginia pushed herself up from the piano bench. "Anything I can do to help?"

Connie's face relaxed. "Thanks, Virginia. Could you make sure Jim Ed gets some dinner? You know how he is. If I don't come back, he'll eat a candy bar or something."

"Will do. Now you go on and drive careful. Tell Patty I'm praying for her."

When they were back in the car, Connie put the key in the ignition, then turned to her daughter.

Julie fumbled with her seat belt. "Mom, I did leave you a note."

Connie stared at her hard. "Julie, what are our rules? Are they that you can leave a note and just run off any old where?"

"No, but I thought Virginia's would be okay."

"What are the rules?"

"That I'm not supposed to leave without permission."

Connie ground the ignition. "Well, you remember that."

The car turned onto Divido Boulevard. The silence inside intensified the buzz of cars moving in the other direction, a motorcycle being gunned, a blare of rock music from a car stereo. After a while, Julie said, "I really hope Aunt Patty's all right."

"Say a prayer with me for her, okay?"

Julie knew this meant her mother's anger had passed now, and she let out her breath. After they prayed for Patty, they were stopped behind a line of cars blocked by road work, and they prayed together for a speedy release from the traffic.

Connie reached over and patted Julie's shoulder. "I was hoping to pin up the hem on your new dress tonight, so you'd have it for Sunday. Guess we'll have to do it next week."

The sun dipped behind a dark line of eucalyptus trees as they turned onto the road to Patty's house. Julie felt a squint go out of her eyes. "Mom, when Aunt Patty married Uncle Wayne, was she in love with him?"

"Oh, I think so." Patty hadn't been the type to get a scholarship to Bible college, didn't dream of setting her sights on a preacher. At the time, Connie had doubts about Wayne, but she told herself that at least he was a churchgoing man. He was big and strong, too. Seemed like he could protect Patty. In Connie's opinion, Patty had sold herself short, but she decided Julie was a little young to understand anything like that just yet.

Chapter 6

To: romey@igc.org
From: juliew@xnn.com
Re: Saturday night
Dear Romey (and I mean that sincerely),
The creek was sooooo cool.
Here's a problem for you:
Find two numbers that, if you multiply each of them by themselves, and add the digits of the result for each one, you get the other. (HINTS below)
Can you come for a sleepover with me on Saturday?
HINT #1: One of these numbers is the same as the age of a certain wonderful person.
HINT #2: This person is tall, with red-brown hair.
HINT #3: This person goes to Divido High.
HINT #4: This person was recently sighted on a Ferris wheel.
People say math is boring and hard, but it's not. IT'S FUN (I'm glad you know that).
I can't believe how lucky I am that I met you.
We won't get to stay up real late on Saturday because I have to sing in church on Sunday. Hope that's okay.
♥ Julie

Even though she had to squint against the glare of the late sun coming through the window, Romey was positive she wasn't making any mistakes reading the screen, reading those words that began with Julie's soft fingertips on computer keys and rode on electric impulses to Romey's eyes. She pictured the reverend with a sneer on his face, wielding a monstrous Bible. She could practically hear what her mother would say about sleeping in the same house with one of those people who picketed the clinic with gruesome pictures of mangled babies, who yelled at the women coming to get their abortions. But, being in the same bedroom with Julie, all night long. . . .

Her mom wouldn't have to know where she was. She could let her think it was Amina's.

Romey grabbed a pencil and paper, did a few quick calculations. Then she clicked the mouse.

> To: juliew@xnn.com
> From: romey@igc.org
> Re: yes!!!
> Dear Julie,
> Yes, I can come over. What time?!?
> I have the fractal picture up on my wall. It looks perfect. Thank you for a great present. I think you must be a mind reader or something because you knew I'd like it (I do).
> Now for the answers to your problem:
> 13 and 16
> 13 x 13 = 169   1 + 6 + 9 = 16
> 16 x 16 = 256   2 + 5 + 6 = 13.
> Here's one for you:
> When you multiply this number by itself, and then add the digits of the result, you get the original number. What is it?
> Hint: The answer ISN'T the same age as a certain beautiful girl. She has dark hair and is the best singer in Divido, though.
> What time should I come?
> Love, Romey

Romey tried to do homework, forced herself to wait at least ninety seconds between checking for new messages. But Julie must have been checking often, too, because in less than a quarter hour, Romey had another message from *juliew@xnn.com:*

> Re: come at six
> Hi Romey,
> Come over at six, okay? We can have pizza. Virginia already got it (don't worry, it won't rot, it's frozen). Hope you like pizza. We're going to be at Virginia's house, not mine. I'm staying at Virginia's because my dad and mom are running a marriage workshop in Eureka. Virginia already said it's okay for you to come.
> Ta da! Here's an answer to your problem:
> 9 x 9 = 81   8 + 1 = 9
> Try this one: What number, when multiplied by itself, increases by no more than when it is added to itself?
> Virginia's address: 4388 Redwood. Hope six isn't too early. But you can come later if it is.
> Love, Julie

To: juliew@xnn.com
From: romey@igc.org
Re: See you at six!!!!!!!!!
Hi Julie,
Six is fine. I'll be there. I can't wait. I love pizza.
The answer: 2. Also, zero works.
Love, Romey

Romey printed out the four messages, folded the paper, and slipped it into her math textbook, for viewing at school as often as she wanted until Saturday. She called Amina, then Elliot, and then went outside and ran four miles, with a giant's stride, legs high, leaping toward the crimson sunset.

Romey decided she couldn't go for a sleepover and stay the whole night without confessing to Julie that she was gay. Only someone sneaky would do that. She promised herself she'd tell.

When Romey arrived, Virginia was out at her prayer group's monthly potluck. It was the perfect opportunity, but Romey couldn't tell Julie in the first five minutes, or even the first ten. She had to kind of get warmed up, like when she ran. And then it didn't feel right while they waited for the pizza to heat up and set out plates. They sat down to eat, and Romey made the interesting discovery that she could eat many slices of pizza, even with butterflies beating their wings in her stomach. Julie told her about the best math Web sites on the Internet, but only half of Romey's brain could pay attention; the other half tried out different wordings of what she knew she had to say, and soon. Then Romey worried that she was being too quiet and Julie was going to think she was boring. But there was so much table between them. Romey decided to wait until after dinner to tell.

Next, they went to the living room and listened to selections from CDs each had brought. Hearing Julie's favorite music and the occasional brush of Julie's fingers when they were changing the discs built up a hot, breathless excitement in Romey. It kept her from interrupting the mood; she couldn't stand to bring an end to the fun.

Virginia was still out when they moved into the guest bedroom. Piles of old sheet music and boxes of cassette tapes were stacked waist-high around the walls, leaving only a narrow walking space around a double bed with maple posts. Romey went to the far side of the bed and turned her back to change into her oversized "Save the Rain Forest" T-shirt. She never turned her back with Amina, or in the locker room at school, but now, here, with Julie, who, Romey knew, didn't go to school, had maybe never been in a locker room, maybe hadn't changed her clothes in front of another girl in her whole life, and definitely not in front of one who was about to announce she was gay, Romey turned her back, pulled her head through the T-shirt's neck, smoothed it down carefully over her body, folded up her jeans and sweatshirt, and stayed with her back turned an extra thirty seconds after she'd stacked her clothes on top of a box of long-play records.

When Romey turned around, Julie was sitting on the other side of the bed, wearing a long-sleeved pink nightgown. Romey perched on the bed's edge. Julie moved nearer. "I'm lucky," Julie said softly, "to have found a friend like you."

The thing unsaid, the thing Romey needed to say, was filling up the air like smoke. Romey felt ready to choke on it. She eyed her jeans and sweatshirt, in case what she was about to say meant she would have to put them back on and go home. Julie smiled what might be the last Julie-smile Romey would ever receive.

"Julie, remember how we said we'd be honest with each other? There's something I need to tell you." Julie was still smiling, that smile with the deep understanding in her eyes, but Romey couldn't smile back. She thought she'd been nervous waiting that night to speak at the school board, but this was much worse. Her face felt like all the muscles were made of concrete. She forced herself to keep talking. "The only reason you don't know is you don't go to school. Everyone there already knows."

"Tell me." Julie slid even closer to Romey, bunching up the bedspread.

"I feel bad I haven't told you before now. It's something I promised myself I would tell people. It's just, you being from the church you are and all . . ."

Julie leaned toward her. Their faces were very close. "You can tell me, no matter what it is. Did you have an abortion?"

"No, nothing like that. It's, I'm . . ." she drew in her breath. The air felt like nails. "I'm a lesbian."

"Gay."

"Yeah."

Romey braced herself for Julie to recoil, but Julie's face stayed close, her smile got even more tender, her eyes never left Romey's, and she squeezed Romey's hand, saying, "Will you still be in love with me even though I can't do lesbian things with you?"

Romey felt the poison chemicals of fear drain out of her blood. "Sure."

"Good." Julie's lips brushed Romey's cheek. Happy electricity squirted through Romey. As Julie pulled away, Romey moved her face to make the kiss last just a little longer.

"I'm glad you told me." Julie's voice took on the velvety quality that sometimes came out when she sang. "It makes me feel like you trust me. And I trust you, too. Will you promise to respect that I want to stay a virgin?"

Romey faced Julie, serious as a juror being sworn in in court. "I promise we'll never do anything you don't want to."

Julie put her arm around Romey. "I love you, Romey. Not like a lesbian. I wouldn't ever love another girl. Just you."

Julie's arm held Romey's arms awkwardly at her side, but Romey didn't want to move. "I love you, too," she said into Julie's satiny hair. "Is it okay for us to hug like this?"

"Of course, silly." Julie turned and put her other arm around Romey. Her breast touched Romey's ribs. "We just can't do lesbian things. Lucky for me, that's going to be easy. I don't even know what any of them are."

Romey knew; she'd read a book her mother had brought home for her last spring.

Slowly, tentatively, ready to draw back at any whisper of hesitation, Romey moved her arms until they were all the way around Julie.

Now they lay side by side in the bed. Julie was turned away, facing the window. Romey was careful not to touch Julie anywhere, but she sensed the warmth between their bodies, the way the space that separated them got larger and smaller, Romey's small breasts so near to Julie's angel-wing shoulder blades, Romey's waist near the place where Julie's buttocks just began to round out from the small of her back, the length of their legs, the larger space between their bare feet.

Outside, doves murmured, settling down for a night on the roof. Was Julie falling asleep? Her breath was so even. Romey wouldn't sleep. Everything she wanted was right here now. A whole night wasn't long enough to memorize the smell of Julie's dark hair flowing across the pillow, the sense of her nearby thigh.

In chemistry class, Romey had learned about electrons orbiting the protons in the billions of atoms of her body. Most electrons stay very close to their protons, but an electron isn't exactly a thing; it's almost pure motion, it's more of a probability, and the probability was that while most of the electrons in Julie's body were whirling in orbits many times smaller than a pinhole, a few were as far away as Bombay. Or Jupiter. Without a doubt, some of Julie's electrons had already zinged into Romey, and Romey's into Julie. She lay stiff and still on her side of the warm space between them, sensing electrons as they pirouetted from body to body.

And the air. The same molecules that were in Julie's lungs a minute ago were now inside Romey, riding through her blood.

A breeze moved like breath over Julie's hair, lifting light strands toward Romey. Far away, a part of the earth shifted, and a tremor sped along a well-established fault line underground, reached Virginia's house, and jiggled the bed. Romey waited to see if the earthquake had wakened Julie. But Julie didn't move or speak. The quake had been too small, too gentle, almost like the earth rocking them to sleep.

Romey rides a horse across a night landscape. Moonlight shimmers on the surface of lakes on either side of a broad, grassy path. She rides, and she is the horse, too. She feels the air entering the horse's lungs as they gallop. She looks down at the ground, and, to her horror, embedded in the path, lying asleep, a trusting smile on her face, is Julie.

The horse's hoof is about to come down and smash the swirl of delicate hair at Julie's temple——

Romey woke with a jerk, and immediately became saturated with wonder. Somehow she had turned the other way, facing the door, and Julie was curled up against her. Julie's arm was around Romey's waist, her knees nested between Romey's calf and thigh, and, through gossamer nightgown and thin T-shirt, Julie's breasts rested plush and warm against Romey's back.

A bar of light burned at the bottom of the door. Romey could hear Virginia moving in the hall from bathroom to bedroom.

Was Julie asleep? How did they get this way? Did Julie know she was holding Romey? Did it count if Julie didn't know? Romey stayed still as granite, afraid that if she moved Julie would wake up, or realize Romey was awake, and end the embrace. The honey of Julie's breath came regularly against Romey's neck, warm and ticklish. Julie's small hand was curled against Romey's ribs, just under the space between Romey's breasts. There was no way Romey could go back to sleep now . . .

Or had it been a dream? Romey had slept again. Now she was turned toward the window, the same way she'd started the night, facing Julie's back. Outside, leaves fluttered and a distant owl hooted. Romey's muscles urged her to curve her body and circle her arm around Julie, just like Julie had held her earlier. Had Julie really done that? And if she had, did Julie know what she'd done? If Julie didn't know she'd curled up around Romey, then if Romey slid her body into an embrace now, it would be like those football boys, those times when Amina had so much beer she didn't know what she was doing. What if Julie woke up, and Romey had to explain how her arm had gotten around Julie, even though Romey had promised not to do lesbian things? Romey shivered.

She'd promised. Julie looked defenseless from behind, small. Romey was strong; she would allow nothing to hurt this tender person, but it was sad to realize what she needed to protect Julie from. It was Romey herself. The lesbian part of her.

When she was little, Romey's mother told her funny stories about shmoos. They were creatures who would turn into a bottle of milk, a new bicycle, whatever you wanted them to be. But now Romey understood those were sad stories, and how sorrowful the shmoo's face must look just before turning into the requested item, because once more, no one welcomed its real shmoo self.

Romey inched her face toward Julie's hair, silently kissed the nearest curl. Julie stirred. Cautiously, Romey cupped her hand over Julie's shoulder. Julie's breath went in, out. Romey's hand remained, warm currents humming through it, until the first light seeped around the curtains and Virginia rapped on the door, calling, "Rise and shine, girls," and Julie turned over with a lazy smile.

Virginia slid a piece of hot cinnamon toast onto Romey's plate. "Can we entice you away from your family's church for one Sunday to try ours? We got the best choir in northern California."

Romey swallowed her hot chocolate.

Julie jumped in quickly. "Romey knows. She heard us at the fair."

"Well, you're surely welcome to come over and hear us again."

"Uh, I, sorry—"

"Well, some other Sunday then, hear?"

Chapter 7

Sometimes, when it's Sunday afternoon, when you haven't slept much the night before, when a colorful Strange Attractor is tacked up next to your poster of women runners, when the sun is coming in your bedroom window and warming your bare feet, when you still feel the imprint on your back, that sense of the breasts belonging to the girl who loves you, at times like this, it's enough just to be you. Romey stared at the ceiling.

Janis's knock, loud as usual, sounded on the bedroom door.

"What, Mom?"

Her mother opened the door, crossed her arms, leaned her shoulder on the doorframe. "Romes? The best way to make sure you're ready for the school board is to keep up practice on your testimony."

The gravel voice, full of practical energy, vaporized Romey's dreamy mood. "You don't seem to be doing much," Janis continued, "so this might be a good time. And you might want to make a change or two, answer some points that were made last time, remind people of what Amina said about cooties, things like that."

Romey sat up. "I don't think I'm going to go."

"What?"

"I just don't want to."

"But you were so gung ho last time. Don't cave in to fear. If we go over what you want to say enough times, you'll do fine."

"It's not that."

"Well, what is it?"

Romey sucked in her breath the way she did when she was running and came to a steep uphill stretch. "Well, remember last week, the girl who was here when you got home? Julie? Well . . ." a long pause, "she doesn't go to Divido High."

Janis looked puzzled. "And, so?" She made a motion with her hands like she was trying to reel something in toward her stomach.

Romey looked at the fractal on her wall. She hadn't noticed before how easy it was to get lost in its swirls of violet and emerald. When she finally spoke, she barely moved her lips. "Julie's dad is that preacher from the meeting."

"*What?*"

Romey wrapped her arms around her shins, pulled them toward her chest, rested her chin on her knee, and avoided her mother's eyes.

Janis walked in and stood over the bed. "And why does that mean you won't testify?"

"If I stand up there and say I'm gay, Julie's dad'll know, and I won't get to keep seeing her."

"What's got into you? You hardly know this girl."

Romey stared past her mother, but Janis moved until she stood in Romey's line of vision. She leaned over. "You're not going to allow this girl to keep you from exercising your free-speech rights. All it takes for evil to triumph is—"

"I know, for good people to do nothing. But Julie didn't ask me not to speak; she doesn't even know I was going to. I decided all by myself."

"But it was your idea to go last time."

"And now it's my idea not to go."

"This is too important. It's discrimination against people just like you, only a little older."

"Stop trying to make me feel guilty. I'm just skipping one school board meeting."

"Come on, Romey. This means giving up all your principles."

"Mom, there's no point in speaking up for the way I love if it gets me cut off from the girl I'm in love with."

"In love with?" Janis looked as if she'd just taken a bite of spoiled food. She thought a minute, then sat down. Her voice came out soft, no gravel. "How many times have you seen this girl?"

"Four."

"Four, huh?"

"And don't try to tell me that's not enough to know I'm in love."

"Okay. Okay, I won't do that. But Romes, nothing good can come of this. Really. Forget the school board. I don't want you getting hurt."

Romey raised her chin. "I'm old enough to make this kind of decision myself."

"You are. That's true. But I still need to be here to help you make a good decision. And when I say you can get hurt, I don't mean only emotional hurt. You know the police told me I'm supposed to wear a bulletproof vest to work. They're worried I might get shot by people who are connected to that church. That church is trouble."

"Julie's not going to shoot me. I don't want to talk about it anymore, okay? I'm not going."

To: romey@igc.org
From: juliew@xnn.com
Re: Squaring the Circle
You know how in geometry it's impossible to square the circle? Well. I proved a way to do it. The file of my proof is attached to this message. See if you can find the place it doesn't work. My Internet teacher couldn't. (He had to e-mail his old professor at Penn State for the answer.)
Love, Julie

To: juliew@xnn.com
From: romey@igc.org
Re: Move over, Pythagoras
I give up. I tried for an hour, but the proof looks right to me.
Want to go inner tubing down the Divido on Saturday? Elliot, Amina, and I are going. It's FUN!!! I have an extra tube for you. Can you come? It's not dangerous when the water's low, like now. And we're going on the safe part. You'll like it, I know you will. And I've had lifesaving, so you don't even need to worry about drowning. Not to mention the fact that the water is only about up to your waist. Hope you can come!!!!
Love, Romey

To: romey@igc.org
From: juliew@xnn.com
Re: inner tubing
I wish I could come, but I have to be at choir practice. I thought maybe I could just learn all my parts on my own and skip practice this ONE TIME, but Virginia says it won't work. Everyone else needs to hear me so they'll sing their parts right.
The mistake in my proof is in the attached file. I love you.
♥ Julie

To: juliew@xnn.com
From: romey@igc.org
Re: wish you could come
I'm impressed. A proof that stumped a college graduate!!! If Virginia changes her mind, you can come at the last minute (hope, hope). Or maybe you can come over next week some time? After school—for those of us who have to get our daily torment—and home school for those LUCKY ones who get to sit around their computers all day dreaming up problems their teachers can't even solve.
Love, Romey

Above the town of Divido, the river was steep, shallow, and rocky. It was too hazardous for inner tubing, and no one had ever tried. Once it reached the town, three creeks merged into the river, and it widened and slowed along gentler terrain for about six miles. Risk-hungry souls inner tubed this stretch of the river in winter and spring, when it was turbulent and thrilling. One had died during the rains of 1997. But by late season, in rainless summer and fall, the river became a lazy float. The Santa Rosa road followed the river, sometimes right by its side, other times swinging high up and away to go around hills. At the end of this part of the river valley was a junction. A narrow winding road headed up into the coastal mountains and, eventually, to the Pacific Ocean. The river headed east. The main road crossed the river over Buck and Doe Bridge and headed southeast to join the main highway north of Santa Rosa, a few miles before the sprawling outlet mall.

Buck and Doe Bridge, built during the 1930s under the WPA, put a lot of men from Divido and the surrounding area back to work during a hungry time. Henry and Helen Kulp, along with several other members of Reverend Wright's church, still remembered their fathers leaving each morning in blue overalls, carrying metal lunch buckets, on their way to haul the bridge's stone and weld its metal.

At each end of the bridge stood two wide gray granite platforms, one on each side of the road, shaped like pyramids with the tops cut off, a geometrical shape both Romey and Julie could identify as the frustrum of a regular quadrangular pyramid. Each side, both girls also knew, formed an isosceles trapezoid. The stone platforms were topped with cast-metal statues. On the right side, a stately buck with eight-point antlers stood sentinel, staring into the distance; on the left, a doe gazed across the road toward her mate.

Every few years, a fad for shooting Stop, Yield, and Deer Crossing signs swept over the town's young men. In 1954, one shot a branch off the buck's antler on the Divido end of the bridge. But otherwise, the four statues were darkened by the years, but intact. The official name was Hufnagel Bridge, after an obscure highway engineer, but everyone in Divido called it Buck and Doe Bridge. College students, soldiers returned from war, adults with big-city jobs coming back for Christmas—all who'd ever been away from Divido—felt they had finally arrived home the minute they crossed the Buck and Doe.

It had taken a lot of planning to organize the inner-tubing expedition. First, Romey and Amina had to convince Elliot, who grumbled that too much exercise early in life might wear out his muscles; in fact, he predicted, Romey might wear hers out before she reached age twenty.

Once he'd agreed, they'd had to find a day when Amina didn't have to baby-sit. They also needed a day when Romey could get Janis's car and Elliot could get his parents' car (all three agreed it was useless to try Amina's parents). One car had to be left at Buck and Doe Bridge, so it would be ready at the end of the trip. Then they had to drive back to the edge of town for their launch.

Now that the day was finally here, Romey was sorry she'd gone to so much trouble. It would feel better to lie in bed and remember the honey of Julie's breath on her neck, to dream about visiting her younger self of last spring, the Romey hunched over the cafeteria table all alone, trying to swallow her lunch, looking up furtively to see who might be watching her. Romey'd whisper in that younger Romey's ear to hold on, because soon a dark-haired beauty with blue eyes would sit on a bed and breathe, "I'm in love with you." Romey could spend the whole morning with the blinds drawn, puzzling over that delicious, "not gay or anything"—yet possibly first— kiss.

But by the time she picked up Amina and they were following Elliot in his parents' battered brown hatchback, under a blue sky with a brassy edge, dusty autumn air streaming hot through the car windows and rock music thrumming from the stereo, Romey was glad.

She could already feel on her skin the coming caress of moving, cool river water.

The fragrance of ripe wild blackberries was in the air. They drove past vineyards at the outskirts of Divido. Plump, purple grapes clung to the vines. Metallic streamers tied on the branches to ward off birds flashed like Christmas ornaments. Air rushed along the skin of Romey's arm, her neck. Everything was vivid today, painted love-bright.

It was the season of thistles going to seed. Bits of thistledown blew across the road, trusting the air to float them to soil where they could grow. Thistledown . . . Romey's finger in the delicate swirl of hair at Julie's temple, and the tiny, vulnerable ladybug with soft tickling legs, but Julie's hair was softer. Romey thought maybe she'd go to that awful church tomorrow, just to see Julie.

"Elliot's getting ahead. Do you think he'll know where to stop?" Amina frowned as the brown car disappeared around a curve.

"I told him this side of Buck and Doe. He'll find it," Romey said. And if he didn't, it would be all right. Everything would, with the sun on her arm, a maple tree aflame in red and gold among the deep green oaks, and Julie, who would be singing in choir practice now, music rising up from the darkness inside her soft throat and flying into the light.

An army-green sport utility vehicle loomed big and close in Romey's rearview mirror. "That guy's trying to crawl up my tailpipe," she said. "I hate that." The headlights and bumper formed a face that seemed to grimace at her.

"I won't speed up when they do that. They just speed up too, and try to make you go even faster," Amina said.

"I want to pull over, but there's no place."

"There's one in about two miles."

"He's a foot away." Romey punched the emergency flasher.

As the cars approached a blind curve, the army-green vehicle pulled out into the other side of the road, whizzed past with tires screeching, missed Romey by inches, and forced her to veer up onto the steep shoulder with a stomp on the brake. The four-wheel drive ripped back into the right lane, in front of Romey, just in time to keep from colliding with an oncoming truck.

Then it slowed way down. Romey braked almost to a stop. "What *is* he doing?"

"Driving slow in front of you to pay you back, maybe. You know who that is? I saw his face when he went by. It's that guy Nick, the one Elliot almost got into a fight with at the school board."

Romey made her voice into a growl. "Duh, I'm better than queers and it makes me feel like a real man. And dude, Jesus sure loves me for it."

"Look at those bumper stickers!"

They both leaned forward. "Hardcore Christian," Romey read.

"Got God?"

"Support the Flag, Not the Fag."

"Omigod. Gross. 'The Miracle of AIDS: Turns Fruits into Vegetables.'"

"God, Guns, Guts Made America Great. Let's Keep All 3."

"'Honk If You Love Jesus.' Maybe he's going slow to make you honk?"

Nick's car also had a metal fish logo, a symbol of Christianity that Romey and Amina didn't recognize. With an ostentatious roar of his engine, he sped on ahead.

Amina sat back in her seat. "He was probably reading all your mom's stickers while he was tailgating you."

Their car had: "I'm Pro-Choice and I Vote," "Parenting by Choice, Not by Chance," "Zero Cut in the National Forests," and a wordless rainbow decal, a symbol of gay freedom that Nick had not recognized.

The river made a big bend here, with hills on the outside. Rising high above the river, the road followed a wide curve for almost three miles. Romey kept her eyes on the road just in front, but Amina could see it over a mile ahead, where the gray asphalt strip curved back around, going almost the opposite of their car's direction. The big army-green four-wheel drive was riding just behind Elliot's brown car. Amina braced herself against the dash. "Oh no. He's bumping Elliot from behind!"

Romey slowed down to try to look.

"He bumped him again!"

Romey pulled over into a wide spot on the shoulder. They watched the army-green car zoom out and pass Elliot, then swing dead in front. Nick slowed, then sped up. Elliot's car stayed right behind.

"Elliot! Let him go!" Romey yelled. She pounded her fist on the steering wheel.

The army-green vehicle slowed to a crawl, and Elliot's brown car immediately pulled out to pass, but Nick sped up and pulled out too, so for a few seconds both cars drove on the wrong side of the road.

"Elliot! Stop!" Both girls yelled at once.

"He's psychotic!"

"Get as far away as you can!"

Elliot's brown car swung out again, revved up, passed Nick, and Nick sped up and passed Elliot again, too close. The brown car bounced onto the shoulder and bumped against a tree, and then the forest was in the way. Romey and Amina could see no more.

Several cars whooshed by. Romey waited, revving the motor, trying to find a break between cars so she could pull out. Finally, she got back on the road and drove impatiently around the big curve to where they'd last seen Elliot's car. Amina stuck her head out the open window to peer down the steep slope. "Romey, stop. There's a car down there."

There was no place to pull off. Romey stopped in the road and put on her emergency flasher.

Amina got to the precipice first. About 200 feet down, Elliot's car lay at a weird angle against a tree, upside down, the gray metal on the bottom looking raw and exposed, motorized guts dangling from the high end, broken. One wheel still slowly turned.

Nick's car was nowhere in sight.

Romey and Amina shouted Elliot's name. It blew away in the air. They waved their arms frantically and flagged down two more cars. Someone called 911 on a cell phone. Romey tried to climb down, sliding, stirring up dust, grabbing tree limbs, knocking down a hail of gravel, but it was too steep. After about thirty feet, she had to stop and struggle her way back up.

Dozens of cars now blocked the road. People got out, milled around, talked in low voices about car crashes past. A line of cars backed up in both lanes. Honking filled the air. Someone got all the stopped cars into one lane and directed traffic in the remaining lane. Minutes dripped away until the rescue crew came. They went down on ropes, cut Elliot from the car, and hauled him up, unconscious. Through the crowd, Romey's eyes fixed on a technician's hand pressing a blood-soaked bandage to Elliot's head. The image stayed in front of her eyes, even after the ambulance left for the hospital in Santa Rosa, siren moaning.

Romey and Amina described everything they had seen to a highway patrol officer.

When Romey called her mother to say she was going to the hospital, Janis insisted Romey come back home and get her. "You haven't had your license long enough to drive all that way. One kid in the hospital is one too many. I'm driving."

The walls of the intensive-care waiting room were painted a too-soothing shade of blue-green. The room was just big enough for a sofa and three chairs; the residue of past anguish clung to the upholstery like smoke. David Novotny, Elliot's father, slumped on the blue sofa. His wife, Sharon, was down the hall making phone calls. David cupped a harmonica over his mouth and blew a series of forlorn notes that didn't quite add up to a tune. He had the same broad, square face as Elliot, but David's was deeply lined by the sun. He wore his thinning gray hair in a straggly ponytail.

Romey, Amina, and Janis rushed into the waiting room. Romey asked, "Is Elliot okay?" just as Amina asked, "Can we see him?" and Janis sat down on the sofa beside David, put a sympathetic hand on his arm, and asked, "How are you doing?"

David set his harmonica on a little end table. "The doctors haven't come out yet. He's still in surgery." He turned to Romey and Amina, wanting to hear every detail about what had happened, especially all about Nick, his speech at the school board meeting, the bumper stickers on the car, the color of the car.

He hadn't finished his questions when Sharon walked in. She was only five feet tall, small-boned, slender, with short gray hair, a mid-

dle-aged gamin. She wanted to hear it all from the beginning, so
Romey and Amina started over. Romey felt as though she'd been telling the story all afternoon, first to the people who'd stopped, then to
the emergency crew, to the police, to Janis, and now, at least three different ways to David and Sharon. The couple grabbed at details, repeating them to each other as if the sequence of events could make
understandable what neither of them could yet understand.

The Novotnys had lived in Divido for over thirty years, had raised
one son there, and were almost finished raising their younger son,
Elliot. They arrived in Divido as hippies and bought land when it was
cheap. They lived easily by growing a little marijuana until the re-
gional representative of the Mafia paid them a courtesy call and informed them they could either become an exclusive franchise, under
Mafia terms, or quit the business. David and Sharon quit.

Now they had a pear orchard and a solar panel distributorship.
Sharon was the leader of a local organization that agitated to protect
good Divido ranch and orchard land from being invaded by vineyards. Her main interest was biological diversity, but she worked
alongside members of Divido Bible Church, who abhorred the drinking of alcohol. The couple had played backup in a shifting series of
country-rock bands over the years.

Romey was describing again how Elliot's overturned car had looked
from high up on the roadside: "Yes, I think it was all in one piece,"
when her mother put a little paper cup of cool water in her hand, then
gave one to Amina. Janis disappeared, then returned with water for
David and Sharon.

Two men and a woman from the Novotnys' band arrived. There
wasn't room for everyone to sit in the waiting room. Romey found
herself in the hall with David, telling the story yet again to the woman
and one of the men. She could hear Amina back in the waiting room,
answering the other man's questions. Two more friends arrived, and
the groups re-formed. Romey repeated the story again. The day was
heating up, and a smell of sweat hung over the people clustered in the
hallway, not the clean saltiness of exertion, but the more pungent
smell of fear.

A white-coated doctor emerged from the intensive care unit. He talked with David and Sharon; everyone else stood a few feet back. Romey couldn't hear it all, but she caught phrases. "A real fighter . . . cranial bleeding . . . trying to stabilize . . . lost a lot of blood . . . brain recovery . . . chances don't look too good . . . wait for . . ."

Romey could see David's knees give way. Sharon and one of the men from the band supported David from each side and led him back to the sofa. Romey felt as if a dentist had injected her insides with a giant shot of novocaine. There was no feeling in there. Amina came to her side. "They should let us in. Elliot's in there all by himself," Amina said. She pushed tears off her cheek with the back of her fist.

Romey squeezed Amina's hand. Sharon had gone back to the doctor and was asking a lot of questions about the surgery, the names of the things that were wrong, possible outcomes, the odds. Romey tried to listen, but the doctor's answers sounded scrambled, indecipherable.

Elliot was being allowed visitors for five minutes per hour. Sharon got David up and they followed a nurse through the door into intensive care.

More people arrived, and Romey told them again what had happened. Her answers were automatic now. Someone gave her a box of apple juice but she put it down after one gulp. It made her mouth stick together inside.

David and Sharon came back. David's shoulders were shaking with dry sobs. Sharon looked dazed. "He's still unconscious," David said, and crumpled onto the sofa.

Sharon's features all condensed toward the center of her face. "I'm making damn sure that fucking punk who ran him off the road goes to prison."

David blew harsh notes on the harmonica. Someone else asked Romey for details about what had happened. The more times she told it, the less real it seemed, and then somehow the five-minute visiting time came around again and Sharon asked her if she'd like to go inside.

Sharon led Romey through a dim corridor. "The doctors said he can't hear or understand anything." Sharon's hands were almost hidden by the sleeves of her big denim shirt. Her jeans were dirt-streaked; she'd been working in the garden when the call came. Romey assumed Sharon meant for them to go in together, but after Sharon opened the door, she let Romey walk in alone.

The blinds were drawn, the light low. Elliot lay on stark white sheets. A big clump of leg in a cast stuck out of the blanket. His head was partly shaved, bandaged. There was a cut on his cheek. His lips were caked and dry. An intimidating number of monitors calmly blinked their electric lights. So many wires were connected to him, and so many tubes; one, Romey noticed with embarrassment, trailed down to a bucket below the bed and must be connected to his penis. So many bandages. His eyebrow ring was gone. Polished industrial surfaces and sterile tubes were part of Elliot now, and he looked like something you weren't supposed to touch. There was no point of contact, no way in. The hand by her side on the gray blanket had an important-looking tube taped to its back, dripping clear liquid. The hand on the other side, though, was free.

Romey stood, picked up her chair quietly, and carried it carefully around the bed. Even though Elliot couldn't hear, it seemed important somehow to be quiet; even though he couldn't feel, it seemed important not to knock the bed, to set the chair down gently. She sat, and slowly slid one of her hands under Elliot's hand, watching all the lights and dials to see if she set off an alarm. They all stayed imperturbably the same: the dials at the same number, the lights blinking or moving across the screen with the same rhythm, or lit constant and still. She put her other hand on top of his. His hand felt heavy, spongy.

The door clicked open. Brisk footsteps. Guiltily, Romey slid her hands away.

"Hello, Elliot, I'm just going to change your IV bottle; you won't feel it. Oh, here, your oxygen has slipped down. I'm going to slide it forward here; that's good, easy. Now, I'm going to crank you up a little, just to give you a slight change of position, okay?"

Romey watched the nurse in confusion. "They told me he can't hear."

"Well, I feel like you can't be sure." The nurse wet a washcloth at the sink and daubed at Elliot's caked lips. "If he *can* hear, it can be awful scary to have someone do things to you without warning. And if he can't, there's no harm in talking." She dumped a bottle into a trashcan labeled "Medical Waste—Hazardous." It hit with a dull plastic thump, and she left.

Romey took Elliot's hand again and asked softly, "Elliot, can you hear me?"

She asked again, as loudly as the nurse.

She put her mouth close to his ear. The skin where his head had been shaved was blue-white. "Don't die."

She watched him breathe.

For a few breaths, she matched her breathing to his. In, out. But his was too fast. It made her pant.

She talked into his ear again. "Elliot, why couldn't you just let him pass you? You should have let him be a jerk." The words got lumped up in her throat. "So what if he was king of the road? You could have been okay."

Yellow and blue bruises on his face. She got up and went to the sink. There was another washcloth there. She put cold water on it and sponged his lips again, the way the nurse had.

The lights stayed the same colors, blinked with the same rhythm. The clock ticked. Muffled voices passed in the hall. Someone in the parking lot ground the ignition of a car that wouldn't start.

She felt a stab of shame because what she'd said sounded critical. She tried to imagine what Elliot felt like as Nick's car roared up at his side. "Maybe you couldn't let one more insult go by. You always act like it doesn't bother you, but maybe it does. But the most important part is, I'm your friend, and I . . ." she stumbled over words that would have embarrassed them both if he were conscious, "I love you. So don't die."

His eyes opened for an instant.

Maybe.

She put her lips near his ear again. "Elliot, if you can hear me, open your eyes."

Nothing.

"Just a blink. Or squeeze my hand."

His hand stayed still, heavy in hers; his face, slack and closed.

The door opened again. The nurse walked in and checked some numbers. "His blood pressure's up."

Romey recoiled from the bed, afraid she'd hurt him.

"We have to watch that it doesn't get too low. It's a good sign that it's up. Could be because you're here."

With a grateful smile, Romey reached for Elliot's hand. But now the nurse was telling her the five minutes were up and it was time to go.

She walked out into the quiet, cold corridor and back to the waiting room. Sharon was telling someone who'd just arrived the details of the surgery. David leaned over his splayed knees, head in hands. Romey sat down in one of the chairs. A single painting hung on the opposite wall, a scene of a window, with homey chintz curtains blowing outward toward a sunny beach. Amina came and sat beside her. Romey stared at the line in the painting where the blue of the sky met the darker blue of the ocean.

They waited another hour, so Amina could see Elliot. Sharon promised to call if there was any news. Janis agreed to bring the girls back the next day. The three rode home silently, just as the twilight was fading into the night. All that was left of the day was a dark red stain on the western horizon.

The police spent most of the afternoon questioning Nick Daggett. For a while, it looked like they might hold him in jail, in view of his just having completed probation, but his honorary uncle, Bob Gahl, the rancher, and his uncle, Reverend Jim Ed Wright, did some hard pleading that persuaded the police to release Nick into their custody.

Back at the house, when Janis found out the girls had eaten nothing since breakfast, she insisted on ordering a pizza over their objections that they weren't hungry.

"You'll be able to eat when it gets here," she said, and poured them each a big glass of orange juice. "At least drink something. You're probably both dehydrated. I know I am." She took her own glass off to the bedroom and called the Remnant.

Romey sprawled exhausted on the sofa, Amina across the easy chair. One would say, "If only he'd let that car pass him," or, "If the nurse is talking to him, there must still be some hope," and the other would answer, "Yeah." Then they'd fall silent.

A jumble of coupons, rubber bands, and stray keys covered the shelf above the fireplace. Magazines and books were piled by the sofa. The walls were liberally decorated with vivid silk-screen posters from Janis's past, posters about stopping the Vietnam War, stopping nuclear war, stopping rape. The colors looked garish tonight to Romey, bloody. For the first time, she noticed that all these familiar posters were about pain and death.

The doorbell rang. Romey got up, pulled the door open, and looked around for Janis's purse to pay for the pizza.

The door hit her hand, swung open hard, all the way around, and banged the bookshelf.

Red-faced, Nick pushed his way in. For the first time in her life, Romey found herself in the same room with a gun.

Gun.

Romey's eyes stuck on the gun, moving into the room with Nick's hand grasping the long barrel, a gun pointed at the ceiling. "Didn't have n-n-n-nothin' to do with that fag g-g-g-going over the mountain," his words spit out hard like bullets. Romey could barely catch them, because he thrust the gun forward, pointed at the ceiling. Hard to think with a gun in the room, the beautiful blue enamelwork gleaming along the gun's butt, his hand not near the trigger. That meant it wouldn't shoot, barrel aimed at the ceiling. Now Amina was moving somewhere in Romey's peripheral vision. Romey's eyes followed the gun, with Nick's hot red face blurred behind it, spewing, "You girls st-st-st-stop your lyin about me, I never . . ." Romey moved one step, beside the fireplace tools. Her fingers touched solid cold iron. She kept her eyes on the gun—hard to hear, hard to think—her mother's voice from the hall, "Who's out there?" . . . and Nick still talking, words rat-tat-tat. "Call that highway p-p-p-patrol now and say you . . ." Her mother materialized in the hall doorway; her mother's voice: "Put that gun down this instant," like Nick was four years old. But he wasn't; he was big and he had a real gun, not a toy gun, a gun swinging around toward her mother, lowering. Nick's hand moved down the barrel, closer to the trigger, and Romey's hand grabbed that poker, felt the right angles of the cold iron shaft bite into the flesh of her palm. She swung it high over her head, grasped it with both hands, brought it down toward the gun. Nick moved forward; she brought the poker down hard, the poker jerked sideways, and Romey jerked with it and the poker fell to the floor as a great noise roared into each ear and met in her brain with a blast.

"Mom! Did it hit you?"

"No, no, I'm okay. Are you?"

"Yes. Amina, did he hit you?"

"I'm okay."

Nick lay on the Guatemalan carpet, his head on the hardwood floor. He moaned.

Janis took a step toward him. "Nick, are you hurt?"

The gun barrel rested on his cheek. He rubbed it against his face, like a child with a teddy bear.

Janis knelt down beside him. "Nick? Romey, call nine-one-one. No, don't touch him."

"I want to take away the gun."

"I think we have to leave it there. The police are going to have to come."

"But what if he sits up and shoots again?"

"Amina, will *you* call nine-one-one right now?"

Amina's eyes darted around the room. "I can't find the phone."

"I don't know where I left it. Use the wall one in the kitchen. Romey, we'll watch him. If it looks like he's going to shoot again, we'll knock the gun away with the poker. No, not the poker. That's evidence, too. Go get the broom."

Romey ran to the kitchen, grabbed the broom, and rushed back holding it like a spear, stick end pointed high, dusty straw at her hip. It felt too big, awkward, flimsy. Amina was spelling out their street.

Janis touched Nick's shoulder softly. "Are you hurt?"

Nick curled into a fetal position around the gun.

Janis looked up at Romey. "I can't see any blood. I don't think he shot himself."

The boy groaned. "Nicky hurts."

"Where, Nicky?" Janis said gently. "Where does it hurt?"

"Nicky's cold." He slid the gun up, so it pointed off toward the corner, and the widest part, with the embossed blue enamelwork, rested on his cheek.

Without standing up or taking her eyes off Nick, Janis leaned sideways, slid the Navajo blanket off the sofa, and started to spread it on his legs.

"Mom, don't cover up that gun!"

Nick whimpered, "They sh-sh-sh-shouldn't let Nicky get this cold. He's *cold*."

Janis tucked the blanket around his legs, torso, and shoulders, leaving his arms and the gun exposed.

Amina walked back in. "They're coming."

"Nicky's awful cold." His voice was a croak. The blanket trembled. Tears dripped down the side of his face and made dark splotches on the hardwood floor. "Nicky's awful, awful cold."

Chapter 8

The paramedics came fast and whisked Nick off to Sutter Hospital in Santa Rosa, the same hospital where Elliot lay, fluids dripping in and out, under the vigilant electronic eyes of the monitors.

The pizza arrived next, but the flat white box sat on the coffee table unopened because the police pulled up just as the pizza truck pulled away.

The police drove Janis, Romey, and Amina to the station, and kept them separated while they questioned each of them in turn. There was only one interrogation room, and the officers were reluctant to put any of them in a cell, so they told Janis to stay in the coffee room, kept Amina in the waiting room under the eyes of the dispatcher, and closed Romey up in an office among regulation manuals bound in green plastic. It was after midnight when an officer finally brought Janis and Romey into the waiting room and announced, "At this point, we're treating it as a self-defense matter," and drove them all back home.

Amina fell right to sleep, but Romey, feeling so tired she was close to throwing up, went to the dining alcove and booted up the computer.

To: juliew@xnn.com
From: romey@igc.org
Re: I didn't mean to hurt him
Oh Julie, if anyone says I hurt Nick on purpose, please PLEASE DON'T LISTEN. I was only trying to knock the gun out of his hand because I thought he was going to shoot my mom and I don't know if he moved or my aim was bad (probably both), but he got hit instead.
I've been at the police station for a couple of hours. But the MOST IMPORTANT thing to me is how bad this must make you feel. I'm sorry. I'm sorry a hundred times. The words are so lame. If I could talk

to you, I'd say it better. I never want to hurt anyone or anything you care about. Ever. Do you know that?

The police say it wasn't my fault. I still feel really horrible and guilty because he is your cousin. I love you. Elliot is very sick. I think I'm still in some kind of shock because of Elliot. It happened so fast. Nick came over here right after I saw Elliot when he couldn't talk. Or open his eyes, even.

My mom's taking me to the hospital tomorrow morning (I don't know what time). I need to talk to you or at least communicate. PLEASE call me or e-mail me if you want to (and I really hope you forgive me & want to). Love, Romey

Pain. Elliot hears pain, tastes it. In a haze of choking dust, he tries to claw his way up the jagged chunks of rubble, but they cut his hands and slip under his feet, he keeps falling back to the bottom of the pit, five stories deep, in what used to be the outlet mall. He's surrounded by fragments of plastic toys, shredded clothing, shattered china, metal shelves twisted into grotesque shapes, mannequins without arms and heads, televisions with their electronic guts spilling out. Smoky fires still burn from the explosion.

He can see his mother, a hundred feet up, a small, slim figure silhouetted against a white sky, standing on a broken slab of concrete. The red windbreaker she wore when he was little flaps against her legs. Black-winged birds swoop behind her. She calls his name. He lifts his leg to climb, but rubble pins him. Frozen wind cuts his face.

Then he's crashing through a forest choked with thorny underbrush. Spider webs gum up his eyes. White worms writhe on rotting logs. A waist-high log blocks his way. He scrambles over it, slips on slimy moss, falls in a hole. His leg bends the wrong way at the knee, opening backward instead of forward, but he goes on, crawls, drags the leg, has to get to where Romey waits for him on the other side of a gray, scummy river. Garbage floats on the river's surface. He starts to cross on some rocks, but they're slick. He wobbles, and then a wall of frigid water slams him sideways. He thrashes around in the water, trying to reach Amina, who has now replaced Romey on the far bank. He can't breathe. Underwater, a rock cracks his head.

Then he's dry and a room opens up, something like the room where the support group meets, bathed in peaceful light. Pain lifts. Elliot's body is whole and smooth and perfect. He takes a step. The clumsiness that has been with him his

whole life disappears and he strides into the room with amazing grace. The air
is full of an elusive, sweet perfume. "What's that smell?" Elliot asks.

"Welcome," says a blond Viking with perfectly chiseled features. He's dressed
in a crisp blue shirt. His mustache is gold as a wedding ring.

"I didn't know welcome had a smell."

"Oh, yes," says the Viking. "And you can look at it, too."

Elliot notices this is true. The air is swirling with rainbows of gorgeous new
colors he's never seen before.

And seated, in chairs much more comfortable than in the old support group
room, are ten of the most attractive men ever. All smiling. An ebony Adonis
takes Elliot's hand and leads him to a love seat. Elliot's stride displays the per-
fection of the human form. He sits down next to an amber-skinned man from
the South Sea islands. The man wears a length of fabric wound around his
waist, patterned in the same new, vibrant colors Elliot sees swirling in the air.
Sweetness radiates from the man's tawny face.

Elliot says, "This isn't an ordinary support group, is it?"

The man on the other side looks familiar, but Elliot can't remember from
where. Then he recognizes him: it's Michelangelo's David, but not in marble
this time, in luminous flesh and toast-brown hair. He smiles at Elliot. All
around him, men smile their resplendent, accepting smiles.

Janis tried to let the girls sleep in the next day, but they woke up
early, and Romey immediately wanted to go to the hospital. Amina
couldn't come; she had to baby-sit the twins. Janis drove Romey to
Santa Rosa.

It was already hot and dusty. The sun fumed in a pallid sky. A big
flatbed truck loaded with tree trunks moved ponderously ahead of
them, gearshift groaning. It trapped them in the center of a slow-
moving, twenty-car tail. Romey's eyelids felt gritty, her neck ached.
Janis dropped her off at the hospital, telling Romey to call her at the
clinic when she wanted to be picked up. Janis would be there working
through her always-large stack of backed-up paperwork.

Romey's steps reverberated as she walked the empty, polished, white
tile floor. There was a bitter smell of disinfectant. No one was in the lit-

tle waiting room. The door to the intensive care unit was locked. She rang the bell. A nurse appeared and told Romey she could go on in.

She opened the door to Elliot's room. The blinds were up and the room was full of pale light. Elliot's mother was holding his hand. His father slumped at the foot of the bed, head bowed, blowing a single weak note on his harmonica. Sharon turned around, face gray, drained, tearless. "It looks like he's just . . . di . . . passing."

Romey stood, unable to move, a few feet from the bed. She wished she knew what she was supposed to do. The harmonica bleated. Elliot was propped up, almost sitting, with his mouth open. His eyes were slightly open, too. It looked to Romey like he was staring in shock at something in his lap.

"I don't think he's breathing anymore," Sharon said softly.

The door opened. Romey's head swung around. It was the same nurse as yesterday. She passed Romey and went to Elliot, felt for a pulse, sighed, and put her hand on the crown of Elliot's head. "This is the last place of life," she said. "It stays warm after everything else goes cold. This is where he is, if any part of Elliot is still with you. If he can take any comfort, you can offer it by putting your hand here."

Sharon kept one hand wrapped around Elliot's stiffening fingers; the other she placed on her son's head. "You're right; it's warmer. David?" She motioned for her husband to join her, but he shook his head and played the harmonica louder, a long tremolo note that spoke of railroad tracks receding into the faraway distance.

"Romey?" Sharon motioned for Romey to step around to the other side of the bed.

Romey obeyed. It felt like the air was made of cotton padding. She wondered if it would be creepy to touch his body. Was Elliot a body already or was he still Elliot? His barely opened eyes stared like a doll's at nothing. The top of Elliot's head on her side was thickly taped, so she set her hand cautiously on skin and bandage at his forehead. The skin was still warm, like the nurse said. She'd never touched Elliot there in life.

In life.

She wasn't positive he'd want her to touch him that way now. What would he want? Jokes? But he liked to tell them more than listen.

The harmonica fell silent. A fluorescent light buzzed overhead, then was quiet. Romey's arm started to ache from holding it in one place, but she didn't know if it would be okay to take it away, okay with Elliot's parents, or okay with Elliot, if he could tell she was there. She'd read that people could tell what was happening as they died; it was like they could look down and see, but she didn't know for how long.

The sound of David's harmonica punctured the air.

She could feel that the only warmth was coming from her hand and Sharon's.

The door opened again. The nurse entered, and Sharon took her hand away, so Romey did, too. The nurse took out the IV, unhooked some other tubes, turned off a monitor. "You can stay here with him as long as you like," she said. "I have some papers here for your signature. I'll leave them. Just ring the call button when you're ready to sign."

The Novotnys were hugging each other. Romey walked quietly out of the room. Her stomach felt like she might be about to get her period, an achy throb, low down. She walked through the hall and pushed the elevator button. The doors opened immediately with a jangly ping. Down at the ground floor, she walked out the front entrance and into the brassy sunlight.

Cars pulled up, stopped, disgorged people who came into the hospital, talked, carried flowers. A man helped a fragile old woman get out of a wheelchair and into the front seat of a van. Romey's legs twitched. She couldn't just stand here. She walked around to the side of the hospital, where sun bounced hard off the yellow wall and stopped at the back, where there was no one. She leaned on rusty metal flashing on the edge of a rough wooden loading dock.

Exhaust fan motors roared around her. The smell of garbage decaying in the heat lifted off two metal dumpsters. Bins of dirty laundry waited on the dock. Scraps of a purple balloon hung from a wire overhead, flapping in the weak breeze. A couple of pigeons pecked at a moldy french fry. Their wings had a greasy, iridescent sheen. Thorny dry weeds pushed out of cracks in the asphalt. Romey didn't believe Elliot was with God, or angels, or with the spirits of his dead relatives.

The big fan motors thudded. Heat rose up from the gray asphalt and down from the bronze sun. The sky had hard edges; the haze was thick enough to suck the color out of everything. Romey tried to get used to Elliot being nowhere anymore.

Nick Daggett's hospital room was crowded with people who had come directly from the eleven o'clock church service, gathered in prayer around his bed. Nick's little brother Teddy's hand was sticky in Julie's palm. Her father solidly held her other hand. She sang the last hymn from the service again for Nick, and everyone joined in on the chorus, voices off-key without her mother's accompaniment on the organ.

Nick slept.

Julie could hear her aunt Patty, who was standing just on the other side of her dad, letting out soft, choked whimpers, like a forlorn little girl. It made Julie shudder. Aunt Patty's weeping was too pathetic; it seemed to carry a hidden message about grown-ups being unable to take care of anybody.

Julie leaned forward to see her aunt. Patty held a tissue to her mouth with both hands; one wrist was splinted and taped. Uncle Wayne stood beside Patty, staring at Nick. Tears ran down one side of Wayne's pitted, bulldog face.

Her father's warm baritone voice intoned prayer after prayer. Heat from many bodies had overwhelmed the air-conditioning. Julie's mouth was dry and she needed to use the toilet. She joined her cousin's little hand with her father's big one and jostled through the bodies to the small bathroom by the doorway.

The toilet sounded loud; she hoped it wouldn't disturb the prayer. She filled her hands with cold water and brought them to her mouth, drank, then wet her face down.

Inching around the edge of the circle, she decided not to push in to stand by her dad again. She walked all the way around to the window. Julie watched pigeons rise and make a sudden turn all together through the washed-out sky. She could hear a low buzz from the exhaust fans.

And down there, leaning against a grimy loading dock, she saw Romey.

Slowly and quietly, Julie made her way around the prayer circle and out the door. Then she flew down the hall, down the stairs, out and around to the back.

She leaned beside Romey on the hot metal. "How's Elliot?"

Romey turned and made a sound that was part moan, part sob. She contorted her long limbs into a half crouch so she could lean her head on Julie's shoulder. Julie tried not to breathe through her nose; the smell of garbage was overpowering. The sun bore down on the top of her head. She put her arms around Romey, and Romey curled tighter, shook jerkily.

Julie had been to the hospital many times before with her father, visiting the ill. "Come with me," she whispered. "I know a better place."

She took Romey's hand and led her around a driveway and through a portal of flowering lime trees in big redwood planters. Lime blossom fragrance filled a little garden that was planted in daisies, pink azaleas, and blue clusters of Queen of the Nile. The yellow stucco walls of the hospital enclosed them on three sides. They sat on a wooden bench in the shade of a green canvas umbrella.

At the garden's center, water curved out of a stone fountain and burbled gently. "I can't stay very long," Julie said. "I have to go back to Nick's room."

Romey looked at the water. "I didn't mean to hurt him."

"I got your e-mail message. But you don't have to tell me. I knew."

"It looked like he was going to shoot my mom."

Julie's arm went around Romey's waist. "Nicky acts like he's worse than he is, but you couldn't know that. He gets in a lot of trouble."

"I'm sorry he's hurt."

"Poor Nicky. It wasn't your fault."

Romey's shoulders uncurled and she sat up. "Elliot's dead."

Julie knelt on the bench, which made her a half head taller. She looked quickly around, saw no one else, and circled Romey in her arms, hugging her as if she could squeeze away everything that had happened since yesterday.

She searched for words to comfort Romey, and was about to say Elliot was in heaven now, with Jesus, when she realized he probably wasn't saved. She frowned and stroked Romey's back. Some of her father's words came back to her then, about no one here on earth being able to decide what would happen in the Afterlife, because "God is the only judge." She sighed, relieved that funny, clumsy Elliot might still be with God, and decided to tell Romey God was the only judge, but she stopped. Romey might not want to hear anything about God. Finally, Julie was surprised to hear herself say something she hadn't even thought of, and she wondered if Jesus had put the words in her mouth, though afterward she realized she'd heard her dad say something like it. "You were a wonderful friend to him. Whatever else happened, he knew he had your love. And that's something really good to have, Romey."

Romey looked up at her. Julie took Romey's face in her hands.

Romey was aware of how sweaty her face was, how smeared with tears, and she drew back and turned her face down, but then Julie bent down and Julie's lips were gentle on hers.

For a long minute, Romey absorbed the kiss, understanding that this was a time-out. It mattered not if she betrayed her hunger; she was allowed, now, to take this kiss, suck every drop of peace and sweetness.

Julie began to talk while their lips still touched. "If there was any way I could stay with you now, I would. But I have to go back."

Her dress brushed Romey's cheek as she stood up.

Romey stayed on the bench. Moving water in the fountain held her eyes. The office where her mother worked was four miles away. She decided to walk, but first she needed more time in the shelter of the green canvas umbrella. She wasn't ready to be under the sky. It was too big.

All day Sunday and into Monday, Sharon Novotny sat in the bentwood rocker, staring out the bay window into the orchard. Her arms felt glued to the curving wood beneath them, and Sharon herself felt glued to the rocker. Tears clotted inside, wrapped around her windpipe in an icy coil.

She rocked mechanically. Her body was taking on the shape of the chair. There was the obituary to write for the newspaper. It felt complicated and impossible.

A shifting cast of friends and band members moved around the room, talking softly. Someone offered to go to the Santa Rosa airport bus to pick up her older son, her only child now. Someone else brought her a bowl of pasta and goat-cheese salad. "You have to eat," a voice said. "Come on, try a little of this postmodern casserole."

Their house was full of musical instruments they'd collected over the years: electric guitars, acoustic guitars, drums from Africa and Polynesia, a hammered dulcimer, and a piano David had built with the black and white keys in an unusual configuration for easier transposition of melodies. At manic speed, David played the piano, then, without bothering to tune it, the dulcimer. He switched to a Caribbean drum, then went outside to hack and dismember logs for the wood stove.

Elliot was being cremated; they'd decided that much. David wanted to bury his ashes in the orchard, so Elliot's essence would become part of the living things they raised and cared for. But Sharon wasn't so sure she wanted to sell pears that were partly Elliot.

And the funeral, or memorial—there had to be something. They had never attended church. Every time they tried to talk about the funeral, a neck-high sludge of exhaustion surrounded them, and they both felt a powerful urge to take a nap.

The phone rang, and one of the band members picked it up, talked a while without any of the conversation registering on Sharon, then passed the phone to her.

"Hello, this is Fran Chakirian, the counselor at Divido High."

"Oh, *Good Cop*."

"What?"

"Oh, that's Elliot's—*was* Elliot's—name for you." In the corner of each eye, Sharon felt one wet tear. It was something. A start.

She listened as Fran offered to hold a memorial assembly "as a way to honor Elliot and also help the students cope emotionally."

Sharon got one of the band members to bring David inside to the extension, and the couple gratefully accepted.

Fran suggested there could be a faculty speaker, the assistant principal, Spencer Grant—

"Bad Cop!" Sharon half giggled, half sobbed.

Would the Novotnys like to speak? Fran asked. They said no. Instead, they'd play music.

Then the counselor asked who among Elliot's friends should speak. David and Sharon immediately suggested Romey Arden. But Fran felt there was a shadow over the Arden girl just now; it wasn't clear what role she'd played exactly in that other young man, Nick Daggett, being seriously injured, although the police had decided not to press charges. Yet. It could complicate the memorial if choosing Romey to speak were interpreted by students who attended that fundamentalist church as condoning her actions; not, of course, that Fran condoned *Nick's* actions, in fact, she thought he should be prosecuted, but it might be better just to leave the whole question out of it. This should be Elliot's day. The focus should be on him. Was there someone else? Well, yes, the Novotnys said, Amina Porter.

Ms. Chakirian called Amina to her office the next morning and invited her (as the counselor saw it) or told her (as Amina saw it) to be one of three speakers at the memorial.

"It's not fair," Amina said to Romey over lunch that day. She shook her head back and forth, and the loose brown curls at her hair's periphery kept moving after her head was still. "You were more of his friend than I was. You should be up there. This is the second time I'll be giving a speech when it should be you."

"It's probably because I'm gay."

"Yeah. I could refuse. Do you want me to? I could tell Ms. Chakirian I won't do it unless they let you talk, too."

Romey stared out across the cafeteria. On the other side of the room, a boy sucked Pepsi through a straw, then pointed the straw across the table and shot the bubbly brown liquid toward two girls. Their squeals, half angry, half delighted, rose above the buzz and clatter.

Romey crumpled up her sandwich wrapper. "No, they might just say you can't speak, either. And someone has to say he was gay. Elliot would have wanted that. I know he would."

Although nothing kept the students from leaving early, few did, and the entire student body, along with friends and relatives of the Novotnys, filled the cafeteria, where the tables had once again been pushed to the side, the chairs arranged in rows. Many had to stand in the back. The American and California flags hung slack on their poles at one side of the stage. On the other, a large wreath of white carnations stood next to a wooden podium. Amina, Meredith, and Spencer Grant sat on the stage on metal cafeteria chairs. A little to one side, David and Sharon were partly hidden behind two music stands and a table with a hammered dulcimer.

Romey sat in the front row beside Elliot's aunt, one of the relatives who'd flown in from the east coast. Romey was saving the seat on her other side for her mother, who was late, but no one tried to sit there. It was the same story as at lunch. Now she was the only openly gay person in the school again, like she'd thought she was until that day Elliot sauntered up to her table, a sardonic smile on his big square face.

A tape of soothing New Age music played on the speakers. The school yearbook and newspaper photographers had put together some slides, which were being projected on a screen at the back of the stage. There were a few baby and little-kid pictures the Novotnys had provided, and two from a family vacation the summer before. Elliot with his dad on a Hawaiian beach. Elliot on a wicker chair, grinning, wearing swim trunks and a white flower lei, holding an icy pink drink with a tiny paper parasol on top, gesturing as if making a toast toward a sign nailed to the trunk of a palm tree: "Watch for falling coconuts." There were also three pictures taken by the student photographers, all of somebody else or a group of somebody elses, with Elliot's face to one side, half hidden. You couldn't even see he had an eyebrow ring, Romey noticed. When the sequence of slides finished, it started all over again.

Just as the overhead lights were switched off, the biology teacher sat down next to Romey. The music and slides halted. Mr. Grant came forward to the podium and welcomed everyone. Tugging on his inch-long beard, he talked briefly about Elliot as a student, about Elliot's wit. "We wish you could be with us today, Elliot, not in the least because we know you'd have something funny and insightful to say to us. Many of us still have things to say to you, too. It is with sorrow that we realize all we get to say is good-bye."

David and Sharon Novotny began their music. At the first soft chords, and the whole audience grew silent and seemed to suck in its breath in order to hear. David's dulcimer laid down a steady pattern. Sharon's liquid flute wove in and out with a curvy, irregular, lingering melody. It made Romey nostalgic for a place she'd never been, a calm mountain somewhere full of spiritual peace, where all kids got to develop to their fullest, unhampered. The dulcimer and flute came together on the last part, and the song ended, but not on the tone the ear expected. Instead it broke off after a long, dissonant, unsettling chord.

Romey felt motion beside her. Elliot's aunt buried her face in her handkerchief. Romey shyly patted the aunt's shoulder.

Amina walked to the podium. She wore a tan suit and her hair was pulled tightly to the back of her head.

"One thing I learned from Elliot is that you can be funny and brave at the same time," Amina began.

"And because he was brave, I know there's something he would have wanted us to remember about him." Amina took a big breath, her eyes on Romey.

Here it comes, Romey thought. She braced herself for the reaction.

"Elliot was gay, and he was proud of being gay. He was one of only two openly gay people in our whole school."

The silence in the audience was like when Romey had the flu and mucus jammed her sinuses. For the first time, the word "gay" had been spoken in a school assembly. She wondered how many kids, like maybe that shy Matt Rodriguez who ate lunch at her table every day now, were going hot in the face, fearing someone might understand the word "gay" applied to them, too.

Amina moved on to repeating a couple of Elliot's jokes. Romey felt the audience exhaling. There was scattered, tentative applause when Amina returned to her seat next to Mr. Grant.

Meredith was next. She began with a poem about a redwood tree cut down before it reached its towering growth. Then she reeled off into what sounded to Romey like pointless generalities that could be true about any young person who died. Romey wondered how she ever could have loved Meredith. Meredith looked so superficial now, her makeup and blonde hair too perfect, rising to the occasion with nauseating platitudes.

Romey uncrossed and recrossed her legs. She crossed her arms. Meredith was saying something about "letting bygones be bygones," about not dwelling on the ways that "he was maybe not perfect, for none of us are perfect, but honor him by remembering him at his best, an outstanding student, a gifted actor, an inspired comedian, and a loyal friend."

Romey wanted to stand up and yell: First of all, Meredith, being gay isn't something less than perfect. And second of all, what makes you think it's such a fucking *honor* to have The Great Meredith talk about Elliot as a friend, loyal or otherwise, The Great Meredith who never talked to Elliot once that I know of, and for sure never sat next to him at lunch?

Mr. Grant rose again. This time, his main point seemed to be that everyone should drive more carefully. "If Elliot's death can stop just one of you from driving dangerously, can save just one of you from an untimely death, he won't have died in vain."

How stupid, Romey thought. One person had to die to save another one? Either way, one person would be dead. How would that make it okay that Elliot was the one who was dead?

And it wasn't even the whole reason Elliot had been killed. He'd been killed not just because there were cars and highways, not just because testosterone beckoned through teenage boys' blood, inciting them to test the limits of the road. As Romey herself had said to the unconscious Elliot, goading Nick wasn't the best thing to do. But it didn't deserve capital punishment. Mr. Grant's safe-driving lecture was covering up the most important thing. Nick had run Elliot off the road because he knew Elliot was gay.

All that was left of Elliot was what she and others who knew him could remember and tell. To cover up the truth was to allow him to die, a little, again.

Amina's saying he was gay wasn't enough. Someone needed to say he died because some people hate gay people enough to kill. Why hadn't Romey thought of it before? Amina would have put it in her speech, even if it got her in trouble.

Mr. Grant was winding down. "So, as you head down the roadway of your young lives, remember that reckless driving can be deadly. Elliot would want you to remember."

Again, there was a scattering of soft applause. No one was sure if they were supposed to clap or not.

Mr. Grant thanked everyone for coming, announced that extra counselors would be standing by afterward for any student who felt the need to talk, and requested a moment of silence.

Romey looked down at her hands, unclenched them.

Sugary New Age music surged up and the slides appeared again on the front screen, Elliot grinning with his frozen pink umbrella drink, Elliot half hidden by someone's elbow at a basketball game. Romey felt achy all over.

Janis was waiting at the back of the auditorium; she'd arrived late. They dropped Amina off at her house. When Romey got home, she sent Julie an e-mail. Then she went into the kitchen, where her mother was making a salad, and said quietly, "I need you to help me go over my school board testimony tonight."

Just before she went to sleep, she checked her e-mail and found Julie's reply.

To: romey@igc.org
From: juliew@xnn.com
Re: Good luck at the school board!!!!
I wish I was allowed to come & hear you. That's one reason I love you.
You do things like that. You're BRAVE.
♥ ♥ Julie

Iris Bernstein opened the school board meeting with a moment of silence in honor of Elliot. Louise Stubbs then followed with an expression of hope for Nick's recovery, which was met, in some parts of the audience, with whispered hopes for Nick's criminal prosecution. Fewer people had attended this time. Even the children were more subdued.

Janis and Amina sat on either side of a numb Romey. Only a month ago, she'd been nervous about what these people, most of whom she didn't even know, would think when she announced she was gay. Now, that seemed like nothing.

Her name was called early. She stood up straight and read her statement slowly, with dignity. She talked about what it had been like for her and Elliot, the only gay kids at Divido High. When she came to the part about Elliot being killed because he was gay, the audience was rapt. Romey enunciated every word. She said the part about being a lesbian herself early in her speech, feeling natural, looking the audience in the eye, determined, as if she'd given a speech like this many times, and paid no attention to the reaction on the right side of the room, where Julie's parents sat with Virginia.

After Romey, testimony dragged on, repeating many of the same arguments from the previous meeting, until just after ten o'clock, when the board voted down Mrs. Stubbs's resolution, four to one. There would be no rule against gay teachers in Divido's schools.

Dark trees whizzed past the car as her mother turned down their street. In the end, Romey realized, the only people who supported Mrs. Stubbs's motion were from Divido Bible Church. Everyone else had been on her side. She puzzled about how all the adults could vote in favor of gay teachers, and yet their high-school children shunned the only gay kids in their midst.

Romey heard a voice inside that was clearly Elliot's: "Romes, they voted to let gay teachers keep their jobs, not to have lunch with one."

Tears needled her eyes. Part of him was part of her now, she realized. Every time she remembered, she kept him alive.

And after the reverend stood in the parking lot and commended his flock for fighting the good fight, after he vowed they would fight again another day, after he and Connie drove a few people home in the Divido Bible Church van, after the only remaining passenger, Virginia, sighed and said, "I could kick myself for letting Julie and that Arden girl sleep over at my house," after Connie responded to that re-mark by turning around in shock from the front seat, after Virginia had been dropped off, when the reverend and his wife were finally alone, Connie said quietly, "I think we need to have a serious talk with Julie."

Chapter 9

Sun from the kitchen window glared on Julie's cereal bowl like a spotlight. Head down, a curtain of dark hair shielding her face on each side, she watched her cornflakes succumb to milk and turn to mush.

"Look at me," her father said. He had those Sunday-sermon eyes fixed on her, flame burning in his deep eye sockets, blue—the hottest flame of all, hotter than yellow or white—a flame that could burn sin clean away. "Now, either this girl has been lying to you, and I'm willing to believe she has, or you've been lying to us about her being a homosexual. That's a lot more serious. Now, tell me the truth, Juliet. Did you know she's a pervert?"

"She's not a pervert! You'd like her if you knew her. She's good in math! She's a year ahead, too. She knows some calculus!"

"That is neither here nor there. Did you know she was a homosexual?"

"Yes, but—"

Connie broke in. "But you didn't tell me or your dad."

"You didn't ask."

Her mother turned to her dad with outrage. "We shouldn't have to."

"I knew you wouldn't understand."

Her dad leaned forward, spoke quietly. "Understand what, Julie? We want to understand everything now, I can assure you of that. Now, I want the truth. Has that pervert girl ever touched you?"

"No! She wouldn't do that. And she's not a pervert."

He stared at her. "The young lady stood up at a microphone and admitted she's a pervert. Well, I'm relieved to hear she hasn't touched you, if you're telling the truth now."

"I *am*."

From outside came the sound of deer hooves on the wooden deck, like a giant wooden drumstick whacking an irregular beat on an enormous drum. Connie popped up from the kitchen table, grabbed a kettle and a big steel spoon, threw open the back door, and banged on the kettle. Her voice was a half note lower than a screech. *"You get out of here! Darn it! Get, get!"*

A full-grown deer stopped munching Connie's potted impatiens and bounded off the deck with a panicky clatter of hooves. It ran across the yard, white rump flashing, and leaped over the fence. "And don't come back," Connie yelled.

She walked back into the kitchen and slammed the door. "As if we don't have enough to worry about right now."

The reverend turned back to Julie. "Let's have the truth about something else. Have you been over to that Arden house?"

Julie stared at the congealing cereal. "Yes."

"You go over there to that house where her mother comes home every day with blood on her hands from killing babies," Connie hissed. "And you lie to us about it. You have a lot to answer for, young lady."

"I'm sorry I lied."

"Sorry isn't going to cut it here," the reverend said.

Connie nodded. "And here your cousin is fighting for his life because she hit him."

"It was an accident! Nick was the one with a gun and—"

Connie crashed dishes into the dishwasher. "You stand up for her when she's wounded your own flesh and blood." Connie tried to get a hold of herself, told herself she should have seen it coming. She'd expected something from all the fuss the congregation had been making over Julie, and Jim Ed treating the girl like a little princess, but never this.

The reverend reached his hand around to the place where a pain was biting into his lower back. "Julie, I thought it went without saying that you'd avoid that girl because she hurt your cousin. Now, it appears you aren't ready for the trust we've placed in you. I'm sorry to learn that. Deeply sorry. So until your judgment gets a little better, your mother and I are going to have to take over. You are not to see her, ever again. Is that understood?"

"Daddy, please, please don't tell me that. She's the most wonderful friend I ever had. It's not fair to keep me away from her. I *love* her."

"Oh, dear Lord." Connie abandoned the dishes and sat down at the table across from Julie. Her fingers moved restlessly over the yellow Formica.

The reverend turned bewildered eyes on Julie. "You've always been such a good girl."

"I still am. I haven't done anything bad. Honest, Daddy. I'm in love with her, but it's not like homosexuals. It's . . . it's . . . *chaste* love. Pure. She's a homosexual, but she would never try to get me to do homosexual things because she loves me too much."

Her mother looked at her with pity. "You are much too young to understand anything about love."

"I am not. I understand Jesus' love. And this love is as good and pure as that."

Her father threw up his hands, sighing.

"The way I feel about Romey is what Jesus meant when He said The Kingdom of Heaven is within you. It's like singing in the choir. I've prayed to Jesus about this and I know it's right."

The ridges above the reverend's eyes grew more prominent. "I don't want to ever hear another word from you comparing your feelings for this pervert girl to Jesus. Now, there's no such thing as a girl being in love with a girl in some unhomosexual way."

"There is too. Lots of people, even people you know, have been in love like this and it wasn't a sin."

"People I know like who?"

The name "Virginia" slammed against Julie's teeth. But she held it there. That day when Virginia showed her Sandy's picture, she'd promised never to tell. "Lots of people. Teachers. People like that."

The reverend shook his head. "Julie, I don't know where you got this idea, but you are sadly mistaken. A girl in love with another girl without being homosexual is like a girl who says she's only a little bit pregnant."

"I'll be too sad if I can't see her. It'll make me want to die."

"Oh, stop overdramatizing," Connie said. "Your dad and I are forbidding you to see Romey. Or talk to her on the phone. Or contact her in any way. Is that clear?"

"Yes." Tears fell into the gloppy cereal.

The reverend reached over and put his hand on Julie's. "You are a beautiful, gifted young lady. You have a good future ahead of you. This pervert girl may not want to corrupt you, but she won't be able to stop herself. Sooner or later, she'll try to pull you into her sick life."

"She won't! She doesn't *have* a sick life." With her free hand, Julie picked up a scratchy paper napkin and wiped her face.

"Homosexuals always have a sick life. Now, you know it is impossible for your mother and I to watch you every minute of the day. Are you ready to promise you'll never see Romey again? Because I am ready to hear that promise."

"No."

"Not ready?" He sounded so disappointed, Julie felt oddly sorry for him.

"No."

"Well, then, go to your room. When you are ready to promise, you can come out."

But the Wrights let their daughter out three hours later, when they received word that her cousin, Nick Daggett, had died at Sutter Hospital. Julie was needed to help, to watch the two younger boys while her parents comforted Patty and Wayne, to fix food and answer the phone and take over other responsibilities they were accustomed to turning over to their daughter when extra demands, like sudden planning for a funeral, were made on their time.

"A teen grief workshop might do you a lot of good. I'll call Pam and see if she knows about one." Janis sat at the desk that had long ago taken over the dining alcove.

Romey lay on the sofa, looking at the cracks in the white ceiling. Through the heels of her socks, she felt the Navajo blanket, folded up at the sofa's far end. The bristly wool brought back a physical sense of Nick in the room, his gun. We should throw the blanket out, Romey thought. It touched a dead person.

"Romey?"

"No."

"No, what?"

"I don't want to go to a grief workshop." Four days. It had been four days since she'd heard from Julie. Not even an e-mail.

Janis walked over to the sofa and sat on the Guatemalan rug, so her face was even with Romey's. She smoothed Romey's hair. "It wouldn't have worked, anyway, with Julie," she said gently.

Romey turned her back, mashed her face into the sofa cushion.

Janis rubbed Romey's shoulder. "There'll be other girls. When you're older, maybe sooner. But you can't even try to keep seeing her. Someone else from that church might come over here with a gun. Plus, Julie's been raised to think it's wrong. She'll probably be so scared of her own feelings, she'll turn right around and get a boyfriend. I've seen that happen. It's a setup. You'll just get hurt. You better stay away."

Into the sofa, Romey said, "You do not understand anything about being in love."

Janis smiled sadly. "I think that's not completely true."

"Don't tell me you're going to side with her mom and dad and keep us apart."

"I'm not siding with them. I've raised you to be the kind of person who can make her own decisions by now. I'm telling you like I'd tell one of my friends. Those Divido Bible Church people are against everything you need to make a good life for yourself. To be in a relationship with the reverend's daughter is just self-destructive."

"You couldn't say that if you knew how we feel when we're together. It's the most un-self-destructive thing I've ever done."

"Hello?"

"Thank Jesus you're home."

Julie's voice. It was as if ropes binding Romey's body were sliced open. She felt herself expand all over. Cell phone to her ear, she walked out onto the front deck.

Sunlight drenched her. If anyone overheard, it might sound boring to stand there and say, "I love you," and "I miss you," and "It's been six days," and "I know," over and over. But it wasn't boring to Romey.

Julie told her about Nick, and the funeral, and being forbidden to contact Romey. "But I'm hoping, now that Mom and Daddy have had some time to calm down and think about it, they'll get used to us."

Romey told Julie about the school board meeting.

"I don't agree with Mrs. Stubbs," Julie broke in. "It isn't fair to fire homosexual teachers. I know my parents think it is. But I'm different."

After a while, they'd told it all, but neither wanted to get off the phone. Romey sat on the deck's warm redwood planks under a honey-colored sun, breathing into the phone, hearing Julie's breath on the other end. For that moment, it was enough.

Romey laughed. An easy, light laugh. "I love you as big as a mountain," she said. It was a game Romey's dad had played with her when she was little.

Julie caught on. "I love you as big as Mount Everest."

"I love you as big as the whole Sierra Nevada."

"Well, I love *you* as big as the solar system."

"And I—"

Romey stopped because she heard a voice in the background. A female voice. Julie's mom. "Juliet Christine, hang up that phone."

Julie, who was seated in front of the computer in the Wright family's home office, swiveled her chair around. Her mother glared at her in the doorway.

"Gotta go," she said into the phone. "But I love you more than the universe when it expands a million light years from now."

Homosexual . . . homosexual . . . homosexual . . . the drumbeat echoed in the reverend's head. Connie had repeated to him what she'd heard of the phone call. He pictured Julie's wrists, so finely turned, so feminine. Her ankles. Homosexual. The word itself sounded polluted. The vise in his lower back ratcheted a notch tighter. He stood up, producing a quick blowtorch blast to his third vertebra, walked from the home office to the bathroom, and swallowed a couple of Tylenols.

Julie, at three, running toward him with uncomplicated glee, butting his knees; he lifted her in his strong arms. . . . A Father's Day card she made one year, with construction paper and glitter glue, that said, "My dad takex me to the church." Homosexual . . . homosexual. A sunny little dark-haired, blue-eyed girl, not even the slightest breasts yet, holding her white leather-bound Bible: "Can I have a lamb, Daddy? See, Jesus has one. Here's the picture." At family meals, father, mother, and daughter were almost always smiling. How was it possible for a family life like his—so wholesome, so loving—to lead to homosexuality?

He started making calls. He soon found out there was a boarding school in Utah that was set up to handle a problem like Julie's. But there were drawbacks. There were drug-addict kids there, for one thing. For another, when he asked about facilities for Julie's continuing her advanced placement math class, the man on the other end of the line snorted and said, "To be honest with you, Reverend, we don't get too many kids in here who need advanced math." More troubling still, not all the staff at the Utah boarding school were saved Christians. There was no choir, and Divido Bible Church's choir would suffer from Julie's absence. He'd have to explain why she was gone, putting a permanent stain at an early age on her reputation, not to mention the family's.

He prayed. "Almighty God, if it is Your will that my daughter be sent away to another state, I will send her. You called me to serve You and I am doing my level best. Surely at a time like this it would be good for a little girl to be near her daddy. I'll miss her awful bad if she has to leave me and her mother. Please, help me find a way here in Divido."

He made more calls. He was discreet about whose child had the problem, giving the impression only that her parents were important and long-standing church members. A fellow preacher in Whittier told him about a local specialist in homosexual reparative therapy, Dr. Howard Oberholzer, "a Christian and the top man in the field."

The Whittier preacher even knew two men, members of his own church, whom this Oberholzer had completely cured of homosexuality. The reverend was able to reach one. The young man was eager to talk, and the reverend listened with rising excitement as the reformed homosexual described living five years in a life of sin, praying to be released, but not able to stop until he found Howard Oberholzer. He'd attended Dr. Oberholzer's two-month workshop, and he still went to weekly meetings. He was saved, and dating a fine Christian young lady.

The reverend asked, "Son, do you think it would have helped you if your parents had taken you to see Dr. Oberholzer at the first sign of trouble?"

"Yes, sir, I believe it would have."

The reverend had to leave a voice-mail message for Oberholzer. But a half hour later, he was on the phone with the man himself.

Oberholzer had a deep, confidence-inspiring baritone voice, not unlike the reverend's own. The reverend briefly outlined the story.

"And where do the other young lady's parents stand in all this?" Dr. Oberholzer asked.

"Oh, it's an atheist single mother who runs the local abortion mill. She accompanied her daughter to a school board meeting and sat there while her daughter announced she was a homosexual."

Oberholzer sighed. "I might have known. The kid's at the stage when sexual identity is most fluid, and here's a mother encouraging her on a deviant path. I tell ya, Reverend, that says it all about how messed up our so-called child protective service system is. By rights, you should be able to turn that woman in, so the other young lady can get some help before it's too late."

The reverend decided he'd found an expert on the right wavelength.

He confessed that the Christian girl he'd described was his own daughter. Oberholzer asked a number of questions about Julie's age, schooling, dating history, interests.

"Has she had any actual homosexual experiences?"

The reverend cleared his throat. "They had a kind of sleepover, slumber-party-type thing, but Julie tells us it was just like sisters sleeping together."

"Well, Reverend, in these cases I've found that where there's smoke, there's usually fire. And if your child is not guided away from temptation, there's a real possibility she'll develop an appetite for this sort of behavior."

He cautioned the reverend not to overreact. "That just makes teenagers dig in their heels."

"Well, my wife and I may have already done a little overreacting."

"Tell her you're praying for her and that you'll keep her problem confidential."

"I'm more worried about the other side of the confidentiality coin. If she's seen around town with this homosexual girl—"

"It could definitely undermine your position, even your church's. No doubt about it. Your best bet is to get some help fast from a Christian counselor. Don't let this fester. If a truck were speeding toward her, you'd get her out of the way. The Gospel is the only known antidote for homosexuality. And the upside is, the prognosis for your daughter is better than for a teenage alcoholic."

But when the reverend asked for a local referral, Oberholzer came up blank, though he had plenty of names in the southern part of the state, and even in Arizona. The conversation turned to the possibility of treatment from Oberholzer himself. He explained that he normally held small workshops. "The ideal thing is if you could gather a group of five to eight teenagers struggling with the issue of homosexuality and I can work with them all at once. Then, the expense for your family will be lower," he suggested.

But when the reverend said there were no others that he knew of, Oberholzer offered to fly in for a few days and conduct individualized treatment. It would be expensive. There was Oberholzer's consulting fee, plus he would need to rent a small meeting room at a Divido motel. "The treatment will be most effective if your daughter is free of the distractions of your home. And, obviously, it would be completely inappropriate for me to treat your daughter in a motel bedroom setting."

The cost for just one day would take the Wrights' modest savings. "And I'll be up-front with you. It generally takes longer than a day, though there are exceptions."

Oberholzer could be in Divido in twenty-four hours. He could work with Julie for up to five days if necessary; then he'd have to return to Whittier for one of his scheduled workshops. He could come back to Divido two weeks later. Or the reverend and Julie could fly down together for follow-up sessions.

"I could also conduct some training with you, Reverend, in the kinds of things we do in our weekly follow-up meetings. It could be helpful to you with other members of your congregation," Oberholzer offered.

The reverend made his decision quickly, while he was still on the phone. Julie's future was at stake, in this life and in the Afterlife. Oberholzer seemed to be the best. As for the money, the reverend just hoped the Lord would provide.

The twenty-four-hour prayer station was turned up loud. The reverend swung the car south onto Highway 101, heading toward Santa Rosa to pick up Dr. Oberholzer at the Airporter. He was beginning to take effective action on his daughter's behalf, and that made him optimistic. The engine was in perfect tune, the road smooth as glass.

Oberholzer was almost a head taller than the reverend, and even more reassuring in the flesh than he'd been on the phone. His soothing baritone rolled out as they drove back. "You have plenty of cause for hope. The more years of homosexual behavior, the harder it is to change. And treatment is most effective if temptation hasn't actually escalated into homosexual activity, which is what your daughter says is the case."

"So she says."

"Treatment will be helpful in getting at the truth. You're absolutely right to nip this in the bud now. It'll be much harder on her if you let her suffer for a couple of years with an untreated problem. If only there were more parents like you."

The reverend switched on his cruise control and removed his foot from the gas. "Uh, can you give me some idea how you'll be working with Julie?"

"We will meet for around seven hours each day. Please send a brown-bag lunch along with her. We'll eat in the same room where I'll treat her. The idea is for us to spend concentrated time in an environment where the only goal is turning Julie away from the homosexual temptation. The majority of our day will be spent in prayer."

A blustery wind buffeted the car with a spray of grit and whipped up the dark roadside eucalyptus trees.

"In between intensive prayer sessions," Oberholzer continued, "I have an array of techniques I use, depending on the individual. Some of my techniques are stronger than others. One thing I need to check with you is if you want to authorize my strongest treatment."

"I want whatever will turn my daughter away from homosexuality. Your best." The reverend smacked the steering wheel.

"Some of my techniques involve a modest amount of pain. Electronic aversive stimulus is a little controversial. Some counselors think it's old-fashioned, but in my experience, it is highly effective. It does include mild, harmless electric shocks."

The reverend slowed down to exit the highway. Sitting in a car for any length of time was hard on his back. It felt like he had a metal claw in there. When the sun hit at this angle, the windshield was smeared. He turned on the spray and wipers. A mile of silence went by. "How much does it hurt?"

"Less than when you spank her."

"Actually, my wife mostly handled spanking, and Julie hasn't needed to be spanked since she was nine. She's always been a good girl. Where, ah, what place on her body, ah—"

"Are the electric shocks administered? To her hands."

"Oh. Her *hands*."

The reverend speeded up to pass a big tanker truck with a red sign on the back reading, "Caution: Explosives." The force of the passing truck sucked the car toward the shiny silver tank. He gave a hard pull on the steering wheel, sending a shooting pain up to his shoulder, then slipped into the right lane just in time to avoid a line of oncoming cars.

Oberholzer cleared his throat. "Reverend, I don't want any misunderstandings here. There are some unethical people working in this field, men who might try to take advantage of your daughter and label that 'curing' her. What I offer is a Christian treatment method. It goes without saying, but let me say it to make things crystal clear: Your daughter will remain properly clothed at all times."

"I—"

"I will remain properly clothed at all times. Proper Christian treatment for homosexuality does not, I repeat, does not, include any so-called 'practice' in normal sex acts."

"No, of co—"

"It never does, but especially not with a child so young."

"I didn't mean to sound like—"

"I know you didn't. I just wanted to clear the air. And you are free to authorize my treatment with or without electronic aversive stimulus. There's a check-off on the release form. I do recommend electronic aversive stimulus, because it can be effective, and you have flown me up here to do what is most effective."

The reverend turned into the Divido Best Western motel parking lot. The emergency brake squealed. "All right, then. I'll authorize everything, even the electrical part. But can you use it as a last resort, start with your other treatments?"

"You betcha, Reverend."

Chapter 10

"Will you pray with me, Julie?"

She nodded. Dr. Oberholzer knelt in front of his orange plastic chair. She did the same, feeling tiny. Her head didn't even come up to the top of those big square shoulders, encased in that gray business suit. They bowed their heads.

Raindrops slapped the full-length windows outside the Divido Best Western motel conference room, but the orange and black drapes inside were drawn tight and muffled the sound. The first fifteen minutes had passed easily. Dr. Howard Oberholzer ushered Julie to her chair, firmly closed the door to the lobby, then returned and sat in an identical chair, at an angle. There was a flip chart on an easel nearby. He asked a lot of questions about math and the choir, and took in her answers with an enthusiastic smile.

Now he started his prayer. "Heavenly Father, I thank you for beginning the process of change in this young lady's life . . ." Julie let out her breath and relaxed at the sound of his deep, smooth, comforting voice, ". . . by guiding her parents to seek help for her. Please help her to come to a place of sexual wholeness . . ."

She jerked her head up, shocked at the word "sexual."

Dr. Oberholzer's head remained bowed. ". . . sexual wholeness in Jesus, we pray. Amen."

He stood up, then sat back in his chair. She copied his movements. He raised his head and looked her in the eye steadily, with deep concern, as if he could read everything inside her, until she lowered her eyes to her lap and let her hair curtain her face.

"Julie, you've been doing things your way for a little while now. Are you willing to try God's way?"

"I do try God's way."

"Good. That's good. Now, Julie, I want to ask you a few questions of a personal nature. And I want you to know that whatever you tell me will remain between us in confidence." He cracked his knuckles. "I will make a report of a general nature to your parents. But I will not reveal any information you confide in me unless I have your explicit permission to do so. Okay?"

"Okay."

His head looked so long and narrow to Julie, almost bullet-shaped. The bald front part had knobby, bony corners. As his head moved, even slightly, the white fluorescent lights overhead made different parts of his forehead shine.

He sat back in his chair. "When you were little, did you play with dolls?"

"Sure."

"A lot? A little? An average amount for a girl?"

"Average, I guess."

"How about house, did you like to play house?"

"Yes."

"Who did you play house with?"

"Different friends. My cousins."

"Were you the mommy?"

"Yes."

"Not the daddy?"

"No. Nicky, my cousin, he was the daddy sometimes. And his little brothers were our kids."

"Good, Julie. Good. Did you play nurse and doctor, too?"

"Yeah."

"A lot?"

"No."

"Now, Julie, many times, children, when they play these games, house and doctor, they get kind of curious about what other kids' bodies look like, and—I'm not going to judge you if you did this— kids will, you know, take off their clothes and look at each other's private parts. Did you ever play this way?"

"No!" Julie's voice was loud with indignation.

"Most children do, actually. The reason I'm asking you this is that the more I know what your experiences have been, the better I'll be able to help you. It's sometimes hard to admit these things. Are you sure you and your cousin, or some other boy, didn't look at each other's bodies?"

"We never, ever did anything like that."

"Or touch each other's private parts?"

"No, no, no. I don't think you should be talking to me like this."

He met her eyes with a look of intense concern. "Julie, we are dealing with serious questions about your sexual future here. You are at risk. To protect your sexual future, we will have to discuss topics that may make you uncomfortable."

Julie noticed the line all the way around his neck where the shaved skin stopped. Thick wiry hairs were matted against his shirt collar. Hair bristled out from his shirt at the wrists, and there were dark tufts on the back of each finger, too. Maybe he was hairy all over. She wondered if it itched.

"We are going," he continued, "to have to squarely face the danger you are in, and not run away from it. We do this because if we turn our backs and pretend you are not in sexual jeopardy, your future will be not just uncomfortable, but one of extreme hardship. Now, when you played with other little girls—and bear in mind that Jesus is witnessing everything you tell me, and that He wants you to tell the truth, even if it could be a little embarrassing—did you ever take off your clothes and look at each other?"

"No." She crossed her arms over her chest, hunched her shoulders so her breasts stuck out less, and stared at the big plastic potted plant in the far corner.

"How about touching each other's private parts, maybe just to play, you and another girl?"

"No."

"No experiences like that, with boys or girls?"

"No."

"Yet your dad tells me you've shared a bed with your friend Romey for an entire night."

She kept her eyes on the potted plant. "It was a sleepover. Best friends sleep over all the time."

"All right, Julie. Now, you strike me as a very mature young lady, so I am going to share with you some information I wouldn't normally share with a girl of fourteen."

She turned to look at him. "I'll be fifteen next month."

He smiled indulgently. "Or a girl almost fifteen. Okay, let's begin. What is God's plan for us as sexual beings? He wants us, if we are female, to marry a husband, or, if we are male, to marry a wife. And he wants us—within the sacred structure of Christian marriage—to freely enjoy the pleasures of our sexuality, and the results of our sexuality. Are you with me so far, Julie? Do you know what I mean by the results of our sexuality?"

"I'm not sure."

"I mean, of course, children. And family life." The look of deep concern for her came over his face again. "Now, your teenage years are crucial to the development of your nervous system for sexual stimulation."

Julie felt her face get hot. She looked down at her hands, twisted them against her blue corduroy skirt.

His voice grew warm and sympathetic. "Girls your age have a lot of passionate, romantic feelings. And mixed in with those feelings, sometimes, is sexual temptation." He stood up and wrote the words "SEXUAL TEMPTATION" with a red marker on the flip chart. "Now, Julie, all sex outside of marriage is abnormal and wrong. Do you understand that?"

She knew her face was bright red. "Yes."

He sat down in his chair and leaned toward her. "It's not just sex outside of marriage that is wrong, but sexual fantasies outside of marriage. These may feel good at the time, but they're nothing but debased lust. And Jesus clearly condemns lust."

She wished the heat would die down from her face.

"We cannot stop ourselves from being tempted by sexual fantasies. Temptation is not our fault. It is not a sin. Giving in to temptation, allowing the lust to develop in our hearts and bodies, that is the sin. Do you see the difference?"

"Yes."

"Now, if a girl—like you, for example—is tempted to indulge in lustful fantasies about another girl, that is homosexual temptation." He stood up again and wrote "HOMOSEXUAL TEMPTATION" on the flip chart, then faced her.

"Being tempted is not a sin. But allowing temptation to progress to lustful thoughts of another girl, into homosexual fantasies, that is a sin." He wrote "HOMOSEXUAL FANTASY" on the flip chart in bold red letters.

Oberholzer turned and drilled his eyes into her. "And if you let temptation go even farther than fantasy, into homosexual activity . . ." the red marker squeaked against the page as he wrote "HOMO-SEXUAL ACTIVITY," "that is also a sin. Do you follow me?"

She picked a speck of lint off her skirt and flicked it away with her fingers. "Yes."

"And if you let fantasies and activity become regular things, then you form," he turned and wrote "HOMOSEXUAL HABITS" on the chart. "Form what, Julie?"

"Homosexual habits."

"Just so I can be clear that you understand, would you please tell me what I just told you, in your own words?"

"I don't think Daddy would approve of you talking to me like this."

"Your dad and I have discussed your treatment. Now, as I said before, you're a mature young lady, fully capable of understanding what I've just told you, and I'd like to hear it in your words."

"You said that doing homosexual things and thinking about it are sins. And keeping on doing them is a bad habit and a sin. I already know that."

"Good. And what about the other part, Julie?" His face registered complete sympathy and he pointed to the words HOMOSEXUAL TEMPTATION. "Is this a sin, too?"

"No, as long as the person doesn't give in to it."

"Okay. I feel we're making some progress here. Let's have a few minutes of silent prayer. No, no, stay in your chair. Seated silent prayer."

The second hand on the wall clock clicked steadily. Outside, the rain slowed to a drizzle, with big drops plopping off the roof and the trees.

After a while, Oberholzer cleared his throat. "Praise the Lord. Amen."

He took off his glasses and rubbed the bridge of his nose. Without glasses, his eyes looked bigger to Julie. They had blue-black circles underneath them. There was a pitcher of ice water on the conference table. He poured a glass and offered it to her, then went to the other side of the room, where the hotel had set up a large coffee thermos and some cups. He poured himself a cup of coffee.

"How's the temperature in this room, Julie? Is it warm enough for you? I can turn up the heat."

"It's okay."

He stood by the flip chart. "All right, let's get back on track here. Now, have you ever felt, with your friend Romey—either by yourself, when you were thinking of her, or when you were with her— homosexual temptation?" He struck the words on the flip chart with a rubber-tipped pointer.

"No! That's why this whole counseling is a big mistake. I love her like a best friend."

"I'm very pleased to hear you haven't felt temptation. I think you'd be wise to leave it up to your parents and me to decide if counseling is a mistake, however."

Light glinted off his glasses. "All right, Julie. Now I need to give you a little more information. Your wedding night with your future husband will be the most exciting of your life." He looked into her eyes. "Jesus has reserved the greatest pleasure of all for you, pleasure available only to married Christian couples."

As his mouth moved to form words, Julie watched the thousands of dark dots moving on his upper lip and jaw. The skin there looked almost gray.

"Now, Julie, if a young person yields to homosexual temptation," he struck the chart again with his pointer, "during these crucial teen-age years, the nervous system may fail to develop normally. Instead, an unhealthy pattern may be put in place. The next homosexual temptation," the pointer whapped the chart again, "will be stronger. And if she yields to that, the next will be stronger still. Homosexual fantasies," he tapped the pointer three times on those words, "will become stored in her memory. Now, if you recall, temptation itself is not sin. But if a young person allows her nervous system to form lust-

ful homosexual habits," he pointed to both HOMOSEXUAL FAN-
TASIES and HOMOSEXUAL ACTIVITY on the chart, "this could
ruin the pleasures of your wedding night."

He paused and took a drink of coffee.

"If homosexual patterns become ingrained in your nervous system,
it could even make you incapable of married life, because your nervous system will be unable to respond normally to your future husband."

Julie's face grew hot and red again.

"Bad sexual habits now could rob you of your chance to be a Christian wife and mother with her own family. Bad sexual habits now can
lead you toward a future of suffering and deviance."

Julie sighed in exasperation and looked at the acoustic tile ceiling.
"But I already told you I'm not doing anything like that with Romey."

"And I'm glad to hear it. Mighty glad. But Julie, you need to trust
that people like your dad and like me know a little bit more about the
Devil and about temptation than you do. Now, I want to make you
aware of the risk you are flirting with here. Your friend Romey is an
avowed homosexual."

"But *I'm* not one."

"No, you're not." The look of extreme sympathy again, almost
pity. "And I'm going to let you in on a little secret. Romey isn't one,
either."

Julie looked at him, confused. She could see tiny images of herself,
slumped in an orange chair, reflected in his glasses. "But Romey says
she is."

"The girl may say she is a homosexual, but no teenager is mature
enough to decide she's a homosexual. There are no homosexual teenagers." He fixed his eyes on her. "There are only young people who are
giving in to homosexual temptation, allowing it to grow into bad homosexual habits. There are only teenagers who are letting their nervous systems get into depraved patterns that will be harder to break
once they grow up."

Julie raised her chin. "Well, if Romey's not a homosexual, then it
should be okay for us to be friends."

"Oh, no, Julie. It's not okay. Not okay at all. Because when this girl tells you she is a homosexual, she is admitting she encourages her mind in homosexual lust," tap went the pointer, "that she perhaps engages in homosexual activity," tap again, "and is willing to become mired in homosexual habits." When the pointer struck the red letters of "HOMOSEXUAL HABITS," it tore the paper.

"But she promised never to do anything homosexual with me."

"Julie, I'm pleased that you don't understand the kind of temptation that will put that promise to the test. But it is a promise she will not keep."

"You don't know her. You don't know that. She loves me."

"Your dad understands she will not be able to keep this promise. That's why he told you to cut off contact with Romey. And what did you do?"

"I talked to her, but—"

"Julie, you *have* learned that disobedience is a sin, haven't you?"

She lowered her head and stared at her navy blue skirt. "Yes, but I thought Daddy would change his mind once he really understood."

"Your dad does understand. That's why he's called me. Your dad and your mother could just let you slip into a life of sin. But they love you too much for that. I'm here with you because your parents have decided not to throw you in the garbage can. The next thing is for you to decide that for yourself."

He watched her. She kept her face down. The rain started up again and beat sullenly on the glass behind the curtain.

"Romey may sincerely believe she loves you. I'm not accusing the girl of consciously lying to you. That would be irresponsible of me. I don't even know her. But one day, her sexual feelings will get the better of her. Or she may respond to your romantic feelings for her by initiating a homosexual act. Or she may be skilled in seduction. Her promise may be part of the seduction process."

Julie picked at the tacks that held the orange plastic upholstery to the arm of her chair.

"Now, Julie, you have a normal need for a close friendship with a girl your age. Nothing wrong with that need. But it's important that you fulfill it in a healthy way. Romey is not an appropriate choice. It would be far better for you to cut off all contact with her, and put your energy into finding a Christian girl to be your best friend."

There was a little piece of paint, or something, on one of the tacks. Julie scratched at it with her fingernail.

Oberholzer stood up and stretched out his arms. "Okay, let's have some silent prayer here. Then I think we'll change gears a little."

The wall-to-wall carpet had a pattern of black, brown, and gray splotches, flecked with orange. Julie stared down at it and prayed to see Romey again. To leave this room forever. She asked Jesus to help her convince her dad and mom.

After a while, Oberholzer said, "Julie, you keep on praying by yourself. I'm going to set up some equipment here."

He unpacked a slide projector, put it on the conference table, adjusted the lens, tested a slide, and moved some of the chairs and the table. He opened the closet door, clamped a board to the doorframe and fastened one of the orange plastic chairs to the board. He pulled the chair from side to side and adjusted the clamps until the chair couldn't be moved. He opened a suitcase, took out a clump of red wires and black straps, untangled them, and arranged them carefully across the clamped chair.

"All right, Julie, have a drink of water, and then you can just move over here," he said, motioning toward the chair with wires.

She sat where he'd directed her. "Put your arm here, please." He wrapped a Velcro strap around her wrist and the chair's arm, then snugly fastened another strap up toward her elbow. "Too tight?"

"A little."

The Velcro made a harsh tearing sound as he loosened it and refastened it. Then he moved to the other side and attached her arm to the chair in the same way. "That better? We don't want your arms to go to sleep."

"They're okay now. Is this some kind of lie detector?"

"That's an interesting idea. In a manner of speaking, yes."

Julie wondered if it could provide evidence that her love for Romey wasn't in danger of becoming the homosexual kind.

Dr. Oberholzer turned off the lights and sat on the other side of the table, facing the same way she was, toward a blank white wall. He clicked the remote and a color slide bloomed.

"What do you see, Julie?"

"A boy and a girl." They held hands and smiled at each other, strolling through a field of daisies under a cloudless blue sky.

"Is this a happy picture, Julie?"

"Yes."

"Would you like to be there?"

"I guess so."

"You guess so. All right."

He clicked again. This slide showed a dingy room. Two girls sat on a couch. One had pimples, and she was about to kiss the other. So this was what lesbians were like, Julie thought. She'd never seen any, except the picture of Sandy that Virginia had shown her. But Sandy looked a lot nicer than these girls. There was something about them, something strange, and mean—

Julie gasped. A hot-metal pain stabbed her palms. "Ow!" She couldn't move her hands; they were fastened to the chair, and when she tried to stand up, she could raise her body only a little. Her hands stayed caught in the slashing pain. She jerked her head sideways toward Dr. Oberholzer, outraged, but he stared straight ahead, his calm profile lit by the greenish glow from the slide.

"That hurts. Stop it!" Her voice came out in a scream.

He stayed impassive, not looking at her.

She twisted her hands the small amount the straps allowed, but she couldn't get away from the scorching corkscrew. Then it stopped.

"This one isn't such a happy picture, is it, Julie?" His baritone was soft and calm.

She swallowed hard. "N-no."

"Take another look, Julie."

"I don't want to."

"This could be your future, if you give in to homosexual temptation. It's important that you face that. Your hands won't hurt this time."

She slowly turned her head toward the image. The girls were old, twenty-five at least, and sloppy-looking. "I would *never* do anything like that," Julie said fervently.

He squeezed the remote. This slide was of a bride turning toward her groom at a sunny church door. Her veil billowed out in the breeze as happy relatives tossed rice.

"How about this, Julie? Would you call this a happy picture?"

"Yes."

"Would you like to be a bride like that some day?"

Julie breathed carefully, in, then out. The truth was, she wanted to live with Romey, like Virginia lived with Sandy before Sandy tried to get Virginia to be a homosexual. But she'd promised to keep Virginia's secret, and she didn't know if Romey would ever want to live like that. They'd never talked about it. Romey would probably want to live with another lesbian instead. Plus, she was positive Dr. Oberholzer wouldn't understand.

"Would you, Julie?"

Second choice would be to get married, so Julie figured it wasn't a sin when she said, "Yes, I want to." But the lie gave her an immediate dirty feeling.

Click. Her whole body tensed against the coming pain. She dug her fingers into the orange plastic on the chair arm.

The same bride and groom appeared on the wall, climbing into a car in the sun, "Just Married" painted on the back.

"Let's just enjoy this one, Julie."

"Okay."

Click. Another dark room. A heavily made-up woman with platinum hair, sitting on a bed with another woman whose head was turned away. The platinum-haired woman's hand was inside the other woman's skirt.

She braced for the pain. Nothing happened.

"Not a very nice picture, is it, Julie?"

Cautiously, she said, "No."

He clicked the projector. Two girls with their arms around each other, their lips ready to meet in a kiss. They looked like nice people, really.

The stabbing in her hands again. Longer, this time. She felt her back jerk into an arch, but nothing she did with her body could move her hands. She moaned. Her eyes were on the ceiling, she wouldn't look again, tears bit her eyelids, and still the pain came, scalding.

"Look at the picture, Julie," he said calmly. "The pain will be over as soon as you look."

She jerked her head down. The knives in her hands stopped. "I'm too young to see these pictures," she whimpered.

A fine sheen of sweat coated her arms. Her mouth was dry.

"Yes, Julie, you're right. You *are* too young. I'm sorry you have to see them. Your daddy will be sorry, too. Very sorry. But this is where you are heading, if you keep up the way you've been. I'm showing you this so it's not you one day up there on the wall."

There were a dozen more slides. The backs of Julie's legs grew sticky. Her face was soaked with tears. The worst part was not knowing when the pain would start. It never came with a picture of a boy and girl, but when the slide was two girls, she couldn't tell if there would be nothing, or if the hot metal was about to jab her hands.

He finally switched off the projector, and when its fan shut off the room seemed deadly quiet. He turned on the lights. The Velcro straps shrieked as he pulled them apart, freeing her arms. She stood up. Everything about her body ached, especially her hands. She turned them over, but there were no stab marks.

She walked toward the door, jerky, dazed.

"Where are you going?"

"To call Daddy."

The door was locked.

"You'll see him at four, when he comes to pick you up. If you want to use the rest room, it's through that door over there."

She went in, closed the door, and tried to lock it. The lock had been taped open with many layers of strapping tape.

Her stomach heaved and she threw herself down on the floor, face in the toilet. Green vomit bubbled up and filled her throat. She coughed and spit. The cold tile floor pressed up through her skirt. She sat for a moment, breathing, waiting to see if more vomit would come, then stood, flushed the toilet, washed her face, blew her nose, and for several minutes stared at her wide, scared eyes in the mirror.

"About finished in there?" He tapped on the door.

Her tears started again as she opened it.

He looked so sympathetic, as if someone else had just hooked her up to wires and hurt her, as if he understood. "Let's have a few minutes of silent prayer, Julie, then we'll break for lunch."

She knelt on the carpet. The gray and black splotches ran together under her eyes. Three years ago, the Divido River had overflowed its banks in the winter rains. The whole church had volunteered to help flooded-out families. On the way to take hot beef stew to another church where people were spending the night, Julie rode in the car with her mother along the river road. The water, the color of chocolate milk, washed up onto the road in places. The river had big logs floating in it, pieces of lumber and pieces of clothing, a shoe, a tire, and then Julie saw the dead dog. Two legs stuck out of the water at a weird angle, and the dog was held afloat by a wet, hairy belly swollen tight as a soccer ball.

Julie prayed to Jesus to protect her love for Romey, to keep it from being washed away by Dr. Oberholzer's dirty torrent of words and pain, whatever happened to the rest of her, to let her keep her love clean. Safe.

After a while, Dr. Oberholzer cleared his throat. "Dear Lord, we know You never command us to obey You without also giving us the ability to obey. We ask you to help this young lady realize she has powerful spiritual resources that will aid her in putting aside this unhealthy relationship. Amen."

He stood up. "Lunchtime, Julie."

They sat on opposite sides of the conference table. Oberholzer thumbed through some papers and occasionally jotted down a note while he ate the chicken sandwich and potato salad he'd had boxed to go at the motel coffee shop that morning. He didn't look at Julie or say much.

She felt hungry somewhere underneath everything, but all she could swallow was her milk; her peanut butter sandwich tasted like wool and glue. She put it down after two bites.

After lunch, Oberholzer reviewed the information he'd presented in the morning. Julie was tense, alert with the fear that he'd make her get into the wired chair again, but he didn't. There were long stretches of silent prayer. The afternoon crawled. Every time she looked at the clock on the wall, sure an hour must have passed, the big black hand had moved only ten minutes.

They finished another prayer.

"Julie," his voice was calm, deep, smooth. "I can feel you have hardened your heart against me. What you need to understand is that if you are not careful, your heart will also harden against Jesus Christ."

She stared down at her lap. Her eyes were narrowed, glittery. "I've prayed about Romey a lot. Jesus doesn't believe loving her is wrong," she said carefully.

"Julie, even men like your dad, who have spent many, many years in Bible study, cannot always say with certainty what Jesus thinks. How do you know Jesus' opinion for sure?"

Julie looked up. Gray hair stubs had sprung up all over his jaw. The fluorescent light glared on the corner of his forehead. More tears pushed out. "Maybe I don't, but that still doesn't mean I'm going to turn into a homosexual."

Oberholzer handed her a tissue.

"Julie, on some things, you're going to have to trust your dad, and me, because we've seen more, we've prayed more, and we just plain know more. You've told your dad you are in love with Romey. You've slept in the same bed with her."

"Just like we were sisters!"

"So you say, Julie."

"It's the truth."

"I believe you, Julie. I believe you. Now, I want you to return the favor, and believe me when I say this puts you at risk for homosexuality, no matter now innocent it appears to you. Now, will you pray with me? No, don't kneel, stay in your seat." He chuckled softly. "These middle-aged knees can't take as much kneeling as your young ones can." He took in a deep breath. "Dear Jesus, please help this young lady realize you are using me to invite her to step back from her risky behavior. Guide her to a healthy and moral response to your invitation. Amen."

He refilled her water glass and his coffee cup, and sat back down.

"Julie, do you have a favorite food?"

Her stomach felt queasy and at first she couldn't think of anything. Finally, she said, "I like popcorn."

"Popcorn. Okay, great."

"Chocolate."

"Fine, fine. Now, here's what I advise you to do tonight, tomorrow morning, all the time you have until you see me again. Whenever a thought about this girl Romey comes into your mind, just gently put it right back out of your mind. Think pure thoughts about other people and other things. If you succeed in doing that, reward yourself with a bit of chocolate or a handful of popcorn."

Julie looked just past his head, toward the wall where the colored slides had earlier appeared.

"If you find it difficult to put Romey out of your mind, you can help yourself succeed by saying 'Cancel-cancel!' whenever you think of her. Will you try that with me now? Please repeat after me. 'Cancel-cancel.'"

She mumbled, "Cancel-cancel."

"Let's hear it like you mean it."

She looked him in the eye. *"Cancel-cancel!"*

"Excellent. Lots of spirit there. I think we're getting somewhere. Now, just try what it's like to live without thoughts of Romey. I think you'll be surprised at how pleasant freedom from temptation can be."

He fixed his look of concern on her again. She could hear the second hand of the clock, toting up the time until she could leave.

"Jesus, let your light shine into the heart of this young lady. Are you praying with me, Julie?"

She was. As she prayed, Julie could see Jesus in a sunny field of daisies, under a cloudless blue sky, dressed in His long white robes, a brotherly, comforting arm around the shoulders of two girls, one at each side. Julie came up only to Jesus' shoulder, but Romey (and Julie did not say "Cancel-cancel!" at the image of Romey), Romey looked happy and strong, walking easily at Jesus' side, almost as tall.

Reverend Wright showed up promptly at four. Julie drooped silently on a bench at the conference room door while her father went inside. Through the window, runny in the steady rain, a neon sign looked like it was dissolving and melting into a puddle.

Oberholzer shook the reverend's hand vigorously. "First I want to share some positive observations with you. Your daughter dresses in a very feminine way. Her hairstyle and the way she holds her body are also very feminine. She's using her body language to say she wants to be a normal young lady."

"Well, Julie never was much of a tomboy. That's one reason this has all been a surprise to Connie and me."

"Her body language provides cause for hope that she will respond positively to the treatment I'm offering her here. The most difficult ones to change are the women who come to my workshops dressed in men's clothing, with extremely short hair. Or men who hold their bodies like girls. Even when these individuals sincerely pray to have their homosexuality lifted, their body language is sending a very different message. Julie doesn't have that problem."

"Praise the Lord," the reverend said quietly.

"What's more, in my best clinical judgment, she's telling the truth when she says she's had no homosexual contact with this Romey."

"Thank you, Jesus."

"However, there is a problem area here. Julie is in deep denial about the risks involved in this relationship with the other young lady. My main therapeutic goal here is to get her to understand that staying in this relationship means choosing to expose herself to danger. And that her whole future is at stake."

"I've tried to tell her that."

"Sometimes young people can hear it better from someone outside the family. Now, Reverend, I want to give you a heads up. If you hear Julie tonight saying 'Cancel-cancel,' out loud, that's an excellent sign of her progress. Just go about your business. Please don't draw attention to what she's saying or joke about it."

"No, of course we won't."

"The second thing is, she may want to eat popcorn or chocolate tonight. That's part of her treatment, too. A positive reinforcement strategy. I suggest you make sure these foods are on hand in your home."

"Okay, thanks; I'll do that. Now, how fast is she progressing? How much longer do you think she's going to need treatment?"

"We made progress today. But our work together is not finished. I recommend we stick to our plan of four more days. If she has a breakthrough, we can always cut the treatment short. And sometime during the four days, I recommend a two-hour conference between myself and you, and possibly your wife. I can instruct you in some techniques I use in my follow-up workshops. You can work with Julie on your own after I leave. That may be all that's necessary."

"All right."

"Then, after a month, you and I can reevaluate Julie's progress and discuss whether further treatment is indicated."

The discussion turned to Oberholzer's fees for the coming four days, which struck the reverend as high.

"Look." Oberholzer made forceful eye contact and the reverend matched him. "A couple of months in boarding school will run you more. I dropped everything and flew up here, brought specialized equipment with me. I normally work with groups, and then the expenses are shared. You were the one who insisted I treat your daughter individually."

"I know that, but our congregation is not a wealthy one. I wonder if you might have a special courtesy rate?"

"Reverend, I think it's a little beneath both our dignity to dicker about this. I'm a professional. This is about your daughter's future."

The reverend sighed. He pulled out his checkbook and wrote the check, knowing he'd have to go to the bank and get a cash advance on his credit card to cover it. Then they worked out a schedule for the following days.

Julie looked small, huddled on the bench in the hallway. The reverend felt a suspicion of pain in his lower back, like a fist closing. He wondered if he could borrow some of Oberholzer's fee from his parents, but he wasn't sure they would have that much saved up, and anyway, he believed strongly that a man his age should not have to go back to his own mother and dad for help.

They got into the car. A tall bush had dropped soggy, rotting purple petals over the windshield. As soon as he turned the key, the wipers gummed up and squealed. His view was obstructed by smeared, rusty-purple mash.

Julie turned her tear-washed face to him. "Daddy, he's hurting me."

"Hurting you how, angel?"

"With electric shocks on my hands. He shows me horrible pictures of ugly girls doing nasty things I shouldn't even know about. Then he hurts me."

Darkness was blotting the last streaks of light from the Divido sky. The reverend finally got the windshield cleared, pulled out of the parking lot, and drove quietly for a few blocks. The windshield wipers swished and squeaked. When the car in front of him drove over deep puddles, it threw up a wall of water that obscured his view. The large check he had just written muffled his doubts.

Finally he spoke. "Dr. Oberholzer is doing that for your own good. Julie, there's something you have to understand here. So far, you know the Lord as an all-loving presence. But God will come back one day as a Judge. What are you going to say to Him on that day, Julie, about your sins? I want you to look up with clear eyes and say you repented. You belong with the angels, not with sinners in hell. The pain you experience now will save you from the far greater pain of hellfire, Julie. One day you will thank me for this, and thank Dr. Oberholzer, too."

They rode through the dark streets, the reverend's back locked in a spasm of pain that would not let up.

"What about choir practice?" Julie asked. The next morning, Saturday, was final rehearsal for Sunday's service.

"I'll take you over to Dr. Oberholzer directly afterward and pick you up like today, at four. And on Sunday, he'll attend our services and you'll start your . . . treatment after lunch. He's agreed to work with you until six on Sunday. He's going out of his way for you, angel."

He pulled the car into a mini-mall parking lot and stopped with a jerk. The emergency brake rasped. "You stay here a minute. I'll be right back." He patted her knee.

A few minutes later, he opened the door and got in. "Dr. Oberholzer said you may be wanting these," he said gruffly, and dropped a bag in her lap.

She looked inside. It was a half-pound of See's assorted chocolates and a package of microwave popcorn. "How long do I have to keep going to see him?"

"Tuesday will be your last day."

"But Daddy, I don't need to see him anymore. I'm not a homosexual."

"Will you promise me never to even try to see that homosexual girl again and to stop all this talk about being in love?"

Julie turned away and looked out the window. On the sidewalk, a man hit a dog across the rump again and again to force the animal to sit. The scene was blurry through rain and tears. "He's going to hurt me again tomorrow. That's what he was telling you, that he was going to keep hurting me, wasn't it, Daddy?"

Howard Oberholzer packed up his equipment and returned to his room. He reflected, not for the first time, that few people realize how a Christian counselor who deals with sexually troubled individuals faces unremitting exposure to depravity, how spending an extended amount of time with those beset by wrongful lusts can inflame the counselor's own involuntary nervous system, how the Devil can use this perturbation of the nervous system to arouse lustful thoughts within the counselor himself, no matter how devoted the counselor is to Jesus Christ.

When Oberholzer first began this work, he occasionally resorted, after a day of intense pressure, to the release of self-manipulation. He told himself the practice was justified because his vocation compelled him to witness an unusually large amount of disturbed sexual energy. But as he gained more experience in his chosen field, as he prayed about and reflected upon this matter, he understood that the temptation to self-manipulation came from the Devil, not God. All of us, he told his clients, must understand the possibility of sin and depravity in our own natures, the cracks in the door that let the wily Devil get his toe in. Dr. Oberholzer counseled his clients against self-manipulation, although he was aware that many liberal Christian counselors did not. He explained that self-manipulation thwarts God's plan for the sex act, which is that the sex act be performed by two people of the opposite sex, united in Christian marriage, and that reserving all sexual energy for marital relations contributes to building a healthy interdependence between husband and wife. If he expected his clients to overcome the temptation to self-manipulation, he could demand no less of himself.

He also realized that practicing self-manipulation was cheating his wife by artificially depleting his sex drive, all of which rightfully belonged to her through the sacrament of marriage. And the lustful images that appeared before him during self-manipulation aroused guilt, which he feared could stunt his spiritual development. For all these reasons, and because he knew God never requires us to do anything we are not capable of doing, Oberholzer decided he must no longer use self-manipulation to gain release.

Now, in his motel room, he knelt on a pillow at the foot of the bed, head bowed and hands clasped on the orange quilted bedcover. He struggled prayerfully to subdue his nervous system and to fill his mind with loving thoughts of his wife, Darlene, along with pure thoughts of other people. After a half hour, he was sure the Devil had been vanquished and another victory could be claimed for Jesus. He washed his hands, strolled over to the motel restaurant, and ordered dinner, which was highly satisfactory: a steak cooked to appropriate rareness, so that when he thrust his knife in to cut the first bite, the white plate pooled with delicious-looking ruddy juices.

Chapter 11

Her body smelled sour. Julie stood under the hot water in the shower until it started to go cold, dried herself, and lay exhausted across her bed, tears dripping onto her ruffled white bedspread. It brought back the memory of another time she had lain across her bed crying, a long time ago, when she was still little. Her mother had just spanked her, which had overwhelmed Julie with a sense of her own sin, a feeling far stronger than the mild pain of the spanking, and then, as she lay sobbing, sure that things could never get any worse, Daddy had come in, scooped her onto his lap, stroked her hair, and told her how much he and her mother both loved her. He had rocked her until she stopped crying and put her arms around his neck. They'd stayed that way until she fell asleep.

This time, no one was coming to comfort her. Talking to her parents and Dr. Oberholzer about her love for Romey was like trying to prove a way to square the circle. No matter what argument she came up with, no matter how logical, no matter how elegant, they would find the flaw, tell her it was impossible.

What was the last spanking about? It was for telling a lie, but what had the lie been? She couldn't remember, but it felt important to try, as if somehow that held the key to the way out. She concentrated hard, but it was lost in the mists of her mind.

She cried more, big chunky sobs.

Finally, she heard her mother calling her for dinner in a cold and impersonal voice.

Nobody ate much of the dinner Connie made, the chicken nuggets, rice, and frozen peas. Julie did the dishes, then asked her mother if she could use the computer to catch up on math.

Her mother followed her into the study. "I'm sorry to have to do this, Julie. I'm sorry you've violated our trust." She yanked the phone cord from the wall and removed the phone. "Now you just do your homework if you want to."

Julie clicked the mouse to open her math, then checked her e-mail. There was a message from Romey. She clicked it onto the screen.

> Re: I love you
> Dear Julie, I miss you.
> Was your mom really mad? If there's any way you can meet me, tell me where & when & I'll be there no matter what. At least call or e-mail if you can.
> xxooxox, LOVE, Romey

Julie clicked "reply."

> To: romey@igc.org
> From: juliew@xnn.com
> Re:
> Romey, my parents still say I have to stop seeing you. I'm trying to figure out what to do. I DID NOT AGREE to never see you.
> Romey, a man is locking me in a hotel room and burning my hands with electric wires to try to make me say I'll stop loving you. I'll never, never say it. My dad is paying this man to pray with me and hurt me. I'm going to

The door to the study opened. Julie clicked the mouse fast to bring up her math.

"Julie, I didn't realize you were in here. What are you doing?" Her father's tired face loomed over her.

"Math."

"What have you done with the phone?"

"Mom took it away. Remember? I'm not allowed to call anybody."

"All right then, I'll just use the kitchen phone." He left the door open as he walked away. Her heart thumping, Julie got up and softly closed it.

> I'm going to ask Virginia to help us tomorrow morning. They're not letting me use the phone. I'll e-mail you as soon as I can figure out how

to get away. DON'T TELL ANYBODY. DELETE THIS MESSAGE after you read it. E-mail me back in the next half hour or not till after
eight tomorrow night, okay?
♥Love, Julie

She changed the e-mail password so no one else could open it.

In the kitchen, the reverend dialed the Best Western.

"Howard, you told me you'd go easy on the electric shocks."

"I am going easy, believe me."

"But on the first day?"

"Reverend, your daughter is not making a conscious choice to become a homosexual. She doesn't experience her feelings for the other
girl as voluntary. But when she tells you she's 'in love' with an avowed
homosexual, she's giving you a loud, clear cry for help. She's telling
you something abnormal is going on in her involuntary nervous system and she's practically begging you to help get it straightened out."

"I see that. But I don't want her hurt unnecessarily."

"Reverend, if her appendix were infected and about to burst, would
you hesitate to have it removed because of the pain of surgery?"

"Well, no, but this is a little different."

"You're absolutely correct. Electronic aversive stimulus is very different from surgery. For one thing, it's less painful. A lot less. The
stimulus was administered at the lowest setting for approximately ten
to twenty seconds. With adults, the setting is higher, and both the
duration and frequency of stimulus are greater."

"But it sounds like it hurt Julie."

Oberholzer coughed. "Our goal here is for Julie to give up her at-
tachment to the other girl of her own accord. You and Mrs. Wright
can't watch her every minute, can you?"

"No, but—"

"And even if you could, she'd be likely to rebel. In fact, she already
has."

"That's true, but—"

"It is far, far better that she understand the risks she's taking and
make the decision to give up the relationship herself. But she can't

make this healthy decision if her involuntary nervous system is held hostage to her pleasant feelings for Romey. Electronic aversive stimulus is highly effective at reducing and removing homosexual patterns from the part of the nervous system that is beyond conscious control. And the younger a person is, the less time the patterns have had to become entrenched, so the easier they are to erase. In that sense, your daughter is an ideal candidate for this type of treatment."

"But—"

"Julie is small-boned, which may intensify the pain. But fear also intensifies pain. And an appropriate amount of fear can be therapeutic in this context. It can be helpful in ridding a young lady of abnormal desires."

"I just want to make sure you try everything else that's possible first."

"And I'm doing that. I don't find administering this kind of treatment the most pleasant experience myself. I'm not doing it to get my jollies. I'm doing it because it works. Reverend Wright, you're in the driver's seat here. I'll sit around and play Monopoly with her, if that's what you want. It's your call. Say the word and I'll stop the electronic aversive stimulus."

"Now, I didn't say I wanted to tie your hands. I just wanted you to assure me you are only using this as a last resort."

"And you have my assurance on that."

"All right, I guess I want you to go ahead."

"Thank you, Reverend. Now you have a pleasant evening, hear?"

"Thanks, Howard, you too."

In the study, Julie waited until she heard her father hang up the phone. Then she e-mailed her math homework to her teacher in Pennsylvania and her message to Romey. She deleted the exchange with Romey and sat in front of the math, symbols and numbers swaying before her eyes.

Julie's message was like a fist crashing through the computer screen into Romey's stomach. It was one thing, Romey thought, to face the consequences of coming out herself, to sit at a lunch table alone, to feel the girls on the track team carve out a zone of no entry around her in the locker room. But coming out could hurt the person you love. She wondered how she could have been so naive that she hadn't understood that.

If only she could somehow erase that night at the school board, not have stood up. The worst part was she wasn't even sure her speech had made any difference. The vote could very well have been the same. She hit "Reply" and typed frantically.

Julie sat at the desk, clicking back and forth between math and e-mail. She squirmed in her seat and fiddled with the brightness of the screen. The math could have been written in Hindi; it didn't make any sense. One foot swung back and forth. Her head itched. Finally, after almost a half hour, there was a message.

> To: juliew@xnn.com
> From: romey@igc.org
> Re: You've got to get out
> SNEAK OUT TONIGHT & I will come and pick you up. You can stay here. I didn't ask my mom yet, but I know it will be okay. Just tell me what time and I'll get my mom's car & meet you wherever you say. Or if that won't work, just tell me what to do.
> Love, Romey

Julie wrote her reply fast, listening for steps outside the study door.

> To: romey@igc.org
> From: Juliew@xnn.com
> Re: PLEASE DON'T TELL!!!
> Romey, if you love me, DON'T TELL YOUR MOM or anyone!!! If I come over there, my dad will just bring me back home and everyone will be madder. Let me talk to Virginia and figure out something. I'll e-mail you when it's safe, but don't e-mail me till you hear from me. You are the only reason I can get through this. I swear, that time we rode the Ferris wheel and held hands, I felt like we were reaching for the edge of heaven. When the electric shocks got the worst, I remembered. It helped!
> L♥VE, Julie

Chapter 12

Before choir practice, Julie pulled Virginia aside. She felt small and light today, something easily tossed in a strong wind. Virginia's feet-on-the-ground solidity comforted her. Talking much too fast, she told Virginia all that had happened in the Best Western conference room the day before.

Virginia listened calmly, silent until Julie finished, then hugged her. "Honey, if you're not going to do anything homosexual, this can't hurt you. And if you are, we better pray it can help you." Her red-rimmed eyes held tranquil sympathy. "Now, your daddy's going to a lot of sacrifice to bring this expert here for you. It appears you and Romey are skating on thin ice."

"But he's hurting me, Virginia."

"Sometimes things hurt now, then later you find out they were good for you. Then they don't hurt so much. You just take this opportunity to learn all you can from your treatment and consider yourself lucky." She took Julie by the shoulders and looked her square in the face. "Now, let's remember what we're really here for. Let's go into rehearsal and use our voices to praise the Lord, okay?"

Julie's mother was seated at the organ in the sanctuary. A muffling fog separated Julie from the choir as it gathered around Virginia. Julie swayed as she awaited the signal to start, but when Virginia blew the pitch pipe, it was the cry of a long-ago foghorn. The sun glared at the weird angle of this season, directly through the red and blue stained-glass cross, searing Julie's eyes. Her mother's opening chords hurt her ears; they came as if from a long tunnel, flat, like the resigned grunts of a dying animal. She blinked in the harsh light. She was sure her voice would come out a wail or a croak, but as she shaped her throat to push out the first note, the sound came out so beautiful it startled her.

Here came her solo, and Julie no longer had to shape the notes. The notes shaped her, Julie was the song, the song was a river and Julie its riverbed, sculpted her whole life by the song's flow.

175

She was sorry the congregation wasn't there; she knew this was one of those peaks the choir reached sometimes, moments that could come only from God's grace. Pain transmuted itself into beauty, poured through her and out her throat; the choir joined her, voices melting into Julie; the song, the whole choir one clear bell. As the strong light bore down through the stained glass, Julie saw, again, her vision of Jesus, His arm curled tenderly over Julie's shoulder on one side and over Romey's on the other, in a green meadow sparkling with daisies, His eyes filled with infinite understanding.

She was on her knees at the Best Western motel, outwardly meek, slightly absent, looking down at the gray and brown splotches on the carpet, the orange flecks. Praying for the speedy arrival of four o'clock.

After they were seated again in their orange plastic chairs, with water for her and coffee for him, Oberholzer gave her two minutes of his deep-concern look. By now, it made her squirm.

"Sometimes," he said, "when we're teenagers, we're a little nervous about, you know, getting to know the opposite sex. Dating."

"My parents don't want me dating till I'm sixteen."

"That's commendable. You should be thankful you have parents who care. But it doesn't hurt—in fact, it can be highly beneficial—to rehearse for dating a little. Now, what kind of boys should you date, Julie?"

"Well, nice ones."

"That's right, but what else?"

"Um . . . moral ones?"

"Yes, but above all, you should be careful to date Christian boys. Now, why would I say that, Julie?"

"Because they're the best kind?"

"Because dating is the first step toward marriage. Kids tend to forget that sometimes."

He took her through an exercise where he role-played a shy young boy calling her for a date, stepping out of character to point out ways she could put the hypothetical boy at ease and places in the conversation where she'd have a chance to get the boy to talk more about himself. He went over some ways she could let a boy know she liked him, without giving the wrong impression. He asked her to brainstorm activities she might arrange with a small group of boys and girls, under appropriate adult supervision, and wrote the list on the flip chart in red marker. Julie contributed:

> Special choir session for teenage members
> Picnic

He added:

> Visit nursing home/cheer patients up
> Water slide/water park
> Video night at church (chaperoned) (pizza)
> Litter pick-up party
> Make popcorn balls (parents present)

He tore off the sheet of paper, rolled it up, put a rubber band around it, and gave it to her for future reference.

They broke again for silent prayer.

"Amen." Oberholzer took off his glasses and cleaned them with a handkerchief, then replaced them. "Julie, do you consider yourself to be someone open to new ideas?"

"Yes. My math teacher says that's why I'm advanced. He says I'm willing to think outside the box."

"Well, I'm not much for math, but I consider this a good sign. We're ready for you to do a little thinking outside the box. Because I'm about to tell you something new. Are you open to it?"

"I guess so."

"Okay. Here goes. Before this is over, you will ask me for electronic aversive stimulus."

Julie's laugh sounded too loud to her own ears.

He raised his hands, palms forward, as if pushing away something. "Now, don't react right away. Let this thought settle in. Let's sit with it for a few moments."

Julie stared down at her lap, one thumb clutched tight in the other hand.

He cleared his throat. "Homosexuality compromises your mental health. It may be hard for you to accept this now. But there are some things you will grow to understand. One, temptation and lust are like a disease. Two, left untreated, they will grow. And finally, you can inoculate yourself against this disease with electronic aversive stimulus. Once you understand all this, you and I will become partners in its administration. When I tell you it is time to stop, you'll ask me to extend our sessions."

"I doubt it."

"I told you this would be a new idea to you. It's natural you're having trouble taking it in right away. But you remember this. It may happen sooner than you imagine. Now, let's pray."

They knelt again, side by side. "Heavenly Father, help this young lady see the hand reaching out to rescue her. Help her to understand she just has to grab it. Amen."

She kept her head down.

He stood up. "All right, Julie. Now, I'm going to give you an opportunity. Will *you* ask me to administer electronic aversive stimulus?"

She wondered how he could imagine his little talk had changed her mind. "No."

"Even knowing it will be more effective if you ask?"

"No."

"Even knowing it could well be shorter if you ask?"

Julie paused.

"You haven't found it in your heart yet? Tell you what. If you ask, we'll do ten slides. If you refuse to ask, it will be twenty."

"How about zero?"

"Sorry, I'm giving you a choice here. Zero isn't one of your choices."

Julie looked up at him. His face was a wall. She looked at the chair, held to the door frame with thick metal clamps, the tangled wires. She breathed out, then in. "Okay."

"Okay, what?"

"Okay, I'll ask."

"Well, then?"

"I'm asking."

"Let me hear you ask. 'Please, Dr. Oberholzer.'"

"Please, Dr. Oberholzer."

"Go on."

"Do the electronic treatment."

"Let's hear it again. You'll be helped more if you're sincere."

"Please, Dr. Oberholzer, do the electronic treatment." She spoke in a dull monotone.

"I want."

"What?"

"Say, 'I want electronic aversive stimulus now'."

"Please, Dr. Oberholzer, I want electronic aversive stimulus now."

"Thank you. That was very good. We're making real progress here. Now just step over to the chair."

She moved toward the chair, snake pit of red wires and black Velcro straps. *It has to get over soon,* she told herself. *Ten slides means maybe five with the shocks.*

As he fastened the straps, Dr. Oberholzer said, "Now, I'm not blind, Julie. I know you didn't really want treatment, this time. But we have to take things in little steps. Asking gives you practice. It's just going to take a little time for your heart and mind to catch up with your words."

It turned out to be four slides with shocks, six without. As the hot metal feeling bit her palm for the third time, Julie noticed, despite her fingers digging into the orange plastic armrest, despite her teeth clamped together, despite her neck pulled into her shoulders, despite her breath stopped dead still, this one slide gave her a different feeling. She memorized that slide, that feeling, for later investigation, and then the pain cut off and another slide, this one of a boy and girl studying the Bible together, blossomed on the wall.

Julie was back in her own room, on her bed. Her hands didn't hurt anymore, but asking for the shocks had left a dirty feeling inside, like a wall of brown floodwater crashing against her head and filling up her nostrils. She wished she were brave like Romey, Romey who stood up at the school board meeting and said she was a lesbian, who wouldn't back down. Romey wouldn't have let herself ask for what hurt her. That was when you were lost, really lost, she thought, when you asked for what hurt you. It had to be sin. Julie didn't know what would have happened if she'd run to the door, banged on it and screamed. Maybe the motel people wouldn't have come, wouldn't have helped. But it bothered her that she hadn't even thought to try. She was so used to obedience.

There was something she needed to remember, but what was it? She felt that tickle inside when she was close to remembering something but not sure what it was. She almost had it, something sweet, something soothing, something that would take away this feeling of having a belly swollen like a balloon, matted wet fur, and stiff legs, and of bobbing on frigid, roiling, filthy water.

The slide.

Yes, the one that came just before the boy and girl studying the Bible. She switched on the slide projector of her mind and let it shine.

Two girls, no harsh makeup, no grotesquely big breasts, no I'm-trying-to-look-sexy clothes, just two girls, in college maybe, a little older than Julie and Romey. One girl's fingers gently lifted the other's chin. An inch of electric air separated their lips. And the other girl's hand curved tenderly around the first girl's ribs, just beneath her breast.

Faint, peach-colored sunset light played across the bedroom ceiling. Julie crawled into the image and brought Romey, too, tried out how it would feel to lift Romey's chin, for Romey's hand to curve around her own ribs, just below her own breast.

The murk inside Julie cleared some. Her muscles had been clutching her bones like kittens on a tree. Now, they loosened, stretched out, and she settled against her white ruffled bedspread. Her breath came out in a long sigh.

She turned the slide around. Romey lifted Julie's face for a kiss, and Julie's own hand spanned Romey's ribs, the web between her thumb and first finger just below Romey's breast. She sat up, felt the luscious rosiness of Yearning spread over her skin. The slide was in her mind and in her body at the same time, it came to life, so her fingers brought Romey's lips to hers with the softest melting of lip into lip. She let her other hand, so vivid in her imagination that it seemed Romey was here on the edge of the bed beside her, let her other hand slide up to cradle Romey's breast. She felt like a Ferris wheel rising into the sky.

The kiss. Julie replayed the scene again. Her hand beneath Romey's breast slowly rose. Again. Again.

She realized she finally had the key. She knew now how to make Yearning come. And she knew exactly how to test if she was right. But was she brave enough to purposely make Yearning go away, so she could know for sure?

She was. She jumped off the bed and knelt by her bookshelf, pulling out books until she found last year's math text. She found paper, and pencil, and lay on her stomach on the floor, not even bothering to turn on a light in the darkening room, solving one algebra problem after another, as fast as she could, until her mind focused completely on math, and Yearning flew off, like birds from a beach, leaving nothing but the search for the identity of the elusive X and Y.

She smacked the book closed and climbed back on her bed. She imagined the scene from the slide again, lifted Romey's chin, felt the electric air between their lips, the softness of their kiss, and (now, again, yes!) her hand sliding up Romey's ribs to hold her breast. Instantly, she was bathed with Yearning.

Shyly, she lifted her hand to her own breast. She knew Romey's would feel smaller, firmer, that strong muscles embraced it from behind. The nipple, would it stiffen against Julie's palm like this?

Yearning was not going to steal away from her on its own schedule this time. She had Yearning now, it was part of her. She could keep Yearning as long as she liked, let her old friend Yearning wash away the dead-dog feeling, the memory of the electric shocks. She was free.

The kiss . . . her hand . . . Romey's breast . . . she wanted this. She did. Wanted to touch Romey in just that way. And she knew for certain that Romey, lesbian Romey, Romey who loved her, was going to say yes . . .

Homosexual fantasies. Homosexual activity.

A deep baritone voice, much like Dr. Oberholzer's, echoed through her mind. She could see the black rubber tip of the pointer hitting the big red letters—HOMOSEXUAL TEMPTATION—on the flip chart.

She realized Dr. Oberholzer had been right all along. Yearning *was* homosexual temptation, luring her to give in to homosexual fantasies. And if she gave in to the temptation (well, to be honest, she already had, hadn't she?) then she'd be . . .

A sinner.

All the Sundays when her dad spoke about sin from the pulpit, ever since she'd been so small in the pew her plump legs stuck straight out, she'd watched him fix sin in his eyes, conjure up sin so sin seemed to strut in the air before him, obscene, a living presence preening before the eyes of the congregation. She wanted not to sin so hard that she held her breath, and the rest of the congregation joined her. Their collective determination to beat sin away from their lives was so strong, sin was forced to flee, disgraced and flayed. The air was left pure in her dad's loving gaze, which reflected the Heavenly Father's gaze from beyond the glow of stained-glass light.

She stood and walked to her bedroom window. Night had almost fallen and she could see herself reflected dimly in the glass. It couldn't be Julie wanting to sin now on purpose. Not Julie.

All the congregation, everyone who'd stopped to talk after services over the years, everyone who'd heard the Lord's love in her singing, the ones she'd given her smiles to, the tired ones, the discouraged ones, the sick, the old, all of them, she could see now, had given her a gift, too, the gift of their approval and love. It went both ways. Now they'd see her as a living example of what must be driven away: sin.

Julie would be the person who must be kept away from children and grandchildren, for fear of corrupting them. She felt as if some substance had already coated her body, slimy, smelly, a substance that would flash like neon to warn everyone away. Of course, there were other churches, churches that blessed being a lesbian, churches that would welcome a new strong soprano to the choir, but Julie would never be allowed to attend one. Her parents always said the people who worshiped there were in for a rude shock on Judgment Day.

She wouldn't lose her mother and dad's love, she knew that. They'd still love her, of course, because she was their daughter and a child of Jesus. But Lord, how they'd hate that sin. And in the end, she'd lose them irrevocably. She'd wither alone, cut off forever from her mother and father, who'd be together with Jesus in the Afterlife.

She would overcome this temptation. She had to.

Julie knelt by her bed and clasped her hands against the white eyelet ruffle on the bedspread her mother had made all those years ago and given her on a magical Christmas morning. Her parents had put her to sleep on some blankets in the office, and the next day, when she woke up, not only were there presents under the tree, but there was also her room made new, with a new bed, the ruffled white bedspread, and a desk, painted pink by her dad.

She put her forehead against her hands and prayed to Jesus long and hard, asking Him to take her sin away. Then she crawled onto the bed and sat cross-legged at the center. She'd succeed, she knew she would. If she started to feel Yearning, she'd just think about math, just concentrate, stifle that sweet glimmer before it dared to flare up. If math didn't work, she'd go back to Dr. Oberholzer and ask for thirty slides, forty—whatever it took to burn this sin away. Her back straightened. She crossed her arms.

A memory stole over her skin, a memory of dry, sunny air by the creek, and the smell of sunshine on redwood, her feet in cool water up to her ankles, the little shy rabbit on the far bank, and that sense of Romey beside her, physical and strong.

Hot, wild tears pierced her eyes. Losing Romey was going to hurt way more than when Nicky died. She flushed with shame then. A good person would feel worse about Nicky. He was her cousin. Sin heaped on sin. She willed the tears to be for Nicky.

She stretched out one pale arm. A little swell of flesh curved below the elbow, then a straight line down to her rounded wrist bone, her small hand. She'd rather have this arm cut off than lose Romey. Both arms. But that wasn't one of her choices here, was it? It was like when she'd asked Dr. Oberholzer for no slides this morning. Her choice here was sin or God.

Her mouth tasted bitter. She took a deep breath, squeezed it all—Romey and that slide of the two college girls and Yearning—way down, compressed it like a Velcro strap tightening around her hand, tighter than Oberholzer ever pulled it, squeezed until it was all no bigger than a fingernail clipping, buried too deep to feel, ever again. She pressed her palms together. *Lift all my sin, Lord. All.*

But Jesus, what was Jesus trying to tell her?

The image came to her of Jesus walking through a grassy field with flowers in every color of the rainbow, Romey on one side, Julie on the other. He stayed that way for many minutes, His arms around both. He was still smiling. He still understood.

Julie let the image from the slide appear, imagined once more lifting Romey's chin to her lips, her fingers meeting the tender swelling of Romey's breast, and gave herself to the swirl of Yearning. She leaned forward, eager, her breath catching. Julie had been saved for almost half her life, since she was nine. Prayer reminded her that she had a long, complicated, and intimate experience with goodness, through her personal relationship with Jesus. And Yearning was an inner good. She could feel Jesus, Who had also once had pain unjustly applied to His hands, nodding His head sagely in agreement. He seemed to be saying, trust yourself.

Lord, she asked, *do You really mean it?*

Julie stood up, walked around the edge of her room along the wall, past her desk and dresser, and turned around when she got to the bed. Back and forth. On one side were her parents, Dr. Oberholzer, the church. On the other, Romey, Yearning, Jesus.

When we take our tangled problems to the Lord, they become clear, her dad had always told her. And now, it was so.

She wanted Romey.

Wanted her more than she wanted not to be a homosexual.

Julie stood and welcomed her own desire, let it flood over her like moonlight. A Holy Presence stayed beside her and within her, big enough to love Julie and her love for Romey, too, real as the breeze that moves leaves of the lemon tree. If this wasn't real, then all those times she'd felt Him at church, or at prayer with her parents—they hadn't been real either.

She moved to the window and looked out into the dark unknown of the night. She said a silent thanks to everyone in the congregation for coming so far with her, and especially for making her their star in the choir. Her eyes were dry now. Good-bye, she thought. I have to go on alone. And Virginia. It would be like with Sandy. In one way, Virginia would keep loving her, but in another, she'd cut Julie out of her heart.

She switched on the bedside lamp. Papers and books were lying on the floor from when she'd pulled out her algebra text. She picked up a copy of the printout of the Strange Attractor, the one that now hung, she knew, on Romey's bedroom wall. Julie sat on the bed and looked at the multicolored swirls edged with bright blazes of fire.

The spanking she'd gotten all those years ago when she told a lie came back to her again. Now, in the way low winter fog dissipates and the Divido hills slowly appear through the whiteness, she remembered the lie itself.

Julie had told her mother she was going to visit Virginia, but instead she went to explore the creek that ran just across the street from the church. It was a wild place then, with tangled bushes, some of which were probably, as her mother said, poison oak, and there'd been some little fishes wiggling in the water. She'd stood on the bank, dipped her finger in a chocolate pudding cup, then stuck it in the cool creek water. Tickly little fishes nibbled the pudding right off her finger. But now that whole creek was surrounded by a subdivision with a 7-Eleven store. Remembering, she knew what she had to do.

"I spoke with Dr. Oberholzer just now on the phone, Julie," the reverend said over dinner. "He says you had a breakthrough today."

"Yes. We did. Kind of."

"So what do you think of Dr. Oberholzer's treatment now?"

She breathed evenly, carefully, met his blue eyes with hers. "I think you were right. It's good for me."

"Well, I'm glad to hear it. Mighty glad."

"I'm sorry, Daddy." She turned to her mother. "I'm sorry. I know you want what's right for me."

"You just pay attention to what Dr. Oberholzer says, angel. You'll come through this okay."

Her mother smiled and reached over to squeeze her hand. "Remember, your dad and I are praying for you."

"I know you are. Can I be excused? I want to do some math."

Her mother stood up and walked toward the refrigerator. "Don't you want some ice cream first?"

"No, that's okay. I'm full."

"Well, you've had a big day already, with choir practice and treatment and all," her dad said. "You've got two services to sing at tomorrow. Don't work too long."

"I won't. I've just got one more problem to solve."

> To: romey@igc.org
> From: julie@xnn.com
> Re: Help me escape
> Romey, can you and Amina come in a car and meet me behind the 7-11 across from the church at 9 tomorrow morning? MAKE SURE NO ONE can see your car from the church OR the church parking lot. And bring a jacket.
> I have a plan. We'll make it look like we committed suicide together and then escape to San Francisco. DON'T TELL ANYONE (except Amina). Delete this e-mail and e-mail me back in the next hour or between 7:30 and 8:30 tomorrow morning.
> Love, Julie

She found a Web site for locating people and clicked until she got an address and phone number for Sandy Galloway in San Francisco. Then she sat in front of her math, typing a few figures randomly on the screen and restlessly moving the mouse over the "Focus on the Lord" mouse pad for twenty minutes. When she checked the e-mail and saw a message there from Romey, it felt like the choir on the big notes.

> To: Julie
> From: Romey
> Re: Yes
> Amina and I will be there. I've got my mom's car.
> Q. How are prime numbers and my love for you alike?
> A. The amounts of both are infinite.
> Love, Romey

Julie typed furiously back:

To: Romey
From: Julie
Re: Tomorrow
Thank Jesus you can come. If I don't get there by 9:15, you'll know I got caught. If that happens, REMEMBER I LOVE YOU, Romey. Delete this message.
♥ Julie

Julie and her mother walked together from the Wrights' house, across the parking lot to the church. Julie wore her blue dress and her short navy raincoat, with all her accumulated baby-sitting money bulging in the pocket. Luckily, her mother hadn't noticed Julie didn't need a coat on this bright fall day, already warm, or that she had on her flat black shoes instead of the little heels.

"It's so much better since we got this lot repaved," her mother said.

"Oh, yes," Julie said heartily. "Way, way better. Now we can walk across instead of around, and nobody has to worry about a big puddle on rainy days, and more cars can fit because they're not having to keep from parking in the big holes, and mud doesn't . . ." she was gushing. Would her mother guess something was up?

She looked sideways quickly, but her mother was intent on a few people gathered at the church entrance, talking; she wasn't looking at Julie, and her expression was Sunday-normal.

Once inside, Julie helped her mother set up the coffee urn in the vestibule. Then she went to the basement and warmed up with the rest of the choir. Her voice came out squeaky at first and too loud a minute later, but to her relief, no one seemed to notice. Soon the time came to go back upstairs. She stayed at the edge of the choir as they gathered at the back of the sanctuary and awaited the signal to file to the front for the first hymn. As soon as her mother was seated at the organ, Julie slipped out the door and darted into the side hall to the ladies' room. She waited in a stall until all was quiet, then tiptoed out, opened the window, and climbed up the sink and onto the window ledge. Outside was about a six-foot drop. She jumped.

She landed on hard concrete, sprang up, ran around to the back of the church, and headed directly away, across the small lawn, and past the children's play equipment, where she'd be least visible from the parking lot for the longest time. She ran through a clump of trees into a vacant lot. Dry thistles scratched her calves through her pantyhose. She concentrated on not tripping on the bumps, and didn't look back until she reached the shadows of a second grove of concealing trees, where she saw with relief that no one was following her.

Instead of heading toward the 7-Eleven, she veered away, across a little wooden bridge over the creek, to where trees opened out into a cul-de-sac street. She ran around the block so she came from the other side, and as she turned the corner leading to the back of the 7-Eleven, tears sprang to her eyes at the sight of Romey and Amina next to the dumpster, inside the little gray car with the rainbow decal and the bumper sticker reading, "I'm Pro-Choice and I Vote."

Romey bounded out of the car, ran to Julie, and threw her arm over Julie's shoulder; it bounced awkwardly as they ran with different strides, side by side, back to the car.

Amina got out to let Julie sit in front.

"No, stay there," Julie panted. "I'll lie down on the backseat."

Romey climbed into the driver's seat and snapped her seat belt shut. "Okay, where are we going?"

"Buck and Doe Bridge," Julie answered from the back.

Romey lurched the car out of the parking lot. Julie threw out her arm and braced herself against the front seat to keep from being thrown to the floor. "Don't drive too fast. We can't get stopped," she said.

Julie watched trees and wires pass overhead as she explained her plan. They'd drive to Buck and Doe Bridge and take the mountain road about a quarter mile further, to just before it turned away from the river. They'd leave their coats and a suicide note at the river's edge. Then they'd double back, cross the bridge, go the other way to Santa Rosa, and get a San Francisco bus.

"I've got the address and phone number of someone there I know will help us. She's a lesbian who went to Divido Bible Church a long time ago," Julie said. "I can stay with her at least till the electric shock man has to go back to Whittier—"

"Julie, I'm not leaving you there. I'm staying, too."

Julie leaned into the well between the seats and reached her arm around so her hand rested on Romey's waist. "I was hoping you'd say that."

Romey pressed Julie's hand. "Amina, you worried about driving back from Santa Rosa alone?" Amina had only a learner's permit.

"I can do it," Amina said.

Romey kept Julie's hand in hers. "I'm not letting them lock you up with that guy again, no matter what."

They stopped the car on the mountain road, at a place where the shoulder widened and a short path angled gradually downward toward a bend in the river. The pebbled riverbank was visible from the road above. Amina looked out through the windshield, watching Romey and Julie disappear down the path. The gray road curved slowly ahead and disappeared. Tall live oaks shaded it on either side, their long branches arching overhead, filling the air with dappled sunlight. Small gray birds twittered. A jay made its jarring call.

Almost at the bend where the road disappeared, Amina saw two men crossing toward the riverside. They wore camouflage gear and carried rifles.

Amina sat up straight, staring.

In a minute, the two men walked back across the road, their guns pointed. In front of them, hands raised over their heads like suspects in a TV cop show, walked Romey and Julie.

The four crossed the road and disappeared into the woods.

Chapter 13

Amina started the car. She wasn't used to the gas pedal. The engine revved to a roar and the tires squealed as she U-turned back toward Divido. She'd never driven alone before. Tears pushed hard behind her eyes; she could barely see.

Amina knew she had to get help, but if she went to the police, Julie would get sent home. If she didn't go, Romey and Julie might get killed. Or raped.

She shoved that thought back down; it was the only way to keep driving.

What if they were already being killed right now? She should have run after them. At least blown the horn. She told herself it was totally stupid, not thinking to blow the horn. It happened so fast. She'd let her friend down. Maybe fatally. Amina had always been told she had a high IQ, but this showed high IQs didn't mean diddly in real life. Stupid, stupid.

When Amina first came to Divido Middle School and saw all those white faces, a few Mexican kids, but no one who looked like her, Romey had wanted to be her friend right from the beginning. That was three years ago, long before Romey announced she was a lesbian, before Romey even knew for sure herself. Romey was good at sports and cute, too. She could have run with the popular kids. But she'd chosen Amina.

The curving road looked runny through her overflowing eyes. A fast truck aimed straight at her from the other side, honking loudly. She'd strayed way over the center line. She swerved back into her lane, then over onto a wide place in the shoulder. She lurched the car into park.

Think.

If only she'd blown the horn. She decided it was stupid to keep thinking about that. She had to do the right thing now and do it fast.

She'd promised not to tell Janis until Julie and Romey were in San Francisco. But wasn't telling the police worse? She'd better go to Romey's house. Janis would know what to do.

As soon as the service ended, Connie and the reverend conferred for a frantic minute. While the reverend shook hands and said good-bye to his departing flock, Connie rushed to the phone in the church office and called the police to report Julie missing.

The voice on the other end was polite, but firm. Teenagers who left of their own initiative had to be gone longer than an hour before the police got involved.

"But you don't understand. Julie's not a runaway. She's the soloist at the Divido Bible Church. She's been brought up in a loving, sheltered Christian home. She's in danger. We're wasting time talking about it right now. You've got to get patrol cars out looking for her immediately." Connie's voice rose toward a shout.

"Now, Ms. Wright—"

"*Mrs.* Wright!" Connie screamed into the phone.

"*Missus* Wright," said the voice, "I advise you to try and keep calm. You and your husband could check the parks in the area, the mall."

"The mall! We can't do that. The next service starts in thirty-five minutes. My husband has to deliver his sermon. I'm needed to play the organ."

"Well, then, Missus Wright, I suggest you search for your daughter after the next service."

"But she could be dead by then!"

"Have you checked your home? Your daughter may have decided to skip church and gone home."

"Oh, don't be ridiculous. She wouldn't do that."

"Have you checked your home phone message machine to see if your daughter has tried to contact you?"

"Of course not, she wouldn't—"

"Have you checked the homes of her friends?"

"Her friends are all here in church." Connie ground her teeth in irritation.

"Well, Missus Wright, any police investigation would have to start with all those things, so I suggest you check them all first."

"Your policy might be all right for children raised in permissive, Godless homes where they let them run around any old place. But this is a saved Christian girl we're talking about. She's not the type to disappear. I demand you do something about it immediately."

"Most youngsters return home on their own after a few hours. If she's not home in four hours, you give us a call."

"Will you please explain to me why we are paying sky-high taxes if the one time we need help from the government we can't get it?"

"Well, if you want to file a complaint—"

"I want you to get out and search for my daughter. Let me speak to your superior."

"I'm sorry, the chief is off for the day. He's reachable only in case of emergency."

"This is an emergency."

"I mean an emergency under department guidelines. Mrs. Wright, I have another call waiting on the line. You call back this afternoon if she hasn't come home and you haven't heard from her. Now, goodbye."

Janis sat in the sunny kitchen, finishing her morning coffee and reading *The Nation*. She liked a peaceful weekend morning like this, with Romey gone, and then again, she liked it when Romey was here. Or Romey and Amina. This article about billions for military hardware was making her so mad, she stood up, went to the dining alcove, booted the computer, and fired off a letter to the President—a real letter, not an e-mail, because she was sure letters carried more weight. She printed it out and found the address in her ongoing file of contact information for important government figures. She addressed an envelope, stamped it, licked it, and smoothed it shut.

The air coming in the window no longer felt cool; it was going to be a hot day. She arched her back and stretched out her arms. Now that she'd done her activist duty, she decided it was time to give the old body its due. She got her gym bag and locked the door. The shopping mall was three blocks away, a pleasant stroll under the calm sun, with a stop to admire a Japanese maple in someone's yard, the leaves in full gold and red glory. She slipped her letter into the mall mailbox, then headed for the health club across the street and changed in the locker room. She hung out there for a few minutes to say hello to a few people. The air-conditioning was already on in the big glass-walled workout room; it was pleasantly cool and her favorite exercise bike was free. She climbed on, propped up *The Nation* in front of her, and absorbed herself in a review of three new books about Palestine and Israel.

Amina pulled into the Arden driveway, lunged out of the car and banged on the front door, but Janis didn't answer. She ran around to the back door and banged again, even went to the side and pounded on the frosted glass bathroom window, listening to see if she could hear the shower running. Nothing. She walked back to the front and sank onto the redwood deck.

The sun stared down on her. Maybe she should just call the police? Probably she should. Where could Janis be, anyway, without her car? Amina could think of only two places close enough to walk, the Safeway or the health club. But one of Janis's friends could have picked her up. Janis could be anywhere. Amina decided to try the Safeway and the health club, then check one more time to see if Janis had come home. If she still couldn't find Janis, she'd call the police.

The car bounced as she backed out of the driveway in unfamiliar reverse gear. Were Romey and Julie still alive? Amina imagined a TV news announcer intoning, "And their friend waited to call the police for a fatal forty-five minutes."

She rushed up and down every aisle at Safeway, knocking down a ten-pack of toilet tissue as she rounded a corner, and searched every checkout line. No Janis. The health club was at the far end of the shopping plaza. Amina half-ran, half-walked, dodged shopping carts, jostled shoppers, darted between cars to cross the road, cut over the lawn, veered through the health club parking lot, and swung open the glass doors to a big mirrored room filled with people running on treadmills and lifting weights. Janis was at the far end, pumping calmly on an exercise cycle, dressed in an oversized "A Woman's Decision Clinic" T-shirt, reading a magazine.

Amina spit out the story. Janis jumped down from the bike and ran to the registration desk to call 911. After the police took the details from Amina, they asked Janis to bring her to Buck and Doe Bridge, so Amina could guide them to the exact site of the crime.

Chapter 14

Connie's hands struck heavy on the organ as the second service started. The sun was a blowtorch on the church roof. Hot air pressed down on the congregation.

As he made his way to the pulpit, the Reverend Wright felt as if he were slogging through Jell-O. The choir bleated a distant and tinny hymn. His muffled sermon rolled out into a great void that lay between him and his congregation, a void filled with darkness, deafness. He could barely concentrate enough to remember what he was supposed to do next, because he was assailed by terrifying and unceasing visions. Trees crashed onto Julie, evil men snatched her and stuffed her into the dark trunk of their car, a mountain lion pounced on her and its powerful jaw snapped her slender neck, trucks ran her down, trains ran her down, an ambulance rushed her to some faraway hospital and she was alone, with strangers; no one even called him as her life ebbed away. His shoulders ached from the effort of shoving each sluggish minute of the hour around the clock.

Finally he stood in the sunlit threshold, shook hands with the last departing family, and wiped sweat from his forehead with his handkerchief. He turned to a couple of trusted church elders he'd asked to stay behind, and called Connie and Virginia to his side. Dr. Oberholzer stepped forward from the edge of the vestibule, where he had been quietly waiting. The group formed a circle and prayed aloud for Julie's safety.

They worked out a search plan with four cars and were about to start when, just as a precaution, Reverend Wright checked the church answering machine to see if Julie had called.

She hadn't. However, an officer of the Divido County Police, sounding extremely apologetic, said he'd had some word on Julie and asked the reverend and Mrs. Wright to come to Buck and Doe Bridge, which was near the scene where, it now appeared, their daughter, along with another girl, had been abducted.

Everyone piled into the Divido Bible Church van.

"The police are just as guilty as the kidnappers," Connie fumed. "I begged them to look for her two hours ago, but would they listen to me? Noooo."

The reverend swung sharply out of the parking lot, throwing Virginia and one of the elders against the side of the van.

Please let her live, Lord, he prayed silently. *My nephew is not cold in the ground, and now my daughter, too. Jesus, I've tried to serve You as best I can. I know I'm not perfect, I'm the first to say that, but, Lord, I'm trying my best. Lift this burden from me, Lord.*

"Now the kidnapper has an extra two hours' start. And why? Because those darned police wouldn't take this seriously," Connie was saying.

Dr. Oberholzer, in the far backseat, stared intently out the window.

The reverend kept up a steady, silent prayer. *Lord, if you are trying to test me as You tested Job, take me. Afflict me. Any illness. Any pain. She's so young. She's hardly lived. Let me go in her place. I will bear any kidnapper's torture. But don't let them use her, Lord, please, don't let them use her.*

Connie turned around to face Virginia. "It's probably all right if they have some rule about waiting to look for runaways when the parents aren't saved. Lord, those people, their kids could leave and they might not even notice."

"If there even are two parents," Virginia chimed in.

"Exactly," Connie nodded. "But when it comes to a child from a saved Christian home, they've got to learn they need to start a search right away, because we believe in supervising our children."

I have tried to be a Christian soldier, Lord. The reverend barely registered what his wife was saying, because his ears were filled up with Julie, two days ago, in the car after her session with Oberholzer, Julie saying, "Daddy, he's hurting me." *Don't let the kidnapper hurt her. I didn't protect her, Lord.* Julie with her delicate wrists and those new breasts not yet in full bloom. *Be a better Father than I have been, Lord. Stay the kidnapper's hand.*

"But do they have a different rule for Christian children? No, they act just as if we're a bunch of heathens, too, letting our kids run wild. If anything happens to her, I'm going to sue them so fast, and for so much money, that no police officer in this whole state will ever, ever tell another mother to check the mall."

Even if she has sinned, let her live, Lord.

Words clumped up in Connie's throat. "I hope they're satisfied now."

Virginia leaned forward and put her hand on Connie's shoulder. "I keep thinking about how little she is. Doesn't weigh but a hundred pounds."

Connie's chest buckled with sobs.

"Let's pray together, Connie Belle, and everyone," the reverend said. "Dear Lord, please let our beautiful daughter be alive, and safe."

"Amen," said the voices from the rear seats.

The reverend went on with his prayer, hoping to feel the Lord's guiding hand on his shoulder, listening for a heavenly Voice in reply, but instead he kept hearing another voice, small and forlorn: *"Daddy, he's hurting me. Daddy, he's hurting me."*

Dotted with brown leaves, the shady path angled for about 200 yards down to the riverbank. The air had a damp, earthy smell. Rushing water drowned out any sound from the road above.

"We could put the jackets here, half in and half out of the water." Romey arranged her purple windbreaker on a rock. "Sort of like they were washed up."

Julie peered down the river. "Or maybe just throw them in and let them really—"

Falling pebbles and dirt rattled the ground behind them, there was a heavy sound of boot on rock, and a deep male voice said, "Okay, ladies, hands up."

Romey whirled around. Two men dressed in uniforms splotched with brown, green, and tan camouflage stepped and slid the last few feet down the rocky slope. They both held guns. Romey put a protective arm around Julie.

"I said, up, not around her," the man barked.

Romey and Julie raised their hands, staring.

He looked like a hairless Santa Claus to Romey, with a pink face and a large potbelly. The other man was younger, with a tan crew cut. Both waved their guns.

"Okay," the bald man said sternly. His rolled-up sleeves exposed doughy arms. Under each, he had a dark sweat circle as wide as a dinner plate.

Keeping his eye on the girls, he walked toward the rock and lifted Romey's purple windbreaker with the tip of his gun. He used his free hand to feel the jacket carefully. Then he removed the jacket from the gun and shook it. He handed it back to Romey.

"Hand yours over," he said to Julie.

She gave him her raincoat.

He found the bulging pocket and opened it slowly, as if it might explode. He pulled out folded-over bills, fanned them, then pulled out the pocket lining. He shook the coat again.

The man in the tan crew cut kept his gun trained on Romey.

The bald man replaced the money in the coat pocket and handed the coat to Julie.

"Better tie those around your waists. We're going to do a little marching. Just walk slow and nobody gets it. No, not up that path. Straight up the bank here and across the road. Ladies first, if you please."

The bank was steep. They grabbed at roots and rocks to scramble up. Their feet slipped on almost every step and sent down miniature avalanches of dirt and small stones.

"Keep those hands up, or we shoot," the bald man huffed.

Romey's heart galloped. She stopped and swayed unsteadily on the steep dirt. "How can we get up without holding something?" She turned her head slightly and almost fell backward. She could see the bald one holding his gun with one hand, bracing himself on a big rock with the other. "You're holding on to stuff. It's not fair."

"Well, you can get handholds, but no tricks, hear? Or we'll shoot you up good."

Romey kept her eyes on Julie's small hand, curling around an over-hanging branch, tightening as Julie steadied herself. Romey could see how hard it was to keep from falling in those church shoes. The delicate bones of Julie's face were half in shade, half in weak sun. If those men lower their guns, Romey thought, I will fall on top of her and shield her from the bullets with my body.

"Where are you taking us?" Julie panted.

"Oh, give me a break," said the bald man. "You know good and well where we're going."

"No, we don't," Julie and Romey both said at once.

"Careful," the crew cut man said to the bald one. "Last week two guys got away with this same trick. And remember that other trick, a few months back, with the ladies?"

Romey stubbed her toe on a tree root. "What are you talking about?"

They reached the road. "Just cross on over, keep quiet, and walk straight by that group of trees there," the bald man ordered.

The terrain was flatter on the other side, and the four moved quickly into the forest. "Now, don't play little Miss Innocence with me," said the bald man. "I'm too smart for that. We're taking you to Company B headquarters."

"Oh," Julie said. "I get it. Are you having a war game?"

In a high falsetto, the man repeated, "Are you having a war game?"

Julie stopped walking. "Well, we're not part of it."

"Yeah, like you're just hanging out in the woods. Well, tell it to headquarters."

A rustling came from some nearby bushes.

"Yee haw!"

Two men bounded out from behind a large gray boulder. They were dressed in camouflage gear topped with orange vests. A third scrambled over the boulder on his stomach. All three lowered their guns and squeezed the triggers.

Romey threw her arms around Julie and knocked them both to the ground, but it was too late to shield either of them from fat, wet splatters of red paint.

"Uncle Bob!" Julie cried.

The three new men lowered their guns. The two captors had gotten doused in red from shoulder to knee.

Bob Gahl extended his hand, helped Julie up. He turned to Romey, but she quickly stood on her own. "Well, Julie. What you doin' here, little girl? How'd you get mixed up with these big bad boys from Company B?"

"My friend and I were just down by the river. They came up and made us come with them."

The bald man wiped red paint off his hands with a camouflage-patterned bandana. "They're not part of your team?"

"Naw," Bob said. "Can't you see they got no guns?"

"We thought it was a trick."

Romey stared at Bob. "What is going on here?"

Bob tipped his camouflage cap in her direction. "We're the Divido County Militia, young lady. And we're conducting our semiannual training exercises right here and now. Sorry, but you walked into a war zone." He leaned his gun against the boulder. "Once a militia member gets shot with paint, or taken to headquarters, he's out for the duration. Company with the most militia left at sunset wins the trophy."

"That doesn't give you the right to make people think they're being kidnapped. Or point guns at us that we didn't know just had paint in them." Romey looked down at the big splotch of red paint on her shirt. "Or mess up our clothes."

Bob adjusted his cap. "Young lady, I'm afraid Zeke here owes you an apology. What you got to say for yourself, Zeke, you no-good, can't-tell-two-pretty-girls-from-a-Company-A-regular, can't-fight-worth-shit—excuse my French, girls—Company B lowlife?"

Zeke's face was hot pink. He tried to wipe the paint off his hands by rubbing them on his round stomach, but it was completely red, too, and he just smeared paint around. "Young ladies, I'm sorry. But it was an honest mistake. Usually no one comes to this part of the woods. So you just naturally assume anyone you meet is part of the Training Exercise. We weren't ever going to hurt you. We didn't mean to scare you."

"Thank you, Zeke. Now you just march on to Company A head-quarters with my lieutenants here. I'll walk these girls back to their car."

Julie shot Romey a worried look. "Oh, no thanks, Uncle Bob, we can find the way."

"Yeah, don't bother," Romey said.

"Well, before you go, ladies, I've got something important to say. This may have spoiled your little outing. And you got some extra laundry to do, I'll admit it. But we're not out here for our health. We are drilling this weekend to protect you and your rights as Americans. That's something you both need to understand."

He motioned for them to sit on a rock. Julie complied, smoothing her red-splattered skirt over her knees. Romey remained standing.

Bob Gahl faced them in a stance of military attention. "You girls are out here for a nice day, taking your freedom for granted. But the United Nations is trying to take over our national forests, and our yellow-livered federal government is ready to knuckle under to them." His voice was stern. "The day you see those foreign soldiers marching into this forest, telling girls like you what you can and cannot do, that's the same day you will see the Divido County Militia spring into action. Foreigners will take over this forest over our dead bodies. Only we won't be the ones dead, because we been out here drilling and practicing, and we're gonna be ready for 'em. You'll be mighty glad we were here this weekend." He stared at each of them until they met his eyes.

"You girls go along enjoying your freedoms in the woods. You just remember your Uncle Bob and all the other Militia, out here working our tails off on our weekends to keep you free. Now, I think when you look at it in that light, a little misunderstanding like this one is a pretty small price to pay, wouldn't you say?"

"Yes, Uncle Bob," Julie said.

Romey dug her toe into the ground. "Let's go, Julie."

Bob reached into the long side pocket in his camouflage pants and pulled out a map. "Now, just take a look here. You go right down the road to the other side of Buck and Doe Bridge, and you'll be out of Official Militia Exercise territory, on both sides of the river. You won't have to tangle with any more freedom fighters today." He reached in his other pants pocket. "Care for a PowerBar, ladies?"

"No, thanks, Uncle Bob. You get back to your exercise. We'll be going," Julie said.

Julie and Romey walked back through the trees toward the road.

"Did I hurt you when I knocked you down?"

"No. Well, maybe a little."

"I was trying to keep—"

"I know."

Sun filtered through the trees in golden bars of light.

"He's not really my uncle," Julie said. "He's just kind of a friend of the family that I'm supposed to call 'uncle.'"

With a screech, a blue jay knocked a pinecone to the ground. They came out of the shadowy woods. Sunlight glared on the empty wide spot in the road where Amina and the car were no longer waiting. Julie watched dust eddy in the air and remembered the feel on the back of her hand as Dr. Oberholzer slid on and fastened the Velcro strap.

Romey's hand now was gentle on her shoulder. "I know some place safe we can go and figure out what to do next," Romey was saying.

A couple of cars whizzed by. Julie pulled Romey back behind the trees.

Romey described Pam's cabin, where the Remnant held its retreats, just a little more than a mile's walk away. They walked first along the road, ducking into the shadows of the woods whenever they heard a car, peeking out to see if it was Amina, but it never was. Once they got to the big granite platform topped by the bronze doe, they hurried on the sidewalk across Buck and Doe Bridge, completely exposed. To their relief, none of the many passing cars stopped and no one inside the cars took any notice.

Soon after the bridge, they came to a wide metal gate at the roadside, held shut with a chain and a padlock. Romey climbed up and over, then took Julie's hand to help her down. Her other hand brushed the thin cotton of Julie's dress as she steadied Julie's hip. Romey turned to continue up the quiet, rutted dirt road, but Julie pulled Romey's hand back toward her, then reached up on tiptoe for a desperate, fast kiss. It was over before Romey realized it had started.

Sun sparkled brightly on green manzanita bushes lining the road. A hummingbird hovered overhead, then flew off in a flash of turquoise and gold. They passed deserted driveways that led to other cabins, but saw no one. At Pam's driveway, there was another padlocked gate to climb over. "They usually park and walk from here," Romey said. This time she held Julie at the waist as Julie jumped down, pulled her close, and kissed her softly, then urgently.

This road was steeper and more deeply rutted, leading uphill for another quarter mile. Romey held Julie's hand as they walked. They rounded a curve and arrived at the little redwood and glass cabin, with a wood-shingled roof that sloped all the way to the ground on one side. The key was under the blue pot of cactus, like always. Romey opened the door.

Julie stepped in. "What a fantastic place."

Inside was one tall airy room, with an open kitchen in a corner, skylights, and two sleeping lofts reachable by ladders. One wall, all glass, looked out on green hills receding into the distance. The land dropped off steeply below it, so that anyone standing outside would be too low to see in. Loops of gauzy white cheesecloth were hung on the other windows, bathing the room in soft, pale light. Dried eucalyptus stood in thick pottery vases on the floor. It filled the air with a woodsy fragrance. The walls were hung with Nepali wood carvings and rainbow-hued embroidered hangings from Central America.

Romey closed the door and locked it from inside. "We're supposed to take off our shoes," Romey said, and so they did, stepping onto the cool lumpiness of a braided rag rug.

Romey faced Julie, moving a silky strand of Julie's tousled hair back to its place. "I won't let that man with the electric shocks get you again," she said fiercely, wondering how she'd be able to fulfill this vow, but confident she'd figure out something.

Julie stared for a moment at the thrilling angles of Romey's face, close now. Then she wound her arms around Romey, pressed her cheek against the stiff blotches of red paint on Romey's shirt, and tucked the top of her head comfortingly under Romey's chin. She could smell fresh, sea-salty sweat. Yearning bloomed within her. She felt Yearning once again like a conscience, another inner voice to help her through life, toward goodness. She'd learned to listen to her conscience. Now, she listened to Yearning.

Julie bumped Romey's chin lightly as she tilted her head up, old words of Virginia's coming into her mind: *Sandy wanted to kiss me like a Hollywood leading man.*

Sundays in the choir, Julie had to think about the notes at first, but sometimes midway through a hymn, it felt like the Holy Spirit took over, and Julie wasn't the one who was doing the singing anymore. The Holy Spirit guided her voice, played her like she was Its flute or violin. Now Yearning guided her lips in the same way, and it was hard to tell who kissed who, Julie or Romey, or if it was all just Yearning, playing them both like an orchestra.

Romey bent over to the kiss, pulling Julie up and toward her, feeling Julie's softness through the thin, paint-matted dress, and she knew she would never end this kiss, Julie would have to stop it if it were ever to stop, she would just keep her lips softly joined to Julie's, discovering with delight that you can keep breathing, both out and in.

That night at Virginia's, Romey had felt her desire for Julie as a danger, a great force she had to protect Julie from. Now she could feel Julie take it eagerly, like a child tearing off shiny Christmas wrappings and bows. Energy surged through Romey, the kind that comes when a person no longer has to use one part of herself to hold back another, and she was aware of the power of the muscles in her arms, circled around Julie.

Neither could have said who ended the kiss, or how, their lips were just apart, cinnamon eyes gazing with seriousness into blue ones.

"Romey, I want to do lesbian things with you," Julie breathed. "But first, we have to be married in our minds."

Tears pierced Romey's eyes. She pulled Julie's face to her chest, breathed in the scent of Julie's hair. "What does it mean, 'married in our minds'?"

Julie pulled away a little and took Romey's hand. "Let's go up there and I'll tell you," she said, pointing to one of the lofts.

They climbed up the ladder, Julie first. Romey followed the blue skirt as it swayed beneath Julie's hips. Julie's pantyhose were torn and there was a long scratch on one leg. The skirt's hem brushed Romey's cheek.

A mattress covered with a quilt filled most of the space in the loft. They sat cross-legged, facing each other, knee to knee. From the skylight, sun drifted down, filtered through boughs of fir and pine.

Julie raised Romey's hand and placed it over her own heart. "It means we love each other enough that if we were old enough to get married and we were allowed to get married, we would."

"Oh, I do. I would."

"Let's promise each other."

"Okay."

They rose a little to kneel on the quilt. Neither Romey or Julie recognized the quilt's pattern, white with interlocking circles patched in pink and gold, but it was traditionally known as Double Wedding Ring. Beside the bed, a richly embroidered wall hanging Pam had brought back from Rajasthan reflected bits of their bodies in dozens of tiny mirrors.

"I love you, Romey, and if we were old enough to get married, and allowed to get married, I'd marry you," Julie said solemnly.

"I love you, Julie, enough to get married if we were old enough and allowed to, and . . . I promise to protect you and cherish you, till death us do part."

"Till death us do part," Julie repeated. She moved closer to Romey and buried her face in Romey's neck, feeling nervous and embarrassed now. She asked, "Will you teach me to do lesbian things?"

Romey laughed uncomfortably. "I've never done any myself, honey," she said, feeling nevertheless a delicious thrill at that word. Honey.

Julie pulled back and looked at her. "You haven't?"

Romey touched Julie's cheek. "No, you're my first girlfriend in my life."

"Then how do you know you're a lesbian?"

"I just know. I know what I've wanted to do."

"Then let's do," Julie kissed Romey softly, "what you," her lips curved into Romey's as they formed her next words, "knew you wanted to do."

She sat back, hands on Romey's shoulders. "And there's something I want to do, too."

"Show me what."

Julie pulled up Romey's T-shirt, gently at first. A thrill shot through her when she saw Romey wore no bra. When the collar stuck on Romey's chin, Julie yanked it, and they both exhaled a hint of a laugh. Julie set the shirt down gently beside her and looked solemnly at Romey, her first sight of this angular, muscled, tawny body.

Even the admiration emanating from Julie could not keep Romey from feeling self-conscious at being the only one half-unclothed. Wordlessly, she reached her arms behind Julie and tried to unzip Julie's dress, but it went too slowly, so they both took kneeling baby steps until Romey was behind Julie. She unzipped the dress, lifted Julie's satiny hair, kissed a little knob of bone at Julie's nape, then lifted the dress over Julie's head. With daring fingers she unfastened Julie's bra and watched Julie willingly slide the straps down her arms.

Julie pulled off her torn pantyhose and turned around. The centers of Romey's breasts were the color of a fawn's spots. Julie remembered the image on the wall of the Best Western motel conference room, the two girls who looked like college students, an image so sweet, the pain of the electric shocks couldn't make it go ugly.

Feeling herself say yes to life in some necessary and elemental way, Julie slid her hand up Romey's ribs and cupped Romey's small breast in her palm. Her hand felt as if it were returning to a beloved place it had been long ago. They sank together against a pile of pillows, Julie half on top of Romey, half at her side.

Yearning took Julie by the hand, led the way. Yearning had dropped its mask and Julie knew its true name now: desire. She discovered with joy that she knew exactly what she wanted next.

Julie started another kiss, soft at first, then building with burning intensity. She felt Romey's hand move softly down her body, hesitating at her waist, then Romey's fingers circled gently to the vigorous, thick hair between Julie's legs. Romey pulled her lips away and drew her face back from Julie's, Romey's eyes wide and still with a question. Julie nodded, smiling, yes. Yes, she pulled Romey's face back to their kiss, and urged Romey's gentle hand deeper, into her own slick, swollen rosiness. A gasp of surprised delight rose toward the skylight, impossible to say from which throat.

To Julie now, it felt right to touch her love's body with her own, thunderingly right, and she knew that from now on, "right" would start here, and "wrong" would be anyone or anything that stopped this. If "right" held any meaning, it had to include Romey's skin warm and soft on hers, had to include, just beneath all that smoothness, Romey's wonderful firm muscles, had to include this freedom to touch wherever her desire led her, flesh to flesh, all along their bodies, this swimming in silk.

Chapter 15

Divido's police department activated their interagency agreement and alerted the county sheriff and state highway patrol. The three law enforcement agencies set up a command post at a rest stop and picnic area at the Divido end of Buck and Doe Bridge. They also established a roadblock to check all cars crossing in either direction.

A news producer from the local Santa Rosa TV channel, who routinely monitored the police band, picked up the story. She diverted a mini-cam van to Divido, reassigning the crew from a low-priority shoot on winter storm preparations. The producer called the California Parents of Abducted Children Foundation for a comment. The foundation dispatched its local representative to the crime scene.

Everyone converged at the rest stop, a wide area open to the hot sun, just beyond the statues on the doe side of the road, mostly bare dirt, with a few trees and some picnic tables connected by asphalt paths. It took the various police officers about forty-five minutes to locate Zeke Honecker, Bob Gahl, and the rest of the Divido County Militia. Initially skeptical about the militia members' story, the police brought both teams to the command post for questioning.

The sun was at its highest. Cars and trucks idling on either side of the roadblock filled the still air with bitter exhaust. In a corner of the rest stop parking lot, the TV camera crew filmed a reporter against a backdrop of Buck and Doe Bridge. She kept her suit jacket on despite the heat and looked soberly into the camera. "Double kidnapping in Divido? Details at six."

The reporter adjusted her hair, blotted her face. The camera crew repositioned its gear. She arranged her features into another earnest look. "Two teens possibly kidnapped outside Divido. Coming up at eleven."

Janis and Amina sat at one end of a weathered picnic table, moving slightly every few minutes to stay in the narrow triangle of shade from a pine tree, as far as possible from the reverend and his entourage.

"If only I had just waited." Amina stared at some dried food embedded in the rough gray wood of the picnic table. Underneath the table, she swung her leg rhythmically back and forth, back and forth.

"You had no way of knowing those men would let them go so fast." Janis reached out and put her hand over Amina's. She took a swig from a plastic bottle of mineral water the TV crew had given them. Then she smiled and passed Amina the bottle. "Don't beat yourself up."

Up until the police had brought the militia back and gotten their story, Amina had repeated over and over, "I should have called nine-one-one right away." Now she said, "They'd be okay if I'd have waited just two minutes."

"So those militia guys say." Janis was still in her "A Woman's Decision Clinic" T-shirt and exercise shorts. Her long hair, pulled back in a low ponytail, weighed damp and heavy in the middle of her back. She lifted it up for a second, but no breeze came to cool her sticky T-shirt. She wished she'd worn a bra while she'd been exercising. She'd rushed out of the health club without even changing clothes. Now, her breasts hung down sweaty against her ribs and swayed with every shift of her body. It annoyed her. She wanted to lift them for a second, to cool the undersides, but there were too many people around.

Heat flared up from Janis's chest and spread over her face. It felt like she'd come down with a sudden fever, or the air temperature had spiked ten degrees in a second. Sweat stung the corner of one eye, and she tried to mop her forehead on her T-shirt sleeve. She looked around to see if the cars idling on the bridge were generating extra heat, and also to see if anyone else had noticed. Amina didn't look all covered in sweat. Janis asked her, "Did it just get a lot hotter?"

Amina shrugged. "It's been hot all day."

"This is all I need," Janis groaned. She was already cooling down, her skin had gone clammy, liquid trickled between her breasts and ribs. From past talks with the Remnant, she realized what had just happened. Her first hot flash.

A man appeared at her side. "Ms. Arden, I'm Marvin Marshall from the Parents of Abducted Children Foundation."

Janis looked up. Everything about him was oblong: face, torso, and the hand he extended toward her. She shook it, winced at the glare of the sun overhead, and looked away.

He sat on the bench beside her. "Ms. Arden, we have a blast fax capability, and if you want to provide me with a photo and description of your daughter, we can put it into the hands of over 1,000 law enforcement agencies and media outlets."

I'm not ready for a new stage of life, Janis thought. My daughter's still missing. This can't happen now.

"Maybe you have a photo with you in your wallet," Marvin Marshall suggested.

A woman should get to welcome menopause into her life in a cool, soft chair, Janis thought. She should be able to contemplate the change over a glass of iced tea. Or even better, a nicely chilled chardonnay.

"And I can just take down her description right here." Marvin Marshall held out his pocket computer.

"What?" Janis squinted up at him. Had Mr. Marshall noticed that every exposed inch of her skin was beaded up with sweat? And why should *she* care if he did? It was just a normal stage of life.

"So we can put your daughter's description out on our blast fax to over one thousand law enforcement agencies and media outlets."

She forced herself to focus on his words. "Oh, well, let's hold off on that for just a little while."

"Time is of the essence here. Statistically, within two hours of abduction—"

With a squeal from his whistle, a police officer motioned everyone to gather at the other end of the rest area, near the portable toilets. Janis, Amina, and Marvin Marshall walked across the picnic area. Janis positioned herself so the TV crew separated her and Amina from the group from Divido Bible Church, even though it meant standing in the sun. Around the periphery stood members of the Divido Militia in red-splattered camouflage.

The police officer climbed up on a picnic bench. "Okay, it appears what we have here is not a kidnapping after all, but a pair of runaways."

"My daughter did not run away," Janis protested. "She's trying to help Julie escape from electric shocks."

Dr. Howard Oberholzer drew back a little from the crowd.

The officer continued, "We're letting the extra law enforcement agencies get back to their regular duties and downgrading our search."

Connie stared at the officer in outrage. "You can't do that! Julie's still missing!"

The reverend put his arm on his wife's shoulder. "Officer, how do you know she hasn't been snatched up by someone else? Or, for that matter, some crony of Mzzzz. Arden here may have both of them stashed somewhere."

Janis rolled her eyes. "Oh, come off it, Reverend!"

Connie waved her hand over her head. "Why haven't you questioned Mzzz. Arden? She has a history of doing harm to other people's babies."

"We spoke with Ms. Arden earlier," the officer said evenly.

Marvin Marshall stepped forward. "Officer, may I interject a word of caution here? As a representative of the California Parents of Missing Children Foundation, I'd like to remind you of a kidnapping a few years ago here in northern California. An officer spoke with the perpetrator. Meanwhile, the young lady was bound and gagged nearby. She was murdered a short time later." Marshall looked meaningfully at the militia members.

The militia erupted in growls of protest.

Marvin continued, raising his voice. "If you downgrade your search now and those little girls are harmed, blood will be on your hands."

"That's right," said the reverend. Connie, Virginia, Howard Oberholzer, the Divido Bible Church elders, and even some militia members nodded vigorously.

Zeke Honecker stepped up on the picnic bench and turned his round, red-stained belly toward the officer. "I am ready and willing to put my militia regulars at your disposal to help with this search," he announced.

Marvin Marshall pumped his head up and down. "This is not the time to downgrade the search and send the Highway Patrol away. If anything, you should call more law enforcement agencies. Why haven't you started a helicopter search?" He turned toward the reverend. "Now, we can help out with our blast fax capability—"

Janis waved her hand as if to shoo him away. To compensate for her sweaty oversized T-shirt and shorts, she stood tall and spoke with maximum authority and volume, which put an extra helping of gravel in her voice. "Officer, the problem here could well be that the girls don't want to be found because they're afraid Julie will get more electric shocks."

The officer turned to the reverend. With sympathy, he asked, "Is the girl mentally ill?"

"No, she's not, she's just confused about her, ah—"

"Sex role identity," Dr. Oberholzer chimed in.

Janis glared at Oberholzer. "Bullshit. Here's what happened. Julie told her parents she's gay—"

"She never, never said she was gay," Connie protested.

Janis kept her eyes on the police officer's face. "Okay, she told them she was romantically involved with my daughter, and so they hauled her off to a quack doctor who claims he can change gay kids into straight ones by torturing it out of them with electric shocks."

"On Julie's hands," Amina added. "She was strapped to the seat."

Janis put her hands on her hips. "So Romey and Julie may be hiding, and they'll stay hidden because they don't want Julie to get hurt again. My daughter wouldn't be out there in the woods," she waved her hand toward the riverbank, "if Julie's parents were taking care of their daughter properly and keeping her away from harm, instead of paying someone to harm her."

"Oh, now the baby killer is lecturing us about harming children!" Connie and her husband exchanged a look of cold fury.

Janis pointed toward the blue and white patrol car. "I have a suggestion. I think you should drive that car up and down the River Road and back and forth across Buck and Doe. Broadcast on your loudspeaker that Julie won't get any more electric shocks." She turned to the reverend and Connie. "That is, if her parents can guarantee she won't."

"Officer, we are wasting precious time here," warned Marvin Marshall.

The reverend drew himself up into his from-the-pulpit stance. "Officer, would you object to my saying a short prayer here?"

"No, Reverend, go ahead."

Janis threw up her hands and backed away a few feet.

Several militia members, Bob Gahl included, joined the circle with Connie, Virginia, Oberholzer, and the elders. All bowed their heads.

"Heavenly Father," the reverend's baritone drowned out the chorus of idling engines at the roadblock, "please watch over our daughter Julie, wherever she may be at this moment, and keep her safe from harm. Please spare the Arden girl from whatever peril she now faces. The Arden girl has been raised in a home where no one ever asked You to watch over her. So we ask now, Jesus. And please lend Your guidance to all of us here, and especially this man of the law, so that we may all do the thing that will bring these two children back to us, safe. Amen."

"Amen," echoed the circle.

The officer was relatively new on the force, which was why he'd pulled weekend duty. He decided to page his chief at the A's game in Oakland to make the final decision. "I'll be with you folks in just a few moments," he said.

While the reverend's group continued pressing for a full search, Janis pulled Amina away from the cluster of people. "I've got an idea," she whispered. "Come with me."

Chapter 16

Romey and Julie lay in the filtered sun from the skylight, all their clothes scattered on either side of the mattress, changing positions slowly as they tried out different ways to touch the most skin. Many kisses had rubbed Julie's lips to the color of coral. Delicious smells rose from their bodies.

Julie licked Romey's bare shoulder. "What I can't understand is why everyone is trying so hard to stop this."

Romey's fingers played with the fine swirl of hair at Julie's temple. Sometimes after a run she could feel every cell in her body dance, yet, as a whole, her body was a lake of contentment. She had a similar feeling now, but to the nth power. She thought they must look beautiful, lying here together, and wished she could both see herself and be herself, though an actual mirror would have been embarrassing.

"I mean, this?" Julie continued. "No one can get pregnant." She slid herself up and across Romey, kissed Romey's nose on the way over, and settled her head on Romey's other shoulder. "We're not hurting anybody. Why would they go to so much trouble to try and stop *this?*"

Romey felt the last words as warm puffs of air against her breast. "I don't know, honey," she said. She lifted and twisted her head to kiss Julie's forehead. "Honey. Honey. It feels good to call you 'honey.' Is it okay," she kissed her again, "honey?"

"Sure, honey. Isn't it a relief?"

"What?"

"To find out it's not a sin." Julie's parents had taught her well how to recognize a blessing when it came her way. At this moment, she knew herself deeply blessed.

With a light fingertip, Romey touched Julie's nose. "I never thought this was wrong. I just worried it would never happen for me."

Julie slid on top of Romey, thigh to thigh, her head between Romey's breasts. "Am I too much weight?"

"Never," Romey breathed. "Are you thirsty? I can probably find some water."

"Yes, but I don't want to stop touching you."

"Then come with me."

They climbed down the ladder. Romey felt an animal freedom, walking barefoot across the floor together, nude. It was like being cats. Or deer in a forest. The kitchen had no running water, but Romey found some bottles of spring water and carried one back to the loft.

With a sharp caw, a crow flew between the skylight and the sun, blinking the room into shadow for a moment. Julie thought she heard voices, far away, outside.

When Romey sat down on the mattress and twisted the lid, the water bottle sputtered. Bubbles rose. Romey offered it to Julie. "Too bad it's not cold."

Julie took the bottle, tipped it to her lips. After drinking as much as she wanted, she took one more sip, leaned forward, put her lips on Romey's collarbone, and let water drip between Romey's breasts.

"Tastes perfect to me," Julie murmured.

"That tickles." Romey laughed and took a drink.

Julie licked the water where it had run almost to Romey's navel.

Romey laughed again. "*You* thought I was a boy that night at the Ferris wheel." She set the water bottle on the floor, reached over, and lightly tickled Julie's ribs.

Julie giggled, ducked.

"You did," Romey insisted.

"No, wait," Julie rolled from side to side. "Listen."

Romey, grinning, held her fingers poised in midair. "I'm listening."

"Well, maybe I did think you were a boy, for a minute." She pushed Romey down on the bed and wriggled her way on top of her until one knee was firmly planted on each side of Romey's boyish hips. Then she held one of Romey's hands against the pillow and, with her other hand, tickled Romey back.

Romey giggled and bucked.

"But I know you're a girl now," Julie laughed, sinking down on Romey, and they rolled over and over, tickling, shaking with laughter, until they slid off the low mattress and onto the floor. "And am I ever glad."

They climbed back on the bed and leaned against pillows, holding the bottle for each other as they drank, quiet, hand in hand, watching the pattern of sun and branches in the skylight. Romey rubbed her toes on Julie's. "I'm getting hungry. Let's see if we can find—"

A fist banged loudly on the outside door, directly underneath the loft, so hard it vibrated through the mattress like a mild earthquake.

"Romey and Julie, are you in there?" Janis's gravelly voice rang out. "Open up."

She banged harder. "I know you're there, because the key's not under the cactus. The police are looking for you, but they're not with us. Amina's here. Let us in."

Romey looked questioningly at Julie. Julie set the water bottle beside the bed and took both of Romey's hands in hers. "I've figured out what I have to do now. About my parents and all. Promise you'll stand by me?"

"Romey!" It sounded like Janis had picked up a board and was using it to pound on the door.

Romey pulled one of her hands from between Julie's and softly touched Julie's temple, where the delicate new hair grew. "I promise."

They exchanged one frantic kiss, then Julie reached for her dress.

"It's okay, Mom. I'm coming," Romey yelled, pulling on her T-shirt.

When Romey and Julie finally opened the door, Janis took one look at the tousled, rosy pair and surmised what had taken them so long. Romey's posture proclaimed her recent ascent to a realm of revelry and pleasure. The girl was almost swaggering with her young ripeness.

It flashed Janis back to her last lover, Brad, before their anguishing breakup, how witty and alive he'd been the final time they made love and it was good, on a spring morning, with a pink flowering plum outside the window, champagne and orange juice to drink. That was over two years ago.

A small furnace seemed to have installed itself in Janis's chest. It was belching heat again now, up into her face and down toward her waist. Both Romey's and Julie's lips looked swollen over their teeth to her, like ripe plums ready to burst their skins. Janis looked down at the ropy blue veins protruding from her large-knuckled hands.

She sternly reminded herself that she'd come of age during an era more drenched in sexual freedom than any other, that she'd taken zestful advantage of those pre-AIDS years, that she'd created for herself a varied and adventurous erotic life, mostly exciting, all of it loving, or at least friendly, give or take a man or two; that even the wrong choices in men had at least been interesting; that these recent two years were probably just a temporary lull, and that she had no reason whatsoever to envy these two flushed teenagers. I will not allow myself, she thought, to go all Snow-White's-stepmother. I just won't.

Romey saw her mother's face. "Don't worry, Mom," she said, indicating her red-stained T-shirt. "This isn't blood, just paint."

"Oh, I know *that*." Janis walked across the kitchen, stomping hard on her big feet, and pulled out another bottle of mineral water. She opened it, tipped a few drops onto the top of her head, and took a big swig.

"I'm sorry, you guys," Amina said. "I thought you got kidnapped."

"Water, anybody?" Janis asked.

"It's okay," Romey and Julie both said at once to Amina. Romey put her arm around Amina's shoulder. "I'd have done exactly the same thing."

They walked toward a sun that was lower in the sky by now, less fierce. Romey, Julie, Amina, and Janis stepped around the broad granite platform at the Santa Rosa end of Buck and Doe Bridge, just below the sturdy legs of the bronze doe, across the road from the bronze buck who was missing one antler tip.

The police had dismantled the roadblock. The four walked on the bridge sidewalk beside steadily flowing traffic. They came in sight of the police cars, the TV van, the church van. Another prayer circle was in progress. Some of the militia were gathered around a poker game at one of the picnic tables. The police were talking with the TV crew and Marvin Marshall. No one paid any attention to the four figures, two splashed with red paint, who were approaching the granite platform on the Divido side of the bridge, where the bronze doe turned her head toward a bronze buck across a strip of gray pavement.

Seeing the crowd still assembled, Janis groaned in exasperation. Amina felt again that it was all her fault. Romey's stomach contracted; she took Julie's hand and squeezed it. Julie looked straight ahead and walked at a steady pace, her expression calm.

Afterward, Romey would not be able to say how it happened, but Julie, who had been at her side, squeezing her hand in return, seemed to have taken only a millisecond to shove her jacket into Romey's hands, scramble up the sheer ten-foot isosceles trapezoidal granite wall, and stand up above them, next to the statue of the doe.

"Julie! Praise the Lord!" Reverend Wright ran over, followed by everyone from the picnic area. The TV crew switched on the camera.

"Stay away," Julie yelled. "If you come any closer, I'll jump."

Everyone in the crowd had passed by the statues in a car. From that vantage, the buck and doe seemed life-sized, but they were actually closer to twice that. Now, next to the doe, Julie looked tiny. Her earlier run through the weeds behind the church had left scratches on her legs. And though everyone knew her dress was splattered with paint, not blood, she looked wounded.

"Julie, you come down this instant!" Connie shielded her eyes against the sun. "We've been worried sick all day!"

Julie stood at the side of the doe that faced the road. Now she inched carefully across the granite in front of the doe's hooves, holding on to a bronze leg behind her back, until she stood against the haunch on the other side. Two feet to her right, the granite platform dropped off over the Divido River, fifty feet down, shallow this time of year, rocky. Julie shouted, "If anyone comes one step closer, I'm jumping."

Air currents rose from the river and rippled her red-stained skirt against her knees. Her hair blew across her face. She reached up to pull it out of her eyes, and Romey saw that Julie's palm was scraped raw and blood-streaked from her climb.

"Julie, come on down, angel." The reverend's voice was gentle, barely loud enough to be heard above the river's burble. "No one's going to hurt you."

"I'm not coming down unless you give me your word I never have to go see Dr. Oberholzer again."

The camera operator from the TV news zoomed in to get a better shot of Julie.

The reverend stood directly in front of her, about four feet away, head bent back. A bolt of pain shot down his spine. "Now, Julie, you just come on down and we'll talk this through together. We'll pray together."

"Not until you promise."

The reverend took a step forward.

Julie stepped toward the edge. "I mean it. Stay away or I'll jump."

The reverend stepped back. Julie returned to the doe's side.

"I believe we could all do with a prayer now," said the reverend. "Dear Lord, thank You for bringing our daughter back to us safely. We are grateful, Jesus."

"Amen," said the church members. They had all bowed their heads, along with some militia members and one police officer, but the reverend kept his up, eyes on Julie.

He continued, "Yes, we are grateful to You for delivering us from these past hours when grief shook our hearts, when we feared harm had befallen our beautiful Julie. And now, Lord, we ask You, humbly, to bring her down to us, safe. In Jesus' name."

Julie watched the prayer, holding down her billowing skirt with her hand. The doe stood solid beside her.

One of the police officers raised his hand. "Julie, if we agree to keep everyone away, will you come back around on this side of the deer?"

"If everyone stays five feet away."

"Okay, everyone, let's move back a little." The officer exchanged a look with his partner.

Everyone shuffled back as the officer cleared a five-foot perimeter. He cocked his head up. "Now, Julie, I did my part, will you please come around this side?"

She ducked under the doe's midriff. But as she emerged on the other side, she saw a police officer rushing the back of the platform. She ducked back under and stood with her toes out over the river on the far granite edge. "No tricks," she screamed. "I mean it. I'll jump."

"Julie, Julie, I'm sorry about the other officer. He acted without permission. Now, you come back to this side."

Julie moved toward the statue, swayed a little, and steadied herself against the doe's thigh. It felt reassuring to rest her palm against the stippled, sun-warmed, bronze muscle. Then she moved back to the edge of the platform, extended half of one foot over the river.

"Don't jump," Romey called. "I don't want you to die. Even if we can't see each other, you'll be alive. Don't, Julie. Come down."

"Listen to your friend," Virginia shouted.

Julie looked at her parents expectantly. She nudged her foot a little farther out.

Romey reached up her hand to Julie, the hand that carried the memory of Julie's inner thigh. So much air separated them now. "Julie, if you jump, I'm going to jump in too."

"I know you, Romey," Julie answered. "You'd never do that."

"But you wouldn't either. Don't. Please—"

Connie stamped her foot. "Julie, if you don't stop all this nonsense and come down, young lady, you'll find out just how sorry you can be."

Julie looked hard at her mother. "Mom, if I'm going to die jumping, what do you think you can do that will make me any more sorry?"

"Now, Connie," the reverend said, putting his arm around his wife, "I think you better let me handle this." Julie looked so little to him, with that bronze doe rising at her side like some pagan idol. Sun glared off its curving neck. He said a silent prayer to Jesus for guidance to do the right thing.

"Julie." He cleared his throat. "You say you'll come down if you don't have to go for any more treatment from Dr. Oberholzer?"

"Don't give in to her," Connie hissed. "Be firm or we'll be sorry later. There's got to be a way to get her down without all this nonsense."

Julie met her father's eyes. "No more sessions with Dr. Oberholzer, and no more electric shocks."

A little murmur moved through the crowd. Romey caught Amina's eye and pointed to the TV camera trained on Julie.

The reverend raised his arms toward his daughter. "Well, you come on down and we'll discuss that. I think it's a possibility. A good possibility."

Connie grimaced.

Julie stood straight against the doe's leg. The sculptor had caught the animal's intrinsic dignity in the angle of neck and head. Staring across at the buck, the doe seemed absorbed in calm contemplation. Above girl and doe in the blue sky hung a brilliant white half-moon.

"No, not a 'possibility.' You have to promise." Julie's face had the same look of confidence it had on Sundays, when she was about to sing a solo. She held her hand up in front of her heart and ticked off her fingers one by one. "No more Dr. Oberholzer, no more electric shocks. And I get to keep seeing Romey. And I get to stay in the choir."

"This is getting completely out of hand." Connie grabbed her husband's shoulder, stood on tiptoe, and cupped her hand around his ear. "Keep her up there till she's tired, then she'll come down."

"If you give me your word on all four, Daddy, I'll come down. But not until."

The blue dress billowed around Julie's knees. "Well, there's certainly no question about your staying in the choir, Julie. It's kind of peculiar that you even bring it up. I can tell you yes to that one right now." The reverend crossed his arms over his chest and smiled at her.

To Romey, Julie looked soft next to the metal deer. *I love you love you love you,* Romey told Julie silently, with her eyes. *I'm proud of you, too.*

To the reverend, Julie looked like a little slip of a thing, no more than a child who'd upended a red paint pot on her dress. When she was small, he could change her mood in a second by swinging her high in the air. Or with just a word or two. Cars slowed on the bridge to see what was going on, and traffic behind them honked. The reverend heard Julie again, from two days before: *Daddy, he's hurting me.*

Only an hour ago he had prayed for her to live, even if she had sinned. For Julie to live, that was the main thing. Everything else could be worked out later, when she was less impulsive and upset. The wind made the red-stained skirt flap against her knee. *Daddy, he's hurting me; he's hurting me.* Lord, let me do what is right here, he prayed. I love her so much.

"All right, angel," the reverend's voice boomed out above the river. "I'll agree. Now you come on down."

"Jim Ed!" Connie's shocked face swung toward him.

"Give me your word," Julie said calmly.

"You have my word."

"Say it, though."

"You have my word, Julie. You won't have to see Dr. Oberholzer. You will be allowed to see your friend Romey. And I already said you may stay in the choir."

"And no more electric shocks."

The reverend winced. He wasn't proud of that part. "No more electric shocks."

Romey and the reverend stepped forward to the platform at the same time. Julie sat down just to the inside of the doe, her feet dangling over the side. "Stand on my shoulders, angel," the reverend said, putting his back to the granite. Julie did, grabbing Romey's hand to steady herself. The reverend bent his knees and grunted as a pain cleaved his spine. In the eye of the TV camera and the disapproving stares of Connie, Virginia, and the assembled members of the Divido Bible congregation, Julie jumped from the reverend's lowered shoulders to the ground, and into Romey's arms. The reverend turned away, hand rising to his face, so Julie did not notice the tears standing in her father's eyes.

On the Santa Rosa station's evening news that night, the story got upstaged by a report about a jackknifed big rig that had spilled a tanker load of used cooking grease across Highway 101. When the segment about the afternoon's events at Buck and Doe Bridge came on, nobody at the scene was quoted. There was just a shot of Julie climbing down with a reporter's voiceover, the reverend's face almost hidden in shadow, Romey's back to the camera, Julie hugging Romey, and then the milling bodies of camouflage-clad militia.

Chapter 17

The following morning, Monday, Julie worked on history for a couple of hours, then Connie administered a quiz. Julie received a grade of 100.

Reverend Wright went early to the Best Western and drove Dr. Oberholzer to the Santa Rosa Airporter. By mutual agreement, they postponed Reverend Wright's training in Oberholzer's counseling techniques. The reverend drove back along Highway 101 under gunmetal clouds that couldn't seem to decide if they were going to rain. The boot-in-the-gut feeling of Julie having been kidnapped wasn't completely gone. Some man's large, dirty hands on her . . . he beat that thought down. The danger was past. Rather than dwell on the worst, he should be giving thanks that the Lord had spared her. And so he did. But that Arden girl, there was this fresh threat of that Arden girl touching Julie in perverted ways, contorting Julie's beautiful character and tender body into something unchaste, putrid, and debauched.

He needed to sit down with Julie and have a father-daughter talk. That was it. Why had he ever thought some professional could do a better job? He'd stay away from scolding her about dipping her toe into sin. Instead, he'd keep it upbeat, describe from his heart how much pleasure he and Connie had found in their marriage, leaving out, of course, the physical details that Julie had no need to hear about until her actual wedding day. Instead of concentrating on the negative—this unhealthy pull Julie felt toward Romey—he'd focus on the positive and motivate Julie to steer herself toward a normal, married future.

There had been few Monday nights when the reverend looked forward more to the release and succor of his own and Connie's marital bed. Yet, when he lay down beside his wife, when he began his familiar preliminary routine of gentle caresses ("It is a wife's duty to always submit to her husband," he told the couples in his weekend marriage workshops, "but if a Christian husband is tender, considerate and loving, if he pays attention to his wife's needs for affection and foreplay, the question of submission need never arise"), Connie lay still, her lips a thin line. He lightly touched his wife's cheek, planted on her body kisses celebrating the return of their daughter, kisses discharging worry and fear, but all he felt in return was her cold submission. He tried touching her in ways that hadn't failed to please her in the past. She cooperated, moved her limbs when needed. Opened her legs. It chilled him, and if he hadn't stored up so much agitation from the day before, for the first time in their long marriage he might have been unable to perform the sacrament of the marriage bed.

When he was finished, Connie put on her robe immediately and knelt by the bed. He joined her and said a long, sincere prayer of gratitude for Julie's safe return to the family.

Connie merely said, "Amen."

The bed was immense that night, wide and long, and their bodies were separated by a comfortless Mojave-Desert expanse of clean sheets.

The next afternoon, as he sat at his desk in the office behind the church sanctuary, Connie marched in, eyes like a Bible illustration of an Old Testament prophet. "Will you take a look at *this?*"

He put on his reading glasses. She handed him a note.

> Dear Mom and Daddy,
> I finished my math and I'm over at
> Romey's. I already made the salad for
> dinner and I'll be back in time to help
> with the rest of it.
> Love,
> Julie

Connie faced his desk, a grim statue. He could not recall a time when Julie had left the house without first asking permission. This was willful disobedience. Just to leave a note, like she was already grown up, like—

"This is exactly the kind of note you'd get from some girl who'd been raised in a heathen household. Like the Ardens'." Connie finished his thought.

They looked at each other, united for a moment in shared indignation. He crumpled the note. "She probably went over there yesterday when we were both out."

"We can't keep giving in to her whims like this."

"I'm going to call up there and tell her to get back home," the reverend said. But after he found the number in the white pages and punched it in, all he got was a recording. As he debated whether or not to leave a message, someone knocked on the office door.

The reverend rose and opened the door to the officer who had presided over the search on Sunday.

"Good afternoon, Reverend. May I come in for a moment? Afternoon, Missus Wright."

Two chairs faced the reverend's desk. He motioned for the officer to take one, and Connie sat down in the other.

"What can we do for you?"

"I'm just making this call as a courtesy, to give you both sort of a heads up." He leaned forward. "Yesterday, your daughter made certain allegations about . . . ah . . . electric shocks. By law, I was required to report those allegations to Child Protective Services."

Connie gasped.

The reverend stood up. The mechanism on his desk chair sprang forward with a squeal. He held up his hands, palms out. "But surely—"

The officer continued, "I'm confident Child Protective Services' investigation will be just a formality—"

"Investigation," the reverend boomed. "Now just a minute here."

The officer kept his tone even and neutral. "An investigation is required by law. But like I said, I'm sure you and Mrs. Wright will be able to clear this up. I wanted to explain it to you before Child Protective Services called. You should expect to hear from them today or tomorrow, and they'll arrange for one of their social workers to make a home visit."

Connie crossed her arms under her breasts and glared at him. "They have no business in our home."

"Just what does this social worker plan to investigate?" The reverend was almost shouting.

"The social worker will make a determination about whether your daughter suffered," the officer looked at them intently, trying to soften the effect of his words, "physical abuse from the alleged electric shocks."

Connie's and the reverend's eyes met again.

The officer went on in his bland voice, "As I said, it will probably be just a formality. CPS does remove children from their homes in cases of serious abuse and neglect, but I could see from your daughter's condition yesterday that's not the case here. The home visit will, in all likelihood, be the end of it. The most that I expect to happen is a recommendation that you both attend a series of parenting classes."

"Parenting classes!" Connie and the reverend spoke at the same time.

The officer gently set some brochures on the desk. "The classes are very good, actually. Many parents who attend them swear by them. Wished they'd taken them sooner. A good percentage of the parents aren't even court-ordered. They come to gain skills to help them through the difficulties all parents face. I've brought some materials about the 'You and Your Growing Teenager' class, just for your own information."

Connie's throat closed up. For some reason, she remembered the time she found a rat swimming in the toilet, slick, gray-brown, and sharp-clawed. Julie was still little then, about four. The county Animal Control Officer, a big blonde Swedish-looking woman in boots, arrived in a truck. She'd captured the rat, put it in a cage, and took it away.

The police officer stood up, straining to lift his waist with the gun and other equipment weighing down his belt. "I kind of hated to give you bad news like this over the phone, after all you went through on Sunday. Just keep in mind, it's a formality." He held out his hand to the reverend.

"Yes, yes. Well, we do appreciate your taking time to stop by," the reverend said. He shook the proffered hand and walked the officer to the door, then to the outer door of the church, then to the squad car.

When he returned to his office, Connie was still sitting. Her lips had disappeared into her head. The twin lines that ran from the corners of her mouth to her chin were stiff, as if they were all that was holding her face together.

He sat down beside her and put his hand on her knee. "Connie Belle, I—"

The phone rang. He picked it up, hoping to tell Julie in no uncertain terms to come home.

But it was a Ms. Santorelli from Child Protective Services, calling to see if three weeks from Wednesday at 2 p.m. would be convenient for a home visit.

He made the arrangement in a detached, professional voice, and penciled it into his calendar. His heart rammed his chest. When he got off the phone, he stared across the room at the locked file cabinet drawer that held the church checkbook and financial records. It reminded him of the cash advance on his credit card he'd taken out to finance the first days of Oberholzer's treatment.

Connie hadn't moved. He walked around his desk, knelt beside her chair, and touched her knee. "I'm going into the sanctuary to pray, Connie Belle. Then, we have some important decisions to make, and I would like to seek your guidance."

Rain thrummed lightly on the roof of the brick and redwood sanctuary. Instead of mounting the pulpit, the reverend went to a second-row pew. The "You and Your Growing Teenager" pamphlet, title printed in screaming red, was in his hand, though he hadn't remembered picking it up. He opened it and read a little, only half seeing. One sentence caught his eye. "Many of us have difficulty facing the fact that our children are becoming sexual beings during these years." With a contemptuous snort, he slammed the pamphlet face down on the wooden seat at his side.

Mzzzz. Santorelli! A social worker who probably had the same warped values as Mzzzz. Arden. Could be an unmarried mother herself. Or even a homosexual. Why not? If there were people in Divido who would let open homosexuals teach in the schools, why not a homosexual social worker?

But whether she was a homosexual or not, she was being paid with his taxes to go around and lecture parents, inform them that their children were *sexual beings,* and help them *accept* their little sexual beings. That one sentence summed up everything that was corrupt and degenerate about the whole interfering government Social Service Gestapo.

Now that apparatus was about to come crashing down on his family. Mzzzz. Santorelli was preparing to come into his house and snoop around, to pass judgment on his child rearing and tell him what he could and could not do to save his daughter from homosexuality. The long tentacles of evil surely had him in their grasp now.

He stood and walked up and down the center aisle, then back and forth in front of the pulpit, pacing in the form of a cross. The stained-glass windows made the rainy light even grayer. He remembered his words of comfort to Patty and Wayne the day Nick was arrested, and later that night, when Nick was rushed to the hospital. But only the Lord could comfort the reverend.

If the government had one lick of sense, Mzzz. Santorelli would open an investigation of Mzzz. Arden for the abuse of encouraging her daughter to be a pervert. There was probably still time to save the Arden girl. But was Mzzz. Arden being investigated? Not a chance.

The dream he'd had last night came back in force. He thought he'd banished it from his mind, but now it replayed, sickening. The doe from Buck and Doe Bridge had come to life, larger than life, half metal and half animal flesh, and leaped down from her stone pedestal. She was monstrous, even larger than she'd seemed with Julie standing next to her. She stank of sexual musk and animal excrement. The huge doe paraded across the Wrights' front yard, stomping her dirty hooves. All Connie's flowers were crushed to pulpy shreds. The doe kicked and pranced and reared, tore up clumps of lawn. Again and again, she thrust her rear end into the air in front of the Wrights' door, and that large rear end was red, grotesquely swollen. "She's horny," said an ominous voiceover. "Horny."

He knelt again in the second pew, in the last of the sickly afternoon light. At first, the only prayer he said, over and over, was "Help me, God."

But gradually, the Lord's light broke over his soul and brought on the beginning of understanding.

"Lord, forgive me. I betrayed You in a misguided attempt to save my daughter. Have mercy on me now, for I acted only out of love for her. I see now that You were testing me. And I have been found wanting. My faith was not strong, like Abraham's. I didn't trust you to spare my child, as you spared Isaac. I pulled her away from the mountain without giving You a chance."

He had been thinking his prayer, but now he spoke it aloud, eyes up toward the last dingy glimmer in the red and blue windows. "And when the Devil spoke through her innocent mouth, the Devil who was put there by that evil child of the baby killer, I gave in when I should have held firm. Forgive me, Lord. Guide me, now, to better action."

The reverend fell silent again. He never went back on his word, and he would not do so now. Yet he couldn't face his congregation with his daughter openly consorting with an admitted homosexual. If he could not get his own house in order, his words would have no standing.

Julie's legs, up on the platform, next to the enormous bronze doe, the edge of her red-stained skirt eddying around them, had been so thin, so delicate. A kidnapper could have snapped one so easily, could have handled her wrongly. That thought had shaken him and had undermined his normally strong capacity to project authority. He'd been so bent on keeping her from any more harm that he'd betrayed Julie to her own self-destructive adolescent demands, and caved in to what was no more than a childish tantrum, at the very moment when she most needed his firm, guiding hand.

And how quickly everything collapses when a father fails in his duty of firmness, he thought. He had a disobedient child on his hands now. And a cold wife. It couldn't be more obvious that the Lord was trying to tell him something.

He understood now how much he'd been swayed by Julie's "Daddy, he's hurting me." But if she scalded in hell for eternity, who would hear then, her cries of hurt?

"Lord, help me make the right decision now, and help me be firm," he prayed. As he continued his prayer, his resolve congealed.

He walked back to his office, but Connie had gone. He turned toward home, crossed the parking lot in the darkening rain, and found Connie back in the bedroom washing down a windowsill, twisting a damp rag.

They prayed. When they heard Julie come in, Connie merely stuck her head out the bedroom door and called to her to put some potatoes in the oven to bake. Husband and wife talked for almost an hour, and when it was over, Connie was bitter and tearful, but with Jesus' guidance, they had made a difficult, but joint, decision, and they were united, as had been typical throughout their long marriage. They stood together now in resolute agreement.

Chapter 18

Romey awoke from a few minutes of honeyed sleep. Her bedroom was full of silvery late-afternoon light, and outside her window rain dripped companionably from the eaves. Inside, a pair of candle flames danced. From the eternally bright world of their poster on the far wall, women runners gazed down approvingly. From the other poster, the crowd at the Gay Freedom Parade cheered. Between them hung the pulsing, bright-colored shapes of the fractal Julie had given her, the Strange Attractor. Romey and Julie lay in each other's arms, nude, exhilarated, spent. Romey yawned, rearranged herself slightly, and sighted downward along the length of their intertwined bodies. From this angle, their arms, breasts, and thighs were folded together like the petals of a rosebud.

Romey now knew these things: There were twin dimples at the base of Julie's spine. Romey could run faster uphill when she was in love. Food wasn't all that important. Julie's body pressed to hers could dissolve Romey into a loose collection of ecstatically bouncing atoms, held together by pure feeling.

Romey didn't know whether she or Julie had actually had an orgasm. The book her mother gave her was exasperatingly vague about how it would feel, and then cautioned the reader not to get hung up on orgasms, with the threatened result a whole list of sexual problems described in a later chapter Romey didn't even want to read. Yet the book made it clear that everyone was constantly trying to have an orgasm. To complicate Romey's ignorance, making love to Julie was already so wonderful, she could not imagine something happening in the middle of it, or the end of it, that could be any more wonderful. Yet, according to the book, this was possible.

When Romey read Julie the relevant passage aloud, the most bewildering part of which was the statement that when your lover "came," she might *do nothing that you could feel or see or hear,* Julie just smiled and hugged Romey tighter. "Sounds kind of like when the Holy Spirit comes into you," Julie said. "When it happens, you just know."

After hearing that, Romey stared at the Strange Attractor on her wall, Julie's gift, that jewel-colored picture of a mathematical formula of a structure found in the human brain, in clouds, and in nature. "Julie," Romey said after a while, "do you mind that I don't feel the Holy Spirit?"

Julie stroked Romey's hip. "Do *you* mind that I do?"

"No."

"Well, I don't mind, either."

Romey's fingers wandered in the softest part of Julie's hair, at the back of her head. "It might matter someday, though."

Julie turned her face so they were eye to eye. "If that time comes, we'll have enough love to get through it. Let's hope." She smiled and touched Romey lightly on the ribs, the slightest hint of a tickle. "No, you hope. I'll pray. Okay?"

All that week, life bubbled and sparkled. The crystal October sunlight, falling sideways, had never looked so gorgeous. Romey felt it would have been a tragedy to have been born anyone else. She walked through charmed corridors and radiant classrooms, possessed of a magical secret that smoldered all day long in the parts of her body that stayed, even when she concentrated on math, slightly swollen with desire.

Julie woke each day long before the autumn sun lightened the black sky. She finished off a whole week of Internet math on Tuesday and tore right in to the next week's assignment. In her other subjects, her mother could barely keep the quizzes coming. Julie did all her regular household chores, usually before her parents got up, plus she made everyone's lunch before she was told, washed and polished the car as the sun rose one morning, swept and hosed down the front porch, polished her mother's sterling silver candlesticks. At 2:30 every day, she hopped on her bike to meet Romey at the high school.

Now, Romey raised Julie's hand to her lips and kissed the center of Julie's palm. "Remember all the ladybugs, after I came to hear you sing?"

"Our first date. You looked so beautiful to me, sitting on that tree behind the stage."

"I never guessed it was our first date."

"Me, neither. But it was."

Romey kissed Julie's small fingertips one by one. "And our first kiss? At Virginia's. The night you told me you weren't gay?"

Julie hugged Romey closer. "It just felt right to kiss you."

"I was so scared that night to even touch you."

Already they had a history, a past that rolled like honey over their tongues.

Romey breathed in a long breath of Julie-smell, of flowers and soap. "I can't believe your parents are letting you come over every day," she said into Julie's neck.

Julie rearranged her body and propped her head up, elbow to pillow, so she could see Romey. "Dad never goes back on his word. I think they're both coming to accept this. Us." She rubbed her toe on Romey's instep. "Basically, there's nothing my dad can do to stop us now."

Janis opened the front door, shaking water droplets off her umbrella and thumping her stuffed briefcase to the floor. It was like a blast furnace inside the house. Romey must have turned the heat way up again. Janis stripped off her coat, stomped over to the thermostat, and turned it down to 65. The whir from the heat vents died away. She walked to the kitchen and ran a glass of water. From her office that afternoon, she'd watched Connie Wright, out in front of the clinic, stubbornly picketing in squishy boots, clutching a plastic bag that contained leaflets covered with horror pictures of fetuses. Connie's dark hair went flat as she shared her umbrella with women who didn't have one and tilted her umbrella out of the way from those who did, hectoring everyone who attempted to rush through the rain to the clinic doors.

In the laundry room, dirty wash was piled up by the machine. Janis decided that if Romey was mature enough to carry on a sexual relationship, she could damn well start washing her own sheets. And towels. Janis strode through the kitchen and living room, throwing her long hair back over her shoulders, intending to inform her daughter of this new rule right now.

But when she arrived in front of Romey's closed door, she hesitated, then turned away.

At the clinic, Janis had counseled hundreds of stricken mothers of pregnant teenagers. The mothers of fourteen-year-olds thought their girls should have waited until they were at least sixteen. The mothers of sixteen-year-olds thought, eighteen. Janis explained to them all that it was just a fact of nature they couldn't change. After puberty, their daughters' bodies were ready to reproduce, no matter what the society surrounding them, or their parents, wanted.

Janis had pitied these mothers, who tried to put their heads in the sand and pretend their daughters' emerging sexuality would just go away. She herself had prepared Romey thoroughly. By age ten, Romey already knew the pros and cons of every method of contraception, was familiar with what they looked like, and understood their most effective modes of deployment. Janis had prepared Romey emotionally, too. Drilled into Romey that she should never do anything sexual with a boy just because he wanted it. Romey had to want it, too. And *use protection*. But if all this contraceptive education failed, and Romey became pregnant, Janis made sure Romey knew her mother would be there, ready to talk it through.

And then, ironically, when Romey turned out to be gay, and there were no girlfriends on the horizon, it looked like Janis was home free. She was going to get what all those mothers at the clinic wanted: a daughter whose sexuality would bloom later, when high school was over, at college maybe, or even after that. And hadn't it been—kind of, she had to admit—a relief?

Soon enough, Romey and Julie would emerge from the bedroom on their own, thin-legged, pink-cheeked, beaming, posture boasting of sated young passion. This sudden florid sexuality grated on Janis's nerves. She felt like some dry husk.

She turned away from Romey's door, went to her own bedroom, picked up the phone and called Pam, who was out. But Peg, mercifully, was home and ready to listen as Janis reminisced about being nineteen, when she gleefully "made love, not war" with her boyfriend, at midnight, on the exquisitely tended, soft, green turf of the university football stadium, right at the fifty-yard line. Peg responded with a story of her own, and then Janis told another, about another boyfriend, with whom Janis drove out to a deserted road in the country one warm night, and even though the gravel hurt her back ("It was pre-women's movement, so of course I wasn't on top," she laughed), she and her boyfriend literally followed the instructions in the Beatles song and "did it in the road."

Janis punctuated her description with raucous laughter, and one phrase recurred again and again, "my boyfriend." My boyfriend, my boyfriend.

"I tell you," Janis said, after laughing until her stomach ached, "the young don't know how beautiful they are. It's like when they're toddlers, and they're so cute, it stops you when you feel like killing them."

Bolstered by the conversation with Peg, Janis felt her equilibrium return enough that when she walked into the dark living room and found Romey and Julie staring dreamily into a fire they'd built, sexual intimacy wafting off them in clouds, she postponed the laundry discussion for another time. At least they were fully clothed. Two days before, they'd wandered into the kitchen to get a snack wearing nothing but long T-shirts. Janis had found it surprisingly unnerving, considering that in the past, Romey and Amina had regularly shown up at the kitchen dressed that way for breakfast.

A log crackled and rolled off the fire with a whoosh and a burst of sparks. Without comment, Janis stepped in front of her daughter and her daughter's lover, pulled the scrim shut so the Guatemalan rug wouldn't catch fire, and offered to bring them back some burritos from the new healthy Mexican take-out place.

Someone blew the paper wrapper off a straw. It shot out in an arc over Romey and Amina's heads and landed in someone's chili at the next table. All around them students laughed, chattered, shouted across the cafeteria, jostled, banged trays, scraped chairs, pounded on tables, and let their knapsacks crash to the floor.

Amina swung her leg back and forth. She tugged a curl out of her cloud of hair, wrapped it around her finger, unwrapped it, let it spring back. She felt the smile on her face was stiff, too bright. She tried to make her voice sound casual. "Am I ever going to see you again except at lunch?" Her question ended with a self-deprecating laugh.

Romey felt guilt billow inside her chest. "Sure, Ameens, it's just, well, this week has been sort of like a honeymoon. How about tomorrow morning?" Julie would be at choir practice.

"I have to baby-sit."

"I'll come over and we can watch them together. It's been a while since I've seen the little ankle-biters."

"Cool." Amina's limbs loosened. She let go of her hair and took a bite of her cheese sandwich.

Romey continued, "And on Sunday, would you come to Julie's church with me? I want to hear her sing, but I'm kind of intimidated to go by myself. I know church isn't exactly fun, but—"

"Sure, I'll come." Amina scooted her chair closer to Romey. "What's it like, to have a lover?"

As their heads bent together, Matt Rodriguez walked up and pulled out the chair next to Amina. With a sweep of his long, curly eyelashes and a deferential hello, he held his lunch tray questioningly over the table. Romey and Amina insisted he wasn't interrupting anything and motioned for him to sit down.

Romey drifted into a hazy, sensuous glow. Even during the parts of the day when she wasn't with Julie, Julie's love changed everything. Romey's body hummed. Amina and Matt's conversation could not dim the brightness around her, although they were discussing next week in biology class, when they were each going to be required to slice open a frog's abdomen and examine its liver, heart, and guts.

"Absolutely not. You are not taking my car to that church. Period." Janis had been at the desk in the dining alcove, writing out checks. She waved the electric bill as if shooing something away.

Romey half leaned, half sat on the side of the sofa arm, legs stretched out in front of her. "But—"

"I'm a supportive mother. There's not one girl in a hundred in America who has the kind of sexual freedom you do. I've opened this house to your girlfriend, in spite of her being from that church. But this is a two-way street. If you want to be treated like an almost-adult, you better start acting like one."

Janis flung her long hair over her shoulders. An irritating image flickered through her mind, the image of Romey and Julie wandering into the kitchen in a daze of sexual afterglow, both barefoot, wearing only their long T-shirts. "Now just think about it for a minute. The people from that church are working night and day to shut the clinic down. I know it's too much to ask you to think about all the teenage girls who wouldn't have a chance to go to college, who'll get stuck in poverty if they have a baby. And I know it's too much to ask you to think of all the grown women who cannot make the most basic decisions about their lives, if they don't have the freedom to control whether or not they have a baby. And I know it's too much to expect you to see that if abortions aren't available, lots of women lose all chance to lead the kind of life you yourself take for granted you are going to lead—"

"Mom—"

"Even if you can't think of anyone but yourself here, you might consider what would happen to you if they close the clinic down. My work there puts a roof over *your* head and clothes on *your* back."

Janis picked up a fistful of bills. "Plus, Julie's parents may allow her to come over here, but you're living in a dream world if you think that whole church won't be dead set against your relationship the second they find out what's going on."

"Mom—" Romey felt an elemental physical superiority, sensed the firmness of her muscles from the inside. She was replete with the natural force that causes seeds to burst into shoots. Her mother looked saggy. Waning.

"You go to that church, and you'll get fed a bunch of propaganda against yourself. They think you need to get married and submit yourself to your husband's will!"

"Come on, they can't make me get married if I go to church one time. I just want to hear Julie. I'm not even going to listen to that other stuff." Romey felt it was sad how her mother didn't get it. Love was a shield the congregation's disapproval could not pierce. "Besides, Amina's gonna go with me."

"Next thing you know you'll be out in front of A Woman's Decision, carrying a big sign with Connie Wright."

"Mom! I'd never do that! It's not the same."

"Well, the answer is, hell, no, my car won't go."

"Okay, I'll take my bike. It's just if it rains."

"If it rains, you'll have to take the consequences for your actions."

It did not rain. The morning was sunny and sparkly, everything washed clean from a storm the night before, the sky perfect blue, the air sweet with recent rain and laced with all the elusive spicy smells from damp earth, leaves, and bark. Romey's seldom worn black skirt kept hiking up as she pedaled her bicycle, and she kept pulling it down, which caused the handlebars to wobble, and then her little black shoulder bag swung forward and hit the handlebars, and Romey shoved it behind her, which made the handlebars wobble even more. Amina, who'd worn pants, started giggling, and when Romey glanced over at her, she started laughing too. It got funnier and funnier, Romey laughed in peals and whoops, and her stomach shook, which made it even harder to control the bike. It wove and shimmied. Finally they had to pull over, rest their feet on the ground, and let out their laughter.

"You're sure doing something that's not like you," Amina said.

"It's crazy, what we do for love," Romey said, panting, smiling, happy and proud to be part of the charmed "we" who are lured into craziness by the depth of their love.

They arrived at the church early, so they decided to lock their bikes two blocks away and walk. They pulled a brush and a pick out of Romey's handbag, repaired the damage that the bike helmets had done to each other's hair, then walked toward the church, breaking into laughter again twice. By the time they mounted the church steps, they were composed and solemn.

A round man in a gray suit stood in the doorway. "Welcome. This your first time here?"

Romey nodded.

"Yeah," said Amina, pulling at a lock of hair.

He handed them each a program. "Well, come on in and welcome to Divido Bible Church. Hi there, Mike and Lori." The man fell into conversation with the people behind them. Romey and Amina entered the sanctuary and sat on the aisle, in the last pew in the back.

It was still ten minutes until the service was supposed to start. Romey knew the soft and somehow mournful music from the organ was Julie's mother playing, but she couldn't see her. Red and blue stained-glass windows threw down a pretty light. The walls were brick to a height of about six feet, then redwood all the way up to the beamed ceiling.

The church slowly filled up. A young couple edged in front of Romey and sat down on the other side of Amina. The woman smiled at Romey over a baby in a nest of pink blankets. Mom was so wrong to get bent out of shape by me coming here, Romey thought. No one's going to say anything. This is harmless.

Music swelled, and the blue-robed choir filed in. Romey found Julie immediately, in the middle, shining like an opal on blue velvet. The hymn began. Julie's eyes met Romey's and stayed there. Her throat shaped the notes the way her fingers, twenty-four hours earlier, had shaped their caress in Romey's bed. The crystalline beauty of Julie's voice broke over Romey, reminding her of the first time she'd heard Julie sing, at the fair, and how she'd understood, then, where humans had gotten the idea of heaven.

When the singing stopped, Romey tuned out, especially when the choir sat down and she could no longer see Julie. Surprisingly, some other preacher, not Mr. Wright, gave the sermon, his voice like a fly buzzing behind Romey's ears. She was busy remembering Friday, the weight of Julie's head on her naked shoulder, how she blew away one of Julie's gossamer dark hairs when it tickled her lip.

Then Reverend Wright himself strode to the pulpit. He had a more commanding presence than the previous speaker, and Romey, along with the rest of the congregation, barely aware of what she was doing, straightened her posture against the hard back of the pew, sat up, and turned her eyes front.

Reverend Wright spoke about how important the Divido community had been all these years he'd had the honor of being pastor at Divido Bible Church, how they'd shared God's work together. He embellished his talk with references Romey couldn't quite get, to things that had happened at the church in the past and more recently. His words made the congregation nod and chuckle. Romey thought she could figure out what he was talking about when he mentioned people working eighteen-hour days to help out the less fortunate during the flood, and she understood completely when he mentioned her mother's clinic and the school board meeting. At those parts, her face felt hot.

The reverend moved on to something about a Call, and the Lord's will, and Romey was about to tune out again when she felt the reverend's eyes glance over her, making the briefest acknowledgment of her presence at the very back, as he said he'd prayed long and hard about this Call, and after listening to the Lord and to the always wise counsel of his wife, Connie, he'd accepted that this was, in fact, the Lord's will. Again, his eyes brushed lightly over Romey, far too quickly for anyone to imagine he knew his words held significance for her, or that she had anything to do with what he was about to say, and then his eyes rested a bit longer on the choir, where Julie was seated. "The Lord's will," his baritone voice echoed off the brick and redwood walls, "is that I accept the Call to take up the ministry at the First Bible Church in Lubbock, Texas."

The congregation had stopped breathing. Now, it let out its breath all together. A murmur rippled through it.

The reverend continued, saying the need was so acute in Lubbock, and Reverend Garner, who had so ably delivered the sermon this morning, was so capable to fill in as interim pastor until a suitable permanent replacement could be found for this fine congregation, that the Reverend Wright and his family would leave for Lubbock this very week.

The choir filed up for the last hymn. Julie's face had a look like a deer who has been grazed by a hunter's bullet in the past, and now glances up from munching flowers to see the red-vested hunter just a few feet away, lowering his gun, aiming at her heart. There were no solos, just the whole choir together, and though Julie's lips moved, Romey could hear no sound coming from her at all.

Chapter 19

A thick silver wedding band with flowers intertwined in relief all around. Romey gazed through the glass into the blue velvet display case. She'd come to the only real jewelry store in town, a room no larger than her bedroom in one of the restored old buildings on the quaint side of the square. The store was hushed and dim, with most of the light coming from glass cases gleaming with silver, copper, and gold. With a sense of being about to commit a daring act, she mentally composed a retort in case that man behind the counter told her she was too young to buy that kind of ring. And the one next to it was nice, too, the same thick silver band, with a more abstract design . . .

"Want to see one of these?" The man, who was around the same age as Romey's mother, looked up from his careful work on some intricate silver earrings. He set down a tiny tool, walked two steps over to the counter, and lifted one of the abstract rings from the deep blue velvet.

It felt solid and hefty to Romey, pleasing to rub the nubby silver texture.

The man's skin was the color of tobacco, and his thick salt-and-pepper dreadlocks hung almost to his waist. He had six earrings in one ear. "Can you tell what the design is? Some people can, some can't."

She looked at the ring more carefully. It wasn't an abstract pattern after all. There, slightly raised in silver, were the tiny silhouettes of the buck and the doe. And circling the ring, the span of—

"It's Buck and Doe Bridge!" Romey turned the ring around and around.

"Far out. You got it. Must mean it's your ring."

"I need one smaller than this, but I don't know how much smaller." Romey described in tender detail how delicate and slim-fingered

Julie's hands were. The man asked how tall Julie was, how heavy. He had Romey try on various rings. Together, they decided that the size that fit Romey's pinky finger would probably be right.

Romey looked at the price tag. The ring clicked softly as she set it back on the glass. "Can you hold it for me until tomorrow?" She had to get her money out of her savings account, and the bank was already closed.

He nodded calmly. In that dim shop with all the jewelry gleaming on lighted shelves, he reminded Romey of an elf (was there such a thing as a giant elf?), or a sorcerer, someone from a fairy tale. He picked up his small tool and went back to the silver earrings.

She turned to go, then realized she needed something else. "Can you hold another one for me, in my size, until I can get some more money?"

He pulled the rings back out of the case. "For sure."

"I might not have enough for a month. Or even two months."

"Tell you what. I'll put this one—this was the one, wasn't it," he held out a ring and she slipped it on her third finger, "on a sixty-day hold."

She turned the nubby ring around so the buck and doe were on the top and admired it. Then she handed it back to him. "Oh, that'd be great."

The next day, there were five people in the bank line in front of Romey, and each seemed to be closing escrow on a house loan or liquidating a stock portfolio. Finally she got her money and crossed the square to the jewelry store.

He handed her the ring. She picked it up again and rubbed the miniature silver filigree of bridge. "Are you sure this is the right size? It feels smaller."

"Well, uh, I thought over everything you told me about the girl you want to buy it for, and, er, I think this one is probably the right size."

Romey looked again at the ring. She slipped it on her pinky, but it wouldn't slide past the knuckle. "But yesterday—"

The big elf eyes were crinkly. "Look, if it's not, you can just bring it back, but I believe that's the size."

She handed over the money and left the shop with the ring, tucked in its bed of blue velvet, resting in her jean pocket against her thigh.

Julie had to work harder that week to see Romey. She got up at four in the morning, three. There were good-bye visits and dinners, a heavy schedule of packing. Still, one way or the other, she made it to the high school every afternoon, and for a couple of hours they were together.

But on Friday, when Romey got to the big eucalyptus tree in front of the school, Julie wasn't there. Romey waited forty-five minutes. She walked repeatedly to the corner and peered down Divido Boulevard in the direction of Julie's neighborhood, then went back to the tree, where she stood tearing strips of rough, papery bark off the trunk and impatiently scuffing up dust with her shoe. Finally, she went home to find a phone message. Julie's parents had insisted she stay home and pack up the last of the study.

Romey went to her room and flopped limp onto her bed, under the poster of women runners making a wild lunge for the finish line. She clicked open and shut the little blue velvet case with the silver ring. She'd saved it for their last time together, but the Wrights' moving day was tomorrow. Their last time together had already taken place. Miles and mountains and deserts would separate them now. It was like a screwdriver in her heart. She pulled the ring onto her smallest finger, as far as the second knuckle, and rubbed the ring's nubby surface. Her body curled into a ball.

Breathing heavily, Virginia wrapped a china plate in a thick layer of newspaper and set it on top of the others in a cardboard box. Her pink and green floral top was streaked with dust. A scrap of strapping tape was stuck to one sleeve. She crumpled more paper, tucked it in around the edges, and closed the flaps. Strapping tape screeched as she pulled it off the roll and sealed the box. With a marking pen, she wrote, "Good china, plates," on the top. She considered the box for a moment. Then on the side she wrote, "May Jesus bless the Wrights' Texas home." Virginia grunted, sighed, blew her nose.

She'd been helping pack for three days, and it seemed like it was never going to end. She hurt all over. She was worried about how the choir would manage minus the organist and best soloist. A few tears splatted down on the writing, blurring the edges of the letters. It was just like when Sandy moved away, Virginia realized. Her tears were on every box.

At 7:30 Friday evening, the Arden phone rang. Julie's voice, breathless and sweet, met Romey's ear. Julie's mother was gone to one last meeting with the Right to Life group, her father to a transition session with Reverend Garner and the church elders.

Romey asked Janis for the car keys.

Janis didn't say anything, just handed over the keys with a sad smile.

When Romey got to Julie's, they huddled in the backyard on a blanket, the edges pulled up all around them, arms entwined. Behind them was the tree that grew outside Julie's bedroom window, blossoms gone, bearing hard little green lemons now.

Overhead the sky was black and moonless, pricked with thousands of stars. One golden star detached itself from the glitter, fell in a graceful arc, and disappeared. A second star fell.

Romey gestured vaguely at the sky. "That something so beautiful is happening up there, and down here, this . . ." she said.

Julie buried her face in Romey's neck.

Romey remembered the night they spent at Virginia's. She wanted to protect Julie then, felt her own desire and love could harm Julie. Maybe she'd been right. She sighed, spoke into Julie's hair. "I feel like I've ruined your life."

Julie pulled back so Romey could see her. In the light from the house, one side of her face was in shadow, one side golden. "Ruined it? You've made my life come to life."

"But you wouldn't have gotten those electric shocks."

Julie kissed Romey decisively. "I'd let him strap me into that chair all over again for one short minute with you."

"It's sort of because of me that you're moving away, too."

Julie sat up, pulled Romey up, and let the blanket slip down so she could hold Romey and kiss her, slowly and deliberately, exactly like a Hollywood leading man. She broke the kiss, drew back, and touched Romey's cheek. "Nothing can ever happen to me that will make me sorry I loved you."

"Loved? Don't talk like it's over."

"No. But when we can't be together, it won't be the same."

Julie looked down, fumbled in the blanket, and turned her eyes back up to Romey, her dark lashes rising from the pale hollows above her cheekbones and reminding Romey, just like the first time in line for the Ferris wheel, of a curtain going up in a theater. "This is for you," Julie said, and handed Romey a small blue velvet box.

Romey snapped it open. "Oh, Julie."

It was a thick silver ring with the pattern of Buck and Doe Bridge.

Grinning, Romey pulled an identical box out of her pocket and handed it to Julie. She watched Julie's face break into that smile with sadness at the corners of the eyes.

Julie slid the ring onto Romey's third finger, left hand. The wedding ring finger. Romey did the same with Julie's.

"They fit," Romey said.

"I knew yours would. That man with the long hair at the ring store? He knew who you were. Had your size. Told me this was the kind of ring you'd *really* like."

For a silent minute they looked at their two young hands, one small, one long-fingered, and at the gleam of silver in the night.

They wrapped the blanket back around them. "Now we're really married in our minds," Romey whispered.

"For always."

"We'll live together. When we grow up. No one will be able to stop us."

"We'll be mathematicians together."

"You'll be a mathematician and a famous singer. And we'll have kids."

"You'll be the one who has them, so they'll be tall and beautiful and smart and strong and run fast."

"No, you'll have them, so they'll be beautiful and smart and graceful and sing."

"We'll let them love whoever they want to."

"Yes. And if it's a boy, we'll name him Elliot." Romey looked down. She thought of Nick.

"It's okay," Julie said. "We don't have to name him for Nick."

Romey moaned and twisted on the blanket. "How can they make us be apart when you can read my mind? It's so unfair."

Just like the first night on the Ferris wheel, Julie smelled to Romey of soap and flowers. Romey inhaled deeply, also taking in the more complex fragrance of Julie's skin. "When we go to college, we can be together. You might even finish high school early. We can start at the same time."

Julie touched Romey's cheek. The sadness was at the corner of her eyes again, but now she wasn't smiling. "My parents are sending me to Bible college."

Romey looked off into the darkness. "Then I'll go, too."

"No. You need to get the best education you can."

"Then we'll find a good college and a Bible college close together. There must be some way."

"Let's not talk about it. College is too long from now. It reminds me of how far apart we'll be. The years." Julie had almost three more years of high school, four of college. She calculated it was almost half the years she'd lived up until now, a wait of half a lifetime.

"And we're still together, this minute," she said. She kissed Romey again. Just as she'd learned to sing the highest notes on Sundays in a way that let the Holy Spirit flow through her, she now knew how to kiss in a way that let all her love and Yearning flow through her and into Romey, unstoppable and natural, like water flowing downhill.

Stars anointed them with elemental, ancient light. "I'm so scared. Your mom and dad, or all those people at the new church, they'll convince you not to love me."

"I won't let them. I'll pray every day for us to be together again."

"Will you still love me, even though I can't believe that will help?"

"Will you still love me, even though I believe it can?"

"I'll remember everything we did together. Every day."

Julie snuggled her head under Romey's chin. "I'm scared, too. You could fall in love with someone else."

"Honey, I'll wait for you. However long it takes."

Romey reached across and rested her left palm on Julie's, so the silver rings touched. "We have to promise each other, no matter what happens, no matter how bad it gets, neither one of us commits suicide."

"I promise."

"I promise, too. Would you have jumped? That day?"

Julie lay back on the blanket and spoke to the sky. "Do you ever do something because there's this force that pulls you, and you don't know if it comes from inside you or outside you? Or maybe some combination? And wherever it's from, it's so strong, you just do it?"

Romey lay down and watched Julie's profile, wishing she understood. Finally she said, "No."

"Well, that's how it was. I don't know if it would've been strong enough to jump. I didn't have to find out."

"But it might've?"

"Yeah."

Romey moved until her lips were next to Julie's ear. She whispered, "Now I'm worried."

"Why?"

"Well, what if some feeling, or force, or whatever it is, happens again? And this time, it's strong enough?"

Julie rolled and slid, rearranging their bodies until she was lying on top of Romey, eye to eye. "It won't."

"How do you know?"

"Because now I know that when it feels like that, I can't just follow it. I have to think first. I have to decide."

Romey held Julie's eyes. "Don't decide to die."

"Don't worry. First of all, we just promised. And second of all, I couldn't leave life. It's got stuff like you in it."

A car pulled into the driveway. The garage door opened.

Julie's sigh lingered sadly in her throat.

They stood up. The blanket fell away from their bodies and they kissed fiercely and quickly. Overhead, another star streaked through the black sky and vaporized to nothing near the horizon.

Julie brought their left hands together again, clicked their rings. "Good-bye, my only love."

"Be strong."

"I'll think about you to make me strong."

"Oh, Julie."

Then Julie went inside to the kitchen, and Romey walked around the house to the front, where she'd left her mother's car with its pro-choice bumper stickers, because it could not possibly matter anymore if a Wright parent saw them or not.

Chapter 20

A hint of the previous night's frost lingered in the Saturday morning air. The sun glared on the eastern horizon but produced only a feeble warmth. On a corner a block from the Wright house, under a single pine tree in a muddy vacant lot, stood a tall, thin figure with short red-brown hair, hands jammed in her jacket pockets. She stamped her feet but still trembled; she'd been there since before cold dawn, unwilling to miss being a witness. Romey could hear the car doors opening even this far away.

She watched Virginia move slowly around the Wrights' blue Dodge sedan, wiping condensation off the windows with a pink towel. The reverend came out the front door with two suitcases and set them in the trunk. Romey had never seen him when he wasn't wearing a suit; it jarred her to see him now in jeans and a tan windbreaker, as if he were just anyone's dad. Julie walked from the door to the car with a duffel bag and a box. After she put them in the car, she headed back toward the house, facing Romey, but she didn't look up. Connie came out and stood talking with Virginia. Julie appeared again, with a suitcase. Her hair gleamed in the sunlight. She had on her navy blue raincoat, the same one she and Romey had tried to leave by the river. From this distance, Romey couldn't see if all the red paint had come out in the wash.

The reverend hugged Virginia. Connie hugged Virginia. Julie put her arms around Virginia and held them there. Compared to Virginia, her parents, and the car, Julie looked small. She sat down in the backseat, and the slamming of the door echoed down the road. Oh please, Romey pleaded silently to no one in particular, handle her with care.

More doors slammed, the motor started, and the blue car pulled away. Romey stared at puffs of white exhaust fumes rising and fading in the sky, where they would mingle with other gases and eat away the planet's protective atmosphere.

Even after the car turned and disappeared, she stood a little longer, staring at the last place it had been. Then she bent down, grasped the cold handlebars of her bike, raised it up from the ground, and swung her leg over to mount the saddle. She saw Virginia standing in the driveway, coat open, mouth open, still holding the pink towel she'd used to wipe down the car windows.

Virginia's eyes were deep crimson at the rims. The white sunlight hurt them. Finally, she turned and walked the two blocks to her own house. The air was quiet, dead almost.

Back home, she took Sandy's picture off the wall and shined its handsome brass frame with Brasso Polish. She liked Brasso because it was the same polish soldiers used on their medals and buttons and such. She got out the tape measure and made a light pencil mark centered just below Sandy, hammered in a nail, and hung up her new picture. It was a formal photo studio portrait of the Wright family posed in front of a mottled, gray, painted backdrop. The reverend was standing, his arm resting on Connie's shoulder, his eyes serious under their prominent ledges, beaming out charisma. Connie was seated at his side, staring with fierce intensity. Julie stood in front of her father, with an angelic, ethereal smile, still a little girl when the photo was taken, three years back. Julie hadn't even begun to develop yet.

Virginia had tried to find a brass frame to match Sandy's, but Sandy's was over twenty years old. They didn't make them anymore. She finally found another one, brass too and just as special.

Sandy's picture had gotten knocked askew when she drove the new nail in the wall. Virginia straightened it, then wiped a few smudges off the new frame. She scooped Leviticus up from the floor, headed for her recliner, sank down, and smoothed a place where the duct tape had folded back over a tear in the black vinyl. She could feel the rough stuffing from the chair's insides. Leviticus must not have been in the mood for a stroking, because Virginia's fingers only smoothed the calico fur along the knobs of the spine once before the cat wriggled free, jumped off her lap, and padded out of the living room, tail in the air. Virginia folded her hands across her stomach and stared for a long time at the addition to her wall. She had the large, padded chair turned at just the right angle.

Low winter sun glared from the southeast, and everyone in the Wright car put on sunglasses.

They passed the turnoff to Patty's house. In the front passenger seat, Connie felt rage pile up in her throat. She was being forced to leave her sister at a time like this, Patty alone with her husband who flew off the handle, her oldest son just killed and, except for her two little boys, no other kin in Divido. It wasn't right.

They were driving the same route Connie had taken for faithful years, every Thursday, to picket the abortion mill in Santa Rosa. No one from the Right to Life group had come forward to take Connie's Thursday afternoon picketing shift. It felt like Janis Arden had won.

She looked slantwise at her husband's profile. His eyes, behind the dark green sunglasses, were locked on the road ahead, on his family's future. She needed to look in that direction too. What was done, was done. She wasn't like some of these wives, disloyal, blaming their husbands when any little thing went wrong. Besides, looked at in one light, this was all Janis Arden's fault. In fact, Connie had wondered more than once this past week if it might not have been a plot on Janis's part to get rid of her, if Janis had put Romey up to seducing Connie's daughter, so the Wrights would have to leave, and Janis Arden would have an even freer hand to murder babies. Connie wouldn't put it past her. And now, thanks to Janis, Patty had to live without her sister's support, without Jim Ed's support, and without her oldest son.

They were out of town now. A deer had been hit. The Wright car sped past the carcass, which had been shoved to the side of the road. Connie felt sorry for the owner of the car involved; hitting a deer could do thousands of dollars in damage. There were way too many deer around Divido, as far as Connie was concerned. In fact, deer were overrunning the landscape all over America, Connie had read that somewhere. Every one of them was an accident waiting to happen.

She looked away from the torn brown hide with its oozing, red-black splotch.

Janis's daughter had been allowed to kill Nick and get off scot-free. The injustice of it all bit into Connie like acid. The police were so blinded by the trashy morals taking over this country that they wouldn't recognize the Devil himself. How much closer to the Devil could you get? A mother who killed babies and a daughter who killed grown boys, and the whole town, saved Christians excepted, went along with everything.

Just before they left, Virginia had handed Connie a good-bye picnic lunch. "There's deviled eggs and homemade apple turnovers in there. Good traveling food," Virginia had said. The brown paper bag was too heavy on Connie's thighs now. She turned and lifted it between the seats. "Julie, can you find someplace for this back there?"

In an odd way, she was going to miss Janis as an adversary. The Devil takes many forms. Although there would probably be an abortion mill that needed her attention in Lubbock, Connie had understood for some time now that her God-given duty had been to fight the Devil in this particular form, Janis Arden. She'd done it well. She'd worked so long and hard to shut down this particular clinic, to put Janis Arden out of a job—wouldn't that have been a wonderful day? For a couple of seconds, Connie's tight lips relaxed into something like a smile.

It had felt like the work the Lord had chosen her to do, and this, to leave, felt like desertion.

There was still Julie's schooling to take care of, of course, and there would be some other work to do for the Lord; there was always plenty. But the final result was that Janis Arden would not have to face Connie at the baby-killing mill anymore. It would be just plain self-deception not to admit that the Devil had won something, this time around.

The Reverend Wright glanced at his wife by his side and looked in the rearview mirror at his daughter. What a relief it was that neither was crying. There had been so many tears this week, and despite being sure he was making the best decision the head of this family could make, he'd felt reproach in those tears.

The windshield was fogging up. He turned on the defrost, and the fan came on with a buzz. Maybe he should never have called Oberholzer in. Then he would be staying in Divido to fight the Godlessness of northern California. But he'd still have to figure out what to do about his daughter being sucked into a life of perversion.

A spasm clutched the reverend's back, tightening itself like a screw boring into hardwood. He gripped the wheel, but after a few seconds the pain seeped away. This long drive was probably going to aggravate his back. Frequent breaks would be the thing. Once they were gone from Divido, there was no reason to rush this trip.

Julie would be in a place now where she could finish growing up in a normal atmosphere. And then again, he was going to have a larger congregation. The reverend was certain no one in Lubbock would support open homosexuals teaching in the schools. He imagined himself already there, seated at a large blond table in an air-conditioned, sunlit conference room at his new church, describing the goings-on at the Divido School Board meeting to a group of incredulous Christians.

Looked at from one angle, you could see Oberholzer as part of the Lord's larger plan for the Wright family, the catalyst that forced the reverend to get Julie to a better place.

In back, Julie wedged the bag with Virginia's lunch on the floor, next to her feet. Since last Sunday, when her dad had made his announcement to the congregation, the unnaturally wise sadness, which used to appear at the corner of her eyes only when she smiled, had been there all the time.

She felt hemmed in by two large suitcases stacked on the seat beside her. She could shove them a few inches more toward the far door, but the effort didn't seem worth it. The Wright car wouldn't pass Romey's house on the way out; it was the other way. But every tree, every street, every flower, every house, every lamppost, even the smashed paper cup on the brown dirt along the shoulder of the road—all of it was where Romey was, and it seemed to Julie, this morning, as if she was leaving hallowed ground.

Romey's ring hung on a chain under Julie's shirt, between her breasts. Julie didn't know why she wasn't crying. Maybe there were only so many tears inside any one person. They were staying with Bible Church ministers every night along the way. Tonight, they'd be in Barstow. The next day, Flagstaff, on Julie's fifteenth birthday.

They passed the auto salvage place where her Uncle Wayne worked off and on, the rusty car hulks and a pile of dirt-streaked tires. She knew she was learning something important about what life was like.

A dead deer lay on the side of the road, its front legs broken, folded on top of each other. How hard and callous I'm getting, Julie thought. She could feel the deer touching a little soft spot in her, but that's all there was. She knew she used to be soft like that all the way through.

There wasn't going to be a computer at the new church. No telling what would happen to her math. Her mother didn't know enough to teach her, but she made it very clear that Julie would not be going to high school.

Lubbock, to Julie, was a place at the edge of a vast, barren plain, with harsh winds blowing dust, stinging her eyes, filling her ears. Lubbock, the end of this journey.

They passed a vineyard. The rows of vines had been chopped back to gnarled stubs amid bare, brown dirt. A hawk perched on a fence post.

She understood now that love had come too soon to her, before she was old enough to earn her own way or decide where to live, and she wasn't able to take care of it. Love did need to be taken care of; she could see that. But some people—she was pretty sure Aunt Patty was one—never had love like this at all, and it was far better to take love when it came, ready or not. She would just have to try to grow up enough, as fast as she could, to be able to keep this love. She'd have to protect the part of herself she'd named Yearning, and something else, too—her integrity. She had to keep it safe, like the smallest doll in a set of Russian dolls, inside a hard exterior of deception and secrets. Her parents had shown her how far they would go to suppress this part of her, the best of her, even uprooting themselves from the home and community they both loved.

The car warmed up inside. She wriggled out of her navy blue raincoat, folded it, set it on top of the suitcases, and shoved them all the way to the other side of the seat.

In youth group, other kids used to say sometimes that their parents didn't understand them. Julie had always felt happy, and—though she didn't mean to be prideful—a little superior to those youth group kids, because she and her parents understood each other so well. It was sad to lose that easy honesty. From here on, her survival depended on making sure her mother and dad couldn't understand her.

It wasn't enough just to keep Yearning safe inside her. She had to do more, give Yearning an inner, sheltered realm in which to develop, until she had grown up enough to walk out into the world and take Yearning along. She didn't know how to do this, and it was important to do it right. If she failed, Yearning might dry up in the hot wind, reduced to bone, to dust. Or grow in some grotesque way, all bulges and flippers and grunts.

She'd have to hide Yearning from her parents, let them believe what she knew they wanted so badly to believe, that her love for Romey had gone away. Julie wouldn't even need to go so far as having a boyfriend. Her parents would like it best, she knew, if she loved no one but them until she was old enough, in their eyes, to get married.

The car turned, and the road stretched out ahead, empty and straight. Starting now, she would have to be who they wanted on the outside.

About a half a mile ahead, she saw Buck and Doe Bridge. For an instant, the bronze doe caught the sun. A tactile memory surfaced in her palms, her fingertips: the feel of the doe's powerful, sun-warmed bronze flank when she stood beside it, ready to jump. Next, she felt a rush of memory of Romey's thigh under her hand, of Romey's body and hers, all their skin touching. It hurt to remember, a different kind of pain than an electric shock. In some ways, an electric shock was easier, and yet, she wanted to feel it, had to feel this memory, this pain.

She put her hands together, pushed together the touch of the bronze doe and of Romey. Her eyes narrowed and the sadness was erased from her downcast face, replaced by an angry smile. Her body filled with the defiant sweetness of Yearning. This position of her hands would have an additional meaning, just to her, from now on. Prayer would be the best cover. She could touch her hands together anywhere, anytime, to conjure up the feel of Romey and of the doe, to flood her body with defiant Yearning. Just let them try to keep her from feeling this. Just let them try.

The Wrights' car passed between the buck and doe at the bridge entrance, and picked up speed. As they approached the far end, Julie kept her eyes on the final doe, separated from the buck by asphalt and traffic, forever solitary on her hard platform of cold stone, steadfast, outlasting weather and time, year after year after year.

The car cleared the bridge with a metallic thump, and the reverend swung it onto the smooth highway toward Santa Rosa. Sunlight glided out of his eyes and warmed his neck and shoulder from the side. The road opened out and broadened here, with light traffic. He took off his sunglasses, looked in the rearview mirror, and saw that his daughter was deep in prayer. Grateful moisture stung his eyes. So quietly that even Connie couldn't hear, just barely moving his lips, he whispered, "Praise the Lord."

Chapter 21

You can't run and cry at the same time. Not really. You're forced to stop doing one or the other. Romey ran.

It was the time between Thanksgiving and Christmas when the knee-high old grass turns yellowish and rust-colored from rain, then falls over in various directions into a patternless mess. It was the time when tender new green was sprouting under the sodden, decaying thatch, but it wasn't visible yet. It was the season of tinsel, of short days, of whipping wind. A thin, chilly haze hung over Divido, a mixture of ground-hugging tule fog and woodsmoke. The pale sun could barely cast afternoon shadows.

She passed a church. It was not Julie's old church, but another one, old-fashioned, made of stone. Romey had never been inside, but it didn't matter; her eyes turned to fuses. She imagined the church bursting open in a fiery explosion. Gray stones bounced high in the air and crashed down into rubble and dust, and the blast hurled flaming pews the length of a football field, crumpled the metal window frames, pulverized the wooden door into splinters and sawdust. Hymnals ignited and their pages blew off in the wind, reduced to greasy ashes. The heat was so intense, fire engines couldn't get within a block of the fire. Stained glass turned liquid, shot up into the sky, splattered down in molten blobs, and sizzled on the damp earth. A toxic black cloud blanketed the town.

Romey didn't want to feel this way every time she saw a church, even the Buddhist temple and United Church of Christ, where she knew gay people were welcome. But she couldn't stop it. All she needed was the sight of a cross, even a religious bumper sticker. Her blood raced and her mind shot blasts of flame, blew up another place of worship.

This morning, when she woke up in the bed where Julie had once made love to her, pain grasped her insides like a vise. She'd kept one pillowcase out of the laundry because it smelled like Julie's hair. She rubbed her face against it. The scent was fainter now, almost gone. Every morning, Julie's absence stunned Romey all over again. At night, in Romey's dreams, Julie strode toward her across a field of sunny golden grass, smiling, no sadness at the corners of her eyes. Ladybugs rose up all around her. Or Julie stood beside a pyramid of gleaming, fragrant apples, all gold and red and jade, twice as tall as she was, and Julie smiled downward, twisting her bracelet on her wrist. Or Julie lay beside Romey, Julie's soft hair touching Romey's shoulder, Julie's small hand on the ribs just below Romey's breast.

Julie, Julie. Romey wrote Julie's name on the margins of her notes at school, on her books, on the back of her hand. Julie, Julie, Julie. Yet sometimes, when she stared at the name she'd written, it felt like the letters that formed the name "Julie" were opening up, that distance was forcing the letters apart until they would fly off into space and meaninglessness.

She wished Amina were coming over tonight. But Amina was busy.

Matt Rodriguez, it had turned out, ate lunch with them every day not because he was on his way out of the closet, but because he was interested in Amina, shyly and respectfully enough to overcome Amina's wariness, to make her forget the football boys.

Tonight was Amina and Matt's sixth date. They were baby-sitting for the twins and watching a video later. Matt understood about having to take care of kids; he had three sisters and a brother, all younger. Between baby-sitting and Matt, Amina wasn't around much. Romey remembered Amina's worry, back at the beginning with Julie, that Romey was abandoning their friendship, and so when Matt sat down next to Amina every day at lunch, and Amina turned to him with that quick, eager look, Romey tried hard not to feel excluded.

The last time Amina had come over to the house was almost two weeks ago. She'd asked Romey, "How will I know if I'm in love?"

It felt miraculous to be experienced enough to have an answer. "You'll know," Romey said. "It'll feel so good and strong and right, you'll just know. You won't have to ask me that question if it's really love."

Then Romey saw herself as if from the outside, preening and crowing about how much she knew. Trying to make herself feel better about Julie being gone by acting like she was so great because she had all this experience in love. It was sickening. It was disloyal to what she and Julie still had. And maybe she was jealous, too. The less important Matt was to Amina, the more Romey might get to see her.

"I'm sorry, Mina-bina. I'm sounding off like I'm this big authority. But it probably happens lots of different ways for different people. We just kind of knew from that first night on the Ferris wheel . . ."

And Amina listened, wonderfully attentive, while Romey told that whole story. Did not mention how many times she'd already heard it. Telling, Romey had found out, kept the time with Julie alive. She felt new sympathy and patience, these days, when her mom repeated the same old stories.

There used to be joy in Romey's muscles during every run, but now she had to keep going for miles, and then she felt only a strange comfort in their ache. Her sock was wrinkled inside her left shoe. It sort of hurt on top, but she didn't stop to fix it. She ran steadily through the old town square, past the jewelry store where she'd bought the buck and doe ring for Julie, and where Julie had bought the ring that now circled Romey's finger, solid and shining. She passed the big gray granite World War II memorial with its blobs of pigeon droppings.

Romey read inscriptions all the time now. She was amazed at how many there were, once you started looking for them. There were rows of names on this memorial. Buck and Doe Bridge had a sign about a highway engineer. A plaque was fastened below the statue of a soldier in the county park. She understood now why people put those signs up. The monuments and statues and plaques said, it may be true that this person was not eternal. But this person was here. Did things. You can never change that. The unchanging fact of having been here, that's what was eternal.

Her pace got easier; she was on a slight downhill stretch. The big rainstorm had left wide dirty streaks of grit and pine needles across the road. Romey wanted there to be some place where Elliot was, some place she could visit. She wished his parents had buried him. She didn't even know where his cremated ashes were.

Romey had remembered the fountain at the hospital, where she and Julie sat the day Elliot died. It, too, had names on a brass plaque. She called the hospital to see how to get Elliot's name put there. The hospital connected her to someone who informed her that the people who'd had the names put on the fountain had paid for the whole courtyard, the fountain, the benches, the lime trees. Romey could tell from the man's impatient voice that he was sure Romey would be too poor to afford it. She hung up abashed and ashamed, like a child reprimanded for trespassing in her mother's purse.

Then one Saturday, trying to exhaust herself into numbness, she ran all the way to the county park. She sat down to rest on a bench before turning around and running home. The park was quiet that day, the live oaks leafless skeletons, with dark green redwood trees whispering in a slight breeze and occasional walkers and joggers. Without trying to, she'd stopped at the same bench where she'd sat with Elliot that Sunday at the fair, after she'd found out Julie was the reverend's daughter. She leaned back and let the corner of the wood bite into her shoulder blades, remembering how Elliot said it made him "swoon" and gave him "the vapors." Her spine rubbed against something bumpy. She turned around and read the embossed metal plaque:

Doris M. Benbow
1929-1987
Mother, Sister,
Beloved Friend

Monday, after school, she called the park and found out that a "dedicated bench" cost a "memorial gift" of $750, and that you didn't have to be over twenty-one.

She swallowed and asked, "Can I say whatever I want on the plaque?"

"Well, let's see, now. First of all, there's only so many letters'll fit on a plaque. And no curse words, of course."

"Is gay a curse word?"

"Beg pardon?"

"Gay. Can I put in the word gay?"

"Oh, I reckon. I'll tell you this much. I'm not gonna stop you. And I'm the superintendent, so the buck stops here."

She told him she'd call back when she got the money, and now she had a job. Saturdays, Sundays, and Thursday nights, at a candle and book shop in the minimall, just until Christmas. She'd asked her dad to give her money instead of a present. Her mom, too. Amina was going to contribute $20. She had Elliot's plaque all planned. It was going to read:

Elliot Novotny

1981-1998

Gay Man,

Beloved Friend

She'd thought a long time about "Boy" instead of "Man." But Elliot would have liked "Man" better, she knew. She wondered if the park really would let her put those words on the bench. But if they tried to stop her, she'd tell her mom about it, and Janis would raise an uproar, probably even get a lawyer. That was the kind of thing she could always count on her mom for.

Elliot, Julie. She wondered if you could wear out your memories by replaying them in your head too much, like when you play a song on your sound system too many times, until it's not beautiful, or even interesting, anymore.

Now Romey rounded a corner, her quadriceps aching. A diesel car passed. The acrid exhaust stung her lungs, but she kept her breathing and stride steady. The stormy wind had split open a tree in someone's yard. A gash in the trunk oozed clear sap. Half the trunk had fallen over onto the asphalt, exposing pale, raw wood, blocking Romey's way. She detoured around it.

Her mother had suggested a support group, found a gay youth chat room on the Internet, left brochures from many colleges on Romey's bed. "It's time to move on. There will be other lovers."

Romey wondered if her mother had known only the kind of love that makes you say, when it's over, well, okay—there's always someone else. If so, Romey felt sorry for her. Romey didn't want another love. This much felt true to her, this much she knew: moving on would be a sin. Not a sin against some god out there, but against herself. Maybe against love, too.

Romey passed an abandoned, desolate, weathered, gray-brown house. Behind it was a crumbling barn with a rusty corrugated roof. So far, Julie didn't have e-mail, but Romey wrote every day, her letters delayed because she sent them to someone named Sandy in San Francisco, who put them in envelopes Sandy made on her computer herself that said "Christian Youth Clubs of America," or something like that, and forwarded them to Julie. Julie had said it was just a precaution. She didn't want her parents intercepting Romey's mail, or realizing how often Romey wrote.

Julie's letters, ballpoint pen on dry paper, insubstantial compared to Julie's tender arms, compared to Julie's smell of soap and flowers, those letters still provided proof, incontrovertible as geometry, of Julie's continuing love. Right now, one was folded into the back zippered pocket of Romey's running shorts, much read, falling apart at the folds.

They'd talked twice on the phone. It was unexpectedly hard to think what to say, because only the most important things seemed worth saying, especially when the pay phone Julie had found wouldn't let Romey call back, so Julie had to deposit more change every few minutes. They spent some of the call in hushed communion; she listened to Julie's breathing, and knew Julie heard hers.

Dampness had darkened the twisted trunks of the live oak trees, stark against the washed-out winter sky. Romey rounded a circle at the end of a cul-de-sac and headed back toward her house. She'd plotted this part of the run at home, carefully comparing the Divido street map to the California and United States maps in the big atlas. On this street, she faced Lubbock exactly. Two points determine a line, that was one of the first principles she'd learned in geometry, and now she faced the invisible line that always connected her and Julie. In Texas it was two hours later, after dinner, and Julie could be facing Divido, facing her.

The sun retreated behind the hills west of town, at Romey's back, leaving the sky deep blue with a few stray gold clouds. She couldn't even glance at it. She kept her eyes down, on the darkening pavement, to make sure she didn't trip on a fallen stick or a plastic bag. Since Julie had gone, beauty wounded her. Anything beautiful— a woman, a painting, a horse, a mountain, and music, especially music. If she looked up at those gilded clouds, that infinite blue, she'd feel the same as if her feet had been amputated, and then she had to watch a group of enthusiastic, sweaty marathon runners rush by her wheelchair.

"You can't just live in the past," her mother had said last night.

"Some people have died for love. So what's so terrible about living in the past for it?" Romey had retorted.

"What's terrible is that it's a waste of your life now." Gentleness in the gravel voice.

"My life was a waste before I met Julie. You think it was okay when nobody loved me, but not okay to keep loving the person who got taken away from me? It doesn't make sense."

Janis fell silent then.

The odds against them were long, Romey knew. She and Julie were up against that great divider, change. The coming years would change them both. Distance might defeat them, or time, or Julie's parents. But Romey didn't have to give them any help. She wasn't going to do or say or think anything that would make this love shrivel. Even trying to keep it and failing would be worth it, because she would know she had done all she could. She would not move on.

Romey touched the pocket on her buttock. Inside, the letter from Julie said, "All we have to do is wake up tomorrow still loving each other. And the tomorrow after. And after, and after, till we're old enough to be together. It's all up to us."

The moment of twilight had arrived when it seems that light does not, as scientists say, travel hundreds of thousands of feet in seconds, but that some of it lingers on pale broken lines painted on the road, on a runner's white T-shirt, on a white rail fence—lingers and makes them glow for a few minutes, as if light wasn't quite ready, yet, to leave them to the night.

The next mile was uphill. The ache in the front of Romey's thighs intensified, but she pumped harder. She knew the most difficult parts of a run made her muscles build their microscopic bits of strength. The heart, too, is a muscle. From deep inside, she sensed her eager muscles overcoming relentless old gravity, taking her into the darkness, propelling her forward against the grade.

ABOUT THE AUTHOR

Judy MacLean's short fiction has appeared in several anthologies, including *All the Ways Home, Queer View Mirror, Love Shook My Heart,* and *Pillow Talk.* She is a contributor to the nonfiction books *Dyke Life* and *Women Take Care.* Her humor and commentary pieces have appeared in *The Best Contemporary Women's Humor,* the *San Francisco Chronicle, The Washington Post,* and on National Public Radio's "All Things Considered." She is a former reporter for *In These Times* and *The Advocate,* and worked on the pioneering lesbian newspaper *Blazing Star.*

Judy MacLean has also written promotional materials—newsletters, annual reports, fund-raising materials, and brochures—for over 75 nonprofit human rights, environmental, gay/lesbian, and social justice organizations. She is an activist for LGBT rights and for peace. She lives in Berkeley, California, with her life partner. *Rosemary and Juliet* is her first novel.